ANDY MALICE

VILLAINS AMONG US

Published By Karnival Kingdom Entertainment Inc. By
arrangement with the Author.

Villains Among Us
Copyright © 2014 Andy Malice

Skeleton Image by George Hodan. Public Domain.

This is a work of fiction. All names, characters, places, and
incidents are either the product of the author's imagination
or are used fictitiously. Any resemblance to actual persons,
living or dead, business establishments, events, or locales is
entirely coincidental. The publisher does not have any control
over and does not assume any responsibility for author or
third party websites or their content.

ISBN: 978-0-9879371-7-9

KARNIVAL KINGDOM

ENTERTAINMENT

****

To Melanie; for all your love, patience, and support.

Happiness is not the same as having fun.

-Knut Hamsun, The Growth Of The Soil

Villains Among Us

Contents

THE FARMER

In the mid-nineteenth century, a two story farm house was built on the fringe of Mississippi's Delta region to house eleven children, a husband, a wife, and two dogs. Since then, the deed to the land has passed from hand to hand, from father to son, for four generations.

One hundred and five years later, what had begun as a cotton farm was now growing rows of corn under the smoldering Mississippi sun. The current owner of the farm, a man known as Chubby Pete, has lived on the land since birth, and learned the trade from his father, who'd been taught by his father before him. With the memory of his lineage stowed in the back of his mind, Chubby Pete strove to make wise decisions concerning the land. Having no children of his own–at least, none who would admit to such an accusation–he was the last in a long line of crop producing DNA.

From his house, the nearest neighbor was a mile away, but the old man never minded that much. Now in his seventies, widowed, he kept a pair of black labradors for company on the vast land. He led a quiet, simple life, and one he wasn't willing to trade for all the money in the world. When his time came, he planned on dying there like the rest of the great men in his family, and there the legacy would end.

The old man sparsely received visitors; a fact he was on good terms with. He enjoyed being alone with his dogs. He thought people had an inane compulsion to complicate things for no other reason than a mean desire for drama. He wasn't keen on drama, and neither were his dogs, so his arrangement was ideal in his mind.

He tended–preferred–to keep to himself, but always strove to think humbly, and be kind and generous in the way he believed the good Lord expected him, and everyone else, to be. Once a week, he left the farm to attend church and stock up on groceries before returning to the endless duties that awaited him day in, day out.

He was happy, and completely unbothered by the happenings of the world beyond the dense maze of corn stalks that surrounded him. Unfortunately, the world proved unbothered by his wish to be left alone when a man named Nick Wilson kidnapped a young girl, drove her out to the country, and settled on Chubby Pete's barn as the perfect stage to commit his terrible crimes. He snuck her in under a waning moon, crept the doors back behind him, and destroyed the poor thing until her body softened like a violated rag. He left the mess to fester in the surging heat of the barn and attempted to disappear in the predawn silence; but only fifteen miles into his escape, his car engine burst into flames as he was crossing a bridge, and Nick Wilson ended his retreat at the bottom of a river.

The following day, returning from church, Chubby Pete parked his car and noticed the barn door ajar. When he pulled on the door and peered inside, the sight left him gasping for air. It was too terrible to deal with. He stood and stared at the mangled mass on the concrete floor, unable to muster enough strength to catch his breath and back away from the horror. He was captivated. Devastated. She was so young, so little, so wasted. The old man's legs trembled terribly, and he swore he could hear a voice inside–something low, almost inaudible–but there. He shook his head in confusion and squinted his eyes, trying to decide if it was real or not. Before he could, however, the sound turned into a piercing wail, and his body stiffened as if he'd been electrocuted. Something hysterical flashed across his face and left him standing pale and confused, and his eyes glazed over like a cadaver's. He glared at the body with a sudden lack of expression. He was as cold as stone.

He shut the door, locked it, and slowly waddled to the house with unconcerned steps. He walked in from the side door, and seconds later, stepped out onto his porch, lit a cigarette, and stared out over the yard like a tired dog.

He puffed generously on the cigarette and flicked the ashes over the railing as though nothing much was happening on his land. Crops were growing decently. Weather's been good. When he finished the cigarette, he lit another, choked it back, and followed it up with yet another. And so it began; for nearly a week, the old man stood there with his buttoned down shirt tucked into his khakis, his red wine colored suspenders taut over his shoulders, his eyes trance-like and aimless. He re-entered the house only twice in that time. The first was to change hats; the second, two days later, was for more cigarettes and a pipe.

The change was drastic. Gone was the polite, clean shaven gentleman of the corn growing Miller family, and in his place stood a dumb beast, unkempt and mephitic, sucking back cigarettes as a source of nutrition.

Day after day, while the girl bulged and burst open in the sweltering heat, he maintained a blissful ignorance of his whimpering dogs scratching at the barn doors, and of the sharp miasmic fog billowing across the yard. He remained in this near catatonic state until a man named Billy Hammond pulled into the drive on a scorching Saturday afternoon. Dressed in a suit, grinning weirdly, Billy parked his car and hustled toward the porch, saying, "Good day, sir. Hot enough for ya?"

He stopped a short distance from the porch and flared his nostrils in the acrid air, instantly nauseated by the stench of rotting girl invading his lungs. He did his best to ignore it, however, and tried to establish a line of communication with the old man. He stood limply, petting the excited dogs sniffing hurriedly at his person, and stared up at the farmer on the porch with a wide smile on his face. The old man smoked his cigarette without expression, not paying the man any attention.

"Sir?" Billy said, and cocked his head to the side. "I hope you don't mind my intruding. I don't mean you any trouble."

The farmer snorted back a breath and blasted out a gob of phlegm over the railing, not meaning any harm by it. He cleared his throat, had a healthy drag of his cigarette, and spoke with smoke billowing from his mouth.

"It's hot!" he declared weirdly, his voice much too fierce for the actual situation. Billy glanced around the yard, suddenly suspicious of threats.

"It is," he nodded. "The sun is punishing in these parts. I'm not from around here, so it takes some getting used to." He laughed, but it felt awkward in response to the old man's lack of expression.

The farmer didn't answer. He took another cigarette from its package and lit it with the cigarette he was just finishing. With a cloud of blueish smoke engulfing his head, he threw the short butt over the railing, and into the inch thick tobacco graveyard covering the ground for a ten foot radius from the porch. Billy stared at it, repulsed by the sight. He wasn't against smoking, but he did believe in self discipline, and this old man's lack of it had given the goddamned ground cancer.

"Right," he mumbled, and shielded his eyes from the sun with his hand. "Ah–anyway, my name is Billy Hammond, and I work for Bigfoot Combine Corporation, in Montana, actually, which is why the heat... Anyway... I was wondering if maybe I could speak with you about your land here and the machinery you might be needing for a great price."

The old man winked his eye at him, his face twitching spastically, and then belched so loudly it echoed off of Billy's car. He smiled happily, flicked the ashes of his cigarette over the railing, flared his nostrils, but didn't catch what the man in the suit seemed to be hung up on.

"Montana?" the farmer said. "Goddamn, boy. You lost! Ha! Ha! Ha! Ha! Ha!"

Now Billy felt his own face twitching, but he wasn't sure if it was for real, or if it was only a psychosomatic response to the old man's grotesque personality. Surely, the man was a lunatic. He cursed himself. Somehow, he'd managed to walk into yet another hidden asylum. He wondered why, in every small farming town he visited across the country trying to sell farming machinery, some-where in the bush, mixed in among mostly normal folks, some bat-shit crazy asshole was holed up in a half dilapidated shack, tripping balls by himself until some stupid tourist crossed the event horizon and was sucked into the lunacy. The sales pitch quickly turned into a desperate attempt to get out of the situation before too much of the weird imprinted itself on his soul.

"Ah–yes, sir, I believe I am lost," Billy said, and smiled crookedly. "Which way is it–ah–back to town, I mean."

The old man stared absently at Billy, who was stepping nervously in place, anxious to get back to his car. With complete disregard to his question, Chubby Pete said, "Sometimes, when I'm sitting in the kitchen, this light comes in through the window and stares at me no matter what I try to get it to leave me alone. The only place I can get away from it is in the bathroom; can't fol-low me in there for some reason. Luckily, it don't happen much out here. Nothing much happens out here."

He puffed on his cigarette again and looked away from Billy, returning his attention to the driveway beyond the car.

Billy shrugged, not understanding, but desperate to remain ignorant of it nonetheless. Shaking his head, he said, "You have yourself a fantastic day, good sir. It was a pleasure meeting you." He turned to head back to his car, but then stopped and stared back at the old man.

"By the way," he said. "Terrible stench around these parts, sir, no offense intended. Do you keep animals in the barn at all?"

The old man ignored him and spat another gob of phlegm over the railing.

"I have trouble walking!" Chubby Pete said, his volume again much too high for the conversation, and then volunteered nothing more beyond the statement.

"I'm–sorry–sir," Billy said. "Would you like me to–"
"Too many hands grab at my feet when I walk," the farmer interrupted, his voice still roaring. "Makes my toes bleed, my feet rot and fall off, my blood turns black, and my tongue grows hair."

Haunted, Billy shook his head and noticed that his hands were trembling and clammy. His legs were a mess of rubber bands, and the wafting odor of decay was suddenly overpowering. Not wanting to risk any further interaction with the old lunatic, he hustled to his car, determined to leave with anger fueled arrogance.

In the driver's seat, he slammed the door shut, jammed the key into the ignition, and turned the switch. Nothing happened. Not even a click. He turned the key back, feeling the foul reality of what was happening creep into his awareness, and tried starting the engine once more.

"Son of a bitch!" he hissed, and glanced at the old man with crawling repulsion. He didn't have a choice; he needed the farmer's phone. "Goddamn it," he whispered to himself, and tried waking the engine once more.

Nothing.

With a sigh, he opened the door, stepped out of the car, and took timid little steps back toward the porch. He grinned as if his heart was about to explode and stared at Chubby Pete with pleading doe eyes.

"I'm terribly sorry to disturb you, sir–um–but ah... My car won't seem to start. Would it be a terrible burden to let me use your telephone for a minute?"

Chubby Pete stared out at a completely different angle, tonguing his browned teeth as though he'd just finished a steak.

"Sir," Billy said curtly now, the old fart's madness irritating him. "I need a telephone. Would you please be so kind as to lend me a helping hand here?"

A cloud of smoke. A tar muffled cough. A clearing of toxic phlegm from the nasal cavity. No eye contact. No acknowledgement.

"Goddamn it!" Billy snapped, and shook his head in despair. He glared at the old man and sighed. The guy wasn't even facing him. He was turned to the side, mumbling nonsense to himself, and leaving Billy to stand there like an asshole with his hat in his hands and his luck up his ass.

He turned and glanced at his car, then back to the old man, and figured it wouldn't make much of a difference either way. The old farmer wasn't even on the same planet; all Billy had to do was use the phone in his own dimension, and everything would be fine.

Gently, he edged away from the porch, heading for the door in the side of the house. Chubby Pete was still mumbling mindless gibberish, staring at a landscape that was not of this world.

Billy lost his breath. The intensity of the stench grew exponentially with his every step toward the door. He waved his way through the foul, fetid fog, and opened the side door to the house. He took a final look over his shoulder before entering; the old man couldn't have cared any less.

Inside, though the stench was far less potent than the dense mist outside, it was no less nauseating. The texture had changed, but something was still, or also, decomposing inside of the house.

Bowing his head in repulsion, he walked down the wood paneled hallway in search of a phone. He passed a bedroom on his left, a bathroom on his right, and came into the kitchen, where a telephone was mounted on the far wall next to the stove.

The room was filthy with rotting food, sifted dust, and rancid liquids long ago spilled and dried to sticky sirups. Billy scoffed and buried his lower face in the crook of his elbow. He wondered how the old man was even allowed to live on his own; he obviously wasn't capable of taking care of himself. This was a maniac's jungle.

The small dining table was covered with coffee cups of all sizes and colors, each growing its own fungi paradise. The air was stagnant, and burned Billy's nostrils when he inhaled. Padding across the room, he noticed some kind of meat in the sink, the whole mess feasted on by a mass of squirming maggots and hysterical flies. Disgusting.

He picked up the phone, listened for a tone, pressed 0, and waited for assistance.

"Operator, how can I help you?" a woman's voice answered.

"Ah... Hello," Billy mumbled. "I need roadside assistance, please. I'm, ah–I'm sorry... I'm at–"

He couldn't remember. He needed help because... What? His car wouldn't start. Right. And he was in a town called...

"Shit," Billy said.

"I'm sorry?"

"Nothing. I apologize. I'll have to call you back; I don't know where I am, I–"

Without warning, a deafening wail pierced through the room and knocked him off balance. Dizzy with pain, he stumbled into the table and knocked over a dozen coffee cups to the floor. They cracked open like eggs and sent a dense mist of spores dancing upward in the air. Billy's panic was seeded in a fundamental instinct for survival. Spores are rarely good, and the possible benefits of those coming from festering coffee cups could only be believed with clear evidence of mental problems.

He left the phone dangling from the wall and bolted across the room with his forearm covering his mouth and his breath held against the toxic air. Cautiously, he re-entered the hallway, but to his grave dismay, he was instantly aware of an ominous change. The narrow wood paneled walls no longer led to the foyer; the end was instead framed by a dark bedroom. Confused and reluctant, he turned and headed back toward the kitchen, but it too had apparently been misplaced in sync with his attention, and the bewildered man soon found himself inexplicably standing in a living room, where a television was on but no one was watching.

"Come on, Billy," he said to himself. "Let's not lose our shit now. Just have to get out of this house."

He glanced about the room with cold terror in his heart. A flower patterned sofa. A matching recliner. A glass coffee table. No photos on the walls. No one else present.

"Where the hell am I?" Billy muttered, and suffered a sudden spell of vertigo. He fought with himself to regain control of his senses, but he felt sedated, unbalanced, and... He shook his head vigorously like a wet dog.

"What is that?" he whispered, squinting his eyes and standing hunchbacked in the room, listening. He was suddenly aware of a voice, barely audible, but it sounded like a little girl chanting an unidentifiable tune.

Sweaty and trembling, he turned to face the mysterious

hallway again, when he was startled to the ground by the presence of the old farmer looming largely over him, grinning weirdly,
smoke billowing from his nostrils.

"Jesus Christ!" Billy screamed and clawed away from the
uncomfortable presence like a backward spider, desperate to find
his way out of the demented house. He'd obviously made a grave
mistake. The old man stared with blank eyes, smiling, amused with
his own blatant madness.

"What do you want from me?" cried Billy. "Please–what's
happening here?"

The farmer's face contorted into a mask of rage and he
began screaming and flailing his arms wildly; but Billy couldn't
hear him over the piercing howl once again filling his ears. Wincing in pain, he closed his eyes and drove flattened palms against
his ears and screamed in defense.

"Stop iiiittt!"

Eventually, the wail receded back to a low, annoying hum, and
when he opened his eyes again he started in surprise. The old man
was gone. The flowered sofa. The coffee table. The television. All
disappeared. He was in a different room, a library, alone. He hadn't
moved; had he? He couldn't remember.

Soaked with sweat, he hurried to his feet, the sound in his
ears ever present in unstable octaves like an uncertain wave. Staring wide-eyed, terrified, he scrutinized the room with the intensity
of a soldier under attack. In the opposing wall was a door, and
without a moment's hesitation he dashed toward it with drunk and
heavy legs.

"Please! Please!" he whimpered, locking his sweaty
palms around the knob. The door swung open and he rushed across
the threshold and found himself standing on the same porch he'd
first approached the farmer; but everything felt wrong–looked
wrong. The sun had long ago set, and the night air was opaque,
indecipherable, and oppressing. He couldn't see his car or the barn
he remembered, and suddenly, the screaming wail rose up again,
and again he covered his ears, but there was no diminishing the
tonal punishment. He was convinced the sound was coming from
inside his head. Stomping his feet against the vinyl floor of the
porch, oozing desperation, the wail receded once more and settled
back into the low level chanting of a child's voice.

The miasma wafting through the night air had magnified
to a potent force capable of knocking a grown man to his knees.
Gasping and crying, he peered into the darkness for his car, for

anything familiar, when from his peripheral he caught a shadow moving in on him with fascinating speed. Instinctively, he flinched, swung his head down, and spun to his left, catching sight of the old farmer arching an axe through the foul air and missing him by a fraction of an inch. The impact with the railing sent an earthquake-like force reverberating through the porch structure.

Billy tried to scream, but before he could fill his lungs with fetid air, Chubby Pete swung his axe again and tried to chop him in half. He jolted backward, tripped over his feet, tumbled over the railing, and fell toward the vileness of the cigarette graveyard below. Face-planting into it, he was instantly certain of his malignancy. Fouled with cancerous mud, he crawled through the mess in a panic, puking and choking, searching for some sort of cryptic understanding of the situation. Reaching untainted soil, he glanced up at the porch, his vision distorted with tears; to his horror, he saw the old man coming over the railing, screaming gibberish and wielding his axe like a Viking warrior.

Unable to control his convulsions, Billy got to his feet and ran aimlessly through the inky night, whimpering nonsense of his own. The air turned caustic suddenly, like breathing in the heat of an explosion, and he could make out the silhouette of the large barn just ahead of him. He hacked forcefully to clear his lungs, but success only meant further destruction. Behind him, he could hear the farmer following, but it was the mysterious voice rising once more that was driving him insane. It kept repeating the same thing, as if caught in an eternal loop.

My voice is so pretty, my voice is so clear, fear not little baby, within you, I'm here.

It was slashing through his mind like lightning and throwing him off balance. The real threat, he knew, was the mad farmer coming for him with his axe like awe-inspiring Achilles, but he couldn't seem to focus on him. The voice was unbearable, and the stench was far too powerful to withstand. With every breath, his stomach twisted, tightened, and punished him with electric cramps.

He tried to muffle the pain by digging fists into his gut, but he refused to stop, or even slow down. He stumbled over a mound and realized with horror that it was the remains of one of the farmer's dogs. The animal had been reduced to a harry sack of oatmeal. He found the other dog in the same condition only a few feet away. Panicked, he made it to the barn doors, but they were locked. He looked back at the farmer; he was still coming at him mechanically, still screaming nonsense at the top of his lungs. A lunatic silhouette in the jaded moonlight beginning to shine through parting clouds.

Billy stepped back from the door and stared at the window next to it. It was big enough to squeeze through. He drove his elbow through it, suffered jagged cuts to his arm, and then crawled through the treacherous opening.

Once inside, he collapsed to the ground with burning eyes and a complete lack of breath. The air was like a billowing cloud of noxious gas. The sound of the voice was worse than ever.

My voice is so pretty, my voice is so clear, fear not little baby, within you, I'm here.

"Stop it!" Billy screamed, but he could barely hear his own voice over the relentless chanting in his ears. The voice was totalitarian; the stench dominating.

He coughed painfully and tried to find a weapon to fight off the old man and get away from him as quickly as possible. Searching with diabolical desperation, he saw a shovel, a rake, a crowbar, a... a body, on the floor, swollen and rotten, foul beyond belief.

He was no longer sure if his mind was making sense of the situation. The sight of the body was grotesque, obscene, but was it real? Was the voice real? He couldn't tell anymore, but surely the farmer was responsible for the festering disaster evaporating on the concrete floor.

Weaker than he'd ever experienced before, he crawled along the floor, trying to inhale as delicately as he could, but it was hopeless. His head was swooning, his vision failing. He reached for the crowbar, but lacked the strength to even pull it toward him. His mind and body were in the grips of atrophy. He convulsed spasmodically and lay on the floor staring at the body and letting the voice tear his mind to shreds. The farmer was no longer on his mind, nor was escaping. He only heard the voice–only saw the body.

...fear not little baby, within you, I'm here.

He felt the temperature rise, as though his blood was turning to magma and his lungs were catching fire. Pain surged in his every molecule. His skin bubbled, blistered, burst, and spewed puss and effluence like a burning sausage splatters grease. He grabbed at his face and his cheeks came off in his hands.

Inside you, I'm here. Inside you, I'm here. Inside you, I'm here.

It wouldn't stop. He tried to scream, express his agony, but nothing came out. He couldn't breathe. He couldn't fight back. He cocked his head and stared at the hole in the wall left by the broken window. Framed within it was Chubby Pete's face, his emotionless eyes staring at him. He puffed on a cigarette and watched as Billy's body bubbled and turned to liquid, ending the terrible ordeal.

The farmer stared a moment longer, then leaned his axe up against the barn wall, backed away from the hole, and walked back to the house. He entered the side door, and seconds later emerged on the porch. He took a cigarette from its package, lit it, and stared like a tired dog over the yard. His eyes empty. His breath controlled. His body calm.

A week following Billy's terrible demise, the stench from the barn grew so potent it could no longer be ignored by passersby. The police received a tip about it and a Sheriff was sent to the farm to investigate. Upon his arrival he discovered a raving lunatic on the porch and a heart stopping stench in the air. Immediately suspecting the barn as the source of the infernal odor, he made a direct line to it, noticing the dried dog carcasses on the way, and stepped through the big wooden doors. He, like Billy Hammond, never came back out. More officers followed, but they too suffered similar fates. Those who'd merely stood back and stared inside were reduced to imitations of the old farmer, staring about themselves like mindless automata. In time, some people attempted to burn the mysterious barn to the ground, but flames seemed to hold no affinity to its wooden walls; instead, those who approached it with billowing torches were caught in sudden gusts of wind, setting themselves ablaze, and performed infernal ballets across the sunburnt yard. Before long, the yard was full of dumbly waddling strangers, meddling about with no direction, no intention. And through it all, the old farmer stared from the porch and smoked his cigarettes, taking no mind of anything unusual.

A short time thereafter, Chubby Pete and the other victims perished, and the residents of the town stopped talking about it all together; for it appeared that those who did so were soon found deceased under suspicious and unexplainable circumstances. No one approaches the land anymore, but the curse continues to grow and claim its victims shortly after the mere mention of it enters their minds.

You can refuse to believe it if you like–but you can feel me now, can't you?

Because I can feel you.

Fear not little baby, within you, I'm here.

The End

OF HUBRIS AND TREACHERY

We came out of the maze of putrid pipes on 12th Street, about a quarter mile from the prison walls. Choking on the caustic stench of thirty year old sewage and rotting rat carcasses, we clambered out of our horrible burrow and welcomed the torrential downpour assaulting the asphalt we rested our tired backs on. Restoring my blood with a fresh stock of oxygen, I stood and told the others to remain silent while I listened for a specific sound I expected to be cutting through the cacophony of the storm. I couldn't hear the alarm yet, but it was only a matter of time. It was about nine in the evening, and after endless months of preparation and four arduous, stamina pushing hours of digging, squirming, and slithering through filthy sewers, we finally stood above ground again, away from the claustrophobic walls of federal prison. We were being beaten by a mean storm, and the lightning tearing up the sky seemed to be either a warning for us to turn back, or a celebration of our imminent success. Natural fireworks. I personally preferred the idea of celebration–it had been hard and nervous work, after all–so it seemed like the only sensible thing to do was to keep going.

After a weird ceremony of screaming at each other, both to be heard over the storm and to get the heartrending anxiety out of our bodies and into the electrified air around us, we found our bearings and headed south toward the docks, hoping to hijack a boat and get off the island, balls to the wall. Suddenly, just as we started running, we heard the hectic sound of alarm in the distance behind us. It was certain now. They knew we were missing, and they would be coming for us like angry hornets looking to punish the idiots who'd stepped on their nest. Whatever the outcome, however, I was content in knowing that the next few hours of my life were going to be rather exciting, life threatening, and nothing like the drab, unconscionable stupidity of life in prison. I'd had my fill of big talking wimps, scatological food, and pretentious pansies in uniforms playing Mr. Authority figure. Many of the latter, if not most, would cower, and plead, and cry if faced with someone like me without their cute little costume and weapons; but behind the safety of bars, armed with guns and back-up–watch out for the big boss!

Yes. Quite enough, thank you.

As a result of the aggressive paranoia awakened by the sirens, the three of us ran in hurried ducking and dodging motions, as if the pigs were already shooting slugs at us from swooping helicopters. The adrenaline was intoxicating, devastating, and it sent my mind reeling with dizzying thoughts and sinister emotions.

Like a marathon of hunchbacks, we made it to the shore, perhaps a hundred feet from the marina, where a row of multi-sized boats floated lively in the rocking waters of the lake. My hands were trembling uncontrollably by then, and I was so thirsty, and so paranoid, that I could barely concentrate on what to do next. I found myself constantly checking over my shoulder, forever expecting to see an angry swat team shooting wildly in our direction; but I refused to give up. I was leaving that goddamned prison forever. Fuck those politician cocksuckers and their privatized ideas of justice! They wouldn't be wasting another day of my life. Not ever again.

"Let's take the black one," Zane said, pointing to the end of the row of boats. "Won't be long before they're right on our asses."

Zane was a killer, thirty two years old, and a nice enough guy in spite of the dramatic list of inhuman felonies attributed to his name. He was serving four consecutive life sentences for the point blank execution of four police officers in an abandoned warehouse. He had called in an emergency, claiming to have found a body, and waited for the police to arrive. He gassed the place, bound and gagged the officers, waited until they came to, and then systematically relieved each of the gray matter they'd spent a lifetime wasting. When they asked him why he had done it, he chuckled and said, "Speeding tickets." People generally kept a fair distance from him, but I thought he was an intelligent man; perhaps too intelligent for his own good, and perhaps even afraid of himself. What intelligent person wasn't afraid of themselves from time to time?

We nodded in agreement to the black boat, and then found ourselves momentarily staring behind us, listening for any sign of oncoming attack. So far, so good.

I'd spent the last six months of my life planning this very moment. The marina was the last step in the first phase of my plan. Get out of prison, and then get off the island. Beyond that, I had vague ideas about what to do, but I dwelt on none of them; because if we couldn't get into a boat and away from the authorities, phase two was as good as non-existent.

"Let's hurry this up!" Marshall snapped, his eyes wide and filled with worry. Time was running out, and we were all terribly aware of it. Marshall, like myself, was a thief, and serving a life sentence for the armed robbery of a bank and the death of a security guard. "You tell them and you tell them," Marshall would say. "It's not worth trying to be a hero when it's not even your money, but people watch too many stupid movies. Everybody only ever cares about being hailed a hero. It's so stupid, isn't it? Nobility is a stupid thing to care about. Self-important pricks."

I agreed with him. Sure. But none of that changed the reality of our lives. None of us were angels. I myself was serving a life sentence for the armed robbery of six East Coast banks, adding a smooth thirteen million dollars to my personal net worth. Of that, only about four million had been seized by the authorities–the rest was still mine–stashed away, and waiting for my greedy little hands to wrap a loving embrace around it. Our escape, our success of it, was going to cause a vicious manhunt aimed at either recapturing us, or, even better for the ratings, shooting us dead on sight. That had the entertainment value necessary to make careers.

This was the meat of the story; roughly four hours ago, at dinner time, the three of us met in the hallway leading to the cafeteria. Using a key I'd managed to file down from a featureless piece of metal, we breached the door that led down to the boiler room, where for the last six weeks, we'd taken shifts at digging out a tunnel through the earth to reach the prison's intricate web of underground maintenance tunnels. Within those tunnels, we were free to run as fast as we could, but it would hardly be that easy all the way. Once we'd taken a left, a right, another right, and then headed down a shaft leading lower into the ground, we arrived at a sewer pipe and managed to punch a hole through it with a variety of makeshift tools. One by one, we squeezed into the filthy twenty-four inch tube. Gagging hopelessly, and desperately trying to keep our hearts from cardiac arrest, we began crawling.

"Why don't we just take this one?" Marshall said, pointing to a different boat as we padded across the dock.

"Just shut up and follow!" Zane snapped, ending the suggestion.

Through those sewer pipes, I only had a vague idea of the direction we were to take. I didn't have a map to rely on, but I did have a compass. All we really knew, or thought we knew, was that we needed to head south. Beyond that, our future was undetermined. We faced every possibility, but my only real fear was taking a wrong turn and getting stuck, or hitting a dead end, and then what? We would die like stranded rats, choked out in a goddamned sewer pipe. A success for the prison, but an unacceptable threat for the rest of us; although, perishing in a shit filled crypt was still marginally better than getting caught. If not in reality, then at least in principle. We were, after all, serving life sentences. In reality, even if we were caught, there was no real way of punishing fiends like us for an escape attempt. All anyone could do was delay the time it took to figure out the next attempt at breaking out. We had nothing left to lose, but having already made it so far, failure suddenly seemed like a terrible tragedy, especially for our egos. Having put in all the work, we felt rather entitled to the fruits of our labors–no? What did those fat donut eating circle jerking power tripping cocksuckers know about putting in the hard work necessary to get the things they wanted out of life? I'd made millions; they worked for the government. I'd worked for that money, and though some may say dishonestly, it felt pretty goddamned honest to me. I'd risked my life countless times; I was risking my life now. How was a nine to five jerk off session in a safe little office five days a week anything honest?

It wasn't. It was completely fucking retarded, in my opinion. I didn't see the value in selling myself to a company. It didn't make me feel good, and I've never understood anyone who claimed that it did. How could anyone be happy slaving away like a responsible ant, unquestioning the rabid lure of the ultimate pheromone–MONEY! Well, if I was going for money, then I was in it for myself, and for myself alone. I believed in hard work, regardless of the ethical implications, and I believed in compensation. I worked hard; I deserved payment. I deserved everything and anything I could acquire through hard work. I deserved it. The TV told me so.

I wondered if I could persuade a jury?

"Yes, I did terrible things. But look at all the trouble I went through to get out; that's got to count for something–doesn't it? I'm entitled to my freedom, goddamn it, I crawled through miles of ancient shit to get it!"

From the dock, we hopped over the edge and into the black boat, and cautiously surveyed our surroundings before continuing. After mutually reassuring nods, Zane got to work on the electrical system. He was a mechanic by trade, (a killer by hobby), and said he could hot wire anything from a car, to a boat, to the lifeless carcass you humped at night and called a wife by day. My heart palpitated horribly in my chest and caused my head to swoon. Initially, I hadn't felt any fear over getting caught, but now that we were in the boat and about to head for the mainland, I was suddenly choked with it. We were too close to fail, too close to go back alive.

"What's it look like?" I demanded of Zane, never moving my attention from the dark and distant perimeter beyond the dock.

"Just give me two minutes," he said, fumbling with a mess of wires in his hands. "I need some tools. Pliers."

"Find him some pliers!" I said to Marshall. "I'll keep a look out."

Peering through the night air, I watched the scene alternate between terrific flashes of lightning and near absolute darkness, and I could still hear the prison's sirens crying helplessly. It sounded like panic. It sounded serious. We knew they were coming, but exactly when was the key to our success. They would waste precious minutes trying to figure out how we had managed our escape. The walls and fences were untouched. No ladders or improvised ropes had been left behind. How had we done it? They would then, purely out of caution, assume that the inmates in question had escaped, and dispatch swat teams and dogs to swarm the prison grounds and look for hideaways. Simultaneously, other teams would hit the ground beyond the walls and search the woods, the houses, the gutters, anywhere and everywhere. There were two points on the island which would require immediate attention. The first was the road joining the island to the mainland, but it was constantly manned by guards anyway, and nearly impossible to breach alive. The second was on these docks, where retired vacationers docked their boats during the off season. Time was a crumbling resource.

"I still don't hear the engine!" I snapped, and wiped a sheet of cold rain from my face.

"I swear, if you rush me again, I'll cut your goddamn nuts off and ram em up your ass. Give me a fucking minute here, all right!"

"You don't have a minute!" I screamed. "Look!"

In the distance, feverish lights bounced across the stifling darkness, undeniably rushing toward our position. Only seconds now. If I had ever believed in anything as easy as God, I would have prayed. Consequently, all I could do was scream.

"Now, motherfucker! Now! I swear to Christ, if you get us caught I'm gonna slit your throat and fuck it! Get us out into the goddamn water!"

Marshall was running frantically around the deck with no real direction in mind. He seemed to want to jump into the water, but it was devastatingly cold; he wouldn't make it five minutes. I swallowed a heavy slab of terror past my Adam's apple, and struggled to focus my attention between our approaching attackers, and Zane fumbling stupidly with the engine. They were gaining ground at a disgusting pace. We were going to get arrested!

We needed a weapon.

Matching the speed of the lightning tearing through the sky, I lunged below deck and began overturning everything I could get my hands on, looking for something we could use for defense. I ripped drawers out of the cabinets, emptied the cupboards, flipped the cushions–all of it was useless shit! I had to hurry, I could hear the sirens and the revving engines of the police cars over the pounding rain.

I tore tables and benches from their brackets, mostly out of rage, and only then did I notice the presence of a survival kit conveniently mounted to the wall. I clawed at it in panic; inside was a flare gun and three cartridges.

"It'll have to do, I guess. What the fuck," I said to myself, and hurried back up to the deck, desperate to do whatever I could to keep the pigs at bay–when suddenly–the engine roared to life.

"Got it!" Zane screamed, panic flattening his voice. "Let's get the fuck out of here."

And there they were. A dozen or so fully equipped officers, foaming at the mouth to put an end to all of our hard work. They were nearly at the dock, guns cocked, voices screaming for us to put our hands up and get down on our knees. Zane leaped to the wheel of the boat, kicked the heavy thing into reverse, and floored the throttle. Instantly, we were thrown forward, staring wide eyed at the approaching soldiers. Then the transmission shifted forward and the reversal of acceleration knocked me off balance. I glanced at Zane, who paid me no attention, and then a tiny explosion went off next to my head and threw splinters of fiberglass into my face.

"Get down!" I screamed to the rest of them. "They're shooting, man!"

Kneeling, I peered over the edge. We were gaining distance from the dock, but not quite fast enough to cleanly escape the officer standing at the end of it. A hero, as Marshall would say, shooting wildly at our boat. The bastard was going to sink us. Again, a bullet punctured the boat. Then another, passing straight through a window and spraying us with jagged shards of glass.

I ducked down and loaded the flare gun. A bullet passed through the wall, maybe a foot to my left. Too close. And then another just ahead of Zane. If I didn't do something soon, we would be killed.

In a single, swift motion, I popped my head up above the edge, aimed crudely in the pig's direction, and pulled the trigger. A flash of light rocketed through the dark night air like a burning asteroid and landed squarely in the cop's face with fantastic fireworks. His body jolted backward awkwardly, his face on fire, and he fell into the water, fighting with himself to make sense of the situation. It was a frantic scene, enough to shock the rest of his team and elicit wild cheering and laughter from behind me in the boat. I had just shot a cop in the face with a flare gun. Along with the escape itself, I was probably going to get into a world of trouble over that. The only proper thing to do was to use it for motivation. Thank Christ the death penalty wasn't legal... Although, it's probably not such a bad thing.

Flying, balls to the wall, we skimmed across the water, heading away from the dock. All around us, bullets missed their target, despite the fierce waves of automatic attack. We remained as low as we could while sailing over the crazed waves, but the bullets were still occasionally spitting through the back of the boat, missing us by luck alone.

Almost far enough to be out of range, another swoosh sped through the boat, and Marshall yelped in agony and bent over his leg. He'd been shot!

"Faster!" I yelled to Zane, but we were already at top speed. Out of the cove, we came into open water, and everything suddenly changed for us. The waves were angry and vicious, and refused to offer us safe passage to the mainland. Water slammed violently into the side of the damaged boat, shifting us around like toys inside a box. It was terrifying, but at least it seemed as though the bullets couldn't reach us anymore; or they'd given up–for a while.

I crawled over to Marshall, trying to see the damage in the dark, but we kept being launched from the bottom of the boat as it smacked savagely into the swirls.

"My leg!" he screamed, crying in pain. "Motherfuckers shot me!"

"Let me see!" I screamed, but there was nothing to see. It was too dark, and too chaotic to make sense of anything.

"This isn't good!" Marshall cried. "This is not good!" It wasn't good. Not at all. What it meant, most probably, was that Marshall's attempt at escaping the reinforced walls of the prison was just about over. Escaping prison was exactly like returning to the animal kingdom. It was survival of the fittest. If you fell behind, you were left behind. It was nothing personal, it was just survival; and for a bunch of guys on the other side of the wall already carrying life sentences on their backs, survival truly was all we had.

Everyone was capable of tragic things. The only real difference was our level of desperation.

Part 2

"Why the fuck would you do that? Are you insane?" It probably wasn't the best question to ask a man who'd ritualistically executed a bunch of cops, but I was furious.

"He was a liability," he screamed back, his tone of voice rivaled the powerful fury of the storm still beating on us with relentless hostility.

"I'm not going back to prison!" He declared. "Not ever again."

This little argument of ours was taking place on the shore of the mainland, which was all good and fine on its own, but what enraged me was the foul series of events that had taken place before we made it. Once we'd realized how badly Marshall had been injured by a stray bullet, taking it right through the shin and shattering the bone, Zane took it upon himself to throw him into the frigid waters. He was as good as dead by now.

"Goddamn it, man," I continued. "This is just adding to the list of felonies; you know that, right?"

"Four life sentences!" he snarled angrily. "Like I give a fuck. You can stay here and cry about it if you want, but I'm getting out of here."

Fantastic, I thought, and began compiling the list in my head. We'd been gone roughly five hours, and in that time, I'd shot a cop in the face with a flare gun, and although he probably wasn't dead, he was most certainly pissed off about the whole thing. And then we'd killed our injured partner by hurtling him from a speeding boat and into hypothermic water. It was all just fucking fantastic, goddamn it!

I watched Zane thrash through a wall of foliage and disappear behind it. I stood alone for a moment, contemplating my next move under the flashing assault of lightning tearing through the dark sky. I looked back at the lake. We hadn't been spotted by any boats, but in the distance I could see a helicopter's search light desperate to spot us somewhere on the water's surface, so far to no avail.

They wouldn't find the boat either–at least–they wouldn't find it anywhere near us. We'd tied down the wheel and sent it zooming across the choppy mess of water at top speed. Where it ended up wasn't important, as long as it was nowhere near us. With any luck, the thing would collapse and buy us precious time while they searched for our bodies. Of course, when they found Marshall, they would search for us too. Damn it, I liked Marshall. Zane was a fucking asshole. We could have left him on the shore; we didn't have to kill the poor bastard.

With a sigh, I pushed through the trees, but Zane had already vanished into the opaque haze of the stormy night. Blindly, I bushwhacked toward an undetermined destination, trying to use my compass in the torrential melee, doing my best to head East. Just keep going East.

I figured that the first place the cops would swarm on the mainland would be the wharf, up the bank about two miles from our position, where it was only logical that we would attempt to land... If we had shit for brains. Why would anyone go through the trouble of accomplishing anything without being original?

Luckily, we weren't so stupid, and decided on steering the boat far away from the wharf, heading East, dumping the boat, and a passenger, and electing to cut through the thick bush, constantly working for our freedom. Surely, with enough time and difficulty, someone in a position of power would agree with that.

Through the dripping horror of trees, it was far darker than standing on the shore. I tripped, and stomped, and forced my way through branches, determined to get as far away from the lake as possible before I physically needed to stop. I needed to keep warm. I needed to keep moving.

Many people, when trapped in similar situations, would focus their minds on their families for that extra nudge of motivation necessary to accomplish great things. They would think of their wives and kids, their parents and friends, but all I could think of was my money. Nine million dollars waited for me. Friends, family, kids, none of that would have been enough for a guy like me. I had no family, and rightfully so, I might add. A man like me shouldn't have one to begin with. I'd caused myself enough pain over the course of my life, there was certainly no use in punishing innocent others simply because they happened to love me. I was a bad man, but at least I was considerate enough to admit it and not impose my selfish urges onto others. Zane, on the other hand, had three kids and wife, qualifying him as a tremendous fucking asshole, among other things.

I hacked my way through the thick brush as quickly as I could, and before long, I ran into Zane again. He was thrashing wildly at branches, cursing in rage, consumed with frustration.

"What fucking direction are we going?" he demanded as he heard me approach him.

"We?" I replied. "I thought you made it clear that you were going about this all on your own."

"Look," he said, stopping his mad assault on the branches. "I'm sorry I threw him overboard, all right? But he was going to slow us down."

"We could have left him on the beach," I said. "Goddamn it, man."

He nodded, but there was little sympathy in his dark eyes. "Maybe," he said. "But it's too late now. We're here, can we just get out of this goddamn bush and as far away from the lake as possible? How long do you think we have before the pigs comb through this place and trap us in like animals?"

"I don't know," I said. "Not long. I guess it all depends on how long it takes them to confirm that we're not dead in the water. Till then, I expect they'll be manning the obvious breach points, plus the helicopter." I pulled my compass from my pocket and wiped the rain from the glass on my sleeve. With the help of the lightning, I was able to confirm that we were still on the correct path. "We need to keep going this way," I said. "From what I remember from the maps, we should stumble onto a highway."

"Then we can steal a car," Zane said, almost excitedly. "Yeah," I said, staring at him awkwardly. "We can get a car. And then we head South again until we can either flip the car for another, or I can call someone, my brother, maybe."

"He can help us?"

"He can help us find a place to hide. I'm just hoping that he will. He's kind of a straight arrow."

"Sounds like a queer," Zane said. "Well, best get going I suppose."

Together we trampled through the brush, hopping over felled trees and ducking under whipping branches. We weren't concerned with making noise as the storm was a thousand times more monstrous. We weren't expecting any search parties or helicopters to swoop above our location. At least, not quite yet.

With bruises, and scratches, and blood drawn from our fight with the forest, we finally escaped the thick horror of the bush and planted our feet on the hard asphalt of the highway. Progress.

We checked both directions before wandering out of the cover of the bush; the road was as dark as the forest had been. The battering storm felt worse, but nothing great was ever accomplished without taking a shit kicking first. I checked my compass again, squinting my eyes in the darkness, waiting for a flash of lightning to illuminate my vision. It came, and we were soon on our way, heading South along the paved road, every step bringing us farther from the drab mundanity of prison, and closer to the freedom our beings were meant to experience. Prison was cruel and unusual punishment. Locking up a bunch of wild animals together under one roof and removing any and all hope of ever being let out, what the hell else did anyone expect to happen? Of course people like us would risk our lives to get out of it, it was basic psychology, like robbing a bank.

We walked for a good fifteen minutes, completely undisturbed. We kept to the shoulder in case any trouble were to arise, so we could duck out into the impossible darkness of the woods. And then, it came.

"Look!" Zane said, and we could see the glare of headlights about to round the corner in front of us. It was heading north, which meant that the odds were that it wasn't a cop, and we could probably hijack the car.

"I'll take care of this," Zane said, smiling. The sick bastard was enjoying every minute of it. "Just hide in the ditch and get ready to help if I need it."

"You sure?"

"Yeah, man. Just go, hurry."

I ducked down into the ditch and peered intently as the headlights lit him up. He waved his arms above his head and stood in the middle of the road. His clothes were filthy with mud, and shit, and blood, but he hardly seemed concerned.

The car honked its horn, swerved slightly at the sight of a man standing in the middle of the road during a violent storm, and then slowed and cautiously came to a stop just in front of him.

"Are you all right?" I heard a man's voice shout out over the storm.

"Yeah," Zane replied, and quickly jogged toward the driver's side with a seemingly friendly gait, just to talk–and then I heard the cries of pain.

"Argh! Mother of–"

"Shut up!" Zane screamed in fury. I hastily clawed up the muddy bank and raced to get to the vehicle before Zane did something stupid–but I was too late. By the time I approached him, he was landing hard fists into an already unconscious face, screaming wildly with the assault of the storm. When he'd finished unleashing his rage on the unsuspecting fool who'd been in the wrong place at the wrong time, he turned to face me and said, "Can you drive? My hands hurt for some reason. Ha! Ha! Ha! Ha!" and then dragged the mangled fool down through the muddy ditch and stashed him just inside the forest's fringe to sleep it off, or die. Degenerate bastard. Perhaps it would be a good time to note that I didn't necessarily agree with the dramatic actions Zane took, but when the pigs were all excited over a simple stroll through miles of shit, escaping assassination, killing one of your partners for being injured, and still being ahead of the game, a man needed to do what he needed to do. We had to get away or else it was back to board games and casual rape in the showers–unconscionably mind numbing.

I jumped into the driver's seat, followed by Zane as a passenger, and in seconds we squealed a sharp U-turn and continued our quest for freedom at top speed.

"Woo hoo hoo!" Zane screamed, slapping the dashboard and smiling widely. "We're on our way, baby! Fuck yeah!"

Seventy miles on the speedometer. Seventy five. The wipers swept across the glass with impressive speed, but it was nearly hopeless in the incessant downpour. Eighty five. Ninety. It was all like some big joke. Escape against all odds, then match the speed of your heart with a car flying blindly through a humbling storm. Stupid, but necessary. One hundred. One hundred and five.

We cleared the crest of a hill and came into a right turn, then eeled to the left, back onto a straight away, pedal to the metal. One twenty. One thirty.

One fifty.

I could taste freedom.

On we forged, like a rocket with no mind.

Part 3

"This is a nice ride, man," Zane said, checking the pockets of the passenger side door. "Nice pick."

In the glaring sun of the early morning, we were in a better mood than ever. Behind us, we'd left hundreds of miles, and now faced nothing but imminent freedom before us. I was certain that the cops were coming down hard back there, desperate to catch a thief and a killer, but the impressive speed with which we had managed to escape was definitely making me feel much better about the whole thing. If freedom was not earned through hard work, perhaps the impressiveness of our escape? Perhaps not.

"Look at all these buttons here," Zane continued. "Goddamn, it's like sitting inside a computer."

Just before dawn we had rolled into a small town named Yorkpark, population 5,600. Our car was nearly out of gas, so, naturally, we needed a new one. In a seemingly abandoned parking lot, a few cars sat idle, and I elected to steal a rather new Jeep. In seconds, impressive, really, Zane had the door unlocked and was toiling away at the wires underneath the steering column; and before I knew it, we were back on the road, heading East on the highway against the rising sun.

I was tired, but stocked full of adrenaline, and refused to stop until we crossed the state line and invited the input of formidable federal agencies into our demented affairs. Why not? Escaping prison was really only a series of lines that needed to be crossed. Most were ethical lines, which were easily brushed aside by men like us, but the important, difficult ones to cross were city lines, state lines, and borders. And with each came an added sigh of relief, because with every line crossed, the bureaucratic stupidity of so called justice demanded that the rules of the game change, which took time, a factor we could fully exploit. Just like with prison security, the authorities' greatest downfall was timing. Their lives and jobs were scheduled, rigid, and inflexible, presenting anyone with half a brain and a big old pair of balls to conveniently schedule themselves straight out of the system. Without timing, their system would fail, and escaping would be much more difficult.

Punctual assholes.

"I used to have one of these Jeeps, you know, the Cherokee," Zane was still babbling. "It was nice, but fuck me, look at all the upgrades they have in these now."

I nodded, but wasn't really in the mood for talk. I just wanted to get out of the state, then we could get the divine rest we both needed. I focussed my eyes on the road, half-ignoring Zane's ceaseless search of every nook and cranny of the vehicle. He snapped open the glove compartment and rifled through it, babbling away.

"I might buy another one of these later on. You know, if the cops don't kill me first." He pulled out handfuls of insurance papers, receipts, travel itineraries. "Man–I can't believe we actually got this far. We're fucking miles from the–Whoa! Check this out!"

From the tone of his voice alone, I knew what had happened; and although I was usually indifferent to such things, there was something about Zane that I found troublesome. He worried me with his unsteady mind. I turned my head and watched him pour his attention over a shiny gun he'd found buried in the glove compartment.

"This is a thirty-eight!" He cried excitedly, and checked the chamber. "Loaded too. Son of a bitch, man! How good can our luck get? You're in trouble now, you pig fuckers!" he declared, aiming the gun out the window and checking the sights. "At least now we've got a fighting chance."

"Yeah," I said, masking my discomfort. I don't mind guns. In fact, I wouldn't even hesitate to shoot someone if I needed too. But something about Zane told me that he hardly waited until he needed to use one. I could tell from his eyes that he was already looking forward to using the ugly thing.

He continued digging through the compartment, when his body suddenly jerked in surprise and he let out a sharp, shrill laugh.

"No shit!" He exclaimed. "Look at this!"
In his hand was a wad of hundred dollar bills, bound tightly with an elastic band. I was flabbergasted. Money! Just what we needed!

"Man, how good can our luck get? Ha! Ha!" he said. "A couple grand and a gun, things are looking up, friend."

Indeed they appeared to be, at least in the phantasmic grip of elation we were still both trapped in. The sight of the wad suddenly returned my thoughts to my own money, my nine million stashed away safely, awaiting my return. Once I got my hands on it, I would never be found again. I would disappear to the Bahamas, or South America, or anywhere there was no extradition treaty, really. It felt good to think about such things after the wretched, nervous fear that had loomed over us during our hectic escape. Already, I could taste the salted air of the beach I was going to retire on. I could see the beautiful women I would do unholy, unforgivable things to with nonchalant regularity. Ah, women. After being forced to waste nearly seven years of my young life in the name of raped morals, and being forced to shower in multicultural sausage fests, the thought of a nice, warm, wet woman was almost as sweet as holding those thick bricks of cold hard cash in my hands.

Almost.

I shifted my weight in my seat and rubbed my eyes with my knuckles. I was exhausted. We needed to rest, but first, we needed to cross the state line. With money and a weapon in our corner, all that was left was to cover a few more miles, buy ourselves some time from the bureaucratic simpletons, and finally close our eyes and escape the harsh reality that we were being hunted.

**

It was dark again. On the edge of a city, about a hundred miles past the state line, we'd taken refuge in a vast, busy truck stop, and slept a solid six hours in the Jeep. Sleeping was always risky business while on the run, but a stupid human necessity, nonetheless. Our grand minds were encapsulated in feeble, untrustable bodies, which were completely incapable of keeping up with our conscious wills. I was out of prison, but none of us were ever truly out of prison. We had too many needs to be tended to, regardless of our intent. It's what some people called, beautiful.

Zane slept in the passenger seat with the gun tucked tightly in his belt. I was still rather uneasy about letting him have the ugly thing, but I sure as hell wasn't about to try and grab it from him. The crazy bastard had thrown Marshall from a speeding boat without the slightest hesitation. I would be a fool to think myself any more important.

With drooping bags under our eyes, I started the engine and drove into the city in search of gasoline and food. Traffic was heavy, but none of that was bothering me. I'd stared at the same four walls for far too long to be complaining about traffic. Smoothly and without rush, I steered the car into traffic and cruised into the city, both of us silent with our thoughts.

I stared at the lights and the people walking the sidewalks, hoping I would get to experience that flavor of freedom once again.

I was out of prison, and in a place the police couldn't quite yet ascertain, but I was far from being free. Until I had my money, and until I had crossed the big imaginary line into a different country, I was considered an armed and dangerous fugitive, to be hunted down like a rabid animal. The journey, as much as I hated to admit it, was only just beginning.

Through numerous hasty intersections and sidewalks lined with busy bodies, we crawled through the city at a comfortable pace. Relaxed, for once. Calm.

"We should hit the strip club," Zane said. "Goddamn what I'd do to have a woman suck my dick for a change."

"Don't be stupid," I said. "We can't afford to stop anywhere for long right now. We need to keep moving. The farther the better. We should probably grab a new ride soon too."

He nodded.
"Yeah, maybe in a few hours we can hotwire a new one."

"Yeah," I said, looking down at the gas gauge. "In the meantime we'll need some gas. And some food; I'm fucking starving."

"Me too. There's a place right up there. Seems as good as any."

In minutes, I pulled the vehicle into the gas station and stopped next to a pump. We scanned our environment, looking for imminent threats, but the place was mostly empty aside from a couple walking out of the store.

"All right," Zane said, and held up the wad of cash. "You pump; it's on me. I'll meet you inside."

I nodded and stepped out of the car, careful to shield my face from the cameras covering the pumps, and trying not to be conspicuous. When I put the nozzle into the fuel tank and started pumping, my anxiety suddenly surged, and my paranoia became strikingly vivid. There was no reason for it. Incessantly, I checked the sights around me as if a swat team was waiting in the shadows until I lapsed in attention. It sent my imagination on wild rides of irrational horrors, and no matter how much I tried reassuring myself, there was no inner comfort to be found. I stared at the display on the pump. It was the slowest goddamn piece of shit I'd ever used!

"Come on, you fucking useless bitch!" I said to the inanimate pump. "Hurry it up!"

When the nozzle clicked in my hand, a sense of relief came over me. The whole ordeal had felt like an experiment in vulnerability, and I was suddenly anxious to get back on the road at top speed.

With the gas cover back on, I turned and headed for the store. I could see Zane through the window loading his arms with excessive amounts of junk food and multicolored drinks. Shaking the jello-like anxiety from my arms while I walked, I opened the door and joined Zane as he was grabbing an armful of potato chips. I followed suit and loaded up on unreasonable amounts of candy bars and exceptionally sized bottles of soda. Seven long goddamned years of not being allowed to disrespect my own body. Fuck it. Like all things in life, living came at a cost. Happiness took sacrifice. Success took risk. Plus, this shit was hardly the worst stuff I'd voluntarily put into my body.

I was so goddamned hungry. My sudden anxiety had rendered me dry–terrorized. My mouth watered when I approached the checkout behind Zane and dumped our haul of corporate poisons onto the counter, trying to smile and act normal.

"You guys on a trip?" the skinny geek behind the counter asked, chuckling at the size of our savage free-from-prison hunger. Above him, a TV played a cheerful commercial for some electric razor... I eyed it suspiciously, hoping it wasn't on some news channel covering our escape. And then, like an electric shock, terror shot through me, and I was suddenly desperate to close the transaction and get back on the road.

"Yeah," I responded to him plainly. "Listen, take like, two hundred bucks for the gas and all this shit, and just keep the rest–sound good?"

He smiled dumbly and cocked his head to the side. "Ah... Sure–I guess. I mean, you don't really have to–"

"Nonsense," I insisted, and tugged at Zane's arm to pay the man and get out of there.

He pulled bills from his pocket and put them on the counter while I stared with shadowed disgust at the television on the wall showing our faces!

Panic.

I loaded my arms with the food and kicked Zane in the leg, urging him to hurry the fuck up. He caught a glimpse of himself on the screen, and his eyes were followed by the clerk's, and suddenly, something went terribly wrong.

It's hard to describe the look on the guy's face. His eyes darkened, and all the color faded from his skin until he looked grey, ill. He stared at Zane squarely in the face, completely bewildered. I backed away from the counter and screamed at Zane to move, but before I could urge him again, the clerk's head blew up all over the wall. He'd shot the guy in the nose at point blank range.

My first thought was, Maybe I shouldn't have let this guy out of prison. I mean, the things he'd done up until then could perhaps have been justified as a man's own self-indulgent desperation; but this was savage. Evil.

"Jesus Christ!" I screamed, dumbfounded. "What the... What the fuck did you do?"

I wasn't a killer. I was indifferent, and mostly rotten at what people considered ethical, but I didn't believe in outright murder. In fact, as my initial shock began to dissipate, I felt quite ill and enraged by the whole thing.

Fuck him, I thought, and dropped the junk food on the floor. I burst through the door, determined to get in the car and leave him in the thick of it. Goddamn idiot! Beyond simply killing some innocent dude when he could just as easily have restrained him for a while, he'd given away our position to our exceptional enemy–the federal government.

"Shit!" I cursed, running across the lot. "Fucking asshole!"

I reached the car and jumped in. Behind me, Zane was almost there. I wouldn't have time to take off without him... And then he stopped. I looked over my right shoulder and my heart walloped weirdly in my chest; a police cruiser had violently jammed his transmission into park and stepped out with his gun aimed at Zane.

Zane shot first, hitting the car, and forcing the cop to duck desperately in avoidance. The cop shot back. Zane rolled on the ground, came back to his knees, and shot another round. Again the cop dodged; but he quickly recovered his stance and fired once more, hitting Zane in the thigh. He fell to the oil poisoned ground, wailing in pain, but still, he crawled away, closer to the gas pumps. I heard the cop warn him again to throw the weapon away and put his hands up. Zane told him to go fuck himself. I started the car, hammered it into gear, and slammed the accelerator to the floorboards.

Behind me, Zane put his gun against the pump's base and pulled the trigger. The resulting explosion was nothing short of catastrophic.

Part 4

"Fucking cocksucking, motherfucking, piece of fucking shit!"

What else could I say? Back there, Zane had caused a horrible scene. That cop was almost certainly dead. As dead as the geek in the store. As dead as Zane.

I'd felt the force of the explosion slam viciously against the car. It was followed by an annihilating ball of fire, and a monstrous, ugly, dark as my soul column of smoke ascending high into the atmosphere.

The bright and violent surprise caused unsuspecting commuters to smash into each other, but I refused to stop. I peeled away from the place, my heart not even beating anymore. My icy hands gripped desperately at the steering wheel as the speedometer tipped past one sixty.

My head was pounding, and I was helplessly confused. What the hell had just happened? Things had been going so well. We were on our way to freedom, and in a matter of minutes, despite not being positively identified by any authority, things had taken a turn for the worse. What was I going to do? I had a full tank of gas, but I was no longer in possession of a gun, or a dollar, or any food for my craving body.

The adrenaline was dizzying. It fueled a terrible fear. I tried to organize my thoughts. In a matter of hours, maybe less, the cops would put together what had happened. Or at the very least, they would carry strong suspicions about Zane's identity. A bulletin would go out, and as a result, one state would cooperate with its neighbor, and piece by piece, they would realize what was going on, and then they'd get to the insane task of finding me, the last remaining maniac on the lam. After what Zane had done, there would be no cost too high for my arrest–or my death.

I was angry when I left the scene and hammered the car down the open road, passing anything that was going slower than one hundred miles an hour. No–not angry–I was insane with rage.

I wasn't what most people would call a good person–but I was far from evil. However, being the only remaining criminal on the run, the consequences of Zane's actions would fall unfathomably hard on my head. Someone had to take the blame, and they certainly weren't about to blame a dead guy for his actions when a living guy could take his place and be made an example of. As far as they were concerned, I was the goddamned devil. Every perspective I could think of led to the same conclusion. I was completely fucked, and I was running out of time. I needed to get my hands on my money, make a couple phone calls, and arrange to have my stupid ass immediately smuggled out of the country. It was my last shot.

Through the inky darkness of the moonless night, I pushed the Jeep to its limits, hoping to get far enough to steal another car and remain anonymous for just a little while longer. I may as well have installed a neon sign on the roof of the Jeep; It, and I, were as wanted as a warm woman in a cold prison bed.

I felt ill. My bowels were irritated and punishing me with spastic, debilitating cramps. I needed to figure out what to do next. I needed a place to hide. I needed a plan; but planning while in the grips of a panic has never done a guy any favors.

***

The highway was mostly clear of traffic. A solid hundred miles beyond the enormous explosion, I was still rapt with anxiety. I couldn't stop thinking about Zane. In reality, his actions were my fault. I shouldn't have helped him out of prison. He was a monster at heart, and a fiendish beast in spirit. What could I say? I couldn't escape prison alone.

I felt bad for the store clerk. The skinny geek was much younger than Zane and I, and he hadn't done anything worth getting his brains blown out. Zane hadn't hesitated for a second. Not one second. I couldn't understand that. Every time I thought of it, I found myself choking up with emotions. I couldn't understand that, either. Guilt was a thing I rarely experienced, and never with much weight at that, so it was a new experience. I felt it burning in the pit of my stomach, unable to get the image of the geek's petrified face out of my mind, or the terrific point blank explosion. Perhaps my change of heart was due to my age. Perhaps time was finally making me human.

Terrible sensations ran through me. I felt unbearable. I wanted to crawl out of my skin. Paranoia invaded my mind like a caustic acid; I couldn't decide what to do. My vehicle was a trap, and one that was closing further in on me every minute. And beyond all that, I was suffering mean pangs of hunger. Starvation! I couldn't remember the last time I'd eaten something, and my body was beginning to warn me that it had had enough of my bullshit. My hands shook terribly, and I felt like my core temperature was plunging, and my vision was getting hazy.

Back in prison, none of these issues had crossed my mind. I'd been filled with rabid overconfidence, convinced by my ego that no one, and no thing could stand in my way. It seemed so simple then. In my fantastical imagination, no one had been hurt. No one killed. No guilt.

No guilt.

Up ahead I saw the lights of another city, and my stomach churned sickeningly, furiously demanding nutrition. I wanted to eat, I wanted to stop my body from eating itself, but it wasn't that simple. Nothing ever was.

I needed a new vehicle before I could stop and eat. There was no sense in doing anything aside from giving myself up unless I managed to switch cars. I also needed some money. And after that I would probably have to keep driving for a few hours before taking a break. It's hard work escaping the law, but it's still better than prison.

As soon as I reached the edge of the city I began looking for a new ride. I looked at the time; it was 11:30 p.m. I passed by closed shops, closed supermarkets, and closed gas stations, frustrated.

"Come on!" I whispered. "Where can I get a car?"

And then I saw it. A strip club. A place filled with drunken perverts, and practically devoid of threats aside from a small gathering of smokers by the entrance. It would have to do. I pulled in, and on my right I caught a flash of tail lights, and then noticed a stumbling fool opening the door and getting into the driver's seat of the car. Opportunity knocks.

I didn't really know what was going through my mind, but I stepped out of the Jeep and quickly padded over to the drunken idiot in the car. Something criminal came over me. The instinct to conquer was suddenly savage.

I came up and knocked quickly, gently, on the window. Inside, he squinted his eyes suspiciously, and terror drained away the features of his face. When he realized I wasn't a pig, his embarrassment, more than the fear he'd felt, quickly turned into something akin to irritable bowel syndrome.

With the demeanor of an experienced asshole, he rolled down his window and barked at me.

"What do you want, man?"

I smiled.

"Do you have a smoke?"

He sighed, annoyed.

"Listen, man," he said. "I don't fucking smok–"
I punched him in the face and attacked the door with vicious, prison honed hostility. With the door open, I grabbed the son of a bitch by the throat and dragged him out of the car. He fell to the asphalt and puked all over himself, but he was still pissed enough to get up and beg for a fight.

As he rose, I grabbed him by the collar and punched him in the face with as much brutality as I could conjure. He went stiff, but before he could even hope to regain his senses, I grabbed the side of his head, and with the ruthlessness of a lion, smashed it rabidly into the side of the car.

Hmm, Hmm, excuse me, everyone. The good sir has been knocked the fuck out.

Trying to hurry, I turned the little bitch over and stole his wallet, stole his car, and continued my quest at a red line pace into the great chaos of the unknown.

I suddenly wasn't so hungry anymore. I was wired with natural speed, electrified with sheer excitement. Already, I could barely remember the events properly. It had all happened so fast. My heart was racing, and I couldn't feel my legs, or my arms.

I had a car! I'd done it! I just needed to clear out of town with one destination in mind. I was going to get my money. I was getting it, and then I was leaving forever–before anyone else was hurt.

Part 5

I drove ten hours straight, stopping only twice to gas up and piss, but I couldn't go any farther. I needed sleep. The more, the better. Tomorrow would be another day of traveling, perhaps eight or nine hours, hopefully tipping things favorably in my direction.

Out of the kindness of his heart, the dude from the strip club parking lot left me a solid four hundred and twenty five dollars in his wallet. Jackpot, baby!

With the sun rising, I rolled into a small town with the sole intention of finding a hotel, having a shower, a meal, and getting some sweet, reality obliterating sleep.

I found one and pulled in. I scanned around me before cautiously walking to the office. Behind the desk stood a smiling old lady who looked like a stereotypical gentle and caring grandmother. My hostile worry was immediately disarmed.

In minutes, I had the key to a room, a smile on my face, and a terrible fatigue overwhelming me. Entering the room, I stripped naked and started a shower, smiling happily. Finally, comfort. The water was warm, the pressure perfect, and the complete lack of fifty other penises flapping around me was quite elating.

Once clean and dry, I called the small hotel restaurant and ordered two cheeseburgers, french fries, and a giant chocolate milkshake. It was all so goddamned delicious!

With my last bite, my eyelids waned in strength. I lay on the bed, absently staring at the television, and without notice I slipped into vivid dreams laced with sensations of peace, and tranquility, and safety.

***

I'd fallen asleep with the television on, and as the lingering, hazy delirium of unconsciousness gave way to reality, I realized that I was staring at my own face on the screen. Like a startled cat, I jumped from the bed and rushed to turn up the volume; but the instant I did, I found myself wishing I hadn't. I'd missed most of the broadcast, but the end of it was enough to cause me illness.

"...if you see this man, please do not approach him. You are directed to call your local emergency services immediately, or the hotline at the bottom of your screen. We repeat, he is armed and dangerous, and will not hesitate to kill. If anyone has any information, even if you do not think it of value, please report the tip immediately.

Wow, Jen. I really hope they catch thi..."

Panic!

Blindly, I ran to the toilet and puked. Horrible, disgusting despair rushed through me. Tears welled up in my eyes, and no matter how much I tried, I couldn't get the news anchor's voice out of my head. I was consumed with a sudden feeling of fatality. A singularity of doom. The walls around me were closing in, they were crushing me, squeezing me, driving me insane. A single, totalitarian instinct came over me.

Run!

I frantically splashed cold water into my face and darted through the room, desperate to recapture the feeling of progress, of freedom. I just wanted to get as far away as possible, but wishes weren't always so easy to make into reality.

I tugged violently at the door, swung it open, and then stopped, paralyzed into a ball of contracted muscles. I grew light-headed and sweaty as my heart raced. A police cruiser circled the parking lot on my left, and even though the pig didn't seem aware of my presence, a man with an ugly list of felonies pinned to his ass is righteous in his fear of any form of authority.

I felt stupid. The sight of the cop was so unexpected it caused me to dance in place as numbness crawled through my legs. It felt like a kick to the chest. I tried to shake it off, get to the car and leave, but I was concerned that my performance had been noticed by the pig. Things were about to sour.

In a moment of inner debate, I decided that I had a better chance in the car than in the room; at least I could run. The cruiser turned a wide circle in the lot and I hustled to my car. I jumped in, started it, and then eyed him intensely in the rearview mirror, hoping he would simply drive off and leave me alone.

He did no such thing.

Instead, he stopped, and though I couldn't see his face through the glass, I knew he was staring at me–waiting.

"Shit!" I hissed. "You stupid cocksucker, leave me the fuck alone. Keep driving, man. Come on."

Nothing.

I took in a deep breath and shifted the transmission into reverse. I backed out of the spot and kept a skeptical eye on the cop. I stopped, shifted into drive, and casually drove toward the highway.

It was torture. The last thing I wanted, or needed, was a

cop riding my ass. My car was most likely reported stolen by now, and in a few seconds that bastard would know it and come down on me with the dedication of a good little authoritive bitch. Impossible!

I rolled out of the lot, frantically looking over my shoulder, terrified. The cruiser remained parked. Seconds later, I had the car floored and flew away from there with every unit of speed physics and engineering would allow me. I pleaded out loud with whatever could hear me; please, please, don't let me get caught. Not after all the hard work.

Fear had a terrible, ugly way of altering one's perception of time. Despite my stern physical speed, the clock insisted on crawling. The torture of relativity.

I was nearly out of time.

Part 6

Seven and a half hours, one stop, and no cops. Good news, but it did nothing to keep me from suffering a raw, crawling anxiety. I was delusional. For most of the trip, I struggled repeatedly to focus on the road. My head swooned, and I felt hypnotized and filled with bad energy. The undertones of imminent capture resonated through every molecule of my body, but on I drove. With diabolical perseverance, I arrived at my intended destination.

Drenched with cold sweat, I stared suspiciously at a quaint log cabin set on the edge of a lake. The well manicured property was surrounded by thick, virgin bush. A neatly trimmed lawn stretched out before the cabin, edging up to the dirt road, and multicolored flowers framed the front of the structure.

The house was once owned by my father. He'd sold it years ago while I was sitting bored and sordid in prison; but before that, when I was on the run from authorities the first time, I'd made an unsuspected visit and buried my hard earned booty just behind the shed, located beyond the house.

I had no idea who the current owner was, but it was undoubtably occupied. An old pick up truck sat in the driveway, and the general activity seemed minimal. I hoped the occupant was an older man, and not one of those hero inclined punks who had been the bane of Marshall's existence.

Bottom line: I wasn't hoping, nor counting, on confrontation. With any luck, whoever lived there would be none the wiser after I was gone. I only wanted my money, and then I would leave everyone alone, forever.

At length, I cruised the dirt roads, trying to come up with a plan. Being mid-afternoon, I'd have to wait until it got dark, sneak in, dig up my cash, and make a smooth escape. That was the best I could come up with. It would have to do. I would have to wait, despite my tortuous, consuming, despicable rush to get it done.

I was out of patience, out of time, and completely out of my mind. It had been a long and hazardous escape from prison, and I'd left a long and ugly trail of carnage in my wake. People had been hurt, and some killed, so that I could achieve my goal. I tried convincing myself that it had all been worth it, but I wasn't so sure. It felt like a chore to think about the future. Wads of cash in my hands. The sun and the beach. The freedom. When did the cost get too high? Where was the line?

I supposed only time would tell.
I remembered there was an ancient logging road just up the road
from the cabin and decided to pull in there and sleep the time
away. Years of growth had rendered it invisible to the unsuspecting
eye. I backed into the invisible road, cloaked with leafy brush, and
rested my weary head against the seat. I suffered horribly at the
hands of ghoulish dreams and wild phantasms.

***

I slept five hours, but I was hardly rested. I'd passed from
one vivid hallucination to the next; imagining cops banging on
the car windows, and the geek with half a head sitting next to me,
blaming me. I felt terrible. I felt tired. I was so tired.

I lit a cigarette and tried to organize my thoughts while
my eyes adjusted to the darkness. My insides crawled with dread,
my mind with repulsion. Back in the days when I robbed banks
without so much as a thought about consequences, I feared nothing. In prison, elbow to elbow with rapists and killers, not once
had my heart skipped a beat. I could hold my own, and I could
be vicious when challenged. All of that had left me, however. I
was alone in the bush, afraid. I was afraid of myself and the ugly
things brewing inside of me. Afraid of the feeling that it no longer
mattered whether I got my money or not, because there were some
things I couldn't pay off, or run away from. Doom. I felt doom.

I finished my cigarette and sighed. I needed to forget
about the sinister things rustling inside of me and get to the task
at hand. When it was all over I could return to my introspective
depression. I needed my money. Pronto!

I started the car and cautiously edged out of the bush and
on to the road. I cruised back to the cabin, passed it, and parked on
the other side of the road. I turned off the engine and waited in the
dark for a minute, surveying, listening. No activity outside. Inside,
the lights were on and someone roamed about. No problems. My
only real fear was of a dog. I didn't know if the owner had one, but
if he didn't, he should damn well get one to keep people like me
out of his yard.

With a small military style shovel I'd picked up at a gas
station, I stepped out of the car and gently shut the door. In the
muted moonlight, I headed for the cabin, my eyes set on the lighted
windows. I heard nothing aside from gravel shifting lightly under
my cautious and meticulous steps. The air was damp, and fresh.

Cool, but not quite cold.

I gained the length of the driveway without incident, stopped next to the pick up truck, and stared at the big bay window at an angle. I couldn't see anyone inside, but I remained vigilant in my progress. I tippy-toed across the grass and headed for the old shed that stood in between the cabin and the lake. When I reached it, I stopped and surveyed the situation. My heart pounded hysterically. My breath was labored. I was standing on the precipice of my imagined freedom, a thing more precious to me than my own life.

I unfolded the shovel's blade, locked it into position, and searched the ground with squinted eyes. When I had buried the money, I'd stood with my back to the shed's wall, stepped out seven steps, and dug straight down. I repeated the ceremony, and, deciding that my presence was still undiscovered, plunged the shovel into the ground. The top was sod, and the ground beneath it was rather tough, but I dug with desperation in my heart. I needed the money more than ever. I had worked for it. I had risked my life for it. And I had sat my stupid ass in prison for years, thinking about it, wondering about it, wanting it.

It was mine!

Every time the shovel hit the ground, I found myself glancing at the house, nervous as hell. Pure insanity had driven me to this hole; it was too important to lose. I could probably deal with being discovered, but I wasn't going anywhere without my money. Not tonight. Not ever.

So close now.

In time my shovel hit something that wasn't soil, and something purely righteous ruptured inside of my chest. I dropped to the ground and began pulling dirt away with my hands, smiling wider than a dope starved heroin addict with a syringe in his cock.

With trembling hands, I pulled a wide duffle bag from the earth, and then another. The inside of the bags were lined with heavy plastic, and they were far heavier than I remembered.

I pulled back on the zippers to confirm the contents, though I had no real doubts. It was a psychological necessity. With them open, even in the dark, I could make out the solid bricks tightly wrapped in plastic, ready to whisk me away to any part of the world I damn well pleased. If anyone wanted to fuck with me now, I was going to put up the fight of my life.

"Yes!" I whispered, completely elated. I felt like crying. "Been waiting for me all this time. Daddy's home. Now let's get out of here!"

Smiling, I stood and began heaving the heavy bags over my shoulder, when I noticed a sight that sent a dizzying shock through my system.

Right next to the wall of the shed, an old man stood with a shotgun trained on me.

"What do you think you're doing?" he asked, offended, and perhaps even a little terrified.

"Listen," I said, glaring at him. "I'm leaving, all right. I didn't mean you any harm whatsoever. I came for something I left a long time ago, long before you even bought this place. That's all I wanted."

He eyed the bags suspiciously.

"What's in them?" he asked, pointing at them with the gun.

"Fuck you, that's what's in them," I said. "I told you, this is all I want. Just let me go, and you can go back to your life. You won't ever see me again, I swear."

"Oh, you swear now, do you?" he replied, but his offended air, which I suppose was fully warranted, was making me hostile. I wanted to waste no more time with this. I had want I wanted, what I had gone through hell for, and all I wanted now was to leave and continue with my life. He wasn't keen on allowing me the simple favor.

"Put the bags down," he said, and raised the shotgun to my head.

"Suck my fucking dick, old man. I'm trying to make this easy on both of us. You don't know who I am or what I'm fully willing to do. Now let me go."

"I can shoot you on the spot just for trespassing."

I was growing terribly angry.

"Then that's what you're going to have to do," I said. "Now either man up and shoot me, or get the fuck out of my way. I'm leaving here with these bags; it's up to you how you want to be left behind."

"Are you threatening me?"

"I'm warning you, you inbred simpleton cocksucker!" I was screaming now. "Get out of my fucking way or else I'll do what I need to do!"

He wasn't a fan of my words. He cocked the hammer on the shotgun, ready to shoot me, but something sinister erupted inside of me. In a flash, I swung one of the heavy bags toward him and hit his gun. It harmlessly shot a slug before hitting the ground, and I was caught in a blind rage!

I kicked him hard in the belly. He doubled over and collapsed to the ground, but what happened next was instinctive, and unguided by rational thought. Before I understood what I was doing, I snatched my shovel from the ground and brought it crashing down on his head with devastating force. I swung the ugly thing over and over with blunt force, blunt psychosis, reducing his panicked resistance to feeble twitches, and then stillness. Blood splattered violently into my face, into my mouth, and eyes. It was evil, unforgivable, but still I swung.

When I finished, he no longer even looked human. He'd been reduced to a broken form in the dark. Motionless and mangled. His fractured skull an open invitation to worms and bugs alike.

What had I done?

I stared at him in shock, disbelief. I felt my arms shaking and barely noticed the shovel falling from my hand. My body convulsed with tremors, my stomach churned, and I closed my burning eyes tightly. When I opened them again, I realized that I was lying on the ground next to the savaged carcass, my face in a puddle of vomit.

Shaking my head, I clambered back to my knees, and then up to my feet.

"What the fuck, man? What the hell did I... Ah, God!" Blindly, I snatched the heavy bags from the ground, hurled them over my shoulder, and with every ounce of energy I could muster, I ran back to the car.

The instinct had come naturally enough. Get in the car, and drive as far away from the pandemonium as possible.

All I could think of was, I'm a killer. I'm a killer. I'm a killer!

Where had it come from?

Part 7

"Look, man. You're all over the news, you know that?"
"Really? I haven't noticed. I've been too busy sightseeing the country. Why the fuck do you think I'm calling you?"

There was a pause on the line.
"I know why you're calling... But–"

"But?" I exclaimed. "No buts! I need your help, goddamn it!"

"Listen..." he said. "I know, all right. I'd be calling you if our roles were reversed, but you need to understand, man. The whole country has a hard on for you. Airports, trains, borders, they're all waiting for you. I love you like a brother, but anyone who tries to help you is going down with you. I have a family now, you know?"

"I've got nine million fucking dollars for your family!" I insisted.

In the car, the blood had been like syrup on my hands, smearing and drying on the steering wheel while I screamed the engine down the narrow gravel road. I gasped for air, exhausted, and I was unsure about the reality of what had happened.

"I'd do anything for you!" I continued. "Anything, god-damn it! I just need a favor!"

Dead silence–the sound of betrayal.
Off the dirt road, I'd raced down the highway, insane with para-noia. I didn't recognize my own eyes in the rear view mirror. I felt like I was watching everything happen without any conscious con-trol. My hands were numb and cold, and my entire body trembled, but it all seemed so distant and surreal. I drove aimlessly, trying to figure out my next move, but something sinister had possession of my mind. I needed to stop and get my head straight.

"Please, man," I broke the tense silence. "You'll never have to work another day of your life, I promise. Just help me this one last time and you'll never hear from me again."

I seethed and heard nothing on the other end; and then, I heard the resolve in his voice.

"I'm sorry, man. I can't do it. I just had a little girl three months ago. I hope you understand. I've made promises. I can't do this to my family."

I sighed and felt a wave of dread wash through me. It was the final nail in the coffin.

"Take care of yourself, man," I said. "Raise your daughter

to be nothing like us."

I hung up and punched a hole in the wall.

After driving for what had seemed like hours, I came across a hotel and parked farther down the street in order to survey the activity in the parking lot. I couldn't walk into the office with blood soaked clothes, so I broke into an empty room while in the grips of a panic attack. I had a long shower and tried to calm my flaring nerves. I was angry, and scared, and choked with panic. In time I turned off the water and dried, and I then made some calls in search of a reliable friend, an acquaintance, or an old contact willing to help me.

That last conversation was with a man named Steven Paxton, a past partner of mine in armed robbery. We'd hit two banks together and gotten away with a healthy haul. Two years after our last job, one he wasn't involved with, I was busted and sentenced to rot in prison for the rest of my life. He was my last call, my last hope for salvation.

Before speaking with him, and after multiple disconnected numbers and various other rejections, I had called my brother, the straight arrow, who not only refused to help me, but promised to report my call to the authorities. I responded with rage induced threats, because I'm a responsible brother, but I'd hardly screamed a sentence before he hung up on me. So... The jig was up. I'd run clear through my list of reliable contacts and came up empty on all fronts. I say reliable, but in reality I had no idea. I hadn't heard from anyone while in prison. I thought I had friends I could trust in times of need; evidently, despite the years, the trials, and the adventures, I didn't mean a goddamn thing to anyone.

I stared absently at the wall for a long time, letting the nightmare of reality rush in like a kaleidoscope. I was screwed. My feeble plan had failed. I had my money, sure. It was right next to me. At will, I could feel it, and smell it, and spend it foolishly; the only problem was, ON WHAT?! What the fuck was I supposed to do with it, wipe my ass? It wasn't even worth that to me. It was useless! It was fucking useless because no one wanted to help me.

I'd been kidding myself. I wasn't getting out of the country. I wasn't going anywhere except right back to a squalid hole in prison. The pigs would never stop hunting me, and at present I was probably right up there with the big boys on the most wanted list, if not in first place.

Look, mommy! First place! Do you love me now?

Fuck me.

I weighed my options. I could give myself up, but every

ounce of my being rejected that idea on principle alone. Never had I given in to authority; there was no use in starting now that I was in the big leagues. Why the hell should they win? Fuck 'em. My other option was to keep running. Make a beeline for the border, take my chances, and if I met with trouble along the way, well, it couldn't be helped. I'd go down to hell with as many of the self-righteous bastards as I could manage to bring with me.

I was never going back to prison.

I ran trembling fingers through my hair, wondering how it had all gone so wrong. How had I ended up trapped in a hotel room, desperate for some type of vague, cryptic salvation? My friends couldn't help me. Deep down, I suppose I knew that. Deep down, I suppose I knew everything was over after I'd caved a man's skull in with a shovel. I'd left him to be defiled and devoured by nocturnal creatures. They probably hadn't found him yet. Maybe no one would find him for days. That thought suddenly made me sad. Maybe I had lost my mind. Surely, I'd lost my soul.

I stood from the bed and paced the room, filled with sordid emotions. I had nowhere to go; no one to see. I was just... In a room. Nothing more. Nothing less. Jesus Christ, and all this time I thought I was a pretty cool guy. Interesting, as it were.

Ha.

What an asshole.

I sat back on the bed, exhausted, and sick of running. I was sick of running from the law, and I was sick of running from myself. Something had shifted in my perception of life. The world was different, somehow.

The truth was that I was a bad man and a dangerous person. Was that my fault? I've tried different paths in my life, different directions, different goals; but all roads seemed to lead back to the same old me. It's fate. Destiny. I was born to end up sitting in grimy hotel rooms, rich as shit and useless as fuck. It was hilarious, like the rest of my life. I was genetically programmed to cause trouble and incite gun toting pigs to abuse me and punish my smiling face. I'd never change; how could I? As much as I hated it, I loved it; it was part of my DNA. It has been since I was twelve and started shoplifting, or when I was nineteen and started stealing cars, or twenty-four and robbing stores at gun point, or twenty-nine and robbing banks, or thirty-nine and escaping prison, killing people, and losing my mind in a goddamned hotel room. I wasn't meant to live in a civilized system. I was programmed for survival of the fittest, eat or be eaten, an eye for an eye and a fist for a fist.

I was born to fail.
I buried my face in my hands and dug my fingers into my eyes. My mind reeled with crude images of a shovel hacking a skull to pieces, splattering blood in all directions. I was no killer. Well... In reality, perhaps, but not in principle. I was just... Desperate. At the time, I felt like I needed to do anything I could to survive, no matter how immoral. A few hours later, however, I was having a revelation; I'd crossed an unknown personal limit. I had finally gone too far. I'd betrayed myself, and it was something I couldn't hide from, I couldn't ignore, and I couldn't lie about.

I thought about the geek from the gas station. Prison no longer seemed like punishment enough.

I pulled the blind from the window about an inch and peered outside. There was nothing happening. No traffic. No cops. No future.

I lit a cigarette, grabbed the complimentary hotel pen and note pad and scrawled, "I'm sorry," on the page.

Was I? I didn't know anymore. I didn't know anything. I sat on the bed and stared pensively at the wall, puffing on my cigarette. I thought, I should do something good for once. I should do the world a favor and do what I know is right. I'd had enough. I was done.

I stood from the bed and crushed my cigarette in the ashtray, then lit another. Taking a hefty drag, I lit the drapes with my lighter, then blazed the bedspread. I calmly took another drag from my cigarette and watched the flames hurtle against each other with increasing violence. The way of life.

In a minute, the walls were ablaze and I began choking on the smoke. The temperature skyrocketed, and I suddenly didn't want my cigarette anymore. It was beginning to look like hell around me.

It was the right thing to do. Goodbye, cruel world. I choked and fought fiercely to maintain consciousness for as long as possible, when a curious thought suddenly crossed my mind. I was offing myself in a hotel room. I'd set fire to a building filled with other people because I was tired of myself. What the hell was wrong with me? I was incapable of not hurting others. I'd just wanted to do something right for once–but I couldn't manage it. I was a walking ensemble of contradictions.

Simian.
The smoke billowed intensely, and the fire alarms screamed shrilly. I couldn't catch a breath; every attempt was like inhaling fire. I

coughed, and gasped, and instinctively dropped to the floor, suddenly desperate for escape.

Curious creatures, we are.

Simian cowards.

My skin blistered and bubbled, and when I couldn't scream in agony anymore, I gave up and lay facedown on the floor. The pain was beyond description; intense, and yet, I felt like I could relax for once. They hadn't apprehended me, after all. Instead, they would find me charred in the middle of the rubble, dead. With the last of my strength, I smiled. My demented ego was fully satisfied.

I thought: If I can't win, then nobody fucking wi–

The End

A FUNNY LITTLE STORY

Stepping out of his combine, the farmer stared at the row of hay stretching out before him with narrow, concentrated eyes. He didn't understand. A few minutes ago, he jumped out of his seat and banged his head against the roof of the machine when a small ball of flames zapped down from the sky and started a fire in his field. Confused, he shielded his eyes from the sun with his hand and stared upward. A long, thin trail of smoke vanished into space; it was terrifyingly beautiful.

The fire was growing in intensity, but with a small effort he managed to suppress it with the extinguisher from the machine. He pulled back his cap, scratched his polished scalp, and looked off in the distance intriguingly. He spat, cocked his head, and stared again at the endless snake of black smoke.

"Some kind of space junk or something," he mumbled to himself. As he stared, however, it seemed as though the other end of the snake, however high up it was in the atmosphere, was dispersing and blackening the sky with dense, apocalyptic clouds. The farmer stumbled back a step with his mouth gaped open, his eyes wide and spellbound. A treacherous wind picked up, and the farmer stumbled, fell to one knee, and then lurched for his machine under the cover of a sky as black as a moonless night.

Desperately climbing up the steel steps, a deafening roar blasted from above and startled the farmer to the ground with his hands over his head as a crude helmet.

The wind intensified, the roar did too, and as the situation approached the farmer's critical point of endurance, the ground beneath him shook terribly and took his breath away. He flailed his arms and writhed with panic. Getting back to his hands and knees, he couldn't believe the sight before him. He twitched automatically, and instantly felt a profound fear of it; a massive machine sat in his field, glowing with intimidating beauty. Smoke billowed around the smooth edges of its walls and rose toward the blackened heavens, filling the farmer's immediate area with an acrid stench.

Choking on the caustic air, he glared and shook his head repeatedly; he'd never seen anything like it in his life.

The thing stood a solid two hundred feet in height, and at least three hundred across. A mechanical football field, thick, and smooth, and constructed with metals the farmer couldn't readily identify. Lights intensified in brightness, then dimmed, but as far as he could tell there were no actual lights mounted to the outside–the glow seemed to come from inside the walls–somehow. It was oval in shape, becoming point-like near the top, like an intergalactic tear drop. It was polished like a mirror, and anywhere the farmer looked he could only see his own figure stumbling around dumbly, simultaneously scared, excited, and baffled.

He took timid steps toward the thing, then something made him stop. A new roar erupted in the sky above him, but this one he could readily identify.

Helicopters.

He searched the sky and found a convoy of choppers coming in from behind him, each with armed soldiers hanging from the sides. Within minutes, the farmer's field was polluted with machines, man made and apparently not, and soldiers screamed at him with guns drawn. A uniformed body approached and grabbed him by the arm.

"Sir, you need to evacuate the area immediately. This is a military order."

But the farmer was too perplexed to make sense of the words.

"What in the hell is this thing?" he asked, but his voice was drowned out in the oppressive noise around them. The soldier slightly tightened his grip.

"Come with me, sir," he said. "Are you injured? Have you been hurt? Have you touched the machine at all? How long have you been out here? What did you see?"

"Easy, fellow, easy," the farmer said. "This is my land, and I demand to know what's happening."

"It's not your land anymore, sir," the soldier replied. "Military orders. This entire area is quarantined and under our jurisdiction. You are trespassing and must leave immediately. Please, sir."

"Trespassing!" the farmer eyes grew wide in offense. "This is my land! I've lived here my whole life. I don't understand how you people can just come here without documentation or invitation and take over my property. I've been–"

"Sir," the soldier interrupted. "I apologize. But this is matter of national security. If you will not leave of your own accord, you will be forcefully removed. There is no offense intended; just doing our jobs, sir."

Dejected, the farmer snorted and stared at the behemoth towering above the mess of helicopters. It wasn't making any noise, or moving, and didn't even seem to be occupied by any living beings. But something had built it, and something had flown it there. He frowned, angry that he was being forced off his land, and curious to see what was going to happen. Would they approach it? Knock on it? Shoot at it? Anything was possible, and seeing as the event was taking place on his land, his rightful claim in the world, he felt he should at least be afforded the opportunity to stick around and find out.

No such luck.

Before he could protest further, a pair of soldiers led him to a helicopter. They strapped him to the seat and shut the door, giving the pilot the okay to take off. The blades gained speed and the chopper lost its grip on the ground. The farmer stared intently at the monstrous machine. The sky above him was clearing up, and now the thing glared with sunlight so bright it hurt his eyes to look at it.

"What in the hell is this thing doing on my land?" he mumbled to himself. As the helicopter picked up speed in the opposing direction, he noticed another small army of choppers making their way to the location he was leaving.

"Goodness," he said. "I've never seen such madness in my life."

Chapter 2

Standing before the long conference room table, around which crowded an assembly of representatives, ministers, and military personnel, the President stared at his advisers, and then at the live feed of the machine on the monitor behind him, unsure of what to say.

"Has anything come out of it?" he asked.

"No, sir," a General replied. "Nothing yet. We're not even sure where the door is, or if there is one. But there was an old farmer present at the landing, ah... There's his photo on the screen. He saw it land, but we removed him as soon as we arrived."

"Good. Good." The President nodded, and the other advisers smiled.

"God," The General said. "Can you imagine? First contact with an alien life form and it's with some greasy old farmer. A nice first impression of humanity. Ha! Ha! Thank God we got there in time."

The President nodded again and bit his bottom lip; uncertainty danced in his eyes.

"Anyone else have an idea they'd like to share?" he asked the room.

"I think we should keep our distance," said the foreign minister, her eyes tinged with fear. The President looked back at the General and pondered the suggestion.

"Personally," the General interrupted the President's train of thought. "I think we need, we must, have a military presence in place; if only to show that we are capable of returning any hostile action they may be thinking of taking."

This too was a good suggestion, but not enough to sway the President either way.

"Sir," the President's secretary poked her head into the room, a guard held the door open for her. "You're getting calls from leaders around the world. They want an update on the situation, and most are demanding a meeting before any further action is taken."

"Yes, yes," the President nodded, stroking his chin with a nervous hand. "Just continue taking messages. We have a crisis on our hands at the moment."

"Yes, sir," she replied quickly. "I also just hung up with the Secretary-General of the United Nations; he is especially keen on communicating with you."

"Very well," he replied. "I will be out to return his call in a minute. Thank you, Jillian."

"Yes, sir," she said, and nodded before thanking the guard at the door and leaving the room.

"Damn it," the President said. "We already have the entire planet knocking on our door. We need a contingency plan, people, before every country in the world gets involved and things get out of hand. This machine is in our country. We are the ones at immediate risk; therefore, regardless of outside opinions, we are handling this our way. You have an hour to come up with something reasonable and efficient to present to the United Nations. Does everyone understand?"

The response was unanimous from the assembly, and the President quickly left the room, feeling slightly ill.

In his office, he first returned the Secretary-General's call and agreed to an international meeting in three hours' time, most leaders attending via satellite transmission.

An hour later, with his team's plan of action in hand, he gave the go ahead to the General to get an armed military presence in place at the landing site, and then boarded his plane and headed for the meeting.

***

"... In addition to the military presence already at the site, we have nuclear armed fighter jets circling a five kilometer radius. Needless to say, the last thing I want to be responsible for is deploying an atomic weapon on my own soil, but the truly unfortunate reality is that we know nothing of this machine, or if there are, in fact, living, thinking beings inside of it."

The President leaned back in his chair, away from the microphone, and stared about the room. It was a virtual meeting for the most part. Faces on screens. Presidents, Prime Ministers, and representatives of various social causes listened to his voice in lieu of mounting their own arguments.

"It sounds like you're trying to intimidate your way into avoiding an attack, in turn risking a strike first reflex from the visitors," one the faces said, and the others became agitated and aggressive.

"Please, let's have order," the Chairman of the meeting said, and with a lag, the voices calmed.

"In my opinion," began a Prime Minister. "Instead of

proving ourselves capable of hostility, we should make a strong effort to actively show that we are intelligent beings with rich and diverse cultures. There is no need to greet anything alien with technological violence. We should greet them as people, as what we are. What other opinion does anyone have?"

"We should shoot first," a President started. "Nuke them on the spot. Friendly or not, there's no need to find out. We have the capabilities, and we have a responsibility to defend our species from outside threats."

"To use nuclear weapons, unprovoked, on unknown visitors?!"

Voices roared with unintelligible protests and supports. "Order!" the Chairman demanded again. "One at a time, please! This is an unprecedented issue, and one which requires cooperation in order to resolve."

"I agree with the Prime Minister," another Prime Minister took up the conversation. "I believe it's important to show them how intelligent we really are. Our ingenuity, our technology, our cultures. I believe that by showing them we are conscious beings, it will be enough to discourage them from an unprovoked attack. However, when I think of it further, what do we do if they're indifferent? What if they don't care about who we are and what our cultures mean? What if they view us as nothing more than cattle? This is a highly volatile situation."

"But how do you show something alien that you are conscious, exactly?" A President replied. "We are judging this narrowly, and only considering things from our point of view here on earth. It may prove to be a grave mistake. In a sense, we should simply keep it isolated and wait for something to happen. We shouldn't crowd it or impose ourselves upon it, and we certainly shouldn't fire any type of weapon against it. We know nothing about how they think, or what they are capable of."

"Hell, we don't even know if there's anything inside. What if it's just a giant robot? How are we supposed to deal with its presence?"

"All right, please, respected guests..." the Chairman was once again attempting to calm the room of bickering computer screens when The President interrupted.

"Excuse me, Ladies and Gentlemen, if I may have a moment with you all."

The volume faded, faces stared, the floor was granted. "I respect all of your opinions, but the fact of the matter is that this thing has landed smack dab in the middle of my country, which means that it is my citizens who are at most risk in this situation. As I've explained, at the moment the site is secured by my military, and it will remain that way for the security of everyone. We are, quite literally, keeping this situation under the push of a button. We will allow a reasonable distance approach to the object, but nothing too close until we conclude processing and securing the site. The first thing the beings will notice, if there are any, is that we are cautious, and simultaneously capable of being vicious. I think that should be sufficient until we make first contact."

The room erupted with protests and promises of military and political retaliation.

"That's all I have to say," the President concluded. "It's the best, and, realistically, the only responsible action we can take at this point. The security measures are necessary to ensure maximum safety for everyone. Thank you all."

"Mr. President," another Prime Minister chimed in. "Though I'm sure we all understand your concerns about safety, this is nonetheless a global event, irrelevant of borders. An alien machine has landed on our planet—our planet—I hardly think the geographical location they chose, or happened to land on, gives any country the right to exclude any other from representing the vast cultures, beliefs, and art inherent to each. If the visitors do prove to be hostile, you can be assured that the global community will have a hand in supporting you in defense, but you have no right to chose how or what first impression we as a planet should imply on these beings. We know nothing of them, and they, presumably, nothing of us. It is thus only fair to assume the unexpected. We need to show them what we are, who we are, and what we represent. The rest is up to them."

A multitude of figures applauded in agreement, and demanded the right to have every country and culture on the planet equally represented. The President took in a deep breath and considered the arguments, but resisted the impulse to give in. He could empathize with their desires, but he was well aware of how quickly things could get out of hand if too many opinions were involved. A firm decision on any subject would prove impossible. He felt a heavy wave of despair wash through him.

"Listen," the President said. "I understand. But what's making me most nervous is the fact that we have nothing to base our decisions on. What if they view the representation of our cultures as hostility? What if they don't care? What if they are simply here for resources, or enslavement?" Suddenly, the screens throughout the room were silent. "You see; we don't know. They could be looking for slaves as equally as they could be wishing to establish a fruitful and mutually beneficial relationship, but we do not know for sure either way. We don't even know if we can communicate. Everything about this situation is a variable, and no logical guesses can be deduced. We are blind here, and all I want is to ensure the safety of everyone. I want to be prepared for as many possibilities as we can, most notably, a hostile attack. I think all of us would feel much better knowing that if they do happen to strike first, we are fully prepared to retaliate. Doesn't that make sense to anyone else? Don't you want to be prepared in the event of an attack?"

He leaned back again, staring aimlessly at the screens about the room. The faces were silent, thoughtful. The decision on how to proceed was terribly unclear to everyone.

"I just," another Prime Minister spoke and scratched her nose uncomfortably. "I don't know how we are supposed to cooperate on this, Mr. President. We all have opinions on what should be done and how, but time is of the essence here, and a global cooperation of this scale has never been proposed before. All we are asking for is the opportunity to have our inputs considered, and have our help accepted. I think we all agree that compromises must be made, but we must also realize that this is a situation which transcends politics, religion, and anything else we are familiar with. The situation is as alien as the machine itself; therefore, I ask you personally–would you consider receiving the leaders present at this meeting to your country in order to assist with the situation as best we can? Anything is possible at this point. But if we are prepared, together, it will be much easier to not only better handle a hostile situation, but also to calm the qualms each country may or may not have in making first contact with an alien entity."

The faces on screens awaited a response, most agreeing with the request. The President sighed and looked at his watch. They'd already spent far too much time debating the situation. Action was necessary. But it was becoming increasingly obvious that he was being pushed into a corner. The leaders were demanding proper representation, and he wasn't in a position to deny them. He was a reasonable man, after all, and if the machine had landed in some other country halfway around the planet, he would be in their position, demanding a first row seat to the event. It was the most difficult and uncertain decision he'd ever had to make.

He leaned forward and approached his mouth to the microphone.

"All right," he said. "I understand, and I agree. Here's what I propose; you are all invited to my country, along with whatever representatives you choose to bring, and I will justly consider your opinions in how we handle the situation–however–the machine is under the command of my military. If the situation does turn hostile, then I will need each of you to pledge your assistance in whatever manner necessary. Is that agreeable?"

Silence permeated the room as the figures on the screens stirred with nervous ticks and profound stares.

"You have my pledge," a President spoke first. "I will arrive in your country just after midnight. Thank you, Mr. President."

"Very well," the President replied. "I appreciate your help."

"I too agree," a Prime Minister said.
"As do I," another President.

Before long, each face in the room agreed to the terms and readied themselves to make the trip.

"I thank you, and look forward to receiving you. Regardless of our individual political disagreements, I hope we can look past our beliefs and careers and ensure that we present ourselves as responsible, sentient, and intelligent beings. I am awaiting your arrivals. Travel well, friends. Thank you for your time."

And with that, the meeting was adjourned.

Chapter 3

The President held his breath, massaged his temples, and exhaled in a controlled manner. His nerves were shot. Things like war, foreign policies, and embargoes could be negotiated, agreed upon, and enforced, but never in his life had he dreamed of being placed in such a chaotic situation. Alien beings cared nothing of human politics, so what was he, or anyone, supposed to do, exactly? Impose an embargo and declare war? It was an impossible situation, and one that was growing in desperation with every minute of indecision.

Four days after his meeting with the leaders, the machine still stood monstrously in the field like an ill-planned tower, and nothing of importance had yet happened. Nothing of importance on behalf of the machine, that was. On the outside of it, madness had been attracted, and the most honest depiction of human nature ever presented ensued.

People from all over the world converged on the scene, screaming wildly, dancing, praying, fighting, fornicating, and foaming at the mouth to have their own cultures, beliefs, and ideas represented at the forefront of the chaos. Throngs of people welcomed the aliens, next to throngs of others demanding their destruction, next to throngs of others begging to be taken away with them. Flags, signs, music, and lights turned nights into loud messes of petty chicanery. Scientists wanted a chance to study the machine up close before it either opened up or took off into space, but the world leaders declined their requests. Religious groups unanimously denounced the machine as a sign of evil and demanded its destruction in the name of their various faiths. It was the first time all religions had unanimously agreed on a major issue. It was them against a machine, a seemingly greater enemy than each other.

The world leaders attempted to resolve the situation from a luxurious underground bunker, but there was little they could do about the sweltering crowds. With a solid chunk of the world's population swarming to the site, force was no longer an option for control. In the face of the brutal inactivity, the leaders' patience began to fail, and tempers flared like volcanos.

"I say we try to open it, and if that fails, blow it open," a President said. "We need to know what's inside of that thing; look at what it's doing to the world. The mystery is oppressive."

"Are you insane?" a Prime Minister roared. "We're still caught up with the same argument as the day this thing landed.

We don't know what's inside; therefore, it's a fool's move to force anything on it and risk a retaliatory attack on scales we possibly haven't even imagined. What if our atomic capabilities are archaic to them? Don't you think they would have some sort of shield against it? Where did they come from? It's almost certainly not from our own solar system, so I think it's reasonable to assume that if they have the ability to travel through interstellar space, surely they have grown beyond an atomic age in both technology and weaponry. That or they've perfected it. Everyone's lives are at risk here; we can't afford to take a blind chance on anything."

"All right, everybody calm down, please," the President said. "Given the circumstances, we are doing the absolute best we can. Everyone has a valid point, which is what's making this situation impossible to navigate clearly. The only real option we have is to continue to wait until we gather enough empirical data to make an educated decision. Without it, we have a responsibility to do exactly what we have been doing. We are not endangering any lives at the moment; not directly, anyway. We can't control everything; in fact, we can't control very much. We must push our egos aside and remain logical. We can't allow our emotions to get the best of us."

The leaders were having another meeting to discuss updates from the quarantined site. The room in which they sat was encased in concrete walls twenty feet thick on all sides, five stories above, and set eighteen stories below ground. White painted walls, LED lighting, and top choice decor; the place was a sprawling underground palace the size of a village, and it was stocked to the seams with the absolute best in comforts, luxuries, and technology. From that facility, the day to day operations of a country, especially one engaged in full on war, could be conducted without the slightest interruption or consequence. It was exclusively designed for the isolation of the powerful.

"Mr. President," an aide stepped into the room. "Major-General Hops is holding for you."

"Thank you, we'll speak with him now."
The aide pressed a button on a remote and a wall length television came to life with the image of a decorated soldier standing at attention, the machine huge and towering in the background. The aide turned the lights off and stood next to the door.

"Good day, Major-General Hops. How are things on site?"

"Hello, Mr. President, and esteemed guests of our country.

I'm honored to be speaking with all of you. Concerning the machine, things are stable and unchanging. Nothing's happening. But the situation outside the quarantine is getting out of hand, sir. There are millions of people out here pressing up against each other, and every minute there are more coming. My fear at the moment is a quarantine breach, sir. Even with the use of force, we are severely outnumbered."

"There is no force authorized on civilians," the President responded. "We are discussing the situation. Continue with your orders for now. Thank you, Major-General. Until next time."

"Thank you, sir. Ladies and gentlemen."

The aide turned off the television and turned on the lights. The present faces were haggard and drawn with fatigue. The last four days had been virtually devoid of sleep, and the hours that were consumed often proved to be filled with nightmares and anxiety. Despite the mental troubles, everyone tried to remain devoted to the cause–cooperation–but evidence was mounting against the possibility of cooperating on nothing. The world was turning savage, out of control, and far beyond the influence of world leaders.

Protests broke out around the globe, and for reasons so varied they cancelled each other out of meaning. Most grew violent, and ended with genuine acts of terrorism indiscriminately strewn upon uninvolved civilians. Places of worship were destroyed by zealous non-believers; in turn, those who'd spent lifetimes preaching peace and love took up arms and returned the terror in the name of whichever deities they ascribed to. The rich and poor were suddenly equals; as were the political and not; the faithful and non. Traditional social customs were discarded in favor of frantically getting each other's hands around each other's throats and strangling the perceived stupidity right out of each other's existence. In consequence, stable economies fumbled, tripped, and fell into the meaningless.

Deep underground, the leaders grappled to find a solution to the chaos, but tempers were proving detrimental to their cause.

"How could this have happened so quickly?" a Prime Minister said. "Nothing has come out of the machine, yet everyone has gone off the deep end. Some of our countries, while we hide here underground, are falling to pirates and thieves. Some of our countries, represented right here in this room, are rumored to have had their governments overthrown. Personally, I would like to leave here and go home. I think we should re-evaluate our priorities. We may have nowhere to go outside of this box."

Eyes exchanged tense glances.

"It's irresponsible to leave," another President piped up. "We must stay here and deal with this situation. We have to represent our respective countries. Order can always be restored. At the moment, we have a situation demanding our immediate attention."

"If you've no interest in your own country, that's your problem, but don't imply that on me," the Prime Minister shot back. "I'm proud of my country, and devoted to it, and I refuse to let it fall into the hands of warlords. It's unacceptable!"

"It's unacceptable to leave! Our countries need us here in case–"

"In case of what? An attack? An overthrowing of our governments?"

"Hey! Hey!" the President attempted to regain control. "Please, let's not succumb to madness down here too. We need to stay focussed on the issues at hand."

"There are no issues at hand; nothing is happening here. Nothing! We are standing around while real lives are being destroyed, and nobody wants to bat an eye. I can't live with myself if that's what's required of me."

"Then go! Just leave!"

"All right!" the President roared. "Okay, let's calm down. Let's all take a break and get some rest. We're too worked up to think rationally at the moment. If something happens we will be notified immediately; until then, I recommend sleep. Read a book. Have a shower. Do what you must, but please, we need to concentrate on working together. All right? Thank you. I will see you all later."

With that, he stood and excused himself from the room, irritated with his guests. They were acting like children, unable to keep calm long enough to talk through an issue. He was tired, and grumpy, and just wanted a few hours of sleep before returning to the debate.

In his suite, he stripped and had a shower, a meal, and then lay in bed and watched the news. There were social maelstroms of violence, hate, fear, and mystics all over the world. It was a terrible situation, and one getting further from resolution with every second the mysterious machine did nothing. He had no idea what to do.

In time he rested his head against the bed's headboard, closed his eyes, and fell asleep.

***

Two days later, the situation worsened. The machine was still silent, inactive, and devastating to the human race. The thick crowd surrounding the machine split into factions and declared war on each other for reasons ranging from religion, to birthright, to freedom, to the unexplainable. None of it mattered. It was a mass return to primitive instincts evolution hadn't yet had time to cleanse. Ethics be damned; people wanted to prove to the aliens how right they were; and they were all right. Bombs tore through throngs, bullets ground flesh, blood made mud, and guerilla warfare ensued.

In the bunker, the madness above them began to creep in. After too many days of tense argument, one leader insulted another, then one declared war on the other, and everyone else picked a side. Within a few hours, the melee climaxed when one President strangled another to death, and a dark mood invaded everyone. They were stuck below ground, scared and dejected, losing the battle against something no one could really define. Humanity. Nature. It was official; the silent alien machine was defeating them all.

Following the strangulation, the President was quickly escorted to his room and quarantined from the rest of the leaders. He couldn't believe it. A room full of world leaders, there to represent symbols of hope, and honor, and respect, had first pledged to help each other, and then literally jumped at each other's throats. Any further effort to save society seemed futile and doomed. They were at war with an invisible force. Ideological insanity.

He felt hope leave his heart as he removed his jacket and tie and sat on the edge of the bed. He couldn't make sense of the lunatic thoughts racing through his mind. Worse than ever, humanity had broken free of paradigms and run wildly with its urges. Volatile beings, drunk with fear, mad with righteousness. It was too much to ponder. He took the glasses from his drawn face and pinched the bridge of his nose with his thumb and forefinger, trying to hold back the welling tears.

He sighed and glanced at the desk pushed up against the far wall. On it was a pad of paper and some pens. He stood from the bed and sat down at the desk. Whenever he found himself in a psychological block, he found it useful, sometimes even cathartic, to simply put pen to paper, and let whatever may come sprawl out.

For a moment, his thoughts were too vague and disjointed to make much sense. He sighed again, closed his eyes, and before long, the pen began scribbling across the pad.

"Terrible things have happened in the world. Things I've never thought possible in my lifetime or any other. In less than a week, society has spiraled into a stew of fear, uncertainty, and violence. The reasons are not understood, and certainly not by any of the offenders. As such, the helplessness I feel in my heart is completely unbearable. Governments have fallen. Citizens are lost. Leaders are non-existent. I will never understand..."

He rubbed his face with the palm of his hand and shook his head. He felt defeated and empty. Failed. He took a deep breath, and before he was aware of it, the pen once again began moving across the pad.

"The bottom line, I think, is that we are too proud a species to ever admit that we are scared; thus, we grapple and fight to find a sense of security and stability, no matter the cost. We all, or most of us, believe in something that makes us feel better about ourselves. Something that gives us hope and strength, no matter how artificial, and the reason is fear. A man who believes in nothing has nothing to fear. Everything simply happens as it does without explanation or consequence. Never once does it trouble him. It is out of his control, and he is wise enough to admit that to himself. These are the people we normally see as heartless enemies, as threats to our social structures. But sitting here now, hidden underneath the mass psychosis, I am truly pressed to decide which person is the bigger fool–the idealist, or the realist. Personally, based on my own life experience, I believe we are our own enemies, on both a personal and social level, and we always will be. We have no other choice but to fight against ourselves, and sitting here now, I can clearly see that we have lost the eternal war. We were always doomed. It just wasn't so obvious before."

Gently placing the pen back on the desktop, he leaned back in his chair and ran his hand through his hair. He still couldn't believe the actions of a President upon another. He still couldn't believe what was happening above ground. With no idea what to do next, he stood and aimlessly paced the room, stroking his chin with his hand. He was exhausted and stressed beyond belief. He'd lost all control, and all hope for the future. A single, inactive machine had been enough to throw them all into turmoil. Regardless of what was to come, nothing would ever be the same again.

Sighing, he looked up at the ceiling and thought of God. God. Where was that belief in all of this? It was eighteen stories above his head, killing non-believers and deeming it righteous.

It was unacceptable; yet no thing, no force, no man nor god was about to stand in the way of it. It would continue on as it always had, only on a far more destructive scale.

"This is the end of the world," he whispered to himself. "Our entire history has been in vain."

Chapter 4

On the screen, they watched crowds of millions throwing themselves wildly in every direction. There were lights, and fires, and explosions, and screams, and chants, and prayers, and dances, and murders, and madness of every kind and flavor. The beings stared at each other, perplexed. They didn't recognize any of the behavior.

With gentle whispers, they churned out a melodious language accentuated with punctuating clicks and groans.

"What do you make of these tiny organisms?"

"I'm not sure. I've never seen anything like them in all of the universe. They seem determined to self-destruct. What kind of stupid planet is this?"

"It's called, (untranslatable). We've never seen it before because it's far too small to detect with most instruments. But it does appear to have what we require. Our analysis of the atmosphere has confirmed our discovery. However, once we go out there we will have to adjust to the severely weakened gravity. We may fall ill, but only temporarily."

"Very good. How long until we may exit the ship?"

"We may do so immediately; but, what about the organisms? What if they're as hostile to us as they are to each other? What if they're intelligent?"

"Look at them!" the other being declared. "Do they look intelligent to you? This is evidence of highly diseased molecular structures. Just look at how ugly they are, for one. Ha! Ha! Ha!"

"Well, I suppose, but I don't understand how they've been able to survive for so long if they're genetically programmed to kill each other. There doesn't seem to be any thought or logic behind their actions. Are we aiming to remove them?"

"Do you think anything is going to miss herds of parasites overcrowding an invisible planet? Look at them, they're obviously not intelligent, and probably not even conscious. How could they be and be so violent? It's an absurd notion. There is nothing interesting here beyond the resources. Let's get our equipment ready and set out. We've hit the jackpot this time; a planet full of resources and no serious threats to hinder our duties." The being stared inquisitively at the organisms on the screen once more, and said, "It's probably too close to its star; the planet is far too warm. The effect obviously causes genetic malfunctions. Homeland will be encouraged by the news. We exit at twelve hundred orbit arcs;

we must hurry and move on."

"Right away. I will get the rest of the team ready."

The being stared at the screen, amused now. For too long they'd arrived on barren planets devoid of useful resources and complex life. Now they'd found one with a healthy chunk of their resource quota, and it had complex life, albeit not intelligent in any obvious manner. They were amusing to watch, however, these underdeveloped little vermin. Unfortunately, they had work to do, and it would be impossible to do with all of those two legged maniacs trying to hurt them at every turn. There were no violent beings inside the ship, after all. They were far too intelligent to be behave in such a primitive fashion.

Another explosion erupted on the screen, tearing a few of the organisms to pieces, and inciting retaliatory attacks. The being before the screen shook its head. "What kind of chaotic mistake is this place? These beings have evolved into unprecedented stupidity."

The being stepped back and looked at the crazed images before him, when the other returned.

"We are ready to exit."

"Very well. Let's get to it. We have a long trip home after this. The quicker the better."

The being took a final glance at the screen and uttered a command, and with a single, brilliant white light, every human cell on the planet was killed. Sterilized.

"Well," said the being with an amused air. "That didn't take much energy."

The beings exited their ship and quickly gathered their fill in a high mood of success. After eons of searching, they'd finally found a useful deposit of resources. They felt lucky; because in the race for survival in the universe, available resources were first come, first served.

The End

THE CHARLIE CALLEN SYNDROME

As a boy, Charlie Callen wanted to follow in his grandfather's footsteps and become a world famous novelist. Always brimming with wild adventures and thrilling fantasies, Grandpa was a master storyteller, and Charlie made a point of visiting him every day after school to listen to a new tale. The boy liked how every time he walked through the door, Grandpa would turn excitedly with wide eyes and glaring teeth, his face bright and wrinkled, and he'd say, "Hey, partner! How're you doing today? Come gimme a hug," and Charlie would run to him and bury his face in his shoulder and hug him tightly.

"Do you have another story today, Grandpa?"
"Well, I do, but I'm not so sure you'll be interested," he would tease, and then say, "All I could come up with today was boring old dragons and giants," or wizards and witches, or any number of uncanny characters.

"Tell it! Tell it!" Charlie would plead, and Grandpa would say something like, "All right... Let's see if I can remember... Something about a magical spell... An oracle... And... Ah yes, here it goes. There once was a boy named Curtis who found a glowing sword at the bottom of a river. To his amazement, he found his name engraved in the side of the blade..." And Charlie would be left enthralled for the rest of the day, and sometimes he'd even dream of the stories with himself as the protagonist.

Living only four doors apart, Charlie dedicated as much time with Grandpa as he could. He watched with fascination throughout the years as Grandpa brushed off colds as mere annoyances and drank weird concoctions of fruits and alcohols as treatment for his various arthritic ailments. He was a wise man, relaxed, happy, kind, and was always remembered for his commanding presence and his charismatic gift for spinning any subject into an unforgettable story.

Whenever Grandpa asked Charlie what he wanted to be when he grew up, he always answered, "I want to grow up to be just like you, Grandpa. Big, and strong, and smart, and I want to write books and make people happy. But I don't know what words to use, or how you get all your great ideas." Grandpa would chuckle and ruffle his hair and say, "Well, kiddo. One day I'll tell you my secret. But I think I'll just enjoy your fascination for a little while longer."

Years went by and the stories kept coming, and when Charlie was twelve, he had lunch with Grandpa in a restaurant. While waiting for their food to arrive, Grandpa told him a story about a young boy and his uncannily intelligent dog. When the story ended, Charlie looked away, shook his head, and fixed a shy smile on his face.

"You didn't like my story?" Grandpa asked.
"I liked it," Charlie answered. "It's just... I don't understand how you come up with so many all the time. It doesn't make any sense, Grandpa."

Grandpa smiled and leaned in closer to his grandson. "Do you think you're old enough to learn one of my tricks?"

Charlie straightened up in his seat, his pupils the size of nickels, his mouth gaped in anticipation.

"For real?" he exclaimed.
"For real!" Grandpa grinned. "But you have to promise me one thing. You can't tell my secret to anyone except your own son or grandson one day. Do you promise?"

"Of course!" Charlie said, and gave Grandpa a silly look. "All right, here it goes. Have you ever stuck a blob of gum under a table?"

Charlie shrugged and nodded.
"Okay. Now take a look around this restaurant, look at the tables, at the people sitting at them; are you looking?"

"Yeah."
"What do you see?"

"I don't know." Charlie said. "People are eating."
"People are eating. They are talking. They are acting. The true magic of a place like this, of any place really, is that from one table to the next there are very different stories, in different styles, and in different structures. A writer doesn't necessarily make up a story; the stories are all around him, all the time, wherever he goes. The trick is in filtering the stimuli around you into a specific story of your own. Now, how do we do that?"

Charlie thought about it, but nothing in particular came to mind.

"Imagination?" he guessed.

"Partly true," Grandpa said. "But it's more than that. Imagination is like a wild wind. It whirls, and twirls, and hurls itself in every direction; therefore, it must be guided in order to pull any sense out of. You must first frame your imagination into a specific context, a specific mood, and let it loose only in that direction. The rest comes out naturally. So, in this case, in the mission of coming up with new stories, the context is easy. Take another good look around. Look at the tables, the faces, the overall tone of the room. Got it?"

Charlie nodded.

"Good. Now, just pick a table, any one in here, and imagine that you are a blob of gum stuck underneath the table top, listening, and let your imagination go only on that idea. Look at this couple over here, for example. He looks big, but soft in personality. She looks vindictive and irritated. It's great stuff. All you have to do is write what they are talking about. Of course, I don't literally mean what they are talking about, because most people are far too boring to say anything interesting, so you have to make that part up."

Charlie stared at the couple for a long time trying to come up with specific words, but it wasn't as easy as Grandpa made it seem.

"Of course," Grandpa continued. "Like all things in life, it takes a lot time and practice. Without investing huge amounts of time and practice in yourself, nothing is good or worthy of other people's time, much less your own."

After that, wherever Charlie went, he was a blob of gum stuck under tables, under shoes, under benches, listening, inventing, creating. He loved the idea, and kept it in mind at all times. He started writing short stories and showing them to Grandpa for review. Grandpa would read them and smile and offer suggestions for little alterations, and Charlie would slap his own forehead and say, "Of course! Why didn't I think of that?"

"Time and practice, my boy," Grandpa would say. "Never stop practicing, and never stop learning."

It was the happiest time of Charlie's young life. He finally had an insight into Grandpa's fascinating mind, and he was determined to be just like him later on in life. His stories and writing skills grew quickly in complexity, and whenever he wasn't with Grandpa, he was writing and reading incessantly.

Then, barely two years after divulging his secret, Grandpa died. It was a cold Sunday morning when Charlie's mother delivered the news, and it felt like something dark and caustic had stabbed him in the heart. Grandpa was seventy-four years old. He was never sick, and never suffered. His heart simply stopped beating in his sleep; at least there was some sort of comfort in that. Somehow.

No one saw much of Charlie after that. Of course, he went to school and spent time with his parents, but he was dedicated to writing new stories, developing his skills, and vying to live up to Grandpa's legendary literary legacy.

Years flashed by uneventfully, until Charlie was eighteen and completed his first novel, and sold it to a publisher. The novel, centered on a deranged man who stared in the mirror one morning, asked himself who he really was, and other people suddenly started answering from within him, shot to the top of the literary world and officially cemented him as the heir of his grandfather's talents. Nothing could have made Charlie happier. From then on, his life changed drastically.

Gone was his quaint, quiet life of obscurity, and in came a dizzying existence of hurried traveling, autograph signings, interviews, and speeches. Though lucrative, the intensity of the schedule was beyond anything Charlie had imagined. Shuffled from one end of the country to the other, he met a vast spectrum of fans ranging from fascinated admirers, to curious readers, to petty, jealous, and untalented hipsters. The healthy mix of positive criticism he received for his work was flattering. He was getting people to think, and it was making a success out of him–until–four weeks into his tour, something happened to change his course once more.

Wrapping up a speech in a packed University auditorium, Charlie left his admirers behind and headed into a cold January night, hugging himself against the freezing air. He padded hurriedly toward his waiting car, but before he could reach it, he was startled by a blaring horn seconds before a car skidded past him on a patch of ice. Panicked, Charlie stood stiffly, stumbled backward, tripped over the concrete curb, and fell to meet gravity with the back of his head. The impact sent an explosion of pain through his skull; a bright burst of brilliant white light before fading to black.

When he next opened his eyes, he couldn't remember a thing. He didn't know where he was. He didn't know how he'd gotten there. All he could do was suffer the choking grip of panic crawling through his chest. In time, he began making sense of the situation. There was a bandage wrapped around his head, an intravenous line in his arm, and a stale, malignant pain burning just behind his eyeballs. He was hurt, he knew that much, but he lacked any memory of a traumatic event. It suddenly felt like a chancrous void inside of him, and just as his anxiety mounted to the fringes of a pungent panic, a doctor walked into the room and surprised him with her presence.

"Oh, good. You're awake," the doctor said.

"I think so," Charlie replied, his voice thick in his throat.

"Have you been having any nightmares?"

"I'm not sure. What happened to me?"

"You had a bad fall and hit your head," the doctor replied. "As far as we can tell there's no serious damage; however, we will be monitoring you for a little while. Head injuries can be deceiving, but I think you'll be all right in due time."

Charlie sighed, winced, and then focussed his attention on ridding himself of the pervasive stupor inhibiting his thoughts. For the life of him, he couldn't remember falling and hitting his head. He vaguely remembered giving a speech to a large crowd. He remembered the applause, the lights, the heat of the auditorium–but nothing beyond that.

Standing next to him, the doctor fiddled with knobs and digital buttons for things he didn't care to understand, when he said, "You know, Julie, it feels like I'm still dreaming."

He wasn't looking at her when he spoke, but when he didn't receive a reply, he glanced at her and noticed the awfully confused expression on her face.

"What's wrong?" he asked, suddenly unsure about everything once again.

"How did you know my name?"

"I'm sorry?"

"You called me Julie," the doctor said.

"Uh huh. Isn't that your name?"

"It is," she said. "But I haven't told you that."

Frowning, he attempted to weigh the value of the situation. She hadn't told him her name?

"I... I don't know," Charlie replied. "I have no explanation."

The doctor shrugged her shoulders and smiled crookedly. "Well," she said. "Maybe it was just a lucky guess. Like I said, head injuries can be deceitful. You should get some rest."

"Yeah," he said, but he suddenly couldn't get it out of his

mind. Her name was Julie Mathews, he knew that, but how? She was from Chicago, the second of three kids, the other two, brothers. "Stop it!" he whispered to himself, and cursed his overactive imagination. None of that could be real; his mind was simply playing tricks. He'd probably knocked the sense out of his brain, and decided that what he really needed was to not think about anything in particular. Just relax, rest, recover. He fell asleep for two hours after that, and when he woke, the doctor, Julie Mathews, was checking on the machines next to his bed, and he couldn't seem to help himself.

"You have two kids," he said, his voice thick and labored. "Jenny and Curtis, seventeen and fifteen years old, respectively. You've been married for twelve years to Harry Mathews, a welder, forty-seven years old, and he hasn't been feeling very well for–"

"Stop it!" the doctor's voice suddenly shrilled, and when he looked at her he saw the terror, and the panic, and the slight tinge of rage masking the naturally soft features of her face. Now she looked hard and drawn, confused and timid.

"I'm sorry, I–"

"That's enough," she cut him off once more. "Listen, I don't know how you know all of that, but please stop. I... I'll be back in a while. I will send someone to speak with you shortly."

With that, she stomped out of the room, feebly attempting to hide her fear with a display of rage, but it wasn't enough. Charlie tried to ask who she would send to speak with him, but she either hadn't heard, or hadn't cared to answer.

He sighed and looked about the room. The burning was still behind his eyes. He felt a dull pain in the back of his head, and when he reached to touch the flat of his head, he winced terribly with a jolt. The skull was incredibly sensitive, pulpy, and the pain stretched down his neck, his spine, his legs, and all the way to the bottom of his heels.

"Son of a bitch," he hissed, and took in a deep breath, attempting to calm the angry nerves firing chaotically inside him. For half a minute, he waited on the cusp of certainty that his head was about to split open like a dropped watermelon, but then it slowly began to pass. He wondered if he truly was all right. The doctor, Julie Mathews, he'd scared her on a level he had never experienced before. He had shaken her core, shattered her privacy, and all from what felt like details from his imagination; like he was a blob of gum somewhere, making up conversations. However, from the doctor's reaction, he was not imagining anything at all.

What could that mean, he wondered. How could he know all those things about a complete stranger? He had never met the woman before, yet he knew her deepest, darkest secrets, far beyond anything he had spoken out loud. It was a strange sensation, surreal, and for the first time since he'd opened his eyes, he seriously considered the possibility that he might be dead. Maybe he hadn't awoken from an accident. Maybe his body was actually somewhere else, here was only his consciousness, his mind, and everything else was nothing but a projection. The fact that there was no possible way of truly qualifying any of those questions scared him. How could he, or anyone, tell if he was actually dreaming or not? Was he asleep before? Was he asleep now? The pain was real, but so what? Pain wasn't real, it was a manifestation; what made us think that anything else wasn't?

He was sharply torn from his introspective nightmare by the entry of a pudgy body in a lab coat, jovial face, glasses sitting squarely on the nose, smiling and nodding until he reached the edge of Charlie's bed and stood staring inquisitively, but in a friendly manner.

"Hello," he said, but Charlie was unable to break away from the flood of images dancing in the back of his mind. He felt his hands tingle numbly, and he couldn't hold eye contact with the man, or fake a congenial smile.

The doctor then said, "Tell me, Charlie, do you know who I am?"

Swallowing a slab of anxiety over his adam's apple, Charlie nodded, and cleared his throat.

"Yes," he whispered.

The doctor nodded, waiting for the continuation of his response.

"Your name is George Williams. You're a sixty-six year old psychiatrist, married thirty-eight years, four children, Henry, Billy, Terra, and Stephanie; thirty-seven, thirty-four, thirty-one, and twenty-nine years old, respectively. You live at eighty-six seventy-five – one eighty seventh avenue, the same house for the last thirty-eight years. Your father was a miner, a solid man, and father to twelve children. Your mother was a house wife, a kind, caring, gentle lady. Both died seven years ago. The father of pneumonia. The mother of loneliness."

From the corner of his eye, Charlie saw the doctor stand stiffly and seemingly ill-balanced, before reaching up to remove his glasses and stare at him in absolute bewilderment. Charlie continued.

"The first time you asked your wife to marry you, she declined, mostly because she was far too shy. You waited nearly a year before asking her again, when she accepted, and you've been faithful to her ever since. Your love is strong. You worry about your children, especially Billy. He screwed up a lot in the–"

"That's very good," the doctor, George Williams, stopped him. He pinched the bridge of his nose and took in a long breath before returning his attention to Charlie. "How in the world could you possibly know any of that? We've never met, have we?"

"I don't think so," Charlie replied.

"Goodness... I'm absolutely speechless. Listen, without revealing any more specific details, and this is purely out of curiosity on my part, how deeply does your knowledge of me go?"

Charlie considered the question intently. How could he know that? How could he know any of it at all?

"I... I don't know, Doctor," Charlie said.

"And what of Doctor Mathews?"

"It's the same. I'm not sure. What's wrong with me?"

"I'm not sure," Doctor Williams replied. "I've never heard of anything like this before. To be frank, it scares the hell out of me. However, from a professional standpoint, what has happened to you is quite fascinating, I must say. I would like to run some tests, both physical and psychological, and perhaps we can figure this thing out for you."

Charlie nodded lightly, his mind occupied with vague things he shouldn't know, but did.

"It's possible," the doctor continued. "That what's happening may wear off on its own. Head injuries often leave the brain sore and slow to recover. Sometimes, certain abilities become apparent as a result of injury, but it is rare, and most often not permanent. It is a tricky instrument, the brain."

"Okay," Charlie said, and then stared at his hands sitting idly in his lap with nothing else to add. He wasn't sure how to feel. While the doctor spoke, sporadic details of the man's life rushed through Charlie's mind, ranging from the mundane to the most intimate private realities. What purpose did something like that serve, he wondered. What reason would he, or anyone, need such an ability? He felt ill. Physically, mentally, and spiritually sick. He was scared, and wondered if he would ever recover; if he would ever be able to have a normal, "private," conversation with anyone. Certainly there were things about people he didn't want to know, especially about his closest friends and family. The truth often ruined solid relationships between people. He would never see anyone quite in the same light again, for no matter what they said, or did, or attested to, he would know the truth. He didn't like that. He'd only met two people while in possession of the ability, and already he'd had enough of it. It didn't do good things for other people. It didn't make them feel good; in fact, it terrified them, and with good reason. He wouldn't like being subjected to the same treatment, and decided that if it didn't go away, he would have to learn to control it. He would have to learn to keep it to himself, and maybe even succeed in stifling its effects on his own feelings toward people.

"My head really hurts," Charlie said to Doctor Williams. "You need more rest," the doctor said, and returned his glasses to the bridge of his nose. "Try not to worry yourself too much. I will arrange for tests to be conducted and we will be seeing each other often in the next few days. I will do what I can to understand what's happening to you."

"Thank you, Doctor," Charlie said. "I appreciate your help."

"Very well, get some sleep now, and I will see you shortly."

Charlie nodded, and, following the doctor's exit from the room, sank his head back into the pillow and closed his eyes. In minutes, he was passing through the subconscious psychosis that was the stuff of dreams.

Two hours later he woke up by himself, still with the sweltering headache, the dizzy confusion, and the numb fear lingering on the forefront of his mind. There was no one else in the room with him, and he sighed in relief. His mind was occupied with his own thoughts, and he suddenly found himself fearful of having to face another person walking into the room. He feared the effortless way his mind was made aware of other people's private affairs. None of it felt any different from simply imagining the life of a fictional character. He didn't have to try for it, or wish it, or want it–his mind just did it, unguided, and unhindered. It wasn't like he heard voices, or saw visions or auras, and it certainly didn't feel like he could read anyone's mind. No; people approached him, and he just knew. It was more of a feeling, an intuition that focussed itself, and all the details he thought imagined were apparently real. He couldn't make any sense of it. Why? Why would he be capable of such a thing? How could it even be possible? Once again, he felt the subliminal terror that came with wondering if he was actually still alive or not. He felt helpless, and desperate.

He reached for the remote and turned on the television in an effort to distract himself. As usual, there was nothing of particular interest playing, and after surfing the catalogue of available channels, he settled on a world news network. Absently, he watched the images of protests and violence from across the world, devastated economies, greedy governments, murder, accidents, and natural disasters all interspersed between upbeat commercials and guilt-ridden charitable begging. The world was beyond insane, Charlie decided. A thousand killed here, a quarter thousand there, and we'll be right back with the story of a terminally ill child right after we hear about how amazing a juicy burger would be right now.

He shifted his weight in the uncomfortable bed and stared at the door, timidly expecting someone to come walking in at any moment. But he was left alone for a good while, and he stayed focussed on the television, ignoring his wandering thoughts, until the doctor, George Williams, came strolling in with a crooked smile and a pair of bright, inquisitive eyes.

"Hello, Charlie," he said softly, smiling, holding a stack of documents in his hands.

"Hi," Charlie replied. "You have tests for me to do?" The doctor nodded, almost amused.

"Yes, I do. Do you feel ready to begin? The first tests are no more than questions for you to answer."

"All right."

"Very well," the doctor replied, and pulled up a chair next to Charlie's bed. He sat, opened a thick binder on his lap, clicked a ball point, smiled, and began asking questions, starting simply, and escalating in depth as he went on.

For the next two days, Charlie faced a barrage of psychological and physical tests. Doctor Williams was especially enthralled with his patient, and seemed determined to define exactly what was happening to him. There is nothing more exciting for a scientific mind than to be faced with something unexplainable, and Charlie was by far the most unexplainable phenomenon he had ever heard of, never mind had direct contact with.

After the blood tests, the x-rays, the MRI, the EKG, the questionnaires, and the assessments were complete, it was established that Charlie Callen, the newly rising literary star, was as psychologically and physiologically healthy as any doctor could hope for. There was nothing wrong with him, and as far as the doctor could tell, he was already well on his way to making a full recovery from his head injury–except–the ability to know everything about random strangers was still there; and, as far as Charlie could tell, it was getting even more acute. During tests, he kept his thoughts to himself, but he knew the nurse hooking up the electrodes to his head was named Linda Stockholm, and she was worried about her ill mother. Peter Davies was the technician who administered the MRI, and he was cheating on his wife with two other women, one of them his assistant, Heather Long, who was madly, hopelessly in love with him. The radiologist was named Derek Dahl, and he was a hypochondriac, a fact that Charlie found amusing given that he worked in a hospital; however, thanks to his unnatural ability, he also knew that the man felt safer there than anywhere else. And beyond knowing each of those people's deepest psyches, as well as everyone he happened to pass in the halls, he knew that Doctor George Williams was growing frustrated with the lack of meaningful definition of Charlie's problem. He felt bad for the doctor. Despite understanding the fact that Charlie was already aware of his thoughts and feelings, George Williams, as per nature, still pretended like he was getting close to an explanation, as though some sort of larger picture was beginning to coalesce before him. Whenever he reminded himself of Charlie's abilities, however, he'd blush and excuse himself from the room, leaving his patient feeling guilty for something he had no control over.

In time, Charlie could see the resentment such an ability would attract from the doctor, as well as anyone else he made aware.

Five days after entering the hospital, he was released with a clean bill of health, a highly damaged self-esteem, and an array of empty reassurances that all would come to pass in due time. At home, he locked himself up for two weeks and tried to understand what had happened to his old self. Where had his confidence gone? His sense of humor? His meaning in life? What was he supposed to do now? How was he supposed to act in the presence of other people? He couldn't piece it together. It was all too disheartening, and terrifying.

He got some rest, avoided all human contact, and when he thought it had finally gone and he was cured, he walked to the store for a pack of cigarettes and had to ignore Glenn, Hilary, Dana, Harry, Jill, Kevin, Dave, Dan, Chuck, Lynn, Agnes, Luke, Steve, and others who passed by him in their cars while he managed the sidewalk. It was hopeless. He would have to learn to live with it and keep it quiet. Perhaps that was beneficial for other people, but what would it do to him, he wondered. How was he supposed to behave around people when they couldn't hide anything from him? It was madness.

So he was a lunatic, he concluded. A freak. A natural abortion. Broken. Defunct. Empty. Sad. Lonely. Angry. He couldn't concentrate enough to write, and he was worried that the accident might have caused a permanent rift in his previous talent for words. It felt like it was all over. His career. His talent. His life.

He couldn't stand going outside, but he couldn't stay locked up forever, could he? Could he live like some cryptic hermit, hunchbacked over a laptop, typing out his magnum opus? Maybe, but the truth was that he did enjoy the company of others. To be robbed of that was a crude blow. What was he to do? His condition seemed a lot like schizophrenia, except the hallucinations, for lack of a better word, were nothing of the sort. They were truth. They were absolutely, and unfailingly correct. The explanation was nowhere to be found, and if anyone was more frustrated than Doctor George Williams, it was he, Charlie, a normally outgoing, determined, life-challenging man. All of that seemed unfeasible suddenly.

Day after day, he'd wake, have some coffee, watch the news, try to write, try to read, try to convince himself that enough time had passed, that whatever had been knocked loose inside of him had finally self-repaired and he was fine, he was healthy, he could get back out there and take on the world, conquer the literary world, give interviews, make friends, and contacts, and secure his name as a capable author–and then–Harry, the post worker, thrice married, father of six, with a soft spot for young ladies, would be standing on his stoop, stuffing his mail into the receptacle while Charlie cursed and raved to himself in pure desperation. It was all too much. He couldn't see how he could keep going. His thoughts came in whirlwinds, in blocks of pure madness, and they were constantly being interrupted by the awareness of those in his vicinity. He was sick of it, and desperate to heal, or wake up, or make sense of what was happening to him.

After great self-deliberation, he met Doctor George Williams for a follow up examination, and it was as though he could feel the doctor's frustrations; as though the man's emotions were his own; as though the sense, or intuition, or whatever anyone wanted to call it, was getting stronger. It was taking over. He was convinced that he was losing his mind, and he knew the doctor couldn't help him in any way. This terrible reality was all on him, served raw.

Without the doctor ever speaking, Charlie said, "Yes, I'll do it. Don't worry about it." And the doctor started with a jolt, then stared intently at his patient's face, his eyes brilliant with astonishment. Charlie had responded to his thoughts, agreeing to meet with the team of specialists the doctor was planning to ask him about. It was a final effort to solve the puzzle, but George Williams held little faith in the matter. Nevertheless, he forgot, or still didn't want to believe in Charlie's abilities, and he said, "You mean... The doctors?"

"Yes," Charlie said. "All the tests you want me to take." And just then he realized that his heart was hammering in his chest, as if he too were astonished. He was feeling another man's feelings, and he didn't know why, or what, or how he was supposed to deal with something like that. Knowing unknowable things about people was bad enough without adding direct emotional ties. He was scared, and confused, and quite unsure about what to do next. He didn't believe that any doctor in the world was capable of helping him. He'd already done the tests, and for all inner and outer appearances, he was as normal and as healthy as could be expected.

George Williams nodded. "Very well," he said. "You know the date and time I had planned?"

Charlie nodded slowly, keeping his eyes locked on the doctor's.

"On the fifth, at two p.m. Meeting with Doctors, Hillary Bain, Peter Lovak, Barry Klein, and Amanda Heath. All neurologists aside from Doctor Amanda Heath, who is a highly respected psychiatrist and has plans to–"

"That's enough," George Williams interrupted him, visibly distraught. Charlie's chest filled with anxiety at what he assumed was the exact same moment as the doctor's. The whole thing was past being fascinating, now it was just getting irritating, both for him and for George Williams. "So you can read my thoughts. Other people's?"

Charlie nodded.

"I don't know how to explain it, Doc. At first, I was just... Aware of people's inner personality and history, but now, I don't know, it's like I know everything there is to know about the people I come into contact with, and I'm somehow responding emotionally to their thoughts. How can... How can that be? You have to do something for me, Doctor. I just... I don't think I can keep going like this. I think it's getting stronger."

The doctor stared deeply into Charlie's eyes, trying to imagine what he was going through, and how he would deal with such an astonishing yet debilitating thing. He was about to speak again, but Charlie once again replied to his thoughts, and when the doctor was taken aback once more, so was Charlie, and he stopped talking and stared back at the doctor with deep horror burning in his eyes.

"You didn't say anything," Charlie said. "I'm talking to you, without you talking to me. How can that be? How can that be?" He pinched the bridge of his nose between his thumb and forefinger, thoroughly exasperated.

"We'll figure it out," Doctor Williams said, completely without conviction, and Charlie already knew he was lying, though he couldn't understand why he would. He supposed it was too difficult a thing to admit that someone else was also in your head, in your thoughts and emotions. How could anyone be expected to deal with something like that?

"Charlie, are you having trouble telling the difference between people's thoughts and their actual voice?"

"What do you think? I'm losing my mind, Doc," he said, supplicating, crying. "Please, Doc. Please, find something."

Doctor Williams had nothing to say. Nothing to think. Fully embarrassed, Charlie decided to leave, despite his very real and justified fear of going out into public. He reassured George Williams that he would be seeing him, along with the team of doctors, on the fifth. Until then, he would call him if anything drastic changed... If he in fact noticed it changing.

At home, he listened to a voicemail from his agent. She wanted to meet with him and see how he was feeling. Charlie didn't necessarily want to meet with her, especially since he felt like he couldn't write anything while dealing with his hellish ability, but she had worked hard for him in the past and he liked her for the most part. He returned a call to her office, but asked if she would meet him at home rather than he traveling to her office. She agreed, and a mere three hours later, he was aware of her arrival a whole two minutes before she rang the doorbell. He fought back tears as he made his way to the foyer and waited for her physical arrival. It was all becoming too much. It was becoming too powerful. Out of control. Unconformable. And once more, he considered the possibility that he was dead, that none of it was real at all, nor was he, nor was anyone else. Hell.

The bell rang and he waited a moment before opening the door so as to avoid arousing suspicion in her. He didn't want to make anyone else aware of his problem. He turned the bolt and opened the door, flashing a fake smile and nodding cordially.

"Hello, Nancy. How are you?"

"Hey, you," she said and smiled widely, but Charlie didn't buy it. She was worried about him, most notably because he was the first big jackpot she'd come across in her career. When assets are good, they demand meticulous tending.

"Please, come in," he said and stepped aside to allow her through the threshold and into his home. Nancy was a woman just shy of forty years old, no children, and no husband. None of that had to do with her physical appearance, however, which was neither to be scoffed nor gawked at. She was unflinchingly dedicated to her goals, and despite Charlie being her first big payoff, she was hardly desperate to make a living without him. She represented many fine authors, and each commanded a fair sized fan base. He only happened to garner a larger following than all the others combined.

He led her from the foyer to the living room, where he gestured for her to make herself comfortable and offered her a drink, which she refused. She chose to sit on his overstuffed leather chair, and he sat opposite on the sofa, trying to stow his towering anxiety.

"So," she began. "How are things, Charlie? You've had a rough time, huh?"

Charlie shrugged and flashed a crooked smile.

"It's been all right," he said. "Just a little bump on the head is all. It could have been worse."

"Well," she said, smiling warmly. "I'm glad you're okay. You gave me a real scare... *'Mister money machine.'*"

This last part she had not spoken, but Charlie hadn't been able to tell the difference.

"I'm sorry?" he said, terribly confused, and slightly offended.

She stared back at him in surprise, her sharp blue eyes darting from side to side while she replayed the words in her mind, trying to discern what she'd said wrong. She couldn't find anything in her memory, so she attempted to recover the previous mood with, "I just... I mean... I'm just happy that you survived the fall and that you're still healthy... *'Although, authors are worth more dead than they are alive.'*"

"What?!" Charlie demanded, and stood from the sofa, shocked. His face flushed hot with rage, and his breath came in quick, shallow quips. "What did you just say?" His voice sounded raw and menacing, and caused her eyes to instantly well up with tears.

"Charlie! What's wrong?"
Her voice cracked, then shrilled, and she couldn't help but press her palm to her chest in astonishment at his seemingly unprovoked anger.

"You basically just said that you'd like it better if I was a dead client instead of a living one."

As quickly as he had, she shot up from her seat and faced him like an equal opponent in a boxing ring.

"I most certainly did not!" she asserted. "Why would I say such a thing?"

And then it dawned on him. She hadn't said a word. She had only thought them, and most likely, the resentment he felt against the idea was her own for having such intrusive thoughts in the first place. He was stunned, and unsure of how to proceed. What could he say? He'd known this woman a few years already–no, more concisely–he thought he knew this woman. In fact, he, like everyone else on the planet, thought he knew lots of people. His friends and family, and their thoughts, and their opinions, and their goals, and their secrets, but as his new ability was proving, no one truly knew anyone else. In fact, Charlie would even say that no one, not any one, even knew themselves. We are all too complex for our own good, he realized, and our behaviors are rehearsed, expected, and faked. There is no such thing as purity except for madness; everything else is wishful thinking, illusion, and self-betrayal.

The impression he'd had of Nancy, his agent, was a favorable one in general. She was a hard working and skilled salesperson with all the right contacts, and the capacity to push opportunities to their ragged ends. But now he could feel her–he damn near was her, in fact–and the realization shattered his perception and left him feeling like a perverted intruder. The unwarranted violation of her mind made him feel ill and disgusting, but he was helpless against the shameless stripping of her layers until her very soul lay bare within him for his unwilling inspection. He saw her raw and defenseless. In direct contrast to the hardened dynamism she exuded on the outside, she suffered from depression and various other anxiety related illnesses on the inside, which was why she dedicated herself so completely to her goals. They were her distraction, her survival, and she'd found a way to channel the negative energy into positive business might.

In truth, she was naturally prone to hostility, drawn to misanthropy, and often leaned toward jealousy and envy of other people when their abilities surpassed hers. This too she managed to use to her advantage, for she had started in the business with the idea of being an author. She'd written short stories and had even once attempted a novel, but her talent for words simply wasn't on par with her love of them; she therefore decided to take on the publishing industry as an agent representing other people's work, helping them shape their ideas, and sharpen their strong points. Fundamentally, she was no more complicated or conflicted than anyone else in the world, and that's what was bothering Charlie most on this occasion.

There she was, a person he trusted, and one who'd worked intensely in his favor. She smiled a lot, and encouraged him, and pushed him to perfect his craft... But there was no room in his new ability for illusions. She thought he had talent, sure, but sometimes she also thought he was an overrated sensationalist that she couldn't, and wouldn't, willingly drop from her repertoire. He represented her solid rock in the middle of an unpredictable business, and she resented him for it, if she were ever to tell anyone the truth; and though she smiled, and laughed at his jokes, and complemented him on a regular basis, his laid-back personality, vicious wit, and spot-on intelligence was a source of irritation for her, despite carrying the same qualities herself. She mistakenly glorified Charlie on a level that simply wasn't real, or even possible. She lived with false perceptions of others, and to his surprise, he realized that he did too. Didn't everybody?

"Charlie, please. Tell me what's going on," she said, her eyes still saturated, her arms still wrapped around herself in an uncomfortable, squirming hug. "I'm not sure what I said that could have–"

"It's fine," Charlie interjected. "I apologize for my behavior. I'm just... I'm still working things out." He stared at the floor, trying to find what next to say, but he couldn't think of anything that would help alleviate the tension in the air. "I... I hit my head pretty badly," he continued. "Doctors say it might take a while to recover."

He felt her fear, her confusion, her resentment. Her mouth remained closed, but he still heard all the suspicious questions. He started shaking when she did; his eyes welled up when hers did; his anxiety skyrocketed on par with hers. He couldn't think straight. All of his thoughts were like glimpses of obscure phantasms, glimpses of her thoughts. A veritable soup of madness from which he could not decide which thoughts and emotions belonged to himself, and which belonged to her. It was too much, and without further discussion or explanation, he began shuffling her out of his home, gently at first, but growing in desperation with every second thereafter.

"We'll have to do this another time, Nancy. I apologize, but I just... I just need to be alone for a while. I hope you understand."

"Ah... Sure... '*You lunatic.*'" She said, and then thought. "Is there anything I can do for you in the meantime, Charlie? Anything at all?... '*Like maybe send you to a sanitarium?*'"

"Stop it!" he snapped, and she jumped in surprise. "I'm sorry, Charlie," she replied, her legs trembling violently. "I was just trying to help you... '*You really have lost your mind, haven't you?*'"

"I'll call you," he snapped. "I'm sorry for my behavior. I'm just going through some things. We'll talk, I promise, but I need you to go now."

"Sure. Of course. It's no problem," she answered, and followed him to the door. She stood for a moment and stared at him with perplexed features masking her face. Seeing the desperation in his eyes, she nodded, and said, "Take good care of yourself, okay? '*Because your name is gold.*'"

Charlie shook this last thought off, somehow understanding that she wasn't so much of a bad person as much as she suffered from insistent, intrusive thoughts; as everyone did from time to time, he'd noticed. He nodded in response, took in a deep breath, pursed his lips, and said, "Thank you, Nancy. We'll talk soon."

She nodded, and as she turned to walk to her car, Charlie heard, '*God, you would be worth a lot more if you killed yourself.*'

"I'm sorry?" Charlie said, and Nancy stopped in her tracks, more confused than ever.

She turned and shook her head. "I... Didn't say anything, Charlie." And her face filled with pity, her heart with sadness. Charlie hated every second of it.

"Right," he said, and chuckled nervously, trying to shake off his embarrassment, and her sadness. Nancy pulled out of the

driveway and waved as she sped away. He shut the door and
returned to the living room where he caught sight of himself in
the mirror on the wall. His reflection felt distant and alien to him.
He walked to the polished glass, stared deeply into his own eyes,
thought about his novel, and said, "Who are you, and what do you
want to do?" However, far worse than the events in the novel, no
one answered at all. Who am I, he wondered. How am I supposed
to make sense of myself if I can't seem to be myself? He was only
partly himself, he realized, and the rest was like a radio tuner picking up random signals from everyone else without sense or reason.
There was no identity to identify with, no certainty to be certain
of. All he knew was that he was alone. No one could help him. No
one could even understand his condition. He was scared, frustrated,
irritated, and alone.

Without warning, a gasp escaped his lips, followed by
another, and before he knew it he was crying at full intensity, desperate for some sort of arcane answer that didn't seem to exist. He
was trapped, and all around him was a smooth, cold, impenetrable
wall, ever closing in.

He collapsed on the sofa and buried his face in his hands.
He cried, and pleaded, and cursed for an hour before finally laying
down and curling up into a ball, convinced that he was trapped in
a nightmare. With all of his being he tried resisting the feeling that
he was about to implode, but the ill-sense seemed unbeatable.

He spent the next four days in a state of utter despair. He
tried to write as a distraction, but nothing original came to him
aside from dark, cryptic moods he wasn't a fan of. Frustrated, completely exasperated, he tried spending his time on the couch watching movies and playing video games, trying his best to ignore his
foul reality, but his problem was proving more powerful every day.
Though he was locked inside of his home, he was captivated by
anyone who walked within a hundred yards of him. It was a keen,
overwhelming sense that he was being overtaken by them, becoming them. Their thoughts and emotions, their hopes and dreams,
their complaints and frustrations, from top to bottom and side to
side, he knew everything, and it was all coming at the cost of his
own identity. He no longer was an individual; he was whoever
was near. His body had become a canister for a conglomeration
of psyches, fouling his soul, ripping apart his very core in jagged
pieces, never to be returned.

On the fifth of the month, he nearly skipped with glee to
meet George Williams and his team of doctors. He tried manu-

facturing hope, forcing naivety on himself, but the truth was that he was depressed; and even that wasn't fully afforded him. The emotion was constantly interrupted by other people's emotions. He couldn't be happy, or sad, or angry, or depressed, or anything else for any more than a few seconds. He was robbed of being human. He was shamed, and humiliated, and reduced to the level of a dumb beast simply reacting to outside stimuli with nothing of his own to offer. Nothing. He was an empty shell, a mindless automaton, moving according to the mechanics of hidden gears.

Walking into the doctor's office, he padded across the small room, trying to ignore Helen, worried about her cold, and Dave, there to follow up on the progress of his broken arm, and Mike, there about the itchy hives making a dramatic appearance on his scrotum. He heard internal voices and mindless thoughts; saw vague images and nonsensical dreams. He stepped up to the reception desk and stared oddly at the smiling woman on the other side. Her name was Jade, twenty-four, a daughter of three, and he had just interrupted her thoughts about Kevin, a guy she'd met last night at the club, with his appearance. Without thinking, he almost blurted out, "I think you should pass on the dude," but she spoke first.

"Hi, there," she said. "How can I help you?"
"Hello," he mumbled, avoiding eye contact, though he didn't fully understand why. "Charlie Callen. I have an appointment with Doctor Williams today."

She turned her attention to the computer screen and hummed a tune, but all Charlie heard was the actual song blaring through his mind, through her mind. He clenched his jaw, desperate to maintain his composure, but all the thoughts and emotions rushing through him was making his head spin, his breath shallow. Above and beneath and woven into it all, he felt a sheer, obliterating panic creep up his spine.

"Yes," Jade said. "You're right on time. I have a note to page the doctor when you arrive. If you'll just have a seat for a moment, please, he'll be out to see you very shortly."

"Thank you," he said, then heard her wonder.
'Isn't that the author guy?'

He glanced at her quickly, then at the counter, and caught sight of his novel sticking out of her handbag next to her chair. She stared back at him and began to say, "Hey, aren't you–"

"That's me," he interrupted her, and she stared with suspicion for a moment.

"I'm sorry?" she said.

"The book, I mean. I can sign it for you if you'd like."
She smiled warmly, slightly embarrassed.

"Oh. That would be... Amazing!" she said, and fetched the
book from her bag. He took it from her and borrowed her pen.

"It's Jade, right?"
"Yeah," she said with a curious stare, but he managed to recover
quickly.

"Your name tag," he said, and lowered his eyes to her
shirt. She followed his gaze and blushed, rolling her eyes in
ridicule of herself. He felt her embarrassment so intensely in that
moment that he blushed too, feeling like a complete fool, before
managing to find his true self once more. It was all too strong to
control. He desperately hoped the doctors could help. He needed
help.

With his hands trembling, he signed the first page of the
book, "To Jade, thanks for your support, and may you find the
answers you need. Charlie Callen" and handed it back to her along
with the pen. She took it from him and read the message. When she
finished, she frowned and stared at him, her mouth struggling to
get the words out. He already knew what she was going to say, and
he smiled prematurely.

"It's... It's like you're a mind reader or something," she
said.

He pursed his lips and grinned, nodding his head. "I guess
it seems that way. You have a good day, Jade. I hope you enjoy the
book."

"Thanks," she said, and reread his message.
He didn't even get to sit before Doctor George Williams appeared
from a door and walked into the waiting room with a big grin on
his face. Charlie could feel his determination and his confidence in
the team he'd assembled for the examination.

"Charlie," the doctor said and extended his hand. Charlie
shook it and said, "How are you, Doctor?"

George Williams chuckled and said, "Like you need to
ask me that," and slapped him on the shoulder as if they were old
friends. Charlie turned back to the listening Jade and winked, but
said nothing. She had no idea what to think; it was making him
dizzy.

"Are you ready?" Doctor Williams asked.
"Let's do it," and with a nod to Jade, Charlie followed the doctor
out of the room feeling more confident and determined than ever

in his life. It took him a while to remember that he was Charlie, not George Williams, and he managed it only a few seconds before reaching the examination room and four other people came rushing into him. More and more, he was losing himself to unexplainable forces. Turning clockwise, he met people he already knew. First was Peter Lovak, a stout man of fifty-eight years with a round face and a compulsive smile. Next was Barry Klein, a sort of antonym to Peter Lovak. Barry was a tall, well built man of thirty-nine with friendly features and a blazing intelligence. After him came Hillary Bain, thirty-five years old with piercing blue eyes and the beauty of a Greek goddess. And finally, he met Amanda Heath, a plump woman of fifty-nine with thick, bottle-like glasses sitting on her nose and her hair pulled back tightly into a bun.

In all, the doctors' spirits were up, and their respective curiosities were at peak levels. They were excited to begin testing, anxious to get to the bottom of what was affecting poor Charlie Callen, and not believing that the answer could elude them. They, like most people, were trained to think that there were reasons for everything, that these sorts of things didn't just happen without a cause; but Charlie, when he was in lucid control of his own mind, was hardly convinced. They wouldn't find a thing. They couldn't. He wasn't even sure there was a "thing" anymore. It felt more like his brain had been reprogrammed in his sleep. There was no tumor, no chemical unbalance, and no misfiring neurons present; only a recrossing of wires, somehow, and the physical self appeared unchanged.

The barrage of tests performed by the team of doctors, just as Charlie had predicted, had been repetitive, intrusive, and completely futile. Furthermore, despite the fact that each had been made aware of Charlie's abilities beforehand, none seemed able to wrap their heads around such a thing. They would suggest that perhaps it was one thing or another, hoping to appease Charlie's anxiety, but their thoughts were in direct contrast to their words. Their intentions were in the right place, and their minds were faithfully concentrated on the task at hand, but the whole thing was ultimately punishing for Charlie. The only person who'd taken Charlie's ability at face value was Doctor Hillary Bain, who spent the entire time telling herself, 'Don't think! Don't think! Don't think!' and smiling nervously. He felt her anxiety, and knew that she was only trying to hide her raging libido from him, but it was no use. The fact remained that she, as well as everyone else, could pretend all they wanted, but none could ever hide. Never again would he be fooled by anyone, and for that, he was growing terribly spiteful. He wasn't human any longer. He was superhuman, and every second of it was tortuous.

For eight hours the doctors scoured through descriptions of rare psychological diseases, uncanny abilities, and literally stopped short of the supernatural for an explanation. They hadn't the vaguest of answers. The experience was intensely morose, and served nothing more than to solidify Charlie's feeling that there was no hope of ever escaping his condition.

In the end, the best the doctors could determine was that the condition affecting him had never been documented before. There was no evidence, or even suggestion of such a thing even being possible; but there he was, able to do it all. In due course, and bringing the patient absolutely no comfort whatsoever, the doctors decided to submit the new condition to be enlisted in the medical lexicon. They called it, The Charlie Callen Syndrome.

Perfect, he thought. There he was, a rising star in the literary world, and now a medical anomaly was named after him. The doctors tried explaining their findings to him, but he stopped them immediately, already aware of everything they had to say, every thought they had, and every sugar-coated encouragement they would try to feed him. He thanked them gratefully, and, filled with dread, made his way home as a crowd of strangers sharing a body.

In his living room, he stared deeply into the mirror, utterly crushed. He didn't know what to do, or where to turn, or whom to speak to. There was no one, no one, and as an ice cold panic flashed up his spine, he broke down in a fit of obliterating sadness. Tears poured from his eyes and his limbs trembled uncontrollably. He buried his face in his hands, and cried, "I can't do this! I can't keep going like this! It's too much!" He choked on his breath and writhed in agony until he felt like all of the energy of his body had left him. All reasons were gone. All hope was abandoned.

Crawling into bed, his face still set in an agonized grimace, he closed his eyes, and almost instantly, consciousness faltered in favor of a strange realm. His mind was haunted with tormented dreams, ghoulish emotions, and desperate wishes, but at least he still perceived himself as he used to be; a human meeting the guidelines of the vast definition of normal; a neurotic mess on legs, clumsy with decision making, and fully incapable of the discipline necessary for unemotional thought.

He'd fallen so deep into the madness that when he woke, he wasn't sure if he was awake or simply getting another dose of subconscious imagination. Feeling exhausted either way, he closed his eyes, and slept another sixteen hours.

When Charlie opened his eyes again, he didn't know where he was; even worse, he didn't know who he was. He wasn't aware of this fact, of course, so the reality of it didn't cause him any alarm whatsoever. He stretched out his body in bed and yawned, feeling relaxed and well rested. He remembered that he had an appointment at the spa today at ten-thirty, and then lunch with Kathy. Then he thought about his wife's birthday; then worried about his company facing bankruptcy; then felt the incredible joy of his pregnancy, and was already thinking of silly names for both boys and girls.

Without any thought or motivation behind it, he threw back the covers, dressed, and left his house with no direction intended or followed. Trudging the sidewalk, he was hundreds of people, filled with thousands of thoughts, and suffered a relentless kaleidoscope of emotions. He continued in this way until he cornered a street and was approached by a mad preacher screaming his interpretation of the Lord's word like a lunatic. He skipped up to Charlie with a devilish grin on his face and waved his arms in the air.

"Good day, sir!" the preacher exclaimed. "You wouldn't have a moment to hear about the Lord today, would you?"

When Charlie set his eyes on the lunatic, he was seized by shock, and his body went rigid with fear. His pupils dilated into black holes and his mouth gaped open.

"Are you all right, my man?" the preacher asked, but Charlie was too perplexed to say anything. After a long minute of tense silence, his face suddenly contorted into a mask of rage, and he managed to say, "Is this some sort of joke?"

The preacher cocked his head back and furrowed his brow.

"You mean the word of God?"
But Charlie didn't acknowledge his question. His heart raced unnaturally, and his mouth was barren, and dry. He was terrified, and trying to fight it with anger.

"What's your name?" Charlie demanded.
"What?"

"Your name! What is it?"
"It's... It's Bradley... Bradley Stock."

With that, Charlie stumbled backward as if the lunatic had shoved him. He stared at the ground, then back up to the preacher, his mind obviously trapped in some sort of nonsensical madness. The preacher shifted his weight uncomfortably, unsure of what was happening. And people called him a lunatic, he thought. He was about to turn and leave Charlie behind when the latter spoke again, but it was only to himself.

"That's... That's impossible," he hissed.

"I'm sorry?" the preacher asked, and frowned, simultaneously repulsed and curious. "What's impossible?"

"You... You can't be Bradley Stock," Charlie said.

"Well, that's me, mister. What's wrong with you, anyway?"

"I'm Bradley Stock," Charlie said, and the preacher was stunned with disbelief. Charlie didn't notice and continued speaking.

"I live at eighty-seven-thirty-four, fourteenth avenue, in the low income shelter. I used to be married to woman named Debbie Dawson, she left me for some fat car salesman and cleaned me out. Then I started drinking, a lot, and far too many years later is when I found Jesus. Since then–"

"Stop!" the preacher screamed, his face pale, his eyes blank, his breath held.

Charlie set his eyes on him and frowned. "What's wrong with you?" he asked.

"How the hell did you do that?" the preacher demanded. "What do you mean?"

"That's my life, man!" the preacher said, growing angry. "How do you know all that shit?" he screamed.

"I'm Bradley Stock," Charlie asserted once more. "And why do you look exactly like me? What's your problem?"

"Hey!" the preacher screamed, and without thinking, threw his bible at Charlie. "Go to hell, asshole!" And he stomped away down the street, furious, and quite rightly terrified. Charlie watched him go, and a second later, he thought about the amazing night he'd spent with his husband; he'd really gone all out for his birthday. He continued down the sidewalk, suddenly late for his meeting with Bill; it was time to ask for a raise.

Farther down the street, he turned left and crossed the lot of a mall, where he caught the attention Suzan Willow, a massive fan of his book. When she saw him, she squinted her eyes for a moment and tried to confirm her suspicion before approaching him hurriedly with an exaggerated smile on her face. Charlie didn't notice her approach, but he suddenly felt terribly excited.

"Excuse me, sir?" Suzan Willow said. "You wouldn't happen to be Charlie Callen, would you?"

Looking around quickly as if being assaulted by gnats, Charlie caught sight of the woman and looked at her strangely.

"I'm sorry?" he asked.

"Um... I just... You look a lot like Charlie Callen, the author."

Charlie stared back with a cold, confused glare, and didn't say anything for a moment. He made her uncomfortable with his eyes, as if he were sizing her up for a fight.

"My name is Suzan Willow," Charlie said. "Sorry." Stunned, Suzan Willow frowned, her mouth gaped and unable to get another word out. In time, however, she managed to recover her train of thought and caught up with Charlie once more.

"I'm... Hi, I'm sorry," she said with her hand grasping his arm. "What did you say your name was?"

"Listen, lady," Charlie snapped. "I don't know what's going on here, or what the meaning of this is, but I don't appreciate this sort of ill-planned farce. Are you stalking me or something?"

"Stalking you?" Suzan replied with an offended snort. "No. I just... I just saw you walking across the lot, figured I'd try and meet you. I had no idea you'd be so rude."

"I'm being rude?" Charlie shot back. "You're the one being rude! How do you explain all of this?" He circled his hand around her figure. "How did you... How did you change your appearance to look like me?"

Suzan contorted her face, bewildered.

"What the hell are you talking about?"

"Look!" Charlie snapped. "I don't know who you are or what you're trying to pull here, but it's very disconcerting. I don't know who you think I am, but you're obviously confused. My name is Suzan Willow, not... Whoever it is you're looking for. Now, if you please, I have my daughter's dance recital to get to. Have a good day."

She didn't understand. Her daughter had a dance recital which she was to attend in an hour's time. Her name was Suzan Willow. Her... Her... Unable to think any further, she watched as Charlie Callen walked away from her in a strange amble, looking about himself as if he were suffering from dimensia. Deeply disturbed, Suzan Willow turned and headed to her car, unable to shake the ill feeling from her guts.

Charlie continued on his way, changing directions and motivations as he passed by more of the unsuspecting public. Within a half-hour, he accused a man of stealing his car, a woman of stealing his children, and a parking attendant of stealing his job. He then entered the mall, and emotions flashed through him like lightning; he was happy, then worried, then bashful, then embarrassed, then sad, then hopeful, then excited, and so on without ever being conscious of the changes.

It wasn't until he reached the bank and went inside that things began going badly for Charlie. Standing in line, he intrinsically knew that his personal account balance was three hundred and fifty seven dollars, then forty-three hundred dollars, and then six hundred seventy thousand. To the observers in the establishment, Charlie seemed unable to stand still in the long line leading to the busy tellers. He turned constantly, nearly dancing in place, and couldn't keep his stare focussed on anything for any more than a second. Here was an obviously deranged man, and after observing him for a few minutes, Jose Constance, one of the two security guards, approached him to see if he was all right and whether he might pose a threat; but when he touched Charlie's shoulder and began asking him for information, something astounding happened, and everyone in the vicinity backed away in awe and terror.

Charlie felt Jose's hand and turned, and in exact sync with the guard's lips, he said, "Sir, are you feeling all right? Is there anything I can do for you?"

With a jolt, Jose stepped back, his eyes blank and searching. He couldn't understand what had just happened, and when he tried to reiterate his concern, he heard Charlie's voice speak his exact words, at the same time, with the same inflections.

"Sir? Is there... Can I... What's your name, sir?" both voices said, and Jose couldn't trust his own mind. He looked back to his partner and motioned with his chin for help, and then stared at the terrified faces of the customers all around them. When he looked back at Charlie, he had the same look on his face, the same confusion running through his mind as everyone else in the place.

"What's happening here?" Dave Nelson, the second guard, said in sync with Charlie, and this second event was met with gasps and yelps from the mob around them. Dave Nelson stared at Charlie, then he and Charlie simultaneously looked to Jose, then back to each other, each as perplexed as the other.

"How... How can..." both voices said, and both bodies began trembling in fear as they realized that there was no conversation to be had, no questions to be posed or answered—only two people speaking the same things—two faces reacting to the same thoughts, contorting in sync as if staring into an inter-dimensional mirror.

"How are you doing–" a woman from the mob began asking, but was cut short by the realization that Charlie was doing it to her too. "My name is Monica," they both said. "I like blue sea turtles perched on top of marshmallow mountains," Monica said, purely as a test, and Charlie hadn't failed.

"Sir, please turn around!... That's enough!... Stop it!" Jose and Charlie said. The guards wanted to escort him from the premises, but couldn't overcome their bewilderment long enough to actually take action. Something primitive had been disturbed in all of them. It unleashed a fundamental fear, an absolute impossibility made real and thrown into their faces. No one was comfortable with it. When someone, anyone, was angry, or scared, or stupefied, so was Charlie, and there was something so intrinsically wrong with that, so uncannily disturbing, that the only reactions left were to either fight or flee.

It happened slowly, steadily. One person backed away from the mob, walking backward with their eyes trained on Charlie at all times, until finally, quietly, slipping out of the bank and into the vast corridors of the mall. In times of fear, people feel the need to inform, and as the first person out of the bank was followed by another, and then another, until the whole place contained only Charlie and two very frightened guards backed up against the wall, the escapees began telling random strangers about the incredible phenomenon they'd just witnessed. Interest was instant, and in minutes, the doors to the bank were crammed with curious eyes, though none dared cross the threshold. They stared and chattered quietly among themselves, until a man name Silvio Piazzo said, "Hey, why are they calling you a freak?" in perfect sync with Charlie's lips. And when Charlie turned to stare directly at him with an expression of astonishment on his face, a clamor erupted from the crowd and turned them into frightened animals. They pushed each other in all directions, trying to get away from an unidentifiable threat, and suddenly, Charlie was also angry, and searching feverishly for the man who was scaring everybody. He had the image of his face in his mind, but failed to match it to anyone he could see. His thoughts reeled wildly, his vision blurred, and when everyone started running, so did he.

Like a cresting wave, screaming bodies ran from him, desperate for escape. They fought and clawed against each other, racing for the doors, checking over their shoulders, but Charlie was doing something that evoked an acid laced confusion in them. He was running with them, checking over his own shoulder for some sort of attacker, his eyes burning with a terror equal to their own.

In the pandemonium, bodies criss-crossed, slammed together, and trampled each other in a blind panic. One of these unfortunate bodies on the floor belonged to a man named George Mack, and he was one of the astonished customers originally in the line that Charlie had disturbed. He was knocked to the ground after tripping over a little girl running with her mother, and just before he could get back up to his feet, he caught sight of Charlie coming directly for him like a panicked buffalo; with the instinct to flee now cancelled, the instinct to fight took over.

George Mack kicked at the floor, braced himself, and landed a heel on one of Charlie's knee cap. The action had the opposite result of his intention. Instead of crumpling to the floor, Charlie flew through the air like a dead weight and crashed on top of his assailant; the panic was instant. Charlie howled with the pain in his leg, and George Mack shrieked as if he were being attacked by a shark.

"Get him off me!" George Mack and Charlie screamed. "Help! Help me! Get him off me!"

When the people around them caught sight of this apparent attack, they soon stopped their exodus, gathered together, and attacked as a pack. Angry hands grabbed at Charlie's body and tried to tear him to pieces. His leg exploded with blinding pain when the mob savagely tugged at it. They proved relentless, and escalated their communal beating to unpredictable levels, trying to kill the thing they couldn't understand. The sole of a boot smashed against the back of Charlie's head and his face bounced off the polished marble floor, releasing a flood of blood from his nose and forehead. He went limp, and was distantly aware of another strong blow to the side of his face. George Mack, wailing and clawing at the floor, managed to crawl from under Charlie's weight, and he was the first to kick him in the ribs. Charlie yelped involuntarily, spitting out chunks of teeth, choking on them, and still, as the crowd howled sporadic insults, calling him a freak, an abomination, an antichrist, in sync with his own lips, all sense of reason was further torn from them. Another brutal blow to his right flank forced his body onto its back, where he stopped multiple kicks with his face, his chest, his legs. A woman's heel landed in his crotch, causing blood and vomit to spew from his mouth and nose, but he could no longer react consciously. His limbs remained limp, heavy, useless. Heels of boots and shoes continued to hammer down on him from all angles, filling the air with the sound of snapping bones, angry voices, and electric terror. The attack went unabated until a woman named Shirley Hanley got her hands on a weighted post, forced herself through the flailing mob, swung it through the air, and landed the heavy base on Charlie's mangled face. The impact caused jets of blood to soil the closest attackers' faces, crushing Charlie's skull, and instantly halting the attack.

Suddenly, all was quiet. Out of breath, and out of mind, the mob backed away and stared at the mess on the floor, trying to make sense of the situation. The body was swollen, broken, limp, and pulpy. Blood escaped from multiple places, but mostly from the head, staining the polished floor, spreading away from the caved skull. The threat was dead, but as the sense of mundane reason returned to the individuals, a heavy, nasty guilt spread through them. Still a mob, they stared in horror, and then looked absently at each other, searching for answers before averting their eyes again. What had they done? A woman collapsed to the floor in an emotional fit and wept, but no one moved to console her. No one moved at all. With their breaths returning, their limbs felt heavy and limber, their pride damaged, their humanity exposed.

Shirley Hanley, the executor of the final blow, began realizing what she was responsible for. She'd lost herself in a frenzy, swept up in the moment, insane. She was no killer; and then there was Charlie. She gasped, and brought her hands up to her mouth, but stopped with a jolt of panic when she saw the blood. Her hands glistened with it, and her face dripped with sticky red syrup. She screwed up her eyes and slumped into a catatonic state, her breath caught in her chest. With a step back, she slipped in the widening puddle of brain and blood and fell to the floor, but she didn't struggle to get out of it. She felt defeated. Evil.

Within minutes, the previously savage gang of killers were reduced to silent tears of disbelief and a complete lack of understanding of what had transpired. While some remained standing, most of the mob sat on the floor, but all continued to stare at the annihilated form once known as Charlie Callen, newly famous author, threat to everything held sacred.

When the police arrived, no one knew what to say, so no one answered their questions. The officers turned pale at the sight of Charlie. They were bewildered by the guilt-ridden crowd around them, and certain that these regular people could not be responsible for such a gruesome crime. How could such a thing be explained? Paramedics soon followed the police and examined those present.

Words were kept at a minimum. A heavy silence still permeated the area like a fog.

One by one, emergency personnel removed those present, uncertain whether to offer words of support or damnation. Most cried involuntarily, hugging themselves, staring at the floor, trembling. In minutes they had most people moved away from the gruesome scene, but one woman was particularly unresponsive to the officer's questions, or presence. The officer trying to speak to her gasped when he saw the extent to which she was covered in blood. She sat in a puddle of it like a monk in a trance, focussed on otherworldly things, unaffected by this dimension. She didn't seem to notice when he put his hand on her shoulder, so the officer decided to try something else to get her attention; familiarity. Finding her purse on the floor, he rifled through it and located her driver's license. He inspected it quickly, matching the bloody face before him to the stern photo on the card. With her identity confirmed, the officer bent down closer to her, and said, "Ma'am? Um... Shirley Hanley? Excuse me? Shirley, are you all right?"

The woman continued to stare at the body, lost in some sort of introspective psychosis. Once again, the officer ventured to place his hand on her shoulder, and he shook her sternly.

"Shirley Hanley!" he repeated. "Are you okay, Shirley?" And suddenly, Shirley's head turned to face her interrogator. The officer smiled when their eyes met, and Shirley followed suit, except her eyes brightened, her face glowed, and a genuine, friendly smile stretched across her face.

"Sam?" she said, and smiled even wider, as if seeing her long lost brother years after having lost touch. "Hey, you. What are you doing here? Isn't this your day off?"

Perplexed, the officer stood straight up and stared at her. His eyes clouded over under his furrowed brow.

"Ma'am," he said, and his voice cracked terribly with fear. He rubbed the nape of his neck with his hand and stared at the bloodied woman on the floor. "Ma'am... How could you know that?"

Shirley stared back, suddenly confused and squinting her eyes.

Shirley Hanley said, "I... I... I don't know. I... I don't know. How do I know that?"

The End

DRIVE!

The blood on my hands was already crusty. On the sidewalk, I stared at the crying woman, spiteful of her hateful glare. As if it was my fault her dog had run a straight line for my tire; maybe the mangled mutt was just tired of her shit. For a moment, I considered the possibility with taciturn amusement. How many men had this woman driven to suicide? How many dogs and/or cats? Was she really so abrasive as to siphon the very will to live out of men and beast alike? She was in my mind, the bitch, but I suppose that's only because she was quite angry with me. What other defense mechanism was I supposed to use aside from spite? When people are angry with you, you're angry with them. It's a primitive response; an ancient mammalian duty that rewards self-defense with alpha confidence. In that vein, I normally, naturally, strive to conquer and destroy with insult and ridicule in the heat of confrontation; however, the stakes are quite different when your opponent personally watched you run over their favorite little poochy woochy lovey dovey ball of fur. Accident or not, there was enough hostility in that situation to warrant a heartfelt altercation–so keeping my mouth shut was probably for the best.

In truth, I wasn't such a bad guy–not as bad as I appeared in the crying woman's opinion, at least. I was only human, and subject to roller coasters of emotions and ideas. I, like everyone, was susceptible to the fundamental chaos that made us individuals; a victim of weather patterns, stress, and middle class slavery. Barely normal, but able to fake it. Normal was always faked. I did care about some things, but I've always had trouble concerning myself with other people's trials and tribulations. Sometimes it bothered me that I didn't naturally feel much compassion toward people in general, but the irritation they usually provided me with was sufficient to overcome those little moments of weakness. I often told myself to stop acting like an asshole, but no one seemed to make it easy for me to simply keep to myself and not bother with the incessant drama. To be honest, I'd love nothing more than to drop the raw, flaring chagrin I feel every time I go outside and just fit in and be happy, but I haven't had any luck finding a doctor willing to perform the lobotomy.

But this time it was my fault. I did kill a dog, and I hadn't done it on purpose... Though I may as well have, judging by her theatrics. I was sorry about it, sure, but above all else, I was angry, because in reality, there was little I hated more than driving. Given this information, one would assume that I would avoid taking employment in the transportation sector at all costs. I was that sensible, without a doubt, but my circumstances weren't even close; therefore, I did what needed to be done. I drove, and screamed, and raged until I found myself standing over some dramatic lady's smothered dog, futilely trying to explain how the thing had come out of nowhere and beelined it for me with suicide in its eyes.

Of course, I would probably get fired for the incident, and honestly, it was about damn time! I was terrible at my job, and possessed none of the qualities necessary for braving the relentless arrogance of clients and commuters alike. Out of respect for my own mental health, I should have quit a long time ago; unfortunately, out of necessity for my physical health, that option was strictly forbidden. I had no choice but to carry the gig straight into the bowels of insanity if that's what it took, because five years ago I enrolled in a prestigious university and completed a master's degree in physics. One hundred thousand dollars later, with my nifty new diploma in hand, I set out into the world in search of work in my field. The plan had been so well laid out in my mind; get a diploma, get a job, and then laugh all the way to the bank for the rest of my life. I was gloriously ignorant of my own naivety, and absolutely oblivious of the fact that we as a society love nothing more than glorifying the past and over-estimating the future. The present always seemed like a lull. It was a waiting period, a hope that things would get better, like they were, like they could be, like they would never be. The great, dreamy veil we pulled over our eyes was rooted in our view of perfection as some sort of absolute success, a final conquering of all hardships. By that definition, however, death is the most perfect of all things–and look at how scared we all are of it. (And look at how devastated the woman with the now perfect dog is.)

I suppose my error was in heartily believing that no matter how many rejections I received, the discipline, dedication, and perseverance would eventually put me on the pedestal I'd spent my whole life eyeing. But six months into it, after having pushed myself physically, mentally, and financially to hold on just a little while longer... I couldn't keep going without a job. In my field of study or not, I had to eat, and résumés lacked a great deal of nutrition. Feeling dejected and embarrassed, I went to a head hunter's office looking for anything that could help me put something other than microwaved macaroni and cheese and dry noodles in my burning belly. I felt like a wounded dog. I felt cheated.

I had a drawn out meeting with a cackling fat lady, took their demeaning aptitude tests, answered their intrusive questions, and signed more paperwork than it takes to be admitted to federal prison. They handed me bus tickets, which I planned on selling, and in only four short hours I was on my way home, pretty sure that I was going to shit my pants. It sounds funny, but it's no joke; malnutrition sucks.

A capitalist system has a way of decimating some people's will to live. It's only natural, after all. There's only one way to live, one way to eat, and those who don't conform either out of will or nature are reduced to starvation, disease, and premature death.

I went to bed that night feeling betrayed. I had gone to school. I had studied my goddamned ass off and put in five years of hard work and borrowed money to get my diploma, and for what? To fill temporary positions? To starve? To allow my dark frustrations to poison my soul? I'd been conned by a common social dream. I felt like a broken man. A failure on all fronts. What had I done to deserve it?

The very next morning, the fat lady called and woke me at eleven thirty. I should've been excited to hear her voice, but all I felt was a gnawing dread at the thought of temporarily working at some dead end job today, and another tomorrow, and another the day after that. She asked if I had a clean driving record. I did. Was I interested in driving a limousine? Only one question mattered... How much?

I'd never thought of doing anything like that. It wasn't a bad idea, and after I agreed to the interview, I even pumped myself up with grand self-assurances. Everything was going to be fine. I'd just hit a stretch of bad luck. It happened to everyone. This job was just in the meantime, just to carry me over to the next job; the one my fancy looking diploma would get me.

The meeting was scheduled for nine the next morning. I woke up at seven thirty, drank a pot of coffee, and then headed to the meeting while repeating encouraging mantras in my head. Everything was going to work out; I just needed to give it some time.

The interview was with a small East Indian man who

spoke quickly and with an accent too thick for me to make any real sense of anything he said; but when he smiled and shook my hand, I understood, assumed, that I'd gotten the gig. He handed me a clipboard with a bunch of names and times bulleted neatly on a crisp page, pointed, and said, "Tonight, seven o'clock, football banquet. You take car number six; see Habib in the shop. Thank you, my friend."

It was done. I was happy. At least I could scrape up some cash. I saw Habib in the shop; he was an eccentric giant of a man who smoked cigarettes in the shop and laughed at everything. He showed me the car with the enthusiasm of a salesman, and then explained to me the finer details of the job. Before I knew it, I was off in a limo for a test drive with Habib. All went well, despite the car handling like a blimp around corners, and it was done. The job was mine.

I went home feeling elated, ecstatic. I had a shower, ate a sandwich, and then sat around terribly impatient. The minutes crawled by. My bowels were irritated, volatile, and my mind reeled with unfocussed thoughts.

At six o'clock, I pulled the long car out of the garage and on to the street, turned it right, and sped away to chauffeur my very first clients. It felt funny. I laughed at myself and made faces in the mirror. "Hello there, I'll be your chauffeur this evening. You'll have to excuse the sharp corners at speed... I just downed a forty of vodka."

I was practically driving a bus. I was nervous, which was why I was fooling around. Not five minutes into the gig, however, an SUV swerved sickeningly into my lane and missed my bumper by a millimeter. I stood on the brake pedal and steered the big bitch away from the moron, suddenly feeling ill, numb, and overcome by a crude sense of paranoia. Annoyed, I drove on through congested intersections, confused commuters, and hundred foot dashes in between red lights. I wasn't making faces or being silly anymore. I suddenly just wanted to get the whole affair over with and go home. Escape.

Nearly thirty minutes later, I arrived at my destination; a huge house with a circular driveway and a five car garage big enough to irritate my feebly stowed envy. I was picking up a bunch of college football players and their girlfriends, seven people in all. With belching voices and the spastic excitement of five year old children, they piled into the back and offered me drinks and women if I played my cards right.

I just wanted to go home with my tail between my legs. Alone. Quietly.

I brought the hulking car back on the street, turned left, and headed for the banquet the animals in the back were destined to attend. Behind me, they screamed, and laughed, and rocked the vehicle from side to side, but it hardly irritated me as much as the assholes driving fifteen kilometers an hour in a fifty zone. My mood darkened to a dizzying mess of volatile hostility and unrestrained self-loathing.

"I fucking hate driving in this city!" I snapped to myself. White knuckles gripped the wheel and I growled like a dog. The car was too big for offensive maneuvers, so I dejectedly crawled along at speeds far below the clearly posted maximum. Behind me, my passengers screamed obscenities at pedestrians and argued about who was going to get the most fucked up out of the gang. I scowled and thought that if they didn't settle down soon, I would do them a favor and fuck them all up well beyond their expectations. Gnashing my teeth, I continued driving fifteen kilometers an hour behind a long line of irritated drivers. I was cut off twice, flipped off once, and arrived at the banquet with bubbling blood and an artery about to explode inside of my head. The streets were sheer madness. Every turn, every block, same insanity.

The goons in the back rushed out of the car and disappeared into the building. According to my contract, I was to wait in the lot and meet whatever reasonable requests the passengers had. God, how pathetic. I wasn't wired for public service. I was just trying to survive. I was just trying to eat. How could this be my life, I thought. Forced to do what I hated most in order to live. Lower middle class.

I parked the car, strolled through the lot, and struck up a conversation with a fellow irritated driver. We complained about the horrid traffic and the rude kids we were hauling around. I'd been a limousine driver for a total of two hours and my sanity was already showing cracks. This other driver had been at it for twenty one years, and it clearly showed in his drawn and sunken face. He held a defeated posture, and his eyes seemed glazed over with a quiet resolve. He was a beaten soul, a desperate victim.

Our conversation was cut short, however. A mere forty five minutes after our arrival, one of my passengers, the quarterback of the football team, came hustling across the parking lot with a girl on each arm.

"Driver, start the car and drive us around the city," he

ordered.

I shook my head and felt an oppressive surge of rage. I wanted to tell him to go fuck himself, but as soon as I was about to open my mouth, I felt my stomach turn violently to one side. It did a backflip, punched itself, and declared that it would soon impose offensive consequences on me if I didn't get on a regular, nutritionally sound diet. It took my breath away. I sighed and bit my bottom lip, reluctantly nodding and staring at the ground.

The kid stood by the door and cleared his throat. "Ah, driver... The door," he said with the arrogant tone of a pompous rap star.

I scoffed, ready to punch the little prick in the throat. I glanced at the driver I'd been conversing with. His eyes avoided mine; I was fucked.

Fury flashed through me as I walked toward them, grinning like an asshole. I opened the door and looked him in the eye.

"Your highness," I said, and gestured with my hand to the back seat. He shoved the girls in before him, and said, "Thanks, bitch!"

Only the pangs of hunger stopped me from ripping his face off. I slammed the door and walked around the back of the car to the driver's seat, hissing under my breath.

"Fucking little cocksucker! I'm about to serve you a free trip to the hospital to get your dick surgically removed from your throat!"

I started the car and pressed the intercom button. "Where to?" I said, incapable of professionalism.

I heard static, then laughing girls, and then, "Just drive around town, man. Go all over the place; just don't stop."

I didn't even reply.

"Fuck!" I snapped, and shifted the car into drive. So it began. On a Friday night, the traffic was manic, lewd, and trying to handle the big car on the freeway was terrifying at times. I wrestled against the shady alignment at high speeds, the squeaky brakes, the lumbering engine, the idiots in the back. I crossed the city like a misanthropic fiend, wishing ill will on everyone, on everything; cursing the kamikaze lane changes, the sudden, unexpected stops, and the brainless bastards who didn't seem aware that beyond themselves, all around, other people existed. From the freeway, I merged onto a secondary and then drove through residential communities. Within an hour, I witnessed an accident, passed by two more, nearly rear-ended three cars, blew two red lights, and began suffering the ill effects of the volcanic-like pressure building inside my veins at nearly every intersection. The whole thing gnawed at my last nerve. I was about to snap.

Eventually, just when I figured it wasn't worth it anymore–that I should stop and hop on a bus and go home–I heard screaming voices in the back. The girls sounded frantic, panicked. It sounded violent, and it somehow made me even angrier than I already was. What the hell was I doing? I had a Master's degree. I should've been working somewhere relevant, not serving as a personal chauffeur to spoiled rich kids at fourteen bucks an hour plus tips, if any. A shit job in the face of a one hundred thousand dollar debt. I was stuck... Probably for life, and I was barely thirty years old.

There was a loud bang in the back, a panicked scream, and then I heard the boy's voice scream maniacally. Good God, I thought. What the hell was going on? Again, more female screams, more bangs, more violence. It was none of my business, I decided, and tried to focus on ignoring the nonsense altogether; then I heard a girl screaming at the top of her lungs for help.

I sighed and threw my hands up in the air in frustration, debating what to do. Should I stop? Should I keep going? Should I throw the keys in the ditch, drag the kid out by the collar, and kick the shit out of him right there on the sidewalk? I wasn't sure, but as I was slowing down, the kid hit the intercom button and said, "Don't you dare fucking stop, asshole. You keep going. You hear me?"

I didn't answer, and I suddenly felt like a terrible person. In the back, girl's were being violated, and though I normally didn't bother with other people's problems, there was a fundamental need to help a young girl in trouble–especially if the offender in question was a nothing more than a pretentious turd with legs–but every time I convinced myself to stop and at least make sure he wasn't killing the poor girls, I felt my other fundamental need burn deeply in the pit of my stomach. As much as I hated it, I needed the job. I needed money. I had no other options. It was this or starvation, homelessness, panhandling.

"Goddamn it," I hissed. What kind of world did we live in when people had to choose between doing the right thing, the decent thing, or survival? It was a broken world; one of superficial goals, undeserved entitlement, rewarded betrayal, and celebrated, glorified, stupidity.

I continued driving, trying to ignore my gnawing guilt.

For the next two hours I drove through gridlock, braved semis on the freeway, and did my best to get out of the way of feverish emergency sirens and lights. Behind me, things eventually quieted, and for a long time I wondered if I was driving a couple of corpses through the city street. I was a bad person. I had no choice.

Back at the banquet, I never even left my seat. I parked in front of the building, allowed the drunken animals to pile into the back, and drove them back across town to the big house with the giant garage. I ignored the screams, and the puking, and the fights. I ignored what had happened. I ignored everything and simply drove. By that time of night, traffic had dissipated and left behind weaving drunks, maniac kids, and idiots with no headlights.

That was my very first day driving. What a disaster. I returned the car to the garage, unwilling to even look in the back. From the noises I'd heard, I fully expected blood, vomit, shit, piss, semen, booze, and cigarette burns to cover everything. The artifacts of modern youth. I had no need for confirmation.

I went home fuming, frustrated. I didn't know what I was going to do. My first night at my new job had nearly caused me a nervous collapse; how could I keep doing such a thing? My stomach tightened in painful knots; how could I keep doing such a thing? I was about to lose my apartment, my health, my mind; how could I do such a thing?

Sleeping was a difficult feat to achieve that night. Every time the fingers of sleep tickled the back of my mind, I heard girls screaming. Memories. Guilt. What was I going to do?

Obviously, I stuck with it. After that night, I managed to convince myself that I'd only had a stroke of bad luck. That those kids were just idiots. Surely not every job would turn out the same. I was bound to have friendly passengers who tipped well and treated people humanely.

Over the next three months... I discovered just how completely full of shit I was. The illusion shattered, and the entire planet seemed to have turned into self-indulgent sadists. Scum.

Day after day I faced congested streets, blocked intersections, overturned vehicles. I had to deal with rude customers, ruder drivers, and endless construction. I witnessed obscene acts of road rage, dangerous stunts, and narcissistic maniacs driving like they were in a video game.

In bed after long, brutal nights, I found myself dreaming of the madness. I was rotting from the inside. I dreamed of Jesus fishes, and Darwin fishes, and bumper stickers with slogans no reasonable person could ever care about. I saw the little family stickers in back windows, as if anyone cared about how many kids, or dogs, or cats other people had. The whole gig was driving me insane, and it was turing me into a bad person. An indifferent sociopath, through and through. Irritated and frustrated to the point where even the smallest inconvenience was enough to set me off on a tantrum. I felt like a ticking time bomb; like a dangerous beast being constantly poked by ignorant instigators.

In the meantime, I continued applying for a real job. Every day I would come home taut with rage, consumed with frustration, which fueled my motivation to lift my spirits, suck it up, and keep trying to get a job in my field. Something that could do more than simply feed me; something that could help me pay the monstrous debts pressing forcefully against my shoulders.

It was hopeless.

I applied everywhere I could think of, pleading for a meaningful post, something to free me from my towering depression, my poverty, but there was always some sort of excuse for why I couldn't have the job. The positions were always granted to people with either less education than me, or the intelligence level of a lobotomized monkey being repeatedly punched in the head. It was typical; everywhere you looked, some asshole was there looking for a handout with no work involved. And even worse, some of them got it; while others worked their asses off, followed the system, and ended up with an education far more useless than not getting one in the first place. At least by now I would have some sort of useful experience under my belt, which was ironically the very thing that stood in my way. I only ever heard one of two responses during interviews.

"Sorry, your qualifications match, but you lack the experience," or "Sorry, your experience matches, but you lack the necessary qualifications on paper."

One of those statements costs one hundred thousand dollars to hear; the other one is free. What's the difference?

My other problem was that I didn't know anyone with meaningful connections; therefore, my degree wasn't even worth wiping my ass with. I was trying to break into an elitist system, formed by and for elitists–the shallow dream we all envy. Superiority–no matter how superficial or illusory.

I tried not letting it get to me. I believed in persistence and hard work, but I was running out of options. Meanwhile, I continued driving, further irritating my volatile temper, my wanton misanthropy, and my darkening insanity. It seemed as if the entire city was conspiring against me. For example, If I stopped at a stop sign in any part of the city with one car opposite me and another on my right and left–no one went first–then everyone went first. Every goddamned time! If I approached a car waiting to merge from a secondary road, it waited, and waited, and waited, until I was three meters away, and then it went, cutting me off at fifteen kilometers per hour. Worst of all, it seemed I was always stuck following some swerving jerk who thought the next exit was his, and then changed his mind, and then committed once more, and then changed his mind. How can so many people not know where the fuck they're going?

I spent my evenings driving personality challenged people. Some of them screamed at me, others laughed, but most insisted on treating me like a worthless slave. Tips? Ha. In my dreams. It seemed that working in the service industry made you less human than everyone else, and more worthless than roadkill. Just because at this point in my life I was forced to work a menial job, for a menial pay, I wasn't entitled to the slightest form of respect. It was all becoming too much to be worth it.

The people I picked up seemed to think that once they crossed the precipice of the limo, no laws could further accost them. Night after night, there was drug use, drinking, sex, fights, and who knew what else just behind the opaque glass divider at my back. I carried on for months, head first into the tailspin, ass backward and emotionally sick; and then something changed. One night, I had to drive a couple to a concert. When I pulled into the driveway, they made me wait forty five minutes before rushing to the back of the car and screaming at me to hurry up or else they would miss the show. On the way, they demanded I run red lights and insisted I push people out of the way in order to serve their holy desires. Then, right in front of me, one car smashed into another, debris landed on the hood of the limo, and one of the cars skidded violently across the lane and completely blocked our way. I felt the veins in my forehead throb vehemently. I didn't care if anyone was hurt or not, all I wanted was for them to get out of my way so I could get these two pompous whales out of my face; but I was stuck with nowhere to go.

The police eventually arrived and insisted on a statement. I was so angry and frustrated that all I could do was scream at the officer, "Listen, this idiot turned this way without looking, and that idiot smashed into him. The only solution I see is for you to pull your weapon and put a bullet in their heads. Cleanse the city."

The cop stared at me, surprised, and frowning curiously. "Sir, what if you were involved in an accident? Wouldn't you want anyone to help you; at the very least, to protect you against libel?"

I sighed and shook my head.

"Do you think they would?" I asked. "You're a civil servant, how nice are people to you? You're out there providing a service, trying to make a difference; do you feel fulfilled? I think most people in this city couldn't be bothered with either saving a life or stepping over a corpse. And even beyond that–" I stopped complaining and snorted in frustration. "Listen, I apologize. I'm just a little frustrated. I'm forced to take this job despite having the black on white paper qualifications to be riding in the back, but such is life. The truth is, through this job, I've learned the truth about this place. It's filled with rude, careless, and pretentious assholes who would take advantage of the rich and poor alike, regardless of the situation as long as it benefited them. I have two of these monsters in the car right now, screaming at me to get them to a concert. They're superficial fools who even went so far as to blame me for this mess here, and pressured me to plow through the wreckage, run over bodies if I have to, just as long as they don't miss their precious little show. The nerve of these fucking people–I'm sure you know what I mean."

The cop nodded and pursed his lips.

"We all have bad days," he replied. "I understand your situation, but maybe you should think about finding a way to relax a little, unwind. I thank you for your patience, and your information, and I won't keep you any longer. But, man to man, I wish you the best of luck in your future. You don't have to keep the job if you hate it so much. In fact, I would advise you against it. Life's far too short, and money far too worthless to be a slave to it." I didn't answer, but nodded apprehensively, staring at the ground. "You can go now. Your statement, minus expletives, has been useful. Have a good evening, sir."

He tipped his hat and I was on my way with a convoluted mess of emotions weighing on me. He was right; what was money? It was an idea attached to a piece of paper, nothing more. You couldn't eat it, nor drink it, nor keep warm with it. The whole idea was only sustainable as long as the rest of the system held up; otherwise, it even made for poor padding as a mattress. But that was the problem–the system was still up and running–and as long as it was, I could feed myself, and drink, and keep warm with money.

It was a necessity; no way around it. I could leave my job, but for what? Was it worth losing my physical and mental health?

What choice did anyone have?

I took in a deep breath and opened the driver's door, zoned into a volatile mood, and conflicted on multiple levels. Not half a second after my ass hit the leather did the bitch behind me start hurling insults.

"You moron!" she snarled. "The show's already started! We'll be demanding a refund for this piss poor service, I hope you know that. Does this company only hire idiots? Are you going to answer me, you worthless little–"

"Listen to me you fucking sow," I snapped, turning around in my seat to face the lunatics. "Sit down and shut up or I swear to God I'll drive this car straight off a bridge after I cave your skulls in, got it? I don't fucking care about you or your stupid concert. If you both dropped dead right there in the back seat it would be nothing more than a minor inconvenience and an early night off. Now, if you don't mind, I have a job to do."

And with that, I closed the divider between us, shutting out the nightmare, and shifted the car into gear. This incident had given me a small personal victory to brood over. I'd had it with these people, every last one of them. The cop was right, I needed to do some serious thinking about my life. This couldn't be worth it. There had to be another way. There had to be an answer for me somewhere.

About a half hour after I'd put the witch in her place, I arrived at their destination, at least half-way through the concert, but I didn't care. The couple was so furious they couldn't even find the words to insult me. Served them right.

Of course, at the end of my shift, there was trouble to pay with my employer. He pulled his hair out in aggravation, screamed at the top of his lungs, and stomped maniacally around his office. I simply sat and stared and never uttered a word, mostly because even after a couple of months, I still couldn't understand anything he said anyway. Deep down, I wished he would fire me. In the end, however, he informed me that business was too good, and his staff too short to let me go–"this time."

"One more chance!" he pointed his finger in my face. "Please, this job is not hard, all you need is patience. This is my livelihood."

In retrospect, I should have asked him for a raise right that instant, but I was so depressed and irritated, I failed to find the necessary grit. I just wanted to go home, curl up in bed, and cry. I just wanted to cry. I wanted some sort of release. I had no other choice but to wait it out. I had rent to pay–debt, interest, more interest, taxes, insurance. I had to keep going on no sleep and the stress level of an unsuspecting antelope suddenly facing a lion. I felt doomed.

On I drove.

To the symphony, the wedding, the play; I forced smiles and transported all flavors of demented tyrants to and fro. I swallowed my distaste, my demonic temper, and simply told myself that I needed to do whatever needed to be done. I had to put my head down, take control of my attitude, and do the best I could while I waited for responses from other prospects. That was life. Tough shit. Take it or leave it.

Everyday I would stare at myself in the rearview mirror and smile, regardless of my mood. I faked it all. I arrived at houses and skipped around the car, grinned widely while holding the door, and whistled while I drove. Ha! Hilarious. Life was better when it was faked. It was the only way to make any fun of it. It was the only way to avoid suicide.

Manufactured zen.

When some old fart would cut me off in the middle of rush hour traffic, I'd take a deep breath and turn the radio up a notch. When an unsure shopper weaved in and out of a lane, I would bite down on my bottom lip and punch myself in the leg in an attempt to stow my frustration. And when a semi would signal left, turn right, and nearly crush me against a concrete embankment, I would look in the mirror and smile. I would become a character. I would play the part.

I would enjoy life.

This went on for days, then weeks. I was feeling good, completely ignoring reality. My level of debt was a minor hurdle. My ravenous temper was only undirected passion. Driving wasn't such a bad gig after all... And then I picked up a woman named Angela Feore. I'd seen her on the news that morning; she was considered a pioneer for animal rights, and I was to drive her to give a speech in some large downtown conference centre.

Her hotel was barely sixteen blocks from the conference centre. A piece of cake. I pulled up to the main doors at seven o'clock, just as my client was walking through the lobby. I shifted the vehicle into park, skipped around the car, opened the door, made eye contact, smiled, nodded my head, and said, "Welcome, ma'am."

She returned my smile and said, "Thank you," and entered the car. I shut the door, skipped back to the driver's seat, and pulled away. I took in a deep breath and looked at myself in the rearview mirror. I smiled and winked my eye. I checked my side-view mirrors and whistled, determined to have a great night–the best since I'd taken the job. There was always a turning point, no matter how bad the situation. It was the one thing that made life worth living; eventually, things changed.

Thank fucking Christ!
Traffic was light for a Friday night, but the directionally challenged fiends were always present. I turned up the radio and watched cars swerve shamelessly across lanes, kissing bumpers, slamming brakes, throwing hands up and screaming unintelligible obscenities at each other like angry children at the playground. In my newly enlightened mood, I laughed and shook my head. I basked in the unreasonable chaos. It brought about a revelation, in fact, and one heavily contrasted with the ambitions of my youth. After high-school, I thought would no longer have to put up with the drama, the gossip, the cliques, the bullies, the douchebags, the meaning-less and often contradictory rules, etc... I'd felt a ravenous opti-mism for the future. I was bright eyed and reaching for the stars. The truth, however, was that we never really did leave highschool. The characters only grew older, childish attitudes intact, and the social nomenclature simply settled into the background and be-came what we called normal. School programmed people to chase after lottery-like dreams with full conviction. It filled their heads with false ideas about success. In truth, fame and fortune only translated into a way out, an end, a distraction; that was the real capitalist dream. The ultimate glory was the complete ignorance of the rest of the world. The right to not participate in the mass psychosis.

The first three blocks were without personal incident, and as I pulled up to a red light, I felt grateful. It was going to be a good night; all the signs were there. When the light turned green, I accelerated through the intersection, and then everything went wrong.

Just ahead of me, a taxi swerved in front of a semi and sent it sailing across two lanes. It caused cars to pile up behind it before it shot up the embankment and turned over on its side. I barely avoided becoming part of the carnage, and I was suddenly tuned in to a wave of scorching anger. The stupidity of it all was too much. I could never explain it; it just got to me on a fundamental level. What was I supposed to do now?

"What's the matter? Is everything okay?" the girl in the back asked over the intercom. I sighed and pushed the button.

"Ah... I'm sorry, Ma'am, but there's been an accident."
"Well..." she hesitated. "Is there any way around it? I have an important appointment tonight."

I gnashed my teeth and shook my head. What the hell was wrong with people?

"Please," she supplicated. "I'm willing to pay anything for you to get me there on time."

I threw up my hands and stared at the wreckage before me. There were at least seven cars smashed into one another. The spaces between them were filled with angry drivers and concerned citizens, most arguing, some trying to help the injured out of vehicles, all adding to the madness.

"Are you going to answer me or not?" she demanded suddenly. "I will give you one thousand dollars cash if you can just get me there on time."

I snorted and looked around me. Vehicles were parked everywhere at odd angles and panicked pedestrians ran amok. I could hear sirens approaching. To my right was an opening I thought I could squeeze through and merge onto a side street and maybe get around the mess. I sighed and shook my head. The things people cared about. I pushed the button and said, "All right, I'll try my best to get out of here but I can't guarantee anything. It's chaos out there."

It wasn't going to be easy. I would have to angle the car and zigzag it in between bumpers, trying to avoid damage. I shifted the car into drive and turned the wheel, slowly released the pressure on the brake pedal, and on we crawled. I had to wait for pedestrians, and didn't acknowledge their scowling glares while I focussed my attention on getting to the side street. Slowly, but with definite progress, we irked across the lanes, mindful of obstructions, and finally merged on to the street just as emergency vehicles were pulling in to assess the mess behind us.

"Ha!" I said and slapped the steering wheel. "Fucking lunatics."

I accelerated and sank back into my seat, but not thirty seconds into it, a truck came flying around an adjacent street with complete disregard for anyone else. He barely missed me and caused my heart to wallop weirdly. Rage. I felt my hands go numb with it. I clenched my jaw and pursed my lips, trying to breathe and stay calm. I was going to have a good night even if it was going to kill me! Goddamn it!

The road ended with a three way intersection, and I suddenly realized that I didn't know where I was going. I turned left and headed in the general direction of my destination, but I soon found myself rolling through residential streets, cul-de-sacs, dead ends, and closed roads. I looked at the clock and sighed. There was only ten minutes left to get my client to her precious little speech. It would be close.

Another cul-de-sac. I followed the curb around and headed back in the direction I'd just come from, bitting my bottom lip in frustration, obsessively pulling at my hair. Ahead of me, serene streets branched off in other directions, but there were so many I couldn't know where they led. I felt like I was driving through a labyrinth. Progress, progress, end, back up, turn around, start over, progress, end. It was driving me insane. I pulled up to a stop sign, waited my turn, then three cars went at once. I laughed, shook my head, punched myself in the leg. Beyond the intersection, I was cut off twice more within a mile; then nearly sideswiped, rear-ended, t-boned, and still, I was oblivious of where I was going. Time was running out, and with it, the very last of my frayed patience. I cursed the drivers, the city planners, God himself. How could all of this even exist? How did anyone ever think that–

My train of thought was violently interrupted by a bang that caused the left side of the car to jump up suddenly, violently. Panic filled my heart. I'd hit something. Fantastic! It was exactly what I needed! Fuck having a good night; this was as good as it got.

Bringing the car to a screaming halt, I slammed the transmission into park and hissed obscenities under my breath. I opened the door, stepped out–and there it was; a broken dog pulled up into the rear wheel-well, pooling blood on the pavement.

"Shit!" I snapped and ran my fingers through my hair. Surely some malicious force was out to get me. There I was, lost, angry, and driving a world renown animal rights representative around town... And I run over a goddamn dog. Beautiful. Just fucking great!

My passenger rolled down her window, her eyes sick with concern. I tried assuring her that it was no problem, just a little accident, be on our way in no time at all, but no sooner did I approach the mangled beast did I hear shrill screams from behind me.

Good! I thought. Why not?

I turned and saw a woman lunging toward me, tears streaming from her eyes, terror contorting her face. There was nothing I could say.

"My dog!" she screamed. Her voice echoed through the street. "Digger! Oh, God, no! Please, tell me he's okay!"

Crazed, blind with terror, she pushed past me, fell to the asphalt, and held a bloody head to her chest, the body still firmly lodged in the wheel well. She cried and hissed angry threats at me.

I couldn't find anything to say aside from mumbled apologies. Not that it would have made a difference, really, because before I could think of something else to say, out came Angela Feore from the car, her eyes wide and angry. She glared at me after sighting the carcass. Her face turned red, and the cords in her neck flexed monstrously under the skin. She was trying to kill me with thoughts alone. It wasn't a good situation.

"Listen," I said, and threw my hands up in the air. "It was an accident–all right? I never saw the thing. I didn't mean to do anything but get you to your destination, Ma'am."

She scowled and became hostile and rabid.

"Are you trying to blame this on me, you incapable idiot!" she screamed at me, military style. I thanked the Lord this woman was not my mother. "Look at what you've done, you moron! You killed a dog! A dog! Look at what you've done to this poor woman, you monster."

Jesus. I was completely fucked. I tried defending myself once more, but before I could get a word out, I saw man approaching the woman on the curb in a hurry and wrap his arms around her, trying to console the inconsolable. He was a beast of a man with arms like tree trunks and the head of a bull.

"He killed Digger!" she wailed, and I was suddenly backing away from them involuntarily, frantic to find a way to settle the score with minimal damage. "He just ran right over him!"

"You!" The man suddenly shot up to his feet. "What did you do? Did you kill my dog?"

I threw my hands up once more, meaning peace, but the beast wanted nothing to do with my offering. He stepped up quickly and leaned his face toward mine. His eyes blazed with a vengeful passion.

"I... It was an accident.. Man," I said, but he wasn't interested in excuses. In a flash, he landed a fist against the side of my jaw and caused my body to follow my head into the side of the limo. I hit the ground and soon found myself locked in a desperate wrestling match with the man. He was thick, and strong, and relentless; I was a physics major. Somehow, mostly by luck, I managed to push the beast back and trip him over the curb. He fell dramatically, comically, onto his back, his limbs flailing like an overturned turtle. I wasted no time. My intentions switched from fight, to flight, and I lunged for the driver's door, feverish to get away from the chaos and avoid my imminent death. The move caused instant rage in all present.

"Hey! Stop that son of a bitch!"

I managed the door and hopped in, completely out of breath. My hands were numb, and my legs were burning, and weak. I got the car started, but before I could shift into gear, someone got into the back.

"Stop the car right this instant!" It was Angela, her voice fierce and determined.

I said nothing and shifted into drive, and then I heard another voice–the beast's.

"You think you can just run away, you little bitch!" he screamed. "I'm not finished with you!"

He banged on the divider, trying to get the thing down before I could take off. Too late. I slammed my foot on the accelerator and shot down the street like a bullet. I didn't know where I was going, or where I should go, but away felt better, at least until the police got to the scene to protect everyone involved.

I swerved through an intersection and turned right, desperate to avoid stopping. Behind me, wrath was trying to get through the wall while screaming threats at me.

"Stop the car, now!" he screamed. "Now, goddamn it!"
"Stop before someone gets hurt!" Angela followed. "You've already caused enough damage!"

I ignored them and continued without destination. I came up to another intersection, but before I could even get to it, the divider behind my head suddenly burst inward, shattered, and a giant hand reached for my throat.

Panic.

I screamed and tried to defend myself against his attack, but it was useless in close quarters.

"Don't!" I yelled. "I'm driving a fucking car here!"

It didn't matter. The beast's hand wrapped around my throat, distracting me from the road, and caused me to press harder on the accelerator and sail into an obstructed intersection on a red light.

I weaved around a car, but as soon as I cleared it, a pick-up truck slammed into the side of the limo and sent it spinning like a top.

Everything was quiet. The air was filled with a metallic, petroleum stench. There was no hand around my throat. No screaming from the back. I looked out of the side window and frowned, trying to get the stars out of my head. People were running in every direction, screaming for someone to call the police. I took a deep breath and rubbed my forehead. I was covered in blood and sported a terrible gash on my brow.

This is it, I thought. The final straw. If I thought my employer was upset over me arguing with clients, imagine what he was going to say now. I was filled with rage, consumed with an urge to break something, or someone. This ridiculous job had taken the very soul out of me. It took my will to live, and my sanity. These people, these foul, desperate, pathetic people had ruined me from the inside out. All I had wanted to do was survive, but it seemed even that wasn't meant to be. I constantly thought about leaving the city, but if I couldn't even bring myself to survive in it, how was I going to leave it? I wasn't. I was to stay, and suffer, and brave the stupidity day in and day out until someone gave me a crack at what I'd spent years working toward. Meanwhile, I was forced to squirm.

In minutes, police cars breached the mess and pulled me out of the car. Before even checking if I was all right, they slapped cuffs around my wrists and threw me into the back of a cruiser. I sat there for a while, fuming, festering in rage and disappointment, watching uniformed bodies rushing in every direction, trying to gain control of the situation.

I glanced around me, looking for sight of my passengers, but I didn't see them anywhere. The police piled into the back of the limo, acting frantically, but they didn't pull anyone out. I sighed and shook my head, suddenly full of questions. Where were they? Were they all right? Would that bastard in the back be charged for grabbing me by the throat while I was driving a car? What was he thinking? What was I thinking? Goddamn it. The more time went by, the worse I felt about the whole thing. How did these things always seem to happen to me?

Eventually, an officer returned to the cruiser and poked his head inside.

"Sir, what happened here?"

"I... Ah," I mumbled. "I was lost, and then I hit a dog–completely by accident. So I got out to set things straight, but before I could do anything, the guy in the back of the limo tried to strangle me. I managed to get loose and into the car, but he and my client climbed into the back, and then the bastard attacked me from the inside. He choked me and I lost control. We were t-boned, and... Well... here we are."

He nodded but said nothing while jotting down notes. When he finished, he turned his head and stared back toward the limo. From the back, an officer exited the car, stared at my interrogator, and shook his head disparagingly. The man before me nodded, and then sighed. Without acknowledging my side of the story, he stared into my eyes and his demeanor darkened.

"Sir," he said. "In addition to being charged with careless driving, you are also being charged with two counts of vehicular manslaughter for the deaths of one Angela Feore, and one John Forsythe. You have the right to remain silent, and it is my duty to inform you that you have the right to retain and instruct counsel without delay"

"Wait!" I exclaimed, suddenly trembling and terribly confused. "What are you saying? Did–did they die back there?"

"You have the right to consult an attorney before speaking to the police and to have an attorney present during questioning now or in the future. If you cannot afford an attorney, one will be appointed to you before any questioning, if you wish. If you decide to answer any questions now, without an attorney present, you will still have the right to stop answering at any time until you speak with an attorney. If you choose to speak without an attorney present, anything you say can be entered into evidence. Do you understand your rights, sir?"

"Just wait a goddamn minute!" I snapped again. A terrible claustrophobic fear encapsulated my heart; my breath became labored. "What the hell are you talking about? They both died? Both of them?"

"Do you understand your rights, sir?" he asked again. "My rights?!" I screamed. "Are you telling me I just killed two people?"

Without answer, he shut the door and left me inside. Calmly, he trotted back to the limo and joined the rest of his team.

"What the fuck?" I whispered. "What the fuck? This isn't good. This... How could this have happened?"

I felt rabid guilt rip through me when I thought of the crying woman sitting on the curb, hugging her limp dog against her chest. Just like that, in a matter of minutes, I'd taken her dog and husband away from her; and for what, my temper? My stupidity? My inability to deal with the general public?

"Shit!" I shook my head and shifted my uncomfortable weight in the seat. It was the most horrible thing I'd ever done. I couldn't come to grips with it, and I burst into a convulsing fit of tears. My body shook violently, and I felt cold. I felt scared. My life was over. Despite the struggling, the irking, the frustration... I had failed. Nothing could ever be more devastating. No matter what I did now, I was going to prison.

Paramedics took the bodies away on gurneys and I was driven to the police station. They booked me, took my prints, and locked me alone in a cold cell with a concrete block to sleep on and an ice cold stainless steel toilet to shit in. It was too real. My soul was broken.

I called a lawyer recommended on the internet and explained my situation. He agreed to defend me at a reduced fee, but warned against expecting an unpunished release; I would have to spend some sort of time in prison.

I hired him, and though he proved to be nothing brilliant, he wasn't fully incompetent either. He handled things well and managed a deal for five years in prison. It was inevitable; I'd accidentally killed two people. I deserved the time. My own stupidity had guided my path there.

I was sorry. I truly was. The people I had destroyed had been just that–people. I hadn't known their hopes and dreams, their fears and regrets, their joys and pains, but I had taken it all away from them anyway. For their families, I would forever stand as a symbol of pain, and evil. I would have to live with that. I felt especially bad about Angela Feore's death, but I was reluctant to take the full brunt of the blame. I had a bad temper, yes, and I had been driving, correct; but it was the volatile mixture of one angry man trying to punish another that had been responsible for the terrible event. I suppose the truth was that life wasn't so much a series of proactive actions as it was a series of defensive reactions. The situation always came first; as such, there was no such thing as control. If there was, we would all achieve our wildest dreams with minimal damage, effort, or sacrifice, and without ever facing unforeseen circumstances. Instead, we were thrown into the chaos to defend ourselves at every turn, trying to glimpse the path we thought correct, squirming to reach our goals with bated breath, and constantly, blindly, waiting for the next outcome to instigate another reaction. It's what we called luck. It was really just called life, and it was a brilliant illusion.

On my first day behind bars I managed a phone call and checked my messages. I had three. The first was a hang-up. The second was a telemarketing computer informing me that I'd won a Caribbean cruise. And the third was a call back from a prominent university letting me know that I'd passed their first interview requirements and they wanted me to come back for a second, more vigorous interview. I collapsed to the floor in a fit of laughter and left the phone dangling above my head. The universe was hilarious. One more day, one more job, one more ounce of patience, and I would have been standing on the precipice of collecting the sweet fruits of all my labor. If a guy couldn't laugh at that, he'd have to kill himself.

On my second day of incarceration I signed up for classes in English literature–completely free of charge. It was the greatest irony of all, and proof of the blatant hypocrisy fundamentally woven into our society. How could I ignore it? I'd wasted five years and one hundred thousand dollars chasing commercialized propaganda disguised as formal education. I'd been socially brainwashed to believe in the reality of television; to think it was acceptable to sacrifice my health, my sanity, and my soul in search of money, adoration, and really, really shiny things.

Turns out all I had to do was kill somebody.
I was such an idiot some times.

The End

THE GREAT LIMBIC WALTZ

One

He smashes a hard fist against the alarm clock. "Shut up!" he croaks, and the thing dies when it hits the wall across the room. He throws back the covers and sits on the edge of the bed, wincing from the pain in his head. He's once again had too much to drink, and it's only Tuesday morning. A long week ahead, no doubt. He rubs the fatigue out of his eyes with sweaty palms and cranes his neck to look at the other side of the bed. Nicole, a woman he'd picked up from the bar a few days ago, is lying there silent and unmoving. A second later, a pungent funk fills his nasal cavity.

"Woo wee, darling. You need a bath," he says, but receives no response from the girl. Shrugging his shoulders, he is sharply reminded of the electric pain zapping through his skull. With a deep breath, he lets his feet hit the floor and heads for the washroom. He spits a thick gob of phlegm into the toilet and dances out an eager stream with a soul soothing shiver. He checks his face in the mirror and notices the graying hair, the deepening wrinkles, the drooping, darkened flesh under his eyes. He fetches a bottle of pain killers from the shelf behind the mirror and pops a handful, drinking from the faucet.

Coughing up another phlegm rocket, he spits it into the sink and turns his head toward the half opened door.

"I think your stay here is about done," he says, and splashes a cool wave of water onto his face. "I'll drive you somewhere when I get home. It's been fun and all, but it's time, I think." His face dripping, he hears nothing coming from the bedroom. He dries his face and mumbles to himself.

"Typical woman; she just wants to sleep all day."
No longer paying her particular attention, he steps into the shower and fights against the alcoholic fog weighing him down. The water works wonders for his hangover, though he's far from cured by the time he shuts off the water and dries himself. Again he exam-

ines his face in the mirror; alcohol abuse is difficult to hide. He stretches out the long wrinkles running away from his eyes with his fingers, and then touches his red nose and his drawn cheeks.

"I'm getting old," he mumbles. "I have to quit drinking so much."

Then, with the catharsis disappearing as quickly as the insight appeared, he dresses and heads downstairs for breakfast. Turning on the news, he makes coffee and busies himself cooking eggs. With the food ready, he sits at the dining table and devours the meal like a starving dog, practically inhaling it. It soothes him beyond expectation. Feeling better, the painkillers kicking in, the coffee taking effect, he yawns and stretches his body, then heads back upstairs.

The girl is still in bed, unbothered by his morning preparations.

No matter, he has to get going.

He steps outside with the kicking pain in his head nearly abated, and breathes in a cool breath of fresh air. The sun is shining, the birds are chirping, and the sky is as clear as an upended ocean.

"Going to be a good day," he says, and walks briskly to his car.

On the windshield, tucked in behind the wiper, someone's left him another flyer. Left him one, as well as his neighbor, and his neighbor's neighbor, and so on all the way down the long street. At least twice a week this sort of thing seems to happen in the middle of the night. He pulls it out and stares at it with mild interest.

Reward: $20,000
Have you seen Monica Holden?
If you have, please call 800-555-5476

He shrugs and crumples the thing in his palm, enters his car, wakes the engine, and pulls out onto the street. His commute is bathed in brilliant sunlight, and the traffic seems unusually light for the morning rush hour. He whistles along to a song on the radio and taps his fingers on the steering wheel. He's in a good mood, glad to go to work, happy with his life on a general level. By the time he pulls into the parking lot, he's smiling as if he's trapped in a bubble, immune from the world around him, ignorant of the scowling faces of the morning rush hour madness.

He walks across campus, scampering around late students with his perpetual smile, and makes his way to his classroom.

Flopping into his great leather chair, the first thing he does is check an ear to the hallway for any incoming intruders–and then sneaks a three ounce gulp of vodka. He's never been much of a vodka man, but it's the only thing that won't betray his breath at work. Returning the bottle to the bottom drawer, he arranges his papers and goes over the sheets he would like to cover in today's class, but before the alcohol can numb his brain enough to allow concentration, students start pouring in.

First in is Julie with her viola; then Andrew with a French horn huddled under his arm. Then comes Ally with a violin, Jessie with a cello, and Roger with a clarinet; before he knows it, the whole orchestra has greeted him and taken their seats, relaxed and ready to practice.

"Good morning, everyone," he says and stands to greet the class. His head swoons lightly when he settles in front of his desk but it's of no of concern–he is ready to teach. "How is everyone on this fantastic summer morning?"

"Good," they say, and smile. The professor's bravado is nothing new to the students; in fact, he's known for it.

"Good stuff," he says, and clasps his hands in front of him, holding a wide smile on his face. "Let's do it."

Thirty two students take their places and stare back at the professor standing before them, baton in hand. After an extended pause, he raises his hands and moves them passionately through the air. A half second later, the music begins.

Waves of harmonies stacked on top of one another flow through the room, and in no time at all, the group is lost as one in a musical orgy. Their bodies sway in sync, their intensity building, and the resulting vibrations are a thing of purity and perfection.

"Yes. Yes. Excellent. Come on, give me some more," the professor encourages, calling them on with his free hand as if in a fight.

Tchaikovsky's Sixth rattles against the walls like an explosion. It climaxes and pours into the halls beyond the theater, and the professor feels something orgasmic render him numb with awe. It is so beautiful.

He's satisfied in knowing that he's the one who has brought these young people to the point of capturing the emotion, the raw power of the music, and executing the piece with perfect inflections and masterful dynamics. In the coming weeks they would move on to Brahms, Mozart, and Beethoven, pushing the limits of genius beyond anyone's true understanding. He can hardly wait.

When it ends, everyone is exhausted. It was a worthy attempt at living up to the composer's expectations.

"Bravo!" the professor cries and claps his hands. "Very, very nice." The room fills with warm smiles and satisfied eyes stare at each other. "Are we ready to continue? One more Tchaikovsky excerpt from his fourth, and then we'll attempt Rimsky-Korsakov's Scheherazade, and that will complete our study of Russian Composers. In the coming weeks, we'll move on and do our best to take on the giants. Sound reasonable?"

The students nod excitedly, eager to expand their understanding of the mysterious and undefinable beauty that music evokes in the human soul.

"Very well," the professor says. "Here we are."
He lifts his hands again, baton ready, and begins moving. Half a second later, the music once again begins. It's tremendously beautiful. He thinks he is truly shaping this younger generation into first class musicians and critics; probably far better than he'd ever done before.

Tchaikovsky's Fourth rattles the room for a solid twenty minutes, and when the session ends, it's time for a break.

"Take fifteen minutes, everyone. Relax, have something to eat, and when we return we will explore the very distinct world of Rimsky-Korsakov."

With that, the students scurry out of the room as a chattering mass, and the professor is quick to gulp another six ounces. Satisfied with the drink, it's time for a cigarette. He scurries through the halls, smiling at everyone who crosses his path, and steps outside into the brilliant sun. Already standing in the smoking section is Bill Warner, a fellow teacher of philosophy, and his occasional smoking partner.

"Good day, Bill," he says, and lights a cigarette in a cupped hand. "How are things?"

"Oh, you know," Bill says. "Same old, same old. It really is a nice day, though. What's new with you?"

"Not much, just wrapping up Russian orchestration this week. What are you teaching your hungry minds?"

"Nietzsche," Bill says. "I wish I could teach it exclusively. The man was brilliant beyond understanding. The Beethoven of modern philosophy, if you will."

The professor chuckles and has a drag of his cigarette.
"Hey," Bill says, changing the subject. "Did you watch the news

this morning?"

"Only passively," the professor says. "Why, what's going on?"

"Seems they've found another woman's body down in the river. They said she's been dead a while, raped. They think the same person dumped four others in there in the last three months. Hope they catch him soon."

Bill wipes his forehead with his sleeve then takes in a drag and squints his eyes in defense of the sun.

"Huh," the professor says. "I haven't heard anything about it. I've been pretty busy lately. Music–I just can't seem to get enough of it out of me. The impulse is there to stay forever."

"Well, at least you're talented," Bill says and slaps the professor on the shoulder. "Otherwise, you'd be teaching philosophy or something like some talentless hack, ha, ha."

They share a laugh and the professor checks his watch. There's only five minutes left of the break. If he hurries back, he's quite confident he can down another three ounces before taking on more Russian brilliance.

"Well, Bill," the professor says. "Nice speaking with you, as always. I'll see you later."

"You take care," Bill says, and waves him off, desperately sucking a final drag from the butt between his fingers.

The professor walks hurriedly down the hall and glances at his watch again. Four minutes left. He reaches the theater and pokes his head in. Fantastic luck! Not a student in sight. Eagerly, he races to his desk, opens the drawer, uncaps the bottle, fills the shooter glass, and gulps the liquid in a fraction of a second.

Safe and sound.

These additional ounces mixing in with the previous six are taking their toll. The professor smiles and lets himself flop down into his great leather chair, relaxed beyond belief. He closes his eyes and smiles, he can hear nothing but music flowing through his mind, but the grandiose melodies are quickly interrupted by the arrival of his pupils.

One by one, they file back to their places, ready to continue with the professor's instruction. Dizzily, he stands before them, his legs numb and pliable, and begins giving background information on Rimsky-Korsakov; he gets no further than the details of the composer's birth, however, before he is interrupted by Dean Miller at the door.

"Excuse me, professor. Could I speak with you for a moment?" she asks in a whisper, visibly regretting the interruption.

"Certainly," the professor says, and suddenly feels nervous. The alcohol is fresh in his veins, and never before had she unexpectedly interrupted his class. "Class, please begin studying the sheet music. I will return shortly. Thank you."

He turns away from the students and calculates his steps carefully until he reaches the door and puts on a pleasant smile. The Dean smiles back and invites him out into the hall.

"What can I do for you, Dean Miller?"
"I'm terribly sorry for the interruption, professor, but I have some rather exciting news for you, and I didn't think it could wait. At least, for you, I didn't think it could wait."

The professor frowns and tries his best to avoid breathing directly in the Dean's direction.

"Well," he says. "What in the world could it be?"
She smiles big and clasps her hands together.

"Professor, you've been invited to conduct your orchestra at Carnegie Hall as part of a showcase to celebrate great professors teaching younger generations the importance of music. But you are not only the guest of honor, they are asking you to headline the event."

Shocked, he stands with his mouth gaped open, searching the Dean's excited eyes for confirmation of what his brain is trying register.

"My goodness," he says. "Is it true?"
"Yes, of course."

"I... I'm not sure what to say. When's the event?"
"In a month's time. Is that sufficient notice?"

"Yes, yes, of course," he says. "I just can't believe it."
"Well, I can," she says, and gently places her hand on his arm. "You are a talented composer and an invaluable instructor. You deserve this, professor, and I am so excited for you."

He smiles and his eyes dart around aimlessly. An event at Carnegie Hall in his honor. It's fantastic! It's–it's a dream come true.

"Th... Thank you, Susan," he stammers. "I'm stunned."
"You completely deserve it," she reiterates. "And, if you need any time off, just let me know, it's no problem at all."

"Yes, thank you. I suppose I could use a few days to get my head wrapped around the idea and get organized."

"Take the rest of the week," she says. "I'll make arrangements for Mr. Duper to supervise your class while you're away."

"I can't thank you enough," he says.

"Please," she says. "This is a great honor for yourself and for the school. If you need anything at all, don't hesitate to ask."

"Yes, of course. Thank you again."

She nods and smiles encouragingly before turning away from him. He stands and watches her go; his mind races with fleeting thoughts, and his chest swells with conflicted emotions. He chuckles and shakes his head, and then returns to his students. They watch him come in, curious about the interruption, but unwilling to ask him about it. He resumes his position before them, clasps his hands together, and smiles.

"Class, I've just been given the most astonishing piece of news." Their heads pop up like curious meerkats. "I–we–have been invited to play Carnegie Hall!"

The room is absolutely silent. Stunned. Carnegie Hall? Really?

"Are you serious?" a young violinist asks.

"To headline!" he says. "And I am just as stunned as you are." He looks about them excitedly, his eyes wide and bright despite the alcohol. "So, in celebration, you all get the rest of the day off! Ha! Ha! I will be away for the remainder of the week getting things in order for this unprecedented event. In the meantime, I ask you all to practice your instruments the best of your abilities. On Monday I will have everything prepared and we can begin practicing a new symphony. I am so excited! Thank you all for your hard work and dedication. I truly look forward to sharing the stage with each and every one of you. Thank you, and I will see you on Monday."

The students are on their feet, chattering among themselves, and congratulating the professor on their way out. In minutes, the room is empty, and the professor slams back another six ounces. He stares at the stage from his chair, stupefied. Drunk.

"Carnegie Hall," he says. "I can't believe it! This is beyond my wildest dreams."

Two

He gulps down the last of his drink and his eyes cross, his body becomes weightless. In addition to the numerous shots at school, he figures he's downed between thirty and forty ounces over the course of the day; consequently, he's about as drunk as a sixteen year old girl at her first drinking party. It's a special day, after all. He's about to present an international audience with the fruits of decades' worth of dedication. He's fifty-two years old, and for the last thirty of those years he's aspired to master the bombastic world of music and make a name for himself. During his first piano lesson at twelve years old, something unexplainable had stirred inside of him, something undefinable, and incredibly powerful. It drove him to practice and to learn the discipline, and by the time he graduated high-school, he was already making waves in the classical community as a talented virtuoso. For a long time it seemed like the whole world lay before him, every dream fulfilled, but in the end the prolonged effort had left him sorely confused and emotionally bankrupt. It was a cruel joke. The universe had allowed him a taste of success, a grueling feeling of being so close to it, so certain of it, and then placed it just out of range to mock him forever.

In truth, he's not okay with the fact that his name will not be remembered after his death, nor with the fact that he's given all of himself to a futile cause, a phantom dream—but that's not to say it's been all bad. Early on, he came to face the harsh reality of all art forms in the modern world; without a solid business sense, talent is utterly meaningless. The masses no longer respect art or skill or originality, for the crafts have been diluted, raped, and rendered mediocre by greedy corporations shoving talentless products down people's throats. He was out of luck on that count; not a business bone resided in his body. But after years of toiling and being forced to stow his burning ambition in the quiet shadows of his mind, an unexpected opportunity did arise... A chance to teach young minds the essence of his passion.

In the heat of a crushing despair, he was offered the opportunity to teach a university's orchestral program, and he couldn't resist. It was that or a regular job, a thought that left a terrible taste in his mouth. He remembers laughing when he accepted the position. Those who can't do, teach, is the old adage; he was grudgingly aware of his nailing the stereotype.

As a result, he swallowed his pride and spent the last

seventeen years teaching young minds the intricacies of music, molding them into professional musicians, guiding them to the zenith of their talents; and what's most important, he thinks, is that he's rather enjoyed the gig. He really does care about his students, and he cares about teaching them properly; but now that the opportunity has come to bring those budding talents to a famous stage to dazzle the minds of an international audience, he's feeling rather anxious about the whole thing. He feels like maybe it's too late. He will be mocked by other, more successful composers. He will fail, he thinks. Somehow, he'll find a way to fail. He's wanted this opportunity for over thirty years, and in all that time it's seemed like nothing more than a distant phantasm, a transparent, formless dream. Nevertheless, there it is, waiting for him, taunting him, making him doubt himself. Professionally, he knows he can do it, despite not having concentrated on something this serious in a very long time. But that's not the issue gnawing at him most. The problem is that he isn't sure if he can trust himself. He's proud of the invitation, but as he looks around now, after forty plus ounces of alcohol poured into his system, he's suddenly aware of how much he's let himself go. Thirty years ago he was a straight laced, concentrated force, dedicated to his dream; thirty years later, like an eroding rock at the foot of a waterfall, that passionate fire has long ago been tamed by addiction.

How much can he trust himself, he wonders. How long can he carry the excitement, the doubt, the stress, the anger, and the tireless hours necessary to pull off such a grandiose event before he's broken by his own weathered mind? In his heightening age, he's picked up many bad habits, some of which he will most likely die with, or from. He's an alcoholic, he knows that, and as much as he's sometimes tempted to pull on his boots and quit, he's rather comfortable with his life too. He functions as an alcoholic, and rarely misses work, but he's now facing a test of will, and he isn't sure he can take it head on. It will take a strong effort to accomplish. Discipline. And with the staggering amount of alcohol in his blood, he decides that he can do it after all, and then laughs.

He puts the empty glass on the bar and glances at his watch. It's 10:50 p.m. He slowly scans the room. It's a quaint sort of bar, but he thinks he might still be able to find himself a companion for the evening. From behind drunken eyelids, he eyes a blonde across the bar, and then catches sight of a brunette walking behind her. He follows her with his gaze as she heads for the washroom, and there, he sees the redhead. He's convinced that it's the greatest day of his life.

He smiles and drools a little on himself. He then cracks his neck, and tries to get his bearings straight. He's not sure he can even speak properly, or intelligibly, but he stands from his stool anyway, determined to make an approach. When his legs hit the ground, it feels like the floor is smacking him in the face, and he realizes just how drunk he really is. He's blasted, and when he takes another step, the room swells and his knees give out. He pukes on the floor and lies face first in the puddle.

***

He wakes up in bed, oblivious of the events beforehand. He can remember flashes, emotions, nothing certain. His head feels like it's been smashed open, and when he tries to move, electric pain flashes through him and he pukes.

"Shit!" he snaps, enraged and disgusted. He jumps out of bed, dizzy and nauseated, and stands with his shoulders to the wall for balance. The woman, Nicole, is gone from his bed. He's not entirely sure, but he vaguely remembers her there when he arrived last night. Maybe not. He doesn't even remember how he got home. But, yes, he does remember a little; she was home, and he had taken her by the arm, and taken her by the leg, and made her leave out the window–but he can't remember why. No linear memories beyond that.

"Whatever," he mumbles, no longer wanting to think about the ungrateful freeloader. At least, that's how he was beginning to feel. He's a solitary sort of man, and he wants to remain that way.

Again he feels his stomach twist and he runs to the washroom with both hands over his mouth as he dives for the porcelain bowl. A terrible upheaval ensues, and when he's done, he drops to his back and stares at the ceiling, holding his furious guts with trembling hands.

What a night. What happened? How had he gotten home? When he can, he'll have to check if his car is in the driveway. He hopes he wasn't stupid enough to drive home; but then, he also hopes he doesn't have to go anywhere to reclaim it. He feels half-rotten on the inside.

Painfully, he crawls over the edge of the bathtub, drops inside, turns on the water, and lies back, completely exhausted. Too much drinking. Too much aging. Yesterday feels like a distant, unimportant piece of the past. Carnegie Hall? That was real, wasn't it? He sorts through his vague memories of the day before; Tchaikovsky, Rimsky-Korsakov, the Dean, the good news, the drinks. He pukes once more.

He spends an hour in the tub before turning off the water and crawling out, desperate for painkillers. He swallows a handful, drinks from the faucet, and then stares at his reflection in the mirror. He looks beyond terrible. His eyes are puffy and red, his face is drawn, and his skin is pale and grayish. His complexion is so bad, in fact, that he feels the need to mumble to himself, "This is what good news looks like to an alcoholic. Idiot."

He rubs his eyes vigorously with the knuckles of his index fingers, throws on his robe, and heads downstairs to make coffee. On the main floor, the warm sunlight streaming through the windows feels like hot needles in his eyes. He squints and tries to adjust to the pain, but it resists being tamed for a while.

He starts the coffee and turns on the television to the news.

"...Police say the bodies were violated for days before being dumped into the river. A manhunt is currently being organized to track down and appre–"

He yawns and quickly stares out the window at his car sitting idly in the drive.

"What the hell?" he says. He can't remember a thing. He can't–wait–the redhead. Yes, he remembers her, but he doesn't remember ever speaking to her. He shakes his head, confused, but the action reminds him of his over-indulgent stupidity and he has to press his palms against his temples to take the pain.

The more he tries to think of last night, the more humiliated he feels. He's a decent drunk by reputation. A man capable of handling his poisons without losing himself in emotionally fueled madness and misunderstood situations. No. He's a quiet drunk, a fun drunk, one with whom another, male or female, comes away thinking their interaction was splendid, and good-natured, and worthy of their time. That was the kind of drunk he was; so what the hell had happened last night? He had puked in a bar; he's sure of it. He'd lost consciousness; he's sure of that too. And as the vague memories begin taking concrete form, he feels humble to the point of losing all self-confidence. He's invited to play Carnegie Hall in a month's time, what the hell was he thinking, getting sloshed beyond reason in a public place and puking himself face first on the filthy floor? It was inexcusable behavior, and if anyone of valor had seen him do it, his big dream would quickly vanish.

On the far wall of the kitchen hangs a mirror, and without putting much thought into it, he walks toward it and frowns at his horrible reflection.

"You're going to screw everything up, you idiot!" he scolds himself. "You need to get your shit together! All your life, everything you've ever tried for, is now in the palm of your hand, and you're going to throw it all away for a good night and a shitty morning? I don't think so! Get your head together! Get organized! There are bigger things in life than your stupid alcohol! You have people to teach, a life to live, a performance to perform. You need to be careful! You can't act like that in public!" He holds his own gaze for a long moment, and then leers coyly. "So I guess you're drinking at home from now on."

Who is he kidding? Drinking has been constant in his life for decades. Carnegie Hall is exciting, promising, but is it enough to quench the mighty beast raging inside of him? Only time will tell, but his confidence in the matter is weak.

He takes a deep breath, closes his eyes, and attempts to center himself.

"It's time to get to work," he says, and pours himself a cup of coffee from the decanter before walking from the kitchen, through the living room, and into his studio.

For the next four hours he sorts through his notes, his sheet music, his recordings, and tries to form an idea of what he wants to do for the show. He knows he wants to do something different, something unique and noteworthy, but he's eventually interrupted by the mean urge for decadence coming back to haunt him. He can't concentrate on anything else; his mouth waters at the thought of alcohol. He's losing his grip already.

He sits in his chair and cracks his knuckles, trying to re-tain his composure, but the compulsion proves too strong, too raw. Standing from his chair, he races upstairs and changes clothes, and before he knows it, he's pulling his car onto to the street.

When he parks in front of the building, his hands are shaking terribly, and his back is slick with sweat. He leaves his car, walks into the store, and buys a bottle of whisky. On the way back to his car for a desperate gulp, he's stopped by a young girl with an armful of flyers.

"Excuse me, sir?" she calls.

"Yes?" he says. "What is it? What do you want?"

"I just want to know if maybe you could help," she says,

and hands him a flyer. "It's my sister, Josie, she disappeared last week. I'm really worried about her."

He stares at the poster, but his vision is so distorted with the promise of alcohol that he wouldn't recognize the girl if she was his own sister.

"I'm sorry," he says. "I haven't seen her."

"Well," she says with a touch of sadness in her eyes. "Can you keep the flyer, just in case?"

"Yeah, sure," he says, and before he can say anything more, he notices something across the parking lot. There's a bar in the far corner of the strip mall, and just outside of it, a pretty redhead is smoking a cigarette and staring off in another direction.

He looks back at the girl with the flyers.

"I'll keep it," he says. "Thank you."

He leaves her and drives his car over to the bar just as the redhead finishes her cigarette and enters the establishment. He follows behind her, and soon finds himself in a crowded room filled with young bodies, drunken leers, and hard dancing. He smiles and approaches the bar. The redhead sits a few seats down from where he is. He orders a whisky and takes possession of a stool, glances over at the girl, and she meets his eyes almost immediately.

"Hi," he says.

She smiles and averts her eyes for a moment before returning the stare.

"Hello," she says.

He shifts over a seat toward her.

"Can I buy you drink?"

"Ah... Sure, why not?" she says. "I'll have a screwdriver."

He nods and orders the drink, and minutes later, they are deep in conversation.

"So, what do you do?" she asks.

"I'm a music teacher and composer," he says. "I conduct orchestras."

"No you don't," she smiles.

"Yes, I do," he winks. "You don't believe me? What do you do?"

"I'm an assistant veterinarian," she says. "It's been a long day. Lost a dog today after he was hit by a car. That always sucks."

"Yeah," he nods. "Animals are precious. It's always terrible to lose one, whatever the circumstances. Do you have any pets?"

"A cat," she says, and smiles awkwardly. "Typical, huh?"

"Nah, I like cats. In fact, I think I prefer cats. I like an animal with

attitude and grace. Cats will stand people, but they won't necessarily love them. In fact, if you stop feeding one, it'll simply stop
caring about you altogether. Ha! Ha! Dogs are needy, emotionally
dependent creatures. They are extremely loyal, but there is something pathetic about it. I'm not sure I'm comfortable with that."

"I agree," she says. "I love my cat. And you're right, she
loves me as long as I feed her, don't stay up too late, don't vacuum,
don't hug her, and pay attention to her only on her terms."

They chuckle, and she gulps down the last of her drink.
"Would you like another?" he asks.

"Sure," she says, and gently rubs his forearm with her
hand. "Thank you."

"No problem," he says, and smiles. "You know, I have a
confession to make."

"Yeah? What is it?"

"Well, I wasn't planning on coming here tonight. In fact, I was
across the lot at the liquor store just about to go home, and then I
saw you smoking and I felt a strong need to talk to you."

"You did?" she asks. "Why?"

"I don't know," he replies. "I suppose I sensed a connection, something cosmic. What do you think about that?"

The bartender stands in wait of their order, but now they
are locked in each other's gazes, ignoring the man behind the bar.

"I think that maybe I should ask if you have any alcohol
at home."

"I most certainly do," he says. "And I could definitely use
some help getting rid of it."

With bright eyes, she thanks the bartender but declines to
order, and then stands from her stool.

"All right," she says. "I don't usually do this sort of thing,
but there's something about you."

He smiles seductively and his heart picks up its pace.
Without breaking eye contact with her, he pays the tab and says,
"Let's go."

Funny, he thinks as he climbs into the driver's seat; he's
just lost all of his discipline in favor of all of his desires. Life is a
cruel thing.

***

He rolls off of her drenched with sweat, out of breath, and
numbed with ecstasy. He lies on his back with his heart pounding

and his limbs feeling nimble and elastic. He smiles in the darkness, panting. When his breath eventually returns, he says, "My
God. That was amazing, darling. You're definitely the last thing I
expected when I woke up this morning."

Next to him, all is quiet. She lies there motionless, inanimate. He shrugs. They had totaled a bottle of whisky, after all, but
he's still feeling rather thirsty. He remembers that the cupboard
above the refrigerator holds half a bottle of vodka, and without a
moment's hesitation, he leaves the bedroom and scuttles down the
stairwell stark naked. Seconds later, he's stretching for the bottle,
his hands trembling uncontrollably.

With the first frantic gulp of the poison, his eyes water,
and the trembling instantly ceases.

"Ahhhh," he says, satisfied enough to die. A solid woman,
a good night of drinking, and Carnegie Hall to come; life was
finally being kind.

He moves from the kitchen to the living room with the
bottle in hand and sits on the sofa. He turns on the television and
stares absently at the screen, allowing his mind to relax, his body
to calm. He thinks he's not doing too badly in his older age. The
woman upstairs is of a type he would only have dreamed of once
upon a time, like Carnegie Hall, but with age and experience under
his belt, it seems he's causing the previously impossible to happen.

He has another healthy gulp of poison and lays his head
against the back of the sofa. He's proud of his recent conquest,
but he still feels threatened by himself. Despite having broken
his oath to get himself in order merely hours after he'd declared
it, he still believes it in substance. If he doesn't begin to mind
his actions, things will quickly fall apart. Addiction pits a man
against the world–against himself. He's well aware of that, but can
he help it? He's not so sure. From experience, he fears the dual
nature of the human animal. Its mind is easily thrown into disar-
ray by compulsions. Discipline is fleeting. And in the grips of a
psychological panic, the body separates from the mind, and each
competes for the satisfaction of its own desires until the only way
to restore harmony is through artificial means–with a drink, with a
hump, with a cigarette, with a tv show; the distractions are endless.
Most people deal with stress in acceptable ways. They socialize,
they watch a movie, they masturbate. He's either immune or he's
a mutant, he thinks, because the ways he deals with the stressors
of life don't seem as innocent as others'; his distractions start off
harmlessly, but they always end by crushing him in their palms.

He's never free, never quite right. Yes, he will have to be very careful, he thinks. This ongoing struggle has never subsided. The beast has never been tamed; why should he expect it now? Many times he's found himself with his face buried in his hands, sobbing convulsively over things he's lost–friends, family, jobs. In such dark moments of emotional madness, he curses himself, condemns his actions, swears to God, to angels, to the very walls that he will change; he will make an effort; he will rise above himself and conquer the evil monsters lurking in the depths of his soul; and then he does, for a while, and then he doesn't, for a much longer while. Even when things are great, he feels temptations sitting on the fringes of his thoughts like staring gargoyles calling his name. Deep down, despite all the years of experience, he's utterly convinced that he's preprogrammed to sabotage his own life. The moment things look up, the old juices start flowing, looking for sabotage. Change was a fantasy meant to remain an unattainable wish. There was no fundamental change possible; there was only the back and forth of ambition and depression, of hope and disappointment. Such was the story of his life. Pleasure to pain, pain to pleasure, then back again with no one else to blame but himself. It was tough to take, but indulgence was not the cause of that war, it was the symptom. It was the soothing, easy bandage for the ugly wounds he didn't want to look at. He's had enough years of morbid introspection to know all of this. He knows better, but even as he thinks it over, it all goes down better with a drink.

He finishes the bottle and wipes his mouth with the back of his forearm. Yes, he decides. He will have to be very careful indeed, especially with the women. Women are a thing of true power and seduction. It's too easy to get sucked in by the insatiable compulsions they cause in him, and then what happens? Anything is possible, but generally, the end game often resembles an airplane meeting a mountain side.

He rubs his eyes vigorously and yawns. Tomorrow, he decides, he will have to get things straight. Get rid of the girl, delay the inevitable drink, and get his music organized for the great Carnegie stage. Yes–tomorrow. Tomorrow is another day. Tomorrow... is the time... to... start.,.

He snores.

Three

With the sun nearing its zenith, he sits on top of a picnic table with his feet resting on the long seat and stares out across the park. This is where he usually comes to get his head straight. It's a city owned park lining the river valley that cuts straight through the middle of the city. The park itself is host to a soccer field, a huge kid's playground, and tucked away picnic areas where one is free make a fire and cook some food. The place is mostly empty now aside from a few pedestrians following the paved path running the length of the river.

Only a few hours ago he awoke on his couch, confused, and in desperate pain. In all honesty, he was angry with himself. The very day he'd told himself, promised himself, that he would relax and stay out of trouble, he ends up at the bar with a strange woman, rivaling the unreasonable drunk he'd had the night before. He was impossible. How was he to gain an upper hand on his emotions, on his thoughts, and on his burning desires to foul himself beyond reason or safety? How was he going to pull it all off? Music was his one saving grace in life, the one constant passion that kept him from all out suicide, but he feels like he's losing his grip on that too. Like everything else, it all seems too distant, too difficult to bother with. He wants to quit drinking, but will he? He knows the attempt certainly won't come today, and maybe not tomorrow, and maybe not ever. He thinks that maybe the desire to quit is nothing more a than false belief in the strength of his will. A false hope. A thing better left until tomorrow, and then the next day, and so on until his insides are pickled, rotten, and irreparably damaged. Maybe he is committing suicide after all; he just didn't realize it.

He sighs, frustrated with his thoughts and emotions. The greatest opportunity of his life has thrown his entire existence into a maelstrom of doubt, uncertainty, and self-loathing. Who is he kidding, he thinks. He isn't meant to play Carnegie Hall before an international audience; otherwise he would have done so years ago, long before he accepted his teaching post.

But he reminds himself that the performance is not only his, it's also his students', and that thought alone will have to remain his last resort. When his own baggage becomes too heavy to lift by himself, he will have to remember that he is not alone in all of this. He has students, eager young minds, looking forward to their futures, to the performance, to prove themselves as worthy musicians. He can't let them down. Too many times they have been his saving grace in life; he has no right to rob them of their dreams in order to hide from his.

He stares off in the distance. He'd had plenty of fun last night, sure, but today he must concentrate. He no longer has a choice; things need to get done. He enjoyed the woman, and even brought her to the park with him, but she's near the path by the river now, and he isn't planning on leaving with her.

Filled with a newly energized dedication to his goals, he glances one last time to where the woman is and then leaves the picnic table. Ambling slowly with his hands in his pockets, he listens to the chirping birds, the buzzing flies, and takes in the fresh air as if he'd just emerged from a sombre cave. Things can look up from here, he decides. All he has to do is put in the effort. Nothing comes out of nothing.

He's whistling when he gets to his car, feeling as straight as an arrow, excited to get to work on his music. He drives home relaxed and enjoying the way the car handles around hard corners. When he pulls into the driveway, his neighbor is outside weeding the flowerbed, and he greets him with a wide smile and a friendly wave. The neighbor makes small talk, mostly about the weather, and he's happy to oblige for a short time before politely breaking off the conversation and entering his house.

Inside, he immediately heads for the studio with an urgent compulsion to get his ideas in order. He sits at his desk and sorts through his sheet music. He'd like to begin the show with a bang, he thinks. Something monstrous in beauty and stature to take everyone aback right from the get go, and then slow it down a little into a soft and delicate movement which carefully mounts back into enormous notes, and finishes again with a bang. Surely he'd written something like that over the years. That piece could then be followed by a Tchaikovsky, and with any luck, perhaps follow that up with a Beethoven, or Mozart piece? It will depend on how prepared his students are.

He sifts through waltzes, dances, concertos, sonatas, and half-finished symphonies of original composition. He gets a few good ideas to sow together, but before he can go any further, his limbs begin trembling again, his mouth gets dry, sweat beads on his back and forehead.

"No," he says to himself. "That's enough drinking. This needs to get done!"

Ignoring the physical onslaught of self-imposed debilitations, he continues to set ideas aside, and eventually moves over to his piano to try a few of them. He forces his mind to concentrate, but it doesn't take long before his old musical salvation kicks in and he's completely lost in the mysteries of music. His limbs no longer tremble, his mind calms, and all he can feel is the music. It's the most wonderful sensation in the world. He plays and plays, stringing one fragment to another, and the next thing he knows, five hours have passed, and he's mostly decided on where and how to take the overall piece to memorable heights.

Soothed, he decides on a break, but he's afraid of stopping because the gnawing at the back of his mind hasn't gone away. The music was enough to abate it temporarily, but now that he's stopped playing, he's once again consumed with thoughts of strong drink.

He spends the next two hours pacing aimlessly, chewing gum, stomping on one foot with the heel of the other, anything to try and gain control over himself–but the beast inside is a formidable enemy. He has a shower, a meal, and another quick attempt at putting a symphony together, but it isn't long before he's clawing at the walls like a desperate dog. It's too big to defy; too strong to stand up to alone.

With the sun nearly set, he gets into his car and pulls onto the street. He decides to drive for as long as he can, trying to remain focussed on the road and distracted from everything else, but he knows that this is only a meaningless act of rebellion against the inevitable. Eventually, he'll be sucking back corrosive liquids from glass bottles, and the worst part is that he won't even feel bad about it then. He hates his addiction, but he's also scared of it. He fears the complete lack of control it brings over him, sinking him further into the pit of madness. He can't concentrate anymore, drunk or sober, and he's not sure what that means exactly, but he is aware of the terrible future it spells out for him. He feels like he's trying to hang on to the tail end of a tornado. It's hopeless and tortuous all at once. It's stunningly powerful.

On the stereo he listens to Beethoven's Ninth, his favorite piece of music, and keeps the speed of his car at a steady forty miles per hour. He claws the steering wheel with both hands, his knuckles white with tension, and refuses to give in to his urges just yet. He tries to control the racing thoughts in his mind, or at the very least diminish their intensity. He stares at buildings, noting new developments, and then waves his hand through the air as if conducting the ninth, but these are only cheap tricks. Feeble solutions to an ironclad problem.

Up ahead, he enters an intersection from the West and nearly gets t-boned by a rogue car blowing a red light. He slams on the brakes and steers defensively to bring the car to a sharp stop. He feels terribly ill. His blood pressure is through the roof, and his temper flares up like lightning in his spine.

He tries to curse, but his throat clamps up, and he's suddenly aware of the violent trembling his whole body is doing. He loses all control, and his mind is plunged into panic. He feels threatened, scared, and the only thing he can think of is pouring half a bottle of whiskey down his throat. He doesn't want to deal with anything else for the rest of the day, he just wants a drink. Now!

He glances around quickly, searching for a bar, but he's left sorely disappointed by the endless string of shops lining the street. Feeling like he's about to collapse, he drives out of the intersection and tries to regain his composure, but his stomach won't have any of it. It's tied in knots, twisting, turning, heaving, and before he can pull over he empties his stomach on the floor of the car.

"Shit," he says and glances around for a place to stop, but traffic is heavy on this street and he's in no condition for fancy maneuvers. Dejected, exhausted, desperate, he carries on like a festering, putrid sore on wheels. His eyes water continually, and his peripheral vision isn't the best, but he checks his speed at thirty miles per hour and champions his way to the liquor store in the foulest, most disgusting car he's ever had the pleasure of driving. He enters the store smelling like a sewer rat.

He grabs four forty-ounce bottles of whisky and places them on the checkout counter, avoiding eye contact with the clerk. He just wants to go home. With no other words spoken aside from the total owed, he pays the clerk, nods, and immediately disappears into the filthy safety of his vehicle. Fundamentally offended by the stench, he opens a bottle, tips the spout into his mouth, and pours free amounts of soul soothing nectar into his stomach. With a quarter of the bottle gone in one pull, the effect is nearly instant. He feels the sweet tingle of carnal satisfaction crawl down his limbs, his face and ears are suddenly warm, and he can finally breathe normally again. Finally–everything is going to be all right.

He starts the car and drives home relaxed and in control. His mouth waters with the after taste of the whiskey, and his stomach feels like it's settling down, ready and willing to take on copious amounts of poison.

No longer caring much about the state of the car, he leaves it in the driveway and dashes for the front door of his house. Fumbling with the bottles on his way in, he leaves three on the kitchen counter and takes one with him to the studio. He enters the room with the bottle raised to his lips and sits down at his desk. Swallowing pure heaven, he stares at the music sprawled before him, his mind strangely eager to organize some sort of tangible idea with it all. He shuffles through pages and tries to make sense of the pattern his mind is trying to make conscious.

"Yes," he suddenly exclaims, and his eyes grow wide. "I can put this one right after this, and all I need is a clever transition in D minor, then lead into the C. Excellent!"

He searches for more ideas, surveying the pages like an archeologist excavating an ancient site, and manages to connect two more incomplete melodies. He then finds an already written bar he can use as a transition. Suddenly quite satisfied with himself, he chuckles at the events of the day. He truly is crazy, and right now, drunk off his ass, he loves it.

He wheels his chair across the room and turns on the stereo. Brahms's third symphony comes pouring out of the speakers like the very example of mastering a man's craft. He sways his hands through the air with his eyes closed and his head follows the music as if he's being electrified by it. He begins sweating, and he smiles and screams, "Yes! Yes! Yes! Louder! Fantastic!"

He stands from the chair and spins around the room in pure glory, pure ecstasy. He downs another healthy measure from the bottle, and his soul suddenly feels like it's trapped in an orgasm. He's connected to the universe through its most perfect medium–music.

Dizzy and out of breath, he drops back down to his chair and smiles. He's so drunk, but so happy. The world is perfect. His life is fine. And very soon, he will accomplish one of his life long goals. Carnegie Hall.

The bottle drops from his hand and rolls up against his foot, spilling the last few ounces on the floor.

Four

When he opens his eyes, he can't move. More accurately, he won't move. The first thing he notices is that his face is plastered to the floor. He smells urine, vomit, sweat, and alcohol. His body vibrates numbly, disconnecting him from reality, or maybe it's the pain doing that. In his skull, nuclear explosions are going off, pulverizing his brain and melting away the back of his eyeballs. He tries to swallow, but his mouth is completely devoid of moisture. Life doesn't get any better than this, he thinks. Yahoo.

He moves his head, but the consequences are unforgiving, and he once again pukes up fermented alcohol. Disgusted, he rolls over to lie on his back and stare at the ceiling with dry eyes. He wishes he had a gun within reach. Suicide is a righteous cure for this kind of hangover, he thinks. This kind changes a man.

He doesn't know what time it is, but he doesn't really care either. He already knows that nothing will save him. He runs through the list in his head. Water will make him sick. So will food. Painkillers will be laughably ineffective. And a shower, well, he isn't in the mood for standing at all, and he certainly isn't about to scale the stairs to the washroom. There's only one other suitable solution aside from suicide; he needs more alcohol.

On the floor next to him lies the bottle from the night before. He claws at it, trying to get a grip, but he already knows it's empty and he sighs in frustration. As badly as the idea sucks, he's going to have to go all the way to the kitchen. Methodically, he manages to get to his hands and knees and crawl slowly across the room. His head feels like it's about to burst open and ooze porridge all over the floor. He continues on, trying to take the pain. It's the worst hangover he's ever had.

In the kitchen, he claws his way up to the counter top, gets a grip on a bottle, and lets himself fall to the tile floor with a thump. The pain doesn't matter anymore, not with the elixir in hand. He tears open the top of the bottle and pours a conservative measure into his mouth, testing the idea with his stomach before going all out. He swallows and the liquid burns his esophagus, but his guts seem to take it calmly. For the next two hours, he remains on the floor of the kitchen, sipping careful amounts of whiskey and letting his body catch up to his willingness to move.

Eventually, he's drunk enough to stand, and even attempt basic tasks. Sorely, tenderly, he walks out of the kitchen and begins climbing the stairs, one slow step at a time, until he reaches the top landing and has to lean against the wall for a moment to catch his breath, right his balance, and calm his guts all at once.

With the whisky bottle still clutched in his hand and his face and chest drenched with alcoholic sweat, he enters his bedroom, then the bathroom, and lays himself on the bottom of the tub. His head spins when he turns on the water, but the moisture is a welcome relief. He lies back with his head against the tub and closes his eyes, feeling every drop of water smack against his body. He's too tired to think, too sick to care, and too pickled to do anything beyond what he'd already accomplished. He coughs and pain electrifies his every cell. He hates himself. He has failed himself on all fronts. The instant the thought of rehabilitation had entered his mind, his addiction had been unleashed like a sleeping dragon desperate to avoid change.

Not even his ego can save him any more. It's a terrible reality, he decides. A joke.

He twitches and coughs under the water for half an hour before gathering enough strength to sit up and shut it off. Climbing out of the tub, he doesn't bother with drying and has another solid pull from the bottle. He crawls out of the bathroom on his hands and knees like a baby, scales the height of his mattress, and face plants the soft pillow.

***

Twenty hours of sleep and still this business with the hangover. He doesn't understand; he's never felt this way before. He certainly hadn't consumed record amounts of alcohol–at least he doesn't think so–and long hours of sleep usually cured his body's persistent punishments. He isn't sure what to think. Maybe he should see a doctor.

Or have another drink.

He swallows a handful of painkillers and washes them down with water from the faucet. He checks his face in the mirror and confirms that he looks exactly the way he feels; like a pissed on bag of shit being stomped on by phantom bullies. Everything hurts. He's tired, and grumpy, and irritated. Without thinking about it any further, he returns to his bed and crawls under the blankets.

"Screw it," he says, and closes his eyes.

***

He realizes that he only has half a day left before returning to work. Over all, despite his groggy mind, he's feeling better. He's slept more hours than he cares to admit, and he is now searching deep within himself for some sort of motivation to get organized.

He sits up and is instantly repulsed by the stench coming from under the sheets. His hair is matted with sweat and his chin's glazed with drool, but at least the gnashing pain of the hangover is mostly gone. He's in desperate need of a shower.

He waddles slowly to the washroom on weak legs and washes himself. Then wearing only a robe, he heads downstairs and drinks a pot of coffee and eats a plate of bacon and eggs. His body sucks up the nutrition, greasing his guts, and helps him wake up from his alcohol induced coma. The symptoms recede, and within an hour he's feeling better.

He dumps the dishes in the sink and heads to the studio, but the caustic stench permeating the room stops him dead in his tracks; before anything else, he needs to clean the floor of the dried vomit and urine.

With the smell of bleach now dominating the room, he sits in his chair and starts leafing through his music once again. He has two thirds of a symphony completed, but a few crucial movements are missing, and he would like to have most of it ready to present to his students in the morning.

Rolling his chair over to his keyboard with fresh sheets of paper in hand, he gets to work on writing a transition to connect two main musical ideas and further develop counterpoints and harmonies. He's feeling decent overall, but after slouching over the black and white keys of his keyboard for nearly two hours, he's suddenly distracted by a terrible itch on his inner thigh. He scratches and ignores the problem as best he can for a while, but it grows in intensity, and eventually forces him to stop working.

"What the hell is going on?" he says, and stands from his chair, scratching his thigh. He undoes the belt, the button, the fly, and pulls his pants down to his ankles. The skin on his thigh is red and irritated, angry looking. He scratches it directly but it only makes it feel more like a burn. He doesn't understand what happened, but he isn't overly worried about it. He soothes the skin with a gentle lotion and gets back to work.

"I have to finish this," he whispers to himself, linking one note to the next, building a self-sustaining structure with its own mood and personality. "I have to finish this."

Five

Animated students pour into the classroom and greet him with smiles and bright faces. He returns the friendly greetings and does his best to ignore his personal health concerns. The vodka is helping him tremendously with that. His thigh isn't any better; in fact, it's slightly worse than when he got out of bed this morning. He figures that all he can do is apply lotion to it; the rest is all waiting and seeing what comes of it.

With everyone settled in their seats, the professor clasps his hands and says, "Good morning, class. How is everybody?"

"Good."

"Very good, very good," he nods. "Well, I trust you've all been practicing in my absence, yes? Yes, good. I've been working hard on getting a new symphony together for the show, and so far it's been a humbling experience, to say the least. Let me tell you, before anyone can critique an artist of any kind, they must first prove that they too can produce a piece of equal or superior quality, otherwise it's a substanceless and pretentious opinion; therefore, I now realize that I am full of substanceless and pretentious opinions."

The pupils laughs along with their professor.

"All right," he continues. "That is not to say I'm giving up. I have the majority of my ideas organized and I was hoping to practice some of them today. Is every one okay with that?"

He receives an unanimous agreement.

"Very well, places, please."

He hands out copies of the sheet music to each musician and in minutes they're all settled and awaiting the professor's instructions.

"Now, as you can all see, we will be beginning the piece in D minor, and then we will go on from there to C major, then E minor. Also, as a side note, I invite you all to come up with suggestions as we go on. This opportunity is ours, not just mine, therefore I welcome any input you may have. Okay? Very well. Here we go."

The professor taps his baton, raises his hands, and begins moving them gracefully through the air. In seconds, he's lost in the melody and sways with the music.

"Very good," he encourages the class. "Keep it going... And here... Boom! Yes! Yes! Excellent, class, excellent."

He guides the orchestra through the complexities of the

piece, but just as they get through the first movement, he's brutally aware of the itch eating away at his thigh. He scratches at it quickly and fights to remain focussed on the music. Through the transition and into the next movement, the pain becomes unbearable, and when he hears the clarinets come in too late, he has no other option but to call for a break.

"Okay, very good," he stops them. "That was fantastic." He smiles big at them. "Let's have a break, shall we?"

The group gladly obliges and leaves their formation for a twenty minute break. The professor waits until the room is empty, downs a few ounces of vodka, and then rushes to the washroom with a bottle of lotion, desperate to get the itch to stop.

He crashes into a stall and drops his pants. The rash doesn't look any worse, but it does nothing to quench his concerns, for a similar thing is starting to spread on his other leg just above the knee.

"What the hell is this?" he whispers to himself. Numb and worried, he applies a generous layer of lotion to both affected areas. When he's done, he's suddenly nauseated, and the intensity of the itch hasn't diminished at all. He takes a deep breath, closes his eyes, and tries to stave off the pain and calm his stomach. With limited success, he pulls his pants up, washes his hands, and returns to the classroom.

Class resumes a few minutes later, but the professor remains seated in his chair, sweating profusely and trying to steady his breath.

"Ah," he says and stands from his seat. His legs are numb and weak. "I'm sorry, class, I, ah, I seem to not be feeling very well today. Uh..." He wipes the sweat from his forehead with his sleeve.

"You're looking a little pale," a young violinist says. "We can practice if you need to go home, professor."

He bites his bottom lip, considers it, but all he can really think about is the pain of the rash; that, and perhaps a good drunk in search of relief. Foul, intrusive thoughts he tries to ignore.

"Yes, I suppose you could," he says and sighs. "I'm really sorry, you guys. I was hoping to get things started well and proper today, but I guess my body has other plans. I feel quite badly about it. I'm very lucky to have such talented and respectable students. I thank you all very much for your understanding."

With that, he shows the class which sections he wants them to practice in his absence, and then leaves knowing that he has nothing to worry about. Tomorrow he will be back and they will learn the rest of the piece. Until then, he will just have to find a way to deal with his physical troubles.

He's feeling tired when he gets to his car, weak, but he remembers that he needs to pick up a new can of coffee, a carton of eggs, and a loaf of bread. Traffic is light and he spends the majority of his time glancing at his leg and scratching intensely. In time, he makes it to the super market and gets the required items without hassle, but before he can get back into his vehicle and drive home, he's interrupted by a woman's voice.

"You got a buck?" she asks, and he stops and turns to face her. She's fairly young, blonde, and slim. Her eyes and cheeks are sunken, but her smile is rather pleasant, despite her filthy hair.

"Sorry," he says. "I'm all out."

"You think I'm going to buy booze with it, don't you?"

"Possibly."

"Well then why don't I make it easier for you? How bout you bring me into that bar over there and buy me a drink? I'm a nice girl, don't you think?"

He looks her over and shakes his head.

"Sorry, but I've no need of the bar. I've plenty of alcohol at home."

"I could drink there too," she says and smiles.

Taken aback, he snorts, not sure if he heard her right.

"I'm sorry," he reiterates. "But I'm not feeling very well today. Maybe if I–"

"I could make you feel better," she interrupts.

He takes in a deep breath and sighs, then glances around the lot and returns his gaze to the girl. She's smiling, awaiting a response, and rubbing his arm with her hand.

"I don't have any money to pay you," he finally says.

"All I want is a drink and some company. I'm a nice girl, no?"

He sighs once more. His leg is inflamed and irritated, but this girl and the filthy lust she's hinting at is powerful enough to take his mind off of it. He knows he shouldn't. He knows he should go home, relax, get a good night's sleep, and return to his students in full form in the morning. But a chance for a woman and booze... the compulsion to indulge in decadent self-abuse is powerful, dominating, even. He knows he's an addict, through and through, but how is he supposed to make a change if this sort of thing just happens out of the blue? He doesn't see it, and frankly, it doesn't matter, for he's already made up his mind.

"Get in the car," he says, and the girl smiles and claps

her hands. She rounds the vehicle and jumps into the passenger's seat, promising him a good time ahead. She completely ignores the putrid stench inside the car; he's yet to soap the vomit from carpet.

He's mostly silent on the ride home, but she just gabbles on and on, using rhetorical questions as transitions between subjects. He's thinking, maybe I shouldn't be taking her home. I am ill, after all; and she's homeless, above all else. But it's too late now. I can't just drop her off. Plus, now I want her. Bad.

He nods in response to her gibberish and takes a breath. A dark, self-loathing mood comes over him. He's a fiend, a hopeless derelict caught in a spiral of self-destruction; but one does not simply step out of a tornado. The winds take on a life of their own and lay waste to previously good things. They shatter people into millions of pieces. They dominate everything.

The pain in his leg is sharp, and stabbing. Between his mind, her incessant voice, and his rash, he's struggling to maintain his concentration on the road, but the lure of soon getting drunk trumps all other concerns. Plus the woman. Another fine night of debauchery and unnecessary risks lie ahead. A few more blocks is all that stands between him and manufactured utopia. He looks at the girl and smiles. She doesn't notice and says something about how this one time she woke up face first on the floor of a basement bar bathroom.

She's perfect.

Around the corner and a left and they're at his door. The instant they enter they're guzzling liquor and ripping each other's clothes off.

***

2:34 a.m. He wakes up with what feels like a knife in his stomach. Dashing from the bed to the washroom, he falls to his knees, empties his stomach, and a terrible fear flashes up his spine. It's all blood. He stares in disbelief, worry, and tries to make sense of the situation. He's still plastered. He and the girl had gone round for round, drink for drink, for just about six hours. He'd fallen asleep after the last carnal bout with the girl, but now he feels like he's in trouble. When he thinks he's done, he sits on the floor and leans against the wall, staring at his leg. The rash has spread like a voracious pathogen, and areas that had been mere spots only half a day before have now quadrupled in size and climbed up his thigh like sinister vines, burning and angry.

"Damn it!" he snaps, and tries putting more lotion on the inflamed areas, but it does nothing to calm the pain. He looks at the toilet once more and the sight of the blood seems to make his heart skip. What's next? He thinks. What now?

"Next is death, you moron!" he says and tries to stand up. He eventually makes it to his feet, but he needs the wall to support his balance. "Death because you drink too much and you're a complete idiot, and now it might just be too late this time. Just great. Fantastic job."

He's slick with sweat, and without further hesitation he decides to have a shower and sober up and maybe get his thoughts in order. He's sick of drinking, he decides. He's been talking about quitting for years; what better time than when you're puking blood? It's the purest motivation of all–fatal fear.

For the duration of his shower, he curses himself. "You idiot! Everything comes to you, you finally get to realize your dreams, and now you're probably going to die. It's what you deserve, you moron. Just couldn't help yourself, could you? No– let's have another drink, that'll keep me away from reality. Yeah, I won't die, not till I'm ninety. Won't happen to me. I'm mister invincible. Stupid fucking asshole!"

Gaining strength in his limbs and clarity in his mind, he dries himself, wraps a robe around him, and leaves the bathroom. In his bed, the girl is buried under the blankets, and he suddenly feels a deep contempt for her, and mocks her.

"Hey, mister. How about you take me home, total stranger that I am, and we can drink and satisfy each other as if no danger exists in the world. I'm a nice girl, I swear," he shakes his head. "You're a goddamn whore is what you are."

No response.
He leaves the room and goes downstairs to the kitchen where he dumps the rest of his whiskey down the drain. He's determined; he is quitting drinking right this instant. He's tired of the puke, and the piss, and the dirty whores, and the hangovers, and the risks of losing his job, and he's sick, he's just, he's sick of everything! Everything.

He shakes the last drops from the bottles and throws them in the garbage.

"Not even worth recycling," he says. "That's how evil you are."

Again his stomach twists and he doubles over in pain, banging a fist against the countertop. It passes in a few seconds, but he's left feeling weak on multiple levels, physically being the least of his worries. In his head, things suddenly seem confused, irrational, and dangerous. He feels broken, like he's broken himself, and hasn't the slightest idea of how to begin putting any of the pieces back together. He's screwed. He had so much to look forward to, but before he could even get his head wrapped around the idea, his body and mind began failing him in terrible ways.

Dry heaving over the sink, he spits and gasps, but nothing else comes out. He downs a tall glass of water, and then another. The water hurts going down, feels nauseating when it reaches his stomach, but he knows he desperately needs it.

He's freezing cold but sweating profusely, and his hands are trembling uncontrollably. Filling the glass once more, he walks to the living room and sinks into the sofa, sighing heavily on the way down. His mind reels with thoughts of death and destruction. He knows he has no one to blame but himself, not even the whore currently in his bed. He decides that he will have to do what he hates doing on a fundamental level; he will have to go and see a doctor. There's no doubt about it.

With that thought, his guts turn and stab him, and before he knows it, he's sitting on the toilet in agony, his eyes watering with the pain. To his complete disbelief, he sees that it's also blood.

"Shit!" he snaps, his heart racing with terror. What's he going to do? He's terribly ill, and terribly tired, and mostly still drunk. He's angry, and doesn't want anything to stand in the way of him and his students getting to the big show–but what's he supposed to do?

In time, feeling stable enough to leave the safety of the toilet, he walks back to the kitchen and starts raiding the refrigerator, thinking that maybe food will make a difference. He finds deli meat and makes himself a sandwich. It's the slowest sandwich he's ever eaten, but the calories do begin calming his stomach by the time he finishes it.

He decides to stay up for the rest of the night, trying to ignore his troubles and concentrate on what to do about the symphony. If he can just focus, just make it to Carnegie Hall, he promises himself that he'll never have another drop of alcohol for the rest of his days. He'll stop picking up strange homeless women. He'll stop giving in to his overwhelming compulsions. He swears!

He shuffles through piles of sheet music in the living room until 7:00 a.m. By then his mind is calmed, or at least, it's busy with thoughts other than blood coming out of his orifices.

Though he has no strength and he's still trembling, and cold, and sweating, he's determined to return to work and get the symphony together and practiced for the big event. No matter what, he's playing that damn show!

He files the papers into a single pile and then goes upstairs to dress for the day. He ignores the girl and goes about his business, and in fifteen minutes he's in his car and driving to work. He'll deal with the woman when he gets back. The drive is punishing. He's having trouble concentrating, and in only two miles of traveling he's already jumped three times in surprise at cars coming out of blind corners–at least, they appeared that way to him. He keeps both hands on the wheel and checks his speed at thirty. Twenty minutes later, he's parked and walking across campus, hoping with every molecule in his body that he won't lose control of his bowels.

With great effort, he makes it to the classroom, sits in his leather chair, and cradles his head in his arms on top of the desk. He begins thinking that maybe coming to work was a bad idea, but it's too late to change his mind. He's there now, may as well give it a go. The symphony isn't going to write itself.

For the first time he can remember, he doesn't want a drink from his desk. He just wants to teach. He doesn't want to see a doctor, or have a drink, or screw another girl, or excrete any more hemorrhaging blood. All he wants is to get the show organized and practiced. It will be the greatest challenge of his life, he's quite sure of that.

In the next ten minutes, students begin filing into class, but he instantly notices their eyes as they enter the room. Worried eyes, repulsed and questioning, stare at him. Inevitably, the questions begin.

"Professor, are you feeling all right?"
"Maybe you should have stayed home again today."

"Is there anything I can bring you? Anything we can do?" The professor shakes his head and raises his hand.

"Just a mild flu," he says. "Nothing to worry about. I just really want to get this thing organized. I'm excited for your young minds to have such a spectacular opportunity, and I want to be the one leading you through it. You understand, I hope? Anyhow, I've come up with a few interesting ideas I would like to try and by the end of this week we should have a performance on our hands, ladies and gentlemen."

The students feign smiles and their eyes scrutinize the

obviously ill professor with worry. They're not sure what to do, but they certainly don't think that he should have come to work today.

"Is everything all right with you guys aside from that?" he asks, trying to deflect their attention away from himself. "Anything new?"

"Well," a young man named David says. "I passed my physics exam. But seriously, sir, you should go home. You really don't look well."

"Nonsense," he says and stands from his chair and rounds his desk. He sits on the edge of the desk, about to explain his new ideas and ignore the questions about his health, but before he can speak, his peripheral vision suddenly grays and he sees racing dots in front of him, then flashes of light, and then he feels the ground, but it feels distant and unimportant. He hears excited voices shrieking, but they don't seem to matter much now that everything is dark.

Six

When he wakes up, he realizes he's been scratching his wrist for some time, unconsciously annoyed, and then he sees the source of the irritation. There's an intravenous line pierced into his arm. Shocked, he jolts his head up and looks about the room. It's bright and the light burns his eyes, and in the corner of the room he notices a broad shouldered orderly staring at him. He swallows hard and his throat erupts in pain, but he tries to speak anyway.

"Where am I?" It comes out dry and weak.

"You're in the hospital, sir," the orderly replies. "The doctor will be in to check on you in a moment."

Confused, he looks down at his body. It looks weak and shriveled, and suddenly, he's convinced that he'll never walk out of this room; he'll be carried out under a sheet. The thought makes his heart labor, and he hears the beeps on the machine next to his bed rise in sync with what he feels in his chest. He feels like he can't breathe, the air is too thick, his entire body is itchy, rotting away, dying. He's dying!

Panicked, he squirms in his bed violently enough for the orderly to restrain him and call out for help. A nurse and a doctor come in, both female, and a calming shot is pumped into his bicep. Almost instantly, he feels a wave of soothing heat wash through him, numbing his limbs, and he's laid back comfortably into bed by the orderly.

The doctor steps back and checks the various monitors surrounding his bed. She adjusts a few buttons, makes a note in her note pad, and then stares at him passively.

"What... What happened?" he asks, and he's suddenly aware that he can't feel any pain whatsoever.

"You lost consciousness at work," the doctor says, and her voice sounds stern, almost angry. "It was a result of septic shock. There are people here who will explain it to you in just a moment. Just relax until they arrive."

He's confused. Doctors usually provide their patients with information, don't they? A few words of encouragement. A reassuring pat on the arm. There's none of that in this woman. She's cold and uninvolved, and he finds himself consumed with a numb fear. He can't feel it, but he can see that he's trembling uncontrollably.

A minute later, two men sporting trench coats enter the room. The first is tall and broad and wears a grey beard like a mane on his face. The second is shorter, but still seems like a formidable opponent to take on in a fight. He spikes his hair, and he's perhaps ten or fifteen years younger than the first man. The doctor nods when they come in and steps away from his bed so the men can approach him from the side.

"How are you feeling?" the bearded man asks, no smile on his face.

"Ah... I'm not sure," he replies. "What's this all about?"

"Just a few questions for you," he says and grins strangely, fakely. The professor is astutely aware of the tension in the room. The mood is dark, as if something terrible is about to happen, and he decides he no longer wants to know anything. He doesn't care what happened, doesn't even care that he's dying, he just wants out of this terrible room. The atmosphere presses hard against him, putting unbearable pressure on his chest. He doesn't think he can speak anymore.

He stares away from the bearded man and catches sight of the other faces in the room. They all hold the same expression. What's their problem?

"You're a teacher?" the bearded man continues.

He nods yes.

"A music teacher?"

"Yes... I... I teach classical music."

"Interesting," the man says and glances to his partner.

"I just want to know what's wrong with me."

"We'll get to that in just a minute," the man replies. "Now, how long have you been a teacher?"

"Ah... Seventeen years."

"Uh huh, and are you married?"

"No."

"Girlfriend?"

"No."

"How about kids?"

"No. I'm sorry, can I ask—"

"Everything will be explained shortly," the man interrupts and looks again to his partner who is jotting down notes in his pad. "Now, what kind of hobbies do you enjoy?"

"Is this a dating questionnaire or something?"

"Just answer the question, please."

"All right, fine. Music. I love music."

"Anything else?"

"Drinking."

"I see. And what else? What about women? Is that why you never married, can't get enough from just one? It's okay, I myself am of the same opinion. I like multiple women. One is never enough."

He eyes him suspiciously from his bed. His eyelids are heavy, his mind clouded, and he's having trouble deciphering where this is all going. Why all the questions? He'd fallen ill and lost consciousness at work. He hadn't caused an accident or anything; at least, as far as he can remember."

"Yes," he says.

"I'm sorry? Yes, what?"

"I also like multiple women."

"I thought so," the man nods, but the response confuses him even more. What the hell is going on?

"Look," he says. "I don't know what you're implying, or trying to imply, but I just want to know what's wrong with me. Am I dying or will I survive?"

"Yes and no," the man replies and grins, which infuriates him.

"Yes and no?" he screams. "What do you mean yes and no? This is obscene treatment of a physically ill patient whose only crime is getting sick and–"

"Quiet!" the man demands, and the action is so unexpected that he loses his ranting train of thought on the spot. "Now–you want to know about your illness–we will tell you."

"Okay..."

"Your doctor here has been quite helpful in explaining all the fascinating implications involved in catching such a rare disease."

This isn't making any sense, he tells himself. What is he talking about?

"Your rash," the man continues. "How long ago has it appeared?"

"I don't even know how long I've been here for."

"Two days," the man replies.

"I've been out for two days?" Panic grips his heart and squeezes. "What... I mean... How can..."

"The rash," the man presses again. "Given the information you now have, how long ago did it appear?"

"Ah..." he thinks but his mind isn't very clear. "It's been, like, four days, I guess. Maybe five."

"Uh huh. And when did you start puking blood?"

"How could you know that?"

"You've been doing it the last two days, man. Please, try to keep up with the conversation, will you?"

His tone is unacceptable and irritating. Who does he think he is, treating an ill man with such disrespect? He doesn't even know him.

"Fine," he snaps. "I don't know, three, maybe four days now."

"And you didn't see a doctor, why?"
"Because I was afraid, all right. Is that what you want to hear? I was afraid, and I have a big show coming up in a month at Carnegie Hall, and all I want to do is survive long enough to play it, and then I'll be ready to die."

"Most people see a doctor to ease their fears," the man says, ignoring his rant. "But you did not. It's very interesting."

"Well, I'm glad you find it amusing," he says. He's now fuming with rage, wishing he had enough strength to attack the rude fool right then and there.

"Well," the man continues to press his buttons. "People like you are amusing, I must admit."

"What the hell is that supposed to mean? Is there something specific you'd like to say to me?"

The man shares a small chuckle with his partner.
"Well, now that you mention it, there is one thing I do want to say to you. But first, I will need the assistance of the good doctor here."

He turns and motions her toward the bed. With quick little steps, she approaches and stands next to the bearded man and glares down at the professor with the same expression of crude and unveiled contempt as the others.

"Doctor, please tell our respectable friend here all about his illness."

"Fine," she says and takes a deep breath. "Your body has gone into septic shock, and whether or not you will make a full recovery remains to be seen. You've let it go on for far too long. Immediate attention was needed about a week ago. Ah, the rash on your body, which you'll notice covers all of your limbs as well as most of your torso, are a result of a disease called Myiasis."

"And there you are," the bearded man cuts in. "Thank you, Doctor. You're free to go now if you'd like."

"Thank you," she says and leaves the room without a further glance at anyone.

"Wait," he says from his bed. "Wait. Myia-what? I don't understand what that means. What does that mean?"

"I will tell you what it mean just as soon as you stop your

little hissy fit," the man says. He calms down and sinks his head into the pillow behind him, trying to avoid the entire conversation.

"Are you all right now?" the man asks, but receives no response. "Fine, it's no matter. I'm going to tell you whether you want to hear it or not, but I do have a final question first. Have you had many sexual partners lately?"

"Excuse me?" he demands, highly offended.

"Have you been fucking lots lately? I didn't think it was a difficult question."

He snorts, frustrated, realizing that he has no other option but to go along with the conversation.

"Fine," he says. "Yes. I have been sexually active lately."

"Uh huh. You sure have."

"Does this have anything to do with my illness?"

"Everything to do with it," the man says, nodding. "Actually, if you don't mind my asking, what type of woman is your preference, exactly?"

"I don't know," he says. "Red heads."

"Um, red heads," the man says. "Very nice, especially with pale skin. Melt a man's heart, am I right?"

He doesn't reply.

"The reason I ask is because this little disease of yours, the rash and the blood, has to do with sex; but it's the kind of sex that we're interested in here."

He suddenly can't breathe and he feels his eyes grow wide. He's staring at the bearded man intensely, listening carefully to every word, brutally aware of where the conversation is going.

"What kind of sex is it that you prefer again?"

He says nothing.

"I'm sorry," the man presses, holding his hand up to his ear as if he'd misheard his response.

"Dead? Is that what you said?"

He doesn't reply.

"The reason I ask, and I think you're finally catching on here, is that your disease, called Myiasis, is often contracted by having sex with a corpse."

He doesn't reply. He doesn't breathe.

"And in your case, multiple corpses, isn't that right?"

He stares, his chest fills with pressure.

"Come on, man. You can tell me. Don't you want to tell me all about it?"

He says nothing.

"No matter," the man shrugs. "You see, we've already searched your home. We found the dead woman in your bed. A fresh one, huh? Only dead a day or two before you collapsed."

He stares.

"We also found the one carelessly tossed from your bedroom window. What happened to her?"

No reply.

"You know, we've been looking for you for a while now. All of those women we've been finding in and around the river valley, you had sex with them too, didn't you? Yes, I know you did. And luckily for us, we're in the process of proving it as we speak. You're a sick little puppy, aren't you?"

He still says nothing.

The man shares another look with his partner, then turns back to him.

"A drinking man," the man says. "A drinking, killing, corpse fucking, sick son of a bitch. And let me tell you something else. If I were you, I would be hoping to die right here in this bed, because if you do live, and it is very much an if at this point, your life will be the epitome of a hellish existence, do you understand me? And then, after you've suffered long enough, lost your mind, your health, your hopes and dreams, then we'll kill your stupid ass."

He stares back at him, unable to speak, unable to think. Is this happening? Is it real? The bearded man and his partner hover over him, leering and egging him on, pushing his buttons and leading him into admittance.

"Not even going to deny it, huh?" the man says. "I don't blame you. It's a terrible thing to admit. And hey, didn't you say you were about to play Carnegie Hall in a month's time? That's hilarious, isn't it? Yes, I think it's quite hilarious. But don't worry, you'll still get worldwide attention once they strap you to the chair. Congratulations, Professor, how does it feel to be famous?"

Seven

The members of the orchestra spend days searching their memories and asking themselves haunting questions. The girls ask things like, "Every time he looked at me, corrected my technique, gave me encouragement, what was he thinking about? Did he ever think about killing me? Having sex with my body? Oh, my God. This is the creepiest thing I've ever heard of."

Now, among the whirlwind of media sensationalism, the students crowd against each other in the benches and face the judge. Only two rows in front of them, the professor sits with his back to them; he appears calm, collected, and glances at no one.

The courtroom is packed with reporters, medical and psychological experts, and mourning family members; most of them demanding death as punishment for the professor's appalling crimes. They hiss hate at him, terrified of the idea of allowing such a man to continue with his life.

"Worthless scum!"
"Kill the bastard! Do the world a favor!"
"Hang him now, right here off the railing!"
"Just let me get my goddamn hands on him!"

The bailiff calls for order and announces the judge's name. Everyone stands and ceases their conversation. The judge is a fat pig-faced man who ambles in breathing laboriously, clearing the grease from his throat with pig-like grunts. He nods and allows every one to sit before lowering his formidable mass into his great chair and spending thirty seconds slopping up and swallowing the drool from his mouth.

"Good morning," the judge croaks.
"Morning," is the unanimous response.
"Counsellors, are we ready to begin?"
"Yes, your honor."
"Very well, let's have it."

The judge seems bored, as if he's already decided to kill the defendant and is just waiting for the required time limit to expire before pronouncing it. Such things are political.

When his attorney begins speaking, the professor zones out. In his mind he's listening to Beethoven's Ninth. He's lost in the abstract beauty of it, the fundamental truth about something no one understands, but everyone knows. He's only been out of the hospital for three days and nearly every second of those days have been spent in this courtroom, listening to lawyers argue like it was a professional sport. Pre-politicians. They bicker about this and that, building a mental structure of events in people's minds, and the best part is, he thinks, a lawyer has yet to ask him a meaningful question of any kind. In reality, the whole fiasco has nothing to do with him; he's simply the context through which other people can argue for unreasonable sums of money.

The bearded man from the hospital is there too, sitting just off to the side. Every time he meets the professor's eyes, he smiles a big, vilifying, malicious smile. But the professor doesn't react. He is cold, calculated, intelligent. He sits in his chair and stares at the judge directly in the eyes, his face devoid of expression. None of the information presented thus far has stirred him, and he offers no reaction when he's referred to. He's a monk, showcased by his stoic calm, his irreversible madness, his desperate need for a strong drink.

At least he's feeling better. It was an arduous road to recovery, and the infection's left irreparable damage in its wake. Six weeks he's suffered, cried, pleaded for the pain to stop, and in the end his body proved strong enough to combat the infection, but he isn't sure if that's a good thing or not. Every day, he hears the bearded man's words echo in his mind; "I would be hoping to die right here in this bed." He does wish it. He doesn't want to live anymore, but it isn't due to any sense of remorse. He isn't going to play music anymore. He will never get another opportunity to play anywhere. He is done, ruined, and that's the only thing that bothers him.

"Professor? Professor. Can you stand please?" the pig judge calls, and to his right he notices the jury coming back into the room. He glares at the judge and doesn't blink, but eventually does get to his feet with the forcible help of the bailiffs. He scratches his forehead with his shackled hands and then calmly stares at the judge, expressionless.

"Has the jury reached a verdict?"
"Yes, your honor."

"Very well, let's have it."
"On seven counts of murder in the first degree, by unanimous vote, we the jury find the defendant guilty as charged."

The crowd erupts in a clamor, applauding, hugging, and hurling insults at the professor.

"Order!" the judge cries. "Order!" and the voices quiet. He addresses the professor. "You have been found guilty by a jury of your peers. I hereby sentence you to death by way of the electric chair."

The lawyers yell for appeals, and the crowd falls into pandemonium once again.

"Burn in hell, asshole!"

"I hope you suffer for the rest of your days!"

"You got what you deserve!"

But the students behind him remain motionless. Most had truly liked the professor, and still couldn't bring themselves to admit that the same man who had taught them had also been capable of such atrocious things. How could that be?

For the first time in three days, the professor turns and looks at each of his students. His face is filled with sorrow, but it's cold, and angry. The students stare back uncomfortably, unsure of what to do, or what to say.

No words are spoken, only cryptic stares that mean different things to different people. Officers shuffle the professor out of courthouse and toward an armored van destined for the penitentiary. The instant they step outside, it's madness with cameras and lights and screaming voices. Every one wants a comment, a thought, a photograph, a way to make money off his face. He stares at the ground and follows the officers' lead through the crowd, ignoring the sea of degenerates trying to pile on top of him.

With blatant contempt, they shove him into the van, shut the doors, and speed away from the animated crowd.

***

He can't believe what he's hearing.

"You're famous," the lawyer says.

"Wait," he says. "What do you mean?"

"I mean, right after you were arrested, someone stole your symphony from your classroom and pieced it together. As of last night, the piece has sold over one point two million copies. They're saying it's stellar."

"What?"

He can't believe it. All his life he's struggled to attain some level of recognition, and now that he's a known killer, his work is seriously accepted? His music has cheated into fame, and he feels sick to his stomach. He truly has destroyed himself on all levels.

"What's the matter?" the lawyer says. "You're not happy?"

"I'm on death row, what do I have to be happy about?"
"Well, your music."

"My music is popular by association. It holds no credence or credibility anymore. That may be acceptable to untalented hacks and greedy business people who'd rather sacrifice the effort of mastering a craft in favor of easy money, but it's unacceptable to me. Please, just leave me alone."

"All right," the lawyer says and raises his hands in the air. "How are they treating you in here, anyway?"

He stares at him coldly.

"I'm a sick man," he says. "I'm not entitled to anything."

***

Nine years later, a crown of electrodes are attached to the professor's skull and a switch is flipped. He had no final words.

People cheer at the news and hug and kiss. He makes international headlines.

A year after that, the epic symphony composed by the so-called "Professor Death" is voted number nine on the top one hundred greatest symphonies of all time.

The End

THE SPYDER LEGEND

I've always wanted stable and fulfilling relationships. By that, I should clarify that I don't just mean relationships with women, but with people from all walks of life. Business and casual. Platonic and sexual. Friendly and hostile. As a young man, I wanted to live and breathe the marrow of our species, to taste the blood that powers our weird habits and irrational behaviors. I wanted to be immersed in passion, electrified by emotion, and enthused by ideological pursuits–but there's always been an obstacle barring me from it all. It seems, and I mean this with utmost honesty, that I am not entirely human. Am I flesh and blood? Yes. Do I have thoughts and dreams? Certainly. But being human is far more than mere physicality, and I seem to be lacking a tremendous part of the overall puzzle. Of course, it seems like a curse to those removed, but in reality I've never been able to consider it anything other than a blessing bestowed upon me by some force with an admirable sense of humor.

You see, I've tried. Believe me, year after year, I've tried to establish and solidify meaningful ties with other people; but none of it ever seems to get past a formal level of interaction because of my seemingly incurable affliction. The thing is, the moment I meet someone I've got their basic personality worked out, and every minute thereafter I notice more subtleties, and then it all happens without any conscious intent. The right words come out, the correct jokes, the perfect amount of charm, and the next thing I know I'm waking up next to a strange girl with pockets full of money and a crude certainty that I've done unholy things I'll never remember nor repent.

The problem, if you can call it that, is that I always get what I want; always, but it sounds better than it actually feels. I say all these wonderful things, act all valiantly, and assume all the correct body language, but there isn't any genuine emotion behind any of it. Trust me, believe me, I love you, these are words to me, tools I happen to use to get the things I want out of life and people.

I see people like mathematical equations, not that I'm a genius
or anything like that, but it's a healthy comparison. I see habits,
vices, and temperaments. I see nothing but patterns on legs. Where
people see fear, I see opportunity for control and profit. Where they
see pity, I see susceptibility to a vast spectrum of advantages. Obviously, I'm aware of this defection, brutally aware, but I just can't
help myself. It's hardwired into me like a fundamental function as
natural and unconscious as breathing. On moral grounds, perhaps
I don't deserve meaningful relationships. Perhaps I deserve a
righteous punishment, and perhaps I will even get it one day; or
maybe, as I think, we're all completely full of shit.

Regardless, I'm only telling you all of this so you can see
the world through my own context, and not yours. The first thing
you should know is that you should never trust anything I say. That
being said, allow me to introduce myself. I currently use the name
Michael Roth, one of many, and most invented out of thin air, just
like the personalities I choose to ease other people into relating
with me. (Or rather, who I am at that time.) Consequently, none of
that is important. What is, is that I am thirty-three years old, and
over the course of the last ten years or so I've managed to amass a
fortune worth over one hundred million dollars. An astronomical,
disgusting amount of money for a middle-class suburban kid, and
one that could easily lead most members of my generation to death
by way of drugs, stupidity, and/or viral infection incurred by the
many daddy issue gold diggers always hanging about.

But none of that applies here... at least not yet. The point
is I've made an obscene amount of money, mostly illegally, and I
won't lie, I had a damn good time making it.

Did I earn it? Come now, how does one earn one hundred
million dollars pound for pound? The last job I had before embark-
ing on my wild journey to riches had my life insured for a whole
twenty-eight thousand dollars. How does an individual righteously
earn one hundred million? Like everyone else in my elite class,
I stole it all. Well, most of it, anyhow. I stole it from companies,
from people, from charities, and I did it without wearing a mask,
wielding a weapon, or threatening a single person's life. Well...
We'll get to that in a little bit. The point is, I used the most powerful weapon available to human beings. Trust. I charmed my
way into a fortune, and I did it without batting an eye or feeling
remorse; and do you know why? I figure it's pretty simple. I know
it's morally wrong, but probably just like yourself, I was stuck
busting my ass day after day, year after year, just to bring home an

unnoticeable portion of company profits–and for what? All around me I saw people willfully giving away their hard earned money for some of the dumbest reasons I'd ever heard of–and that's when it hit me. If people were more than willing to hand over money without question just because it seemed to appeal to an innate part of them, then I was more than willing to accept handfuls of it and quit wasting my health and time in order to make some other asshole rich.

In college, I developed a burning interest in the secrets of magic, so I convinced a grumpy old wizard called Ernesto The Great to train me in the basics of the art. I say convinced, he called it blackmail, but it's not my fault he was married and took an animalistic interest in the girl I paid to play with his wrinkled magic stick. Anyhow, despite recognizing the potential of scheming and cajoling, at that time I was only interested in blatant theft, so I had Ernesto train me in slight of hand. (Away from my magic stick.) I wanted to have the ability to calmly walk into a store and fill my pockets without anyone being the wiser, or pay a cashier and then switch the bills at the last second without getting caught.

"Ninety-nine percent discount you say? Why, thank you, Ma'am."

Of course, it was juvenile stuff, but I was only about twenty years old then, and it seemed like a talent that could not only make me money, but also get me laid. My inner voice was firmly reassured on that point. Learn magic, steal chocolate bars, get dick sucked. Pure science. My friends were going to be so jealous!

Things were great for a while, until I got caught stealing a diamond ring when I stupidly pulled my hands from my pockets and out came this two carat monster hung up on the button of my sleeve. It fell to the floor with a terrible, tinny clunk, right in front of the clerk. The store owner was a solid mass of hairy Armenian muscle, and that crazy cocksucker kicked the shit out of me. Rightfully so, I should add, for Ernesto was clearly a terrible teacher.

It was a good thing in the end, because it didn't take me long to realize that doing all the dirty work was a shitty way of making money, even if you're stealing it. Charming words and charisma worked far better, and if I could somehow place myself in the middle of two other people making a transaction, facilitating the deal somehow, then I would be making some easy money. So my mind began tearing through ideas.

How can I make the most of my efforts, I asked myself.

What line of business is worth getting into? There are many options in the theft industry, but what struck me most was the idea that if you're going to steal, you may as well go big; because in the eyes of law there is little difference between stealing one hundred thousand dollars and a million dollars. The punishment all comes down to the same, so why waste time and effort chasing after little fish? Jewelry, cars, and even scams are profitable prospects; but if you're going for the big money, there is nothing on the planet worth more than art. Some people love to pay obscene sums to bask in their own ego. Steal a good painting once and all future jobs are optional. Of course, it's not that easy. It's a tough world to get into. Items need to be physically removed, the security involved is usually unreasonable on multiple levels, and then someone rich and crooked enough has to be found to exchange the goods with for an offensive price tag.

I'd learned my lesson, so I stayed out of physical theft and all that exciting stuff, and instead stood in the middle of it all as a broker, connecting poor thieves to rich thieves, closing deals, and taking my percentages home. I was some weird hybrid being in a position that didn't necessarily need to exist, but I was rather good at promoting it–and exploiting it.

In the beginning it was all about networking. I hit the streets, climbed up the ladder of thieves, made contacts, and eventually found regular buyers for stolen art, antiques, diamonds, and gold. In time, I found myself sitting pretty on top of an enormous fortune. But as with all things good and bad, they don't last forever, and it's all influenced by forces we as individuals have absolutely no control over. Nevertheless, the ride to the end amid a whirlwind of unstoppable forces doesn't always spell disaster. Sometimes, like a caterpillar, the old form dies and a new one emerges. The trouble, I find, is our inability to consider the unknown as a good thing until a butterfly emerges from the cocoon and we realize that flying across the land is far more efficient than crawling, regardless of the amount of legs that previously carried us.

So that's the story I'm here to tell you. The end of one paradigm, and the beginning of another. For the denouement, however, I first need to introduce you to two of my most loyal clients; a buyer named Henry, and a thief named Freddy.

I first met Henry through another buyer of mine, and we quickly forged a strong affiliation. I loved the man, because he was the most gullible bastard on the face of the earth. He was loaded with inherited riches, born shitting money, and had never done anything of consequence in his life. He was rich, and that was all he was, despite his fanatical fondness for thinking himself the world's greatest gift to art collection and criticism. He abused unfortunate visitors with pompous opinions and unveiled jealousy of other artists, but he personally wasn't capable of anything aside from boring the living shit out of a lobotomized dog. Of course, to listen to him without much knowledge of the subject, the man sounded like an expert–professional, and definitive in his critical arguments–but it was all icing on top of a layer of shit. I know that, because for years I sold him the most worthless, unimportant, uninteresting pieces of crap failures in art for hilarious sums of money. It's the nature of the industry, and like many other industries, if you're going to get into it unprepared or mistaking your ego for skill and knowledge, you'll be bled dry. As well you should be. If I hadn't done it, someone else would have, and I'd still be busting my ass for some jerk I've never even met. Does that make me a sociopath? Maybe. Is that a bad thing? Not necessarily.

It sure is profitable.

But I'll get back to Henry in a moment. For now, allow me to introduce the other pertinent character in my story. I met the thief, Freddy, when I was first starting out in the business. He'd stolen a bunch of antique fine china for no other reason than he thought they looked expensive; he was correct, but he had no idea what to do with them. He'd gotten a hold of my number through another thief I was acquainted with and called me. He sounded harmless enough so I agreed to meet him and we made a deal. I found him a buyer, got myself a healthy twenty percent commission, and after that he started coming to me with everything he came across and decided to steal on impulse. The difference between Henry and Freddy was that Henry didn't necessarily need my services, whereas Freddy would have been completely screwed without me. No matter what kind of retarded piece of antique looking turd he snuck out of some place, I was usually successful in finding him a buyer. There are people who will buy anything; you just need to find them.

So the forces were put into motion. Freddy would steal, Henry would buy, and I just stayed comfortably nestled in the middle, making phone calls; literally, just making phone calls and collecting healthy sums for my efforts. It was a nice gig, especially once I managed to expand and diversify my client list. Before long, the thieves calling me were daring, and they were looking for daring buyers, but I always paid special attention to both Freddy and Henry because one was incapable of not stealing things, and the other was incapable of not buying them. I viewed it as passive income with no initial investment at risk. It's no coincidence that corporations have the exact same profit models as organized crime–it's the proven formula.

Things were good for years. I bought a house and worked from there. I never needed to leave, though I was free to if I caught the notion. Finally, I was free of the soul-crushing mundanity of the rat race. Wake up, have a shower, go to work, go drinking, go to sleep, and repeat. Gross. No, I was free. Free of bosses, and free of bullshit. I had pulled my weight in the right direction and money had come falling out. It was a terrible system, I admit, but it was still the system. You can only beat it by going with it, not against it. With it, change is possible. Against it, misery is the only possibility.

So there I was, on top of the system, manipulating it to my will. I did what I wanted, didn't do what I didn't want to, and all in all, I felt rather invincible. Shit, who am I kidding? I still feel invincible... But I'm getting ahead of myself.

One day, I woke up with a jolt next to three women I didn't know. It was the telephone ringing. I slowly rolled over a soft and warm body, and then another, and finally answered the call.

"Hello."

"It's Freddy. Listen, can I come over?"

I looked at the clock. It was 7:30 a.m.

"Sure," I said. "What time?"

"An hour?"

"Sounds good," I said. "Is it any good?"

"You'll love it."

I hung up the phone and jumped back into bed, waking the naked strangers.

"All right, girls. I have time for one more round, but I'm afraid you'll have to go after that. I have some business to tend to."

They obliged, I obliged, and about an hour later, sure enough, Freddy knocked on my door. The girls were in the process of leaving when he came in wide eyed and smiling, nodding to the girls and staring dumbly. The girls left and Freddy and I moved to the dining table where he placed a burlap bag and pulled from it a fantastic vase. The thing was an example of impeccable craftsmanship, decorated with excessive detail, and sufficiently aged to demand a fortune. I figured I could leach a solid half-million out of Henry for it. I would start at three quarters of a million; he was a cheap bastard with all that money he'd never earned.

"Fantastic!" I said. "What do you know about it?"
"Nothing," Freddy said. "But look at it. You can't blame me for taking it, can you?"

I could not. If I had the moral integrity to steal things for myself I would also have considered it. I examined the details closely. The rim was painted gold with minuscule naked people and odd symbols. It was a beautiful piece, and the first in a long time that I was going to sell to Henry. I had to give the man items that were actually worth something once in a while. Besides, if push ever came to shove, they could always be stolen back.

"Where'd you get it?" I asked.
"Please, you know better than that. I got it off your mother after I fucked her, as usual."

"Well, it's good to know mom is getting some. There are too many lonely ladies out there, you know. You're providing a valuable service, my friend."

"You're sick."
"And I have a doctor's note. Don't fuck with me. I'm liable to eat your face."

This type of camaraderie was a staple in our exchanges. We liked to joke around, and it added pleasure to the business at hand. Freddy was always looking for the next thing to score with. He was a slob by nature, filthy, and pretty disgusting in every hygienic sense, but I had to give it to him, he was doing quite well for himself. He was making more money than I was; of course, he also did work for it. I did nothing but phone calls. It was wonderful.

I scrutinized the vase methodically for a long time, and when I looked up and caught Freddy's eyes I noticed what I thought was a glimmer of misery. I couldn't imagine why; I'd just told him he was going to be half a million dollars richer. Why else would he have stolen the damn thing?

"Are you feeling all right, Freddy? You want a drink? I've got some great whiskey."

"Sure," he said, shuffled in his seat, and feigned a smile. I poured two drinks and brought them back to the table. We toasted and downed the wonderful liquid.

"You look sad," I remarked. "You just made a lot of money."

"I know," he said, and then shrugged. "I'm happy about

the money. I'm just having some trouble at home."

"Woman?"

"Woman," he confirmed. "I think the bitch is cheating on me. I'm pretty sure she is, anyway. I mean, I put myself on the line, buy her everything she wants, treat her like a princess, and what does she do? She goes and fucks some fat balding cocksucker. Well, you know what I mean."

I did. His wife had a penis. No, but seriously, it was why I was single. Well, it was the way I rationalized my inability to have a normal relationship with a woman, anyway.

"I just... I guess I just want to be happy. The money is great, but... I don't know."

"Ha! Happy. How naive," I said. "Life is an experience, not a chore. It's good, it's bad, it's everything in between, and it's supposed to be ruthlessly explored across the vast spectrum. What's the point otherwise? No sad memories to counter the happy ones? No hate to balance the love? No rage to counter the peace? Makes for awfully boring people if you ask me."

"Don't you want to be happy?"

"I am happy. I'm also sad, and angry, and horny. Life, my friend– that's what's flowing through these mighty veins. Look at yourself, stuck on happy. Don't you know your longing for it will end up being the very thing making you unhappy? It's very ironic–and in my opinion–rather self-evident."

He stared at me with a furrowed brow, unsure how to respond.

"What I'm saying is, just be yourself, man. Be you. Don't worry about being happy, it'll come when you're comfortable with who and what you are. The more you fight it, the worst off you'll be. You're looking for something superficial. A delusion. Also, dump the fucking whore. You're the only one responsible for your happiness, not her, and not anyone else; so whose fault is it?"

"Why, thank you for your analysis."

"It can't be helped," I said. "Take my advice, it's solid; quit being a little bitch."

"You're very professional, Doctor."

"I'm only honest. I apologize, it's not the norm."

"That's for sure," he said. "Everyone has to be a fucking liar these days."

"Don't let it get to you," I said. "Get rid of the girl. You're rich. What's the problem? Girls are available to you at any point in time."

"Yeah," he said, but had nothing else to add to the subject. "Anyway, let me know what happens with the vase."

He stood and walked toward the door.

"Will do," I said. "I'll have answers for you tomorrow. Like I said, I think I can get a half million for it."

"Let me know," he said. "Thanks for the drink."

"Anytime."

The next morning I called Henry, and, finding him in an exceptionally good mood, I secured a respectably crooked seven hundred thousand dollars for the vase without much resistance. I loved my job. Hanging up with Henry, I called Freddy, but he didn't answer. An hour later, still no answer. That night a car came and took the vase in exchange for a cash filled suitcase–there was still no answer. It didn't make any sense. I started thinking he'd done something stupid. Maybe he'd been arrested. Maybe he was dead.

Four days later, I was pushing myself into a lady's tabooed orifice when the door bell rang. Unalarmed, I continued wrestling with the girl, hoping the unexpected visitor would go away. I was in the middle of an impressive feat of balance when I heard the bell again. I hurried then, pushing the girl into a ball of animalistic lust; and two minutes later the door could be answered.

It was Freddy. He looked haggard and crazed, and he was staring nervously around me, avoiding eye contact.

"Hey, man," he said. "Sorry to just show up like this. Am I bothering you?"

"Not anymore," I said, and stepped aside to let him in. "I've been trying to get a hold of you. Did you lose your phone or something?"

He nodded quickly, and then shook his head.

"Ah... I'm kind of in trouble," he said, and ran his hands through his hair.

"Why? What happened?"

"I, ah... I caught the bitch cheating in my own bed," he said, and his eyes welled up with tears. "That fucking cunt! How could she do that to me?"

"Ah, shit, man," I said. "I'm sorry to hear that. You obviously love her a lot, but it's–"

"That's not all," he interrupted, and shook his head. "It's not important. Never mind."

"Okay, well, why don't you make yourself comfortable for a minute. I just have to go upstairs and take care of something.

Drinks are on the bar. Help yourself to as much as you like."

"Thanks," he said, and sort of walked around in a circle, not sure what to do with himself.

I went upstairs and tried talking the girl into leaving, but she wanted more. Fair enough, I gave her another round; and far too long to be polite later, I came downstairs with the girl, saw her to the door, and had a cab drive her home.

I came into the living room with a crooked smile. "Sorry," I said.

"No worries," he said. "I came unannounced. I'm sorry I ruined your night with the girl."

"Nonsense. I've accomplished all of my goals for the night. The rest is for relaxation."

His eyes were glossy and I could tell he was a little drunk already. His whiskey glass was filled to the brim, and I wondered how many of those he'd had already. I poured myself a healthy measure and sat down on the chair opposite him. He seemed en-raged, but it was an internal, introspective anger.

"So," I continued. "Ah... What else were you going to tell me? You caught your woman..."

"Yeah," he said, and nodded slowly. "I caught the bitch. I was going to kill 'em. Honestly, I was going to stab 'em and piss on 'em."

"But you didn't?"

"I couldn't get my hands on 'em," he said. "They must've heard the door when I came in because by the time I got upstairs I was just in time to watch her dumb ass climb out the window. They took off in a panic, and I was going to chase 'em and sideswipe the motherfuckers right off the road, but I was shaking so bad I couldn't have driven very far before I lost it and just killed myself instead."

"Jesus," I said. "Listen, man. I know it sucks, but it's just a relationship. There are women everywhere, and a lot better than her, at that. Don't let that bitch do this to you. Don't let anyone do this to you. It's not worth it–things always work out eventually."

"It's too late for that," he said, his voice crackling. I frowned. "Why?"

He gulped half of his glass and stared deep into my eyes, but it seemed like he was staring straight through me.

"I, ah... After they left, I smashed the room to pieces. I was so fucking angry. I couldn't take it. I tried having a couple of drinks to calm down, but it had the opposite effect. I became more hostile, and thirstier than ever for blood. Eventually, I decided to go for a walk just to get out of there, and I went down a narrow alleyway cutting in between two blocks of buildings. It was dark and I was thinking that the first homeless guy to ask me for change or a cigarette was going to get the shit beaten out of him. It sounds childish, I know, but I didn't know what else to do. I just wanted to beat the shit out of somebody. Anybody."

I nodded, not interrupting, but indicating that I fully understood the impulse. Sometimes you just need to smash something before things start feeling better. And sometimes, if you keep from doing it, the memory just sits there for years, gnawing at you, and all you can think is, "I should've smashed that fucking lamp against the wall. I would feel so much better today!"

"Anyway," he continued. "So I'm walking, smoking a cigarette, and sure as shit this dude comes out of nowhere and asks me for a smoke. When I looked at his face I realized that he was no older than I am, and for some reason that enraged me even more. Before I knew it, I punched him in the face as hard as I could. He fell to the ground coughing and spitting out chunks of teeth, and then I pounced..."

"You beat him?"

"I beat the living shit out of him," he said. "Well, I was in the middle of it, anyway, until I felt a hand grab my shoulder and tear me away from the homeless motherfucker."

"What?"

"Yeah. It was just this random guy. I guess he was walking by, heard the commotion, and decided to be a hero. Anyway, I'm so pissed at this point that I start fighting with this new guy. The homeless dude is dead to the world on a pile of garbage; and then this piece of shit pulls a knife on me–nobody pulls a fucking knife on me!"

He was getting intense, and I was already done my drink, but I didn't want to interrupt his rant. I sat and listened.

"So I tell this guy, 'Listen, man. If you want to fight, we'll fight, but don't be pulling a fucking knife on me cause I swear to God if I get my hands on it for a single second I'm going to plunge it right into your throat.' Of course, the tough guy doesn't listen. He comes at me slashing wildly–no idea what the hell he's doing. I dodged him, kicked him in the balls, landed my knee in his face as he went down, and before I knew it I had all of my weight focussed on the knife handle."

I was stunned.

"You killed the guy?"

He nodded and stared at the floor, dejected.

"It wasn't my fault. But I'm in trouble now, because I took the knife and put it in the homeless guy's hand and covered it with blood; but when I cleaned up later on I noticed that I'd been cut on the forearm. I must've left some blood there. I'm totally fucked! And all because of that goddamn slut!"

"Jesus," I said, but quickly found myself with nothing to add. What could I say? I understood his actions, didn't even condemn them, in fact, but he had assessed the situation quite correctly. He was fucked. A single drop of blood would seal his fate. I stood from my chair and held out my hand, indicating his glass, and walked to the bar to fill them.

"I just..." he continued. He was deep in some introspective nightmare, practically dancing in his chair with anxiety, and I could see his hands trembling from across the room. "I just, I thought I could come here and see you, and that maybe you could help me out somehow. I know we're just business friends, but I don't know anyone else that I trust, and I don't know what else to do."

I nodded and thought about it. I had a sip of my drink and stared at him. His face was drawn, ashen, his eyelids puffy. He held the posture of an abused dog and kept rubbing his forehead compulsively with the back of his hand.

"Do you think you can help me?"

I pursed my lips, had another sip, and straightened up in my chair.

"What do you need, exactly?"

"I need... I don't know. I need a place to go, first of all."

I nodded. I wanted to help the man, but I certainly didn't want him staying in my house. It was too risky; plus, despite dealing with him for years, I didn't fully trust him. I considered the implications for a while and thought I had a solution for him.

"Just let me make a phone call," I said, and left him in the living room. In the office I called Henry and told him a friend of mine had been cleaned out by his wife; did he have a place for him to stay for a little while? He thought about it, rightfully wary at first, but I was able to get him to agree to it as a personal favor to me. And just like that things were set. Henry had another house in the city–a mansion, I should say–which he paid to keep up but never took the time to actually enjoy. He seemed glad to help by the end of the conversation. I hung up with him and returned to the living room with the news, but when I got there I found Freddy already fast asleep on the couch with his legs tucked in close to his torso. I chuckled and shook my head. What was a man to do? I figured it was probably the first comfortable sleep he'd had in a few days, so I decided to let him sleep the rest of the night. I fetched a blanket and threw it over him before going upstairs, smoking a joint, watching a movie, and falling asleep.

When I came down the next morning I found Freddy in the kitchen with a giant spread of eggs, bacon, pancakes, and what have you all out on the table. It was the last thing I expected, and it made me smile.

"What's happening?" I said.
He turned quickly from the stove with an apprehensive smile on his face.

"Oh, hey, man," he said. "Listen, I'm really sorry about falling asleep last night. You should've just kicked me out."

"No trouble at all," I said. "It's a big house, and I'm glad to help."

"Coffee?" he asked, holding up the decanter.
"Black, please," I said, and sat at the table before the vast feast.
"So I made a phone call last night and I've got everything settled for you."

"Yeah? How do you mean?"
"Well, first off, I got you seven hundred thousand for the vase."

"No shit! That's awesome, man. Well, keep the extra two hundred grand; I truly appreciate everything you've done for me."

"That's very kind of you," I said, nowhere near humble enough to protest the offer. "I also found a place you can stay until you get straightened out. Your very own mansion, in fact. Host to no one but yourself."

"How'd you pull that off?"
"I know a lot of people," I said. "Anyway, if you want, after breakfast I'll drive you there. You're welcome to stay until you can get back on your feet. I told my contact that you were cleaned out in a divorce and needed to get away for a while."

He smiled. "You're a good man," he said. "I don't know how to repay you."

"Don't worry about it," I said. "If I ever need you, I'll come and see you. Otherwise, we're only being friendly."

He sat down at the other end of the table and we ate. The food was delicious, and I had a suspicion that Freddy spent a lot of time cooking, but I wasn't interested enough to ask him. I only told him how good it was. Afterward, we took one of my cars and drove to the mansion. The place was a sprawling palace some-where around fifty thousand square feet lining a vast lake; beautiful was an understatement.

We made our way up the drive, staring at the meticu-lously manicured gardens on the way, and parked in front of the monstrous dwelling where we were greeted by waiting servants. The head butler gave us a tour of the forty bedroom house and both Freddy and I were taken aback by how many valued items the place contained. The paintings on the walls were exquisite, some unimaginably important and valuable, and I began thinking that maybe Henry did have some art sense after all. The stairwells were lined with immaculate marble statues of Greek gods, and the prop-erty showcased an olympic sized pool, a golf course, a tennis court, a theater, a bowling alley, an ice cream bar.... There was nothing missing.

With the tour over, I shook hands with Freddy and told him that he could call me any time he needed, and that I hoped he was able to overcome his troubles and return to being a reliable supplier for me. We chuckled, and I was off. I returned home and found that I had two new paintings out for tender, and I had just the buyer for one of them. If the other couldn't be taken care of, I'd simply call Henry about it.

I didn't think about Freddy for the rest of the week. I was focussed on closing deals. I'd taken care of the first two paintings fairly easily. One was being shipped to Turkey, the other to Egypt. I didn't care; I'd throw them into the ocean if I was being paid for it. And then a new piece fell into my hands, a Matisse, for which I would have to push the limit of my contacts in order to find someone rich enough, and appreciative enough, to buy it. Someone like Henry had the money, but he was too dumb to fully appreci-ate the mastery of the art. With works like those, you want a buyer with a private gallery, and who is able to take the utmost care of it; because one day it will be stolen again, or the owner will die, and then someone like me can double up on the same item. It truly was the greatest business on the planet.

Six days after I'd last spoken to either Freddy or Henry, I received an urgent call from Henry, and he was angrier than I thought his personality could allow.

"Who the hell did you put up in my place?" he demanded.

"It's nice to speak to you too, Henry. Jesus, what's the matter with you?"

"Don't fuck with me!" he said. "That son of a bitch you

put up in my house robbed me."

"What?" I was shocked. Was Freddy really that impulsive? I supposed he was, but I hadn't expected him to screw me
after the lavish favor I'd done him.

"He robbed me!" he reiterated. "The paintings, the statues, a whole goddamn truck load of stuff, just gone. Now who the
hell is he? How do you know him?"

"All right, Henry, just calm down for a second."
"Don't patronize me, you asshole! This is your fault!"

"Henry, I wouldn't go so far as saying–"
"It's your fault, you bastard!" he screamed. "Now I want this
settled, and I want my stuff back, unharmed, and I want it now!"

"Listen–"
"Right now!" he roared, and I couldn't help but smile. I can't
remember ever getting so emotional about anything; forgive me if I
find it amusing.

"Look," I said. "He's a guy I know–I told you this. He
needed a place to stay. Now, I'm sorry he took your–"

"You're sorry?" he said. "Not yet you're not. I'll give you
something to be sorry about, you little–"

"Goddamn it, Henry! Don't worry about it. I'll find out
what happened and I'll get your stuff back." I was thinking that if I
was lucky I might be able to help Freddy disappear, and then resell
all of Henry's stuff right back to him. "All right?" I continued. "I'll
make a few calls and get back to you."

"I'll tell you what you're going to do," Henry said, his
voice shaking with rage. "You have two days to find this bastard
and bring him, along with all of my property, to me. If you do that,
I will forget your involvement and deal with this prick myself. But
if you don't, things aren't going to go very well for you."

"Come, Henry. It's Sunday; it's no time to be threatening
people."

"I'm not fucking around!" he snapped. "Two days, that's
all you get. If you don't have the man and my things back to me by
six p.m. on Tuesday, there will be a price out on your head."

"A price on my head? What are we gangsters now? Henry,
we've been dealing together a long time, I just need you to trust
me."

"I am trusting you. I'm trusting you for two days. After
that I'm taking care of the whole business. I'm waiting for your
call, good-bye!"

I hung up and sighed. Ah, Henry. He was always so

dramatic. Of course I would find Freddy, and I would find Henry's things, but as far as helping Freddy any further, I didn't think I could. The man obviously wasn't satisfied with the depth of his grave and thus decided to dig it a little deeper. Some people couldn't be helped.

So it began. The game was on, and I wanted to please Henry; because even without Freddy supplying me with junk to sell him, I could easily find other sources to keep him supporting me. I searched high and low, called everyone I thought could help. I checked credit card statements, and even hired an investigator with the distinct instruction to find the idiot before six on Tuesday; but Freddy had become a phantom, a shadow, a figment of my imagination. He'd disappeared from the face of the earth.

Tuesday, at six on the money, Henry called.
"And?" he asked.

"Look, Henry. It's going to take a little more time to find him."

"So you don't have him or my property is what you're are saying?"

I decided to take it delicately. The man on the other end was obviously balancing on the sharp edge of insanity.

"Well, no," I said. "But it hasn't been long enough, he's bound to come up–"

"I don't want to hear it!" he declared. "You had your time, and I had my terms. You have failed–now my terms come into play."

"Please, Henry, let's not be unreasonable," I tried saying, but he would have none of it.

"Watch your back!" he spat into the phone. "Your time is up."

I was going to protest again, but he hung up long before I could get another word in. Fair enough, the man was angry. I could understand, but I certainly didn't expect him to follow through on his threat.

Two nights later, while entertaining a couple of ladies in the shower, I heard a bang out in the hall. Not able to ignore it, I left the girls to play with each other while I stepped out into the bedroom. There I stopped and listened intently to the halls beyond for something. Nothing came. I walked to my closet, unlocked the safe, took out my forty-five, and cocked it. I wasn't a violent man by nature, but when threatened I sure as hell was going to shoot. I stepped out into the hall, gentle on my feet, and held my breath while scanning the area. I wasn't absolutely convinced of someone having breached my home, but I wasn't taking a blind chance at it either. The hall was clear. I took careful, calculated steps down the stairs and stopped on the main floor. There was no one in the living room, but when I turned into the kitchen I found a man pointing a gun at me. Surprised, I leveled my weapon to his chest.

"What are you doing in my house?" I demanded.
"Sir, put the weapon down."

"I'll blow your head off! Who are you? What do you want?"

"I'm just a guy," he said, and smiled, but never lowered his weapon. "Just a guy with a job, and I'm afraid I have to–"

I shot him. His chest tore open and a dark plume of sopping gore splattered against the wall behind him. He stumbled backward like a limp marionette and crashed to the floor, dead as a rock. I snorted with wide eyes, suddenly out of breath. I'd only shot the gun once before, and that had only been at a propane tank; this had made a far bigger mess.

I rushed back upstairs and found the girls out of the shower and on my bed. They smiled when I came in and one of them said, "Hey, we need you. This plastic thing is bullshit. We want the real thing."

"Not now," I said, pulling on my hair. "Get out. You girls need to leave."

"What? Why?"
"Didn't you just hear a bang?"

They looked at each other, then back to me.
"No," one of them said. "Although she was straddling my face."

"Never mind," I said. "You need to go. Get your shit together, put some clothes on, and I'll call a car to bring you home."

Confused, rejected, they did as I asked. I called for a car and it showed up only minutes later. Still half-dressed, I pushed them out the door and into the car.

"Yes, yes, it was fun. Thank you. Here's a gift."
I threw about two thousand dollars into the car and shut the door. I then gave the driver five hundred and ensured that none of them had ever been to my house before–correct? Correct; and off they were. Back inside, I packed a bag of clothes and headed for the airport. I didn't even bother with the man in the kitchen; mostly because I had no idea what to do with him. I figured Henry would take care of it in due time. Meanwhile, I chartered a private jet and went straight to Panama.

It was hard to worry in a place like Panama. The sun was brighter there, it seemed. The people were friendly, the culture relaxed, the celebrations abundant. The women were exotic, and I was especially capable, as a foreigner, to keep my room stocked with them for as long as I wanted. For three weeks, I didn't see or hear a thing. Henry, as far as I could tell, hadn't found me. I wondered if he was going to spend the money to track me down. He was sort of a crackpot, but he had never appeared capable of being so hostile. I guessed only time would tell... And then I got my answer.

I was sitting on the patio of a cafe drinking a martini and chatting up an almond-eyed beauty, when I caught sight of something from the corner of my eye. Some guy was taking photos of me–I was sure of it. Instantly, the overwhelming urge to flee burned in my limbs, and I politely excused myself from the gazing beauty for the washroom.

I ran.

I returned to my room, collected my things, and headed back to the airport. I flew to London and stayed for a week before I caught someone else staking me out. I moved again, to Paris, and decided it imprudent to remain in the same place for any more than a few days before moving on. So the adventure began. From France I hit Italy, Germany, Austria, Russia, Japan, and then back across the continent to Spain, down to Africa, West to the Caribbean, and on through South America. I couldn't help but send Henry the occasional post card. At the beginning of this ordeal I was rather annoyed by his self-righteous stupidity, but only a few weeks into the thing I was having the time of my life. I'd tasted the food, the drinks, and the women from nearly every continent in the world– and how fantastic I felt about it all. I saw the attractions, immersed myself in the cultures, and, inevitably, what had begun as a threat had evolved into a blessing.

But even in the thick of my adventure, I couldn't fully get it out of my head. I wondered about Freddy; where was he, and what had he done with his treasures? I was his broker, after all. Perhaps he'd left me for another man, the cheating bastard. I wondered if Henry was still after me. Was he still pouring money into settling a useless quarrel? It wasn't like I had orchestrated the theft myself, but it made little difference in his mind. He was convinced of being an important man, and someone had to pay for the deplorable crimes committed against him. The fool.

Things were quiet for a while, until, on my second night

in Peru, I met an exotic beauty at a dance club and walked her back to my exotic hut on the beach. We were busy exploring each other's proportions on the way, infatuated, distracted, and when we reached the hut, we surprised a man breaking into my room. The girl screamed; I didn't. I punched him in the side of the head and ordered the girl home in an outrageous display of domination. She vanished with a devastated yelp, unnecessarily hysterical, and I turned my attention to the moaning sissy writhing on the ground. I politely invited him in. "Get in here, you motherfucker!" and asked him to sit, but he seemed to prefer lying on the floor. I got in his face.

"Who are you?"
He only moaned.
"Speak! Why were you breaking into my room?"
He moaned again, and it suddenly all made sense. I had broken his jaw when I punched him–the bastard couldn't tell me shit... But he could still nod. He thrashed under my weight like a dying fish, wildly flailing his limbs, his eyes burning with rage. I couldn't risk being overpowered by a rush of adrenaline, so I grabbed him by the chin and squeezed. The reaction was outstanding. He stiffened like a corpse and howled like the wolf pack slut in heat with no wolf dick around for miles.

"Listen to me. Are you listening? Nod. Good. Now, nod to my questions or else I'm going to punch you in the fucking jaw again. Got it? Good. Do you know who I am? Yes? Yes. Were you sent by Henry? Uh huh. That stupid cocksucker. And you were supposed to kill me? Yeah. Well, then... I suppose it's only fair that I kill you. No? Stop howling. Stop it! You hypocritical bastard. All right, fine; I'm not going to kill you. But I will have to break your legs. Yes. No, I don't care about your jaw; I didn't really mean that one. Hey, it's better than getting killed, isn't it? Shut up, you were here to kill me; at least take it like a man, you goddamn pussy."

Fortunately for him, I've never desired a vacation in a foreign prison, so I didn't desire to shoot him with his own gun. Much more pleasantly, I smashed his kneecaps with a cricket bat I'd bought earlier that day; a useful souvenir for once. He shrieked and convulsed with the pain of the first strike; but by the second a deep, peaceful sleep descended on him and he lied comfortably on the floor like an angelic baby with horribly swollen legs. Of course, I hadn't done it out of rage or malice; like everything else I do, I do out of practicality, not emotion. It was time to stop my aimless travels.

The way he was lying on the floor was really quite inconvenient for packing. Limbs splayed out in all directions, his head rolled back, I kept jumping over him back and forth across the room, collecting all of my belongings in the suitcase on the bed.

"This isn't the kind of exercise I was planning for tonight, you inconsiderate bastard," I said to the inanimate body. "I was expecting to hear screaming and moaning, just from a higher pitched voice, is all. I guess what I'm saying is, you totally cock-blocked me tonight, and I don't appreciate it. Have you seen the women around here? Jesus, guy, what's wrong with you? You're a workaholic, that's what. Come to paradise to kill people. For shame, mister. For shame. You're a foreigner. You should be busy sliding your throbbing vein cane into exotic orifices; instead you're here with me, sleeping on duty, wasting your employer's funds, and you've already failed you're whole mission. God, it must suck to be you. You really are a bad person; I hope you know that."

With all of my clothes and knick knacks packed, I took a final look at the fool on the floor. "Well, no harm done. I've been thinking about going home for a while anyway. You know, get my life back in order, my business back on line, my enthusiasm unmarred by paranoia. Of course, I'm going to sodomize your girlfriend before I do any of that; but don't you worry, you big lug, I hear gringos are never lonely in prison around here."

With that, I left the room, and before hailing a cab I managed to pay a young woman to call the police and report an attempted rape in my room. Then, finally, all the pesky formalities over with, I made my way to the airport. Checking in was a breeze seeing as you couldn't forge my forged passport. It was the real thing, aside from the identity, because literally anything is possible if you have money. It's truly pathetic. I sat at the gate for about an hour and amused myself watching travelers rush to and fro; I then boarded the plane, smiling and nodding to anyone who met my eyes.

The guy sitting next to me was a business development manager for a drill bit manufacturer. To him, I was a sales manager for a software company, and we'd even stayed in the same hotel, and of course I'd heard of his company–I was the one who'd sold them the software they used. Incredible coincidences the sort he'd never heard of. Suddenly, we were the best of friends, and he willingly told me all of his secrets as if, somehow, as a stranger, I was safe. He could trust me. It couldn't possibly hurt him.

Hilarious.

To complete the deal, I nearly made him cry when I told him about the time my mother's ex-husband's cousin decapitated my dog on the front lawn as vengeance for the divorce settlement. A few months after that, my mother killed herself, and I was sent to live with my drug addicted uncle who fed me cocaine pancakes for breakfast and meth laced kool-aid for lunch. It was all a very sad, and truly very stupid story, but it didn't matter. He ate it all up, because people are too quick to trust strangers. An extra hour on the flight and the guy would've let me spend the night tremendously expanding his wife's sexual comforts. Ah, yes. Despite numerous examples in the news of people like me lurching across the globe like phantasms in the shadows, leaving havoc in our wakes, making rubble of people's lives, they still falsely believe in some sort of fundamental good in society, an inherent civility based on respect. It never dawns on them that some people are simply born predators, and the thought of morality never crosses their minds as anything other than an advantage, a tool, to decimate unsuspecting prey. This reality, in legal form, is called capitalism; and those predators are called successful.

We exchanged numbers after landing, bid each other good luck in our respected professions, and went our separate ways. I hailed a cab and headed home, though I wasn't planning on spending any appreciable amount of time there. No. It was time for a new strategy. I figured the best thing to do was to get back in the good books with both Henry and Freddy. A feat that wouldn't be easy, to be sure, but it could be done, and I would do it. Henry, most of all, had grossly underestimated the size of my ambitions, and he was about to pay hefty price for it. I was willing to go to extravagant lengths to get what I wanted out of life, and it seemed to me like the solution to my problem required something precisely extravagant. I needed to get organized.

At home, to both my surprise and delight, the body in my kitchen was already gone. I was particularly happy about this, because who wants to have to deal with that shit? The law makes it quite difficult to dispose of a heap of dead cells in some gutter. The blood was still there, however, dark and crusty, but no other evidence. In the bedroom I packed a suitcase with new clothes, a gun, a multitude of legal passports, and I loaded it all in one of my cars and checked into a hotel. Was I in town for the conference? Of course I was. A pass for free food, compliments of the company? Why, thank you. I swear some days I could stand on a sidewalk with my hand out and every moron out there would hand over their lives to me. I had this big, beautiful trust magnet in my head.

My first order of business was to find an inconspicu-ous base of operations. A place where I could hide comfortably, invisible in plain sight, and manipulate my marks like the master puppeteer I was born to be. I would either win, or I would die in the process. I'm kidding, of course I'd win; I'm me.

I didn't want to stay in hotels for long, even under an assumed identity, because Henry had a lot of eyes looking for me, and it was only a matter of time before I was found out. Where could I go? Where could I stay and remain anonymous? It was a question I'd wrestled with since leaving Peru, and one I was still short a viable answer. I could buy a warehouse, a house, an apartment building, but even renting one of those would take an eternity. No, I needed something better, something that would im-mediately allow me to get to work–but what?

I got my answer while taking a walk the morning after my arrival. On the edge of downtown, lining a long and forgotten alley, I came across a sight that seemed to kick me in the head with obvious appeal–a hostel. Yes! Of course, I thought. It was elegantly simple. Here was a place free of identity, filled with a consistent stream of strangers coming and going, and even the building itself was hidden from the sight of most citizens. I wasted no time, and when I walked through the doors, my suspicions were instantly cauterized. It was perfect. I could pay with cash and leave no paper trail. I could mingle with the young travelers of the world and use them to my own ends. And best of all, in my opinion, I was going to have sex with the young desk clerk long before the sun went down. I was on top of the world.

I spent that evening mingling with the other international residents and taking part in an erotically drunken party even I had never seen the likes of. The next morning I woke up next to the desk clerk and some other girl I didn't know or remember. I had a terrible hangover and a vicious compulsion to foul my innards with greasy foods. I went out for breakfast alone and destroyed a plate of eggs, bacon, sausage, hashbrowns, and waffles. The greatest hangover cure known to man. Feeling much better, I labored aim-lessly down the sidewalks, meditating on my next move. I knew where to find Henry, but what of Freddy? I needed to find him. Naturally, he would probably avoid me at all costs, purely out of guilt, but that would not do. Since I was paying for his stupidity, I felt he should also be contributing to the purchase price. Of course, I also half-expected him to be either dead or in prison already, as tends to happen to impulsive people, but I would have to be sure. How? Where? I would need time to figure it out.

Coming out of my introspective daze, I returned to the hostel in high spirits, and found the desk clerk staring at me with palpitating love in her eyes. I gave her a sensuous wink, a sly smile, and passed on to my room–where I found a paper heart cut-out stuck to my door with my fake name on it. I burst out laughing and shook my head. "Well," I said, and read the lovely little poem inside. "Fuck this shit."

It was time to move on.

I moved to a hostel only a couple of blocks away, and as soon as I entered the building I knew I'd found a special place. Being a crooked and infinitely ambitious bastard, my mind raced with the potential business opportunities this place could offer me. First, there was the building itself. It was four stories tall, rectangular, with a terrace on the roof, and a courtyard in the middle of the whole structure. Sixty-four rooms, one hundred and ten beds, twenty-nine toilets, two kitchens, three lounge areas, one games room; and despite its large size, it was practically imperceptible from the street. I could traffic art, drugs, diamonds, whatever I wanted, hidden in plain sight. Yes–I was very impressed with the whole impression. The next day I made inquiries and discovered that the business was privately owned. Five days later, I presented the owner with a very generous purchase offer; and just like that, I had a new place to indulge in my shady business affairs. I got to work.

My dear thief Freddy had to be found. Dead or alive, imprisoned or not, I needed to know before a plan could be put into action. Given that the legal system is a hive of guarded informa-tion, I would need some help to find out. I had the gall to meddle with the authorities, so I did, and two officers quickly fell into my grip. The first was a single mother who could use twenty-thousand dollars in exchange for checking prison registries for Freddy's name. Rather harmless, after all. The second was a father of three, married twenty-two years, who blatantly refused a bribe in exchange for checking arrest reports for Freddy and his two other legal pseudonyms; but he soon accepted the offer in light of the evidence I had of his secret homosexual meeting from two nights before. I tell you, if people weren't so ashamed of who and what they are, my life would be so much more difficult.

Freddy had not yet been arrested, but he was wanted for the cold blooded murder of a good samaritan in a back alley.

The fool. Compulsive people are good for nothing; they just act on the spot and then whine about the consequences. If he'd taken the time to plan a proper murder, he would be free and clear. As it was, he was still roaming the gutters like the sewer rat that he was; and according to the credit card statements I received from the properly motivated officer, it seemed like good old Freddy boy was hunkered down in a shady neighborhood. His exact location was unknown, but it didn't take me long to figure it out. I canvassed the streets and questioned the underground characters, the drug dealers, the thieves, the hustlers, the homeless, and, surely enough, after exhausting the list of suspects, I got my answer from a prostitute. I should have known to ask them first. I found out that the slimy bastard hiding in some shit hole apartment with a junkie whore and three starving dogs, but I didn't want to just show up at his door and scare him away. No–I wanted to surprise him and get him firmly in my claws. It was time to enlist the help of some younger folk bent on adventure.

At the hostel, I observed certain individuals for a several days, trying to pick up on those most open to the proposal I was planning to offer. There were three guys I liked–two Australians and a Frenchman–and I wasted no time in getting them assimilated into my plans. I held identical interviews with each of them.

"What are you plans for your life?"

"I... I don't know. I'm like twenty-two."

"Uh huh. And? Is that too young to know what you want out of life? I was a millionaire by your age."

"No shit–really?"

"Yeah, but that doesn't matter. What I want to know is this–are you planning on staying here for any amount of time?"

"In the country?"

"In this very hostel. My hostel. Would you like to stay?"

"Ah... I mean... I had plans to go–"

"What if I paid you fifty thousand dollars to stay here and work for me?"

"Shit! For real? I mean, I would, but I don't have a visa for–"

"Fuck the visa–this is all cash. Are you ready for your first mission? Here's what we're gonna do..."

With the three boys secured, I put my plan to lure Freddy out into action. It was all very simple. I instructed them to go out into the neighborhood and approach him with a tantalizing offer.

"I want you to ask him to pull a heist with you guys. Say

you've heard of him on the streets, and make sure you flatter him a little. Tell him he's like some infamous thieving legend, or some stupid shit like that, it'll grease up his ego nicely. Of course, being in deep trouble already, he will flat out refuse and try to blow you off. To get around this, I want you guys to act like amateurs; which, of course, you are. So just be yourselves, and as you meet his objections, I want you to talk too much. You know, give away information that you shouldn't be giving away. And one of you will have to be the voice of reason, telling the others that they shouldn't be talking about this in front of this guy. In this way, I want you guys to leak where the heist will take place, which is at this address here, and what you will be stealing, which is... Ah... Let's say some paintings–one of which is a Picasso. That'll give the stupid bastard a boner. Do you understand? Yes? Good. You do well and you'll only end up making more money as time goes on. Now go get him."

Get him they did. They came back reporting that Freddy had acted pretty much as I had expected. He feigned disinterest, refused to carry on the conversation, but every time one would tell the other he shouldn't be talking about this information openly, Freddy's ears perked up. I had the bastard in my palm, and it was time to crush him. Instead of surveilling Freddy, I simply parked in front of the building where the fake heist was supposed to take place two days later. I knew Freddy would come that night, being a compulsive asshole and all. The building was an abandoned warehouse that used to manufacture boat accessories. The boys had told Freddy that it now belonged to a wealthy businessman who used it to hide his greatest collectibles, and like a mindless puppy dog who sees nothing of the dangers around him for want of the juicy slab of meat dangling in his face, the gullible prick behaved as mechanically, and compulsively, and pathetically as I had expected. I watched him pull up in front of the building and cautiously scan his surroundings before getting out of the car. With a smile on my face and a shake of my head, I entered the building on the opposite side and waited for him with my gun cocked. The place was filthy and caked with dust, bird shit, broken glass, and squatter leftovers shoved into the corners. In minutes, I could hear the slow shuffling of Freddy's timid steps. I watched his creeping shadow turn to flesh, a jittering silhouette caught in the grips of frenzied endorphins. I could almost hear his teeth gnashing with the rush of indulging his compulsion. He stopped to listen for threats before entering the room. With my gun leveled to his head, I said, "Hello,

Freddy."

I may as well have fired a shot. His body jerked convulsively, spastically, and he turned in a circle, ducked, and ended the performance face first on the floor. I burst out laughing.

"You're a real tough guy," I said, and stepped out of the shadows so he could see me. He was whimpering something about me not killing him when he finally realized who I was.

"Jesus... Jesus fucking Christ, man! You scared the shit out of me! What the fuck are you doing here?"

"I was waiting for you, you dumb prick."
He stood quickly and dusted himself off, his eyes filled with worry, with guilt, with shame.

"Look," he said. "I'm really sorry about what I did."
"Not yet you're not."

"No, seriously," he pleaded. "I didn't mean to cause any trouble. I just... I was just living in that place, and it was practically a museum; I mean–"

"I've been around the world because of you."
"What? Why?"

"Why? Did you think my friend, Henry, the one whose house you robbed blind after he did you a favor, was just going to let me off the hook for your actions? The bastard is trying to kill me. There were assassins everywhere I went."

"Okay... But look... I can make it–"
"I should kill you right now and be done with it all. I trusted you, Freddy. I actually thought you had a little more brains than that."

"I wanted to find you, but I'm sort of in a bit of trouble right now."

"On multiple fronts," I interjected. "Yes. With the police. With Henry. And with me. You've dug yourself a big old grave, and now look at you, digging it deeper. Coming here to steal when you know so many people are out for your head. Why shouldn't I shoot you here, now? Seems to me I'd be doing you a favor."

"No!" he gasped, and fell prostrating at my feet. "Please. I don't want to die. I feel terrible about what I did to you. If I could take it back, I would. I was being selfish, not thinking of those who actually helped me out when I needed it. I fucked up real bad, and I'll make it up to you. I swear to God, no matter what happens, I'll make it up to you."

He broke down in a convulsive mess of sobs. It was truly pathetic. When I do something, I do it, consequences be damned; but if they do eventually catch up with me, well, I knew of them prior to committing the offense. It's the way of the universe. Sometimes, despite your best efforts, you just lose. You need to be a man about it.

I sighed and shook my head while he moaned at my feet like a child.

"Please. I'll make it up to you. Just don't kill me. I know I deserve it, but I'll do anything you want. Please."

"All right," I said and took a step back. "Quit acting like a bitch and listen to me. Are you listening, Freddy? Good. Now look, I'm not going to kill you."

"You're not?"

"No. It's really not my thing unless it's absolutely necessary. In this case, you're still of some use to me."

"I'll do anything."

"That's a respectable attitude. Now tell me, what do you know of Henry?"

He was a nervous wreck when he spoke, as though all the stress he'd suffered over the last few weeks threatened to blow him up from the inside. He said he didn't know much about Henry, but of all the people chasing him, Henry was feared most. If he was caught, he was dead, and this fear had rendered his life a paranoid exercise in cosmic cowering. Everywhere he went, everything he did, Henry was over his shoulder, behind his back, he was practically the disease riddled whore he was balls deep in every night. It was unbearable, and as much as he wanted to get to the man first, he didn't have enough freedom to get himself organized and gather the information he needed.

"Organize," I said. "I didn't think it part of your lexicon."

"What?"

"Nevermind. Look, I'm going to help you with this."

"You are? But... Why?"

"Why? Because even though you fucked me over, I still hate Henry more. He's trying to kill me, after all, and something needs to be done to teach him a lesson."

"I want to kill the fucker!" Freddy snapped.

"Good, because that's exactly what I want you to do."

He sized me up, searching and finding in my eyes the honesty I was so skilled at faking. He stopped crying and stared pensively at the floor. He knew the cops would eventually get him, but he felt he could deal with prison. An unknown assassin was a greater threat, and if I could help him eliminate that threat, he was more than willing to get his hands dirty.

"I'll put a plan together," I said. "But I need to know you're on board, and I need to be able to reach you at all times."

"Yeah," he agreed vehemently. "Of course. No problem. Anything you need."

"Good. Then give me a day or two and I'll come back to you with a plan. But know this, Freddy. If you try to skip out or I can't get a hold of you when I need to, I will blow your head off. Do you understand?"

"Yes. It's what I deserve. I'm sorry I fucked you over, man. I'll make it up to you."

"This is all I need from you right now. Do we have a deal?"

"Yes. Of course."

There it was. We shook hands and I promised to be in touch shortly with a plan to get rid of Henry once and for all, freeing us both from his unreasonable and undeserved tyranny. He seemed relieved that I'd let him live, though I didn't understand why. If I was him I'd want nothing more than to end my miserable existence. Luckily, I was me, and it was time to get to work. I returned to the hostel and immediately after entering my room, I called Henry. The surprise which I beheld on the other end is difficult to describe. As soon as he realized who was calling, he started offering all sort of flattering compliments. Saying I had awfully big balls; I was so stupid I was genius; I was an asshole of divine proportions; and other such ego stroking words. It's always nice when others acknowledge my qualities.

"You're fucking dead, I hope you know that," Henry spat into the phone.

"Henry, listen," I said. "I've found a way to make it up to you. We can forget all of this ugly business and move on from here. I just want to wipe the slate clean."

"Oh yeah? And how do you think you can do that?"
"I can give you Freddy."

"What?"

"Freddy. I know where he is. I just spoke to him not twenty minutes ago. I know where he is, I know where your stuff is, and I really just want to put an end to all of this. It's really boring, Henry. Aren't you tired of chasing phantoms? I can give you Freddy, and then we can call it even, can't we?"

Nothing.
"Henry? Do we have a deal?"

"Yes," he finally said. "We have a deal. But I'm warning

you–"

"No need," I said. "There are no games here. I like you, Henry, despite our differences, and I never planned for any of this to happen. I want this guy to go down as much as you do. I was trying to help him out of a bad spot, as were you, and look at how he's repaid us. This is serious stuff. Let's get this done together, and then we can move on with our lives."

That evening, not without a little anxiety, I made my way to Henry's palace and faced the man who'd been trying to kill me for the last several weeks. He welcomed me amiably enough. We sat, had a drink, and I commented on a few new pieces of art he'd picked up during my absence. It was all very formal, but that atmosphere didn't last long, for once I began talking about Freddy he was overwhelmed with a wrathful passion. He was full of threats, rage, and determination to delete Freddy's DNA from existence. He grilled me with incessant questions, some I had to sidestep in order to remain in control of the operation, and he demanded that the whole thing be done as quickly as possible. I assured him of it. No time to be wasted. I even had a plan, which he readily accepted with only one contingency: he wanted to kill Freddy himself. So vexed and vindicated he was, he aimed to strangle the bastard with his bare hands. Fair enough, I thought, because although I often act as a puppeteer, I rarely like to place myself in a responsible situation when others are more than willing to do so for me.

"So when are we doing this?" he asked.

"Well," I said. "I met him in an old warehouse where he's stashed all of your things. I figure why not kill two birds with one stone. I'll call him in for a meeting with me, where he'll find you, and after you deal with him your stuff can be carted out and returned to you immediately."

"That sounds good–but when?"

I shrugged my shoulders. "Two nights?"

"Two nights–Wednesday night. What time?"

"Well, I'll have to set it up first, but let's say seven. You show up as early as you need to be ready."

We shook hands, and it seemed like I'd sated his concerns, but he was still bursting at the seams with anxiety. With the deal done, however, he apologized for trying to kill me, and said that he always did like me, but surely I could understand where he was coming from. I said I could, and I did–that was why I was helping him. I told him I was terribly embarrassed about the whole thing, overcome with guilt, and expressed a lot of other weak emo-

tions normal people have to help him drop his guard. We had another drink, and he then gave me a proper tour of his house. It was
a sprawling establishment crammed with a wide array of collectibles, some worthless, some priceless, all of it beautiful. If he ever
wanted to sell some of his collection, or if it was robbed outright...
Ha. I was rotten to the core, a twisted romantic. I complemented
Henry on his taste in art, ignoring his utter ignorance of the subject, and we concluded the tour in his library, where a mish mash
of valuable paintings, ancients statues, and rare books peppered the
room. I eyed the artifacts like a hungry wolf, thanked Henry for his
hospitality and willingness to mend old wounds, and assured him
that our plan would go off like clockwork.

So it was done. I would bring Freddy and Henry's
bloodlust together and let the chips fall where they may. Perhaps,
I thought, I should take bets from those in the hostel. Put your
money on the man you judge best. Only one can live, so don't bet
on the dead one; death is a worthless investment unless you own an
insurance company.

I felt good about my plan, despite the fact that after meeting with Freddy a second time to inform him of my arrangement
with Henry, the whole thing took on a rather annoying turn. My
phone rang incessantly: first Henry, then Freddy, each with their
own concerns, and each expressing the same determination to get
to the other first. It became intolerable. "Yes, Henry. We'll kill him
soon; Yes, Freddy. Relax, it's all about the timing; Henry, please,
just shoot the guy, there's no need to flay a man alive; Freddy–
I know you're angry, but you don't cut off a man's dick. No–it
doesn't matter, Freddy–it's just not something you do."

Children!
Meanwhile, in between dealing with the two rabid dogs, I busied
myself at the hostel. I would need help with a new endeavor I had
in mind. The idea had come to me while I was meeting with Henry.
In addition to the three people I already had at my disposal, I was
in need of three more to drive vans, and two more bodies to assist.
Having no problems finding assistance in the face of exaggerated
compensation, I rented three moving vans, made sure everyone involved was aware of their responsibilities, and I was ready to make
the whole puzzle come together like the beautiful pieces of art I
shamelessly shuffled from crooked hand to crooked hand.

The next morning I called Henry and informed him that
Freddy would be at the warehouse at seven p.m. I also offered him
my services. Once he was done with Freddy, he could call me and I

would be more than willing to assist him in moving his things from the warehouse to his house. Of course, not knowing that his things weren't anywhere near the warehouse, he readily accepted the offer, and even thanked me earnestly for everything I'd done to make things right. I was once again a good name in his books. Fantastic.

I called Freddy and told him the plan. Henry was expecting him at the warehouse at seven. He was expecting to find him alone and off guard. He planned to kill him on sight, so be prepared. Freddy beamed with excitement and thanked me profusely for everything I had done for him. He would make it right–I would see. I assured him of my lack of doubts–by the end of the night, everything would be settled.

At six-thirty, my eight helpers and I crammed into the rented vans and drove across the city. At ten to seven, just as I was sure the meeting between Henry and Freddy was taking place, we pulled up in front of the house and I made a phone call.

"What's your emergency, please?"

"Oh, my God!" I screamed into the phone. "There's been a shootout! Multiple shots fired in a warehouse on 97th and Main. Oh, God! Please hurry!"

I hung up, smiled, and nodded at the others.

"Let's get to work."

We casually strolled from the vans to the house, broke a window, unlocked the doors, and started hauling our lot. Henry simply had too many things to keep locked out of sight. Some people were willing to pay astronomical amounts for large parts of his collection, and I felt a duty to collect those sums as settlement for all the stress he'd put me through over the last few weeks. There were like two nights where I didn't get a full eight hours of rest–someone had to pay for that.

We filled the vans with rare paintings, vases, statues, medieval arms, diamonds, and a whole shit load of various precious stones. It was beautifully done, and the whole operation was over with in a mere thirty minutes. Calmly, we drove back to the hostel and I had my workers empty the vans and lock the contents in the basement. Meanwhile, I got into my car and drove to the warehouse, where I found a manic scene. An entire city block was cut off by emergency personnel. Uniformed bodies ran in every direction; helicopters circled above. I pulled over and walked the sidewalk–and then I saw him–Freddy–being led out of the building in handcuffs, his face and torso covered with blood splatter. Exactly as I had promised Henry–the thing had gone off like clockwork. I watched as they put him in the back of a cruiser and I smiled. It was all over. No longer would I have to worry about either Henry or Freddy. A new chapter in my life had arrived. I was now a legitimate business owner, and I had the potential capital to expand that business all the way across the globe. Henry was right after all; I was so stupid I was a goddamned genius!

Quietly, I returned to my car, drove to the hostel, and retired to my room. I lit a cigarette and stared out the window at the timid street below. I had pulled it all off with an admirable level of deception and betrayal. Henry was dead. Freddy was in prison. And I had come out of it with far more than I could ever have imagined only a week before.

I think it's only fair that I should point out my thought process behind all of this; especially concerning Freddy, whom I truly did like. It's not that I thought he deserved any sort of justice for what he'd done to me. I carried no ill will or feeling against him. On that front I was indifferent, as always. But what I did was necessary, because it was my only insurance policy. If Henry had somehow managed to kill Freddy, who was dumb enough to end up that way even with all the odds in his favor, then at least Henry would have been arrested for his detestable crime, and probably even have faced the death penalty. Plus, Freddy was already fucked. It was only a matter of time before the system ate him up. I only happened to speed up the process for my own ends. At least the socially responsible members of the city could feel better while watching the story on the news. They could feel secure in knowing that one less psycho was on the streets, one less creep was in the shadows, and one less person with a complete disregard for the laws and ethics of our civilized world was removed from their midst.

Ha. Ha.

In the years that followed, there were many changes in my life. The people I had working for me remained loyal, and they became my family, the so-called relationships I'd always longed for. They became my friends, and with them, I was able to expand my business into an international entity that was legal on the surface, and crooked as fuck in the thick of it. It worked well, and I was happy. Before long, I became a sort of legend in the underground, a phantom in the shadows, manipulating society itself through my exploits, and no one was ever the wiser because of it.

My hostel became the place for young travelers looking for a change of pace, or a change of life. I became known as one name, and any time an unsuspecting backpacker made it to my hostel and witnessed my extravagant antics, they would ask someone, "Who is that guy, anyway?" And someone would answer, "That's Spyder. He owns this chain of hostels. He is the greatest man I've ever met."

So a new life began and the legend crept through the gutters of society. Toward the future I forged with a loyal army at my back, and a united dream to conquer the world in my own twisted way. I made untold millions, took care of my new international family, and pushed the bounds of crime with daring capers too bizarre to make any sense of.

Then, one day a man named Richard Knox came through my doors, and his life and mine were thrown into a terrible whirlwind. But I'll let him tell you the story. He's far more dramatic about the whole thing.

Until then, should you find yourself wanting to get rich, get the person of your dreams, or dominate the competition in whatever you choose to take on, I have a small piece of advice for you. The key to unlocking all of your potential lies in two simple words.

Trust me.
You can practice that on your own, or you can always just come and see me. Take the trip of a lifetime. Live a little. Live a lot. Explore your existence, and I will help you achieve your wildest dreams.

Just trust me.

The End

THE HERMIT OF ROSETHORN

Chapter 1

Right Ascension: 05h 55m 10.3053s : Declination: +07° 24' 25.426" Constellation Orion–the mythical Greek hunter. The hermit peers through his telescope and bites his bottom lip. Betelgeuse. He squints his eye automatically and smiles. The red supergiant always has a way of tickling his sense of wonder. He pulls away from the lens, turns to his computer, and enters information into his sky chart. Betelgeuse observed–9:17 p.m.

He turns back to his telescope with a grunt, looks once more at the star, adjusts the focus as best he can, and snaps a photo with his new CCD camera equipped telescope. In seconds, the image appears on his computer screen labeled, Photograph #5

"Beautiful," he says, and sips his coffee. Finished categorizing the image, he turns back to the telescope for a final glimpse before moving on.

Readjustment. Right Ascension: 05h 35m 08.277615s : Declination: +09° 56' 02.9611" He peers through the glass and stares at faint Meissa, the head of the hunter. 9:20 p.m. Photograph #6.

He scrutinizes the image on the computer screen, nods, and files it in its proper folder.

"Now," the hermit says, leaning back in his chair and staring absently at the print of the Deep Field View mounted to his wall. "Time to have a look around."

From Meissa, he aims the lens downward and to the right, to Bellatrix, snaps a photo, then moves down to Mintaka, the edge of Orion's belt. From there he crosses over to the left, photographing Alnilam, and Alnitak, completing the belt, then moving down to Hatsa, to Saiph, and finally back across to the right for a glimpse of the magical Rigel, the triple star system, and the sixth brightest light in the night sky.

Satisfied with the images, he returns to the telescope and focuses on the coordinates, RA 05h 35.4m : DEC -05° 27' and snaps an excellent photo of the Trapezium Cluster. At RA 05h 35m 17.3s : DEC -05° 23' 28" he catches the stunning Orion Nebula, smiles widely at the shot, and decides to finish christening his new telescope with an incredibly detailed photograph of the awe inspiring Horsehead Nebula.

"Best money I've ever spent!" he declares, and squints his eyes while admiring his newest attempt at sophisticating his passion for exploring the great beyond. First, there's the room itself; it's an observatory he's just finished adding to his house, complete with a roof made of removable glass panes that allow him to expose the unobstructed sky in three directions. The structure fills him with a sense of accomplishment, but the real pride of his set up is the brand new CCD monochrome camera, cooled to 45 degrees below ambient temperature, and equipped with filters for building composite digital images on a computer. The best on the market. Unable to stop smiling, he browses through his photos and finishes his cup of coffee. He's been looking at the dark skies for the last twenty-two years as an amateur astronomer, and for the first time he's now able to take composites, save them on a harddrive, and study them with a wide array of digital tools.

Turning back to his computer, he completes his notes in his sky chart, and then opens a text file from his desktop. Sporadically, he's been working on a memoir of sorts, mixing his passion for astronomy with his thoughts and experiences over the years. A wall of text appears on the screen. He stares at the blinking cursor for a moment and allows his vague thoughts to coalesce before rushing his hands to the keyboard.

"These days, I busy myself as an amateur astronomer, surveying the heavens with utter awe. It's my way of staying humble. It fascinates me to try and conceive of the true size of it all, the absolute beauty of space. It is a complex, yet elegant, and graceful thing. It waltzes together at its own ancient speed, never rushing, never slowing, never caring. It is a thing we can look at, go into, explore, and yet, there is no mind capable of truly conceiving of its reality. It's right there, but we can't believe it. It's too much, too big, and far too intimidating to understand. That is the source of my, and many others' passion.

When I point my telescope to the sky in the shade of the sun, I gasp at watching planets near us on their own trajectory, carrying on their own existence. I shudder at the sight of massive stars much too distant to reach in a thousand lifetimes, their masses already past the edge of our abstract capabilities. It's a psychological experience for me, a powerful rush of awe, an absolute reminder of how microscopic not only our planet is, but our entire galaxy. The whole disk is a dimmed half pixel on the map. It fills me with such an intense appreciation of my awareness, of my ability to even recognize the impossible mystery of it all, that I can't help but smile, take in a deep breath, and feel at peace with myself. No matter how small, I'm still a part of this immense system I will never understand. The feeling is as undefinable as..."

What next? He isn't sure, but he knows it'll come to him when the time is right. He's too excited about his new equipment to concentrate on anything else for very long. Stretching in his chair, he waves his arms through the air, stares at his telescope, and nods his head. It's the best equipment he's ever owned, and he feels a compulsion to use it.

He points the things to RA 0h 42m 44s : DEC 41° 16.152' 9" and snaps multiple filtered shots of the great Andromeda Galaxy. He stares at the image and giggles; it's all so impossibly beautiful. Moving on. He moves the lens to coordinates, RA 01h 33m 50.02s : DEC +30° 39' 36.7" and captures a photo of the great pinwheel, the Triangulum Galaxy. His heart rate rises. Incredible technology. From there, he moves over to RA 12h 56m 43.75s : DEC +21° 40' 58" and sights Messier Object 64–The Black Eye Galaxy. He runs through his filters and marvels at the photos that appear on his screen. It's the greatest night of his amateur career.

He labels and categorizes each image as if it's the greatest honor to do so. It's certainly the greatest pleasure, and he hums an aimless tune while going about his duties. He's smiling perpetually, compulsively, and the thought of stopping for the night seems like a bitter shame. Utter nonsense. There's too much up there to explore; too much to gawk and wonder at. Only an arrogant fool could ignore it.

He turns back to his equipment and rubs his hands together.

"Let's see what this thing does with local objects," he says.

Facing East, he captures a photo of Mars and stares at the image on the monitor. Exquisite quality. Iron-red, it sits there like a infallible beacon in the impossible darkness. Satisfied, he raises the lens and catches Venus, glowing blue-white, then nails an enormously colorful shot of Jupiter. He smiles and shakes his head. Why had he waited so long to acquire such fantastic tools for the night sky? From Jupiter, he runs his filters through on Saturn and builds a composite shot of the ringed world and most of its relatively tiny moons.

He glances at the clock on the wall. 11:23 p.m. Time passes too quickly when he's immersed in his passion, he decides. He yawns and stretches once more, and then sets his recently acquired photographs as a slideshow and watches them with waning attention as they go on in a loop.

Time for a break.

From the desk drawer he pulls his pipe and lights the bowl. He inhales, coughs painfully on the exhale, and blows a dense cloud of bluish smoke toward the opened ceiling. His eyes redden and his vision blurs. He's numb, comfortable, and happy that his two plants grew good and potent last year. He has another lungful, then feels his body become one with the chair while he stares at the ongoing slideshow. They're the most beautiful, most detailed, most fascinating images he's ever been able to take.

Another lungful of the pipe brings about a harsh coughing fit, and he suddenly craves liquid for his dry mouth; but when he turns from his computer with an amused grimace on his face, he elbows the telescope and throws his coordinates out of whack.

"Shit," he says, and then smiles. Nothing damaged. "Well, one for good luck, I suppose."

He snaps a picture and the image interrupts the slideshow when it appears on the screen. It's pinpricked with indefinable lights interrupting the eternal darkness. He brings his face closer to the screen and stares. Impossible. How can such a thing be real? How can the universe exist? All these worlds, these objects, these unfathomable distances–how can it be real? Thousands of years of the same question; thousands of years without an inkling of an answer. The malignant, incessant conscious affliction.

He stops at the washroom on his way to the kitchen, then fills a tall glass with orange juice and returns to the office. He comes in humming a tune, feeling comfortable, and relaxed. He drops himself into the chair and spins around once with a stupid smile on his face. He then stops, has a drink of juice, and stares at the blind photo he took. Billions of lights. Trillions. Probably more, there's no way to ever tell for sure. Aliens worlds. Distant systems. Unexplainable mysteri...

"Wait," he says, interrupting his train of thought. He squints his eyes and leans in closer to the monitor. "What is that?"

Near the bottom right of the photograph, in amongst the ridiculous amount of stars, and nebulas, and galaxies, there is a peculiar dot that catches his attention. He can't make sense of it.

"Where is this?"

He turns to the telescope, buries his eye into the eyepiece, snaps another photo, and then turns back to the monitor. The pale dot is still there, but there is something wrong with it; as far as he knows, as surely as his experience has taught him over the years, that thing should not be there.

He grabs a pad of paper and a pen and writes down the dot's approximate location. Right Ascension: 06h 45m 23.8796s : Declination: 06° 17' 24" and then stares at it through the lens once more.

He's baffled.

It's not a star, nor a planet, nor a supernova, nor anything he seems to be able to pull from his wealth of knowledge. It appears to be pulsating, causing him to shake his head and frown. At his monitor, he pulls up both images and snorts in disbelief. It's not exactly in the same location from one photograph to the other. He looks to the clock on the wall. It's only been, what, a little more than thirty minutes? At most. How fast can something like that move? It must be fairly local.

The confusion causes drastic excitement to stir within him. As an amateur astronomer, any astronomer, the discovery of something previously unknown is the holy grail of the passion. Of course, the possibility of that happening in modern times are as astronomical as space itself, but as with all things in the universe, regardless of statistics, it does happen.

Isolating the dot on the computer screen, he blows up the image and scrunches up his face. It makes no sense to him, so he checks the online astronomy community to see if anyone else has noticed an anomaly near his coordinates. Nothing. He sighs, leans back in his chair, and lets his mind reel. Is this real, or is it a manufacturer's defect? Is he too stoned? Is he dreaming?

He runs a shaky hand through his hair and looks out into space again. It's still there, pulsating rapidly, but not like a star would, or should. Its color isn't consistent. It continues to shift hues, completely out of sync with the pulsations, turning from white, to whitish blue, whitish yellow, whitish red, and then green, and then back again. At least it seems to have some sort of pattern. Patterns are always good; they can be measured.

He snaps multiple images of the mysterious object, running through all of his filters, and merges them together on the computer. To him, it appears far away; then again, it could be close, and small. He can't decide on it either way, and shies away from rushing to post the images online. It could give his name a little respectability in the scientific community as equally as it could make him look like a fool. He decides to survey it first, at least for another night, and see what happens.

He's not sure what to do. Perhaps he should take a break, maybe try to sleep, but he's filled with anxiety. He's been trying to quit for the last two weeks, but he now feels like he no longer has a choice; he needs a cigarette!

He pulls a pack and an ashtray from the bottom drawer of his desk. The cigarettes are stale and dry, but they'll do. He lights up and guiltily savors the first drag like it's a shot of heroin. He blows a thick cloud to the voided ceiling and chews on the tip of his thumb, staring distantly at the image on the screen.

He feels weird–antsy–and a little bit nauseated. Razor winged butterflies in his stomach. He crushes the cigarette in the ashtray and stands from the chair, only to sit back down again and stare compulsively at the image. He isn't going to get any sleep.

Hunchbacked over the telescope, he watches the tiny light. He can't see it moving by eye, but the photographs suggest otherwise. He decides that he will have to stay up all night photographing at intervals and triple checking the coordinates.

When the sun rises in the morning, he's dizzy with exhaustion and even has impossible results to consider, but before he can do anything further he falls asleep with his face flattened against the desk.

Chapter 2

Doorbell. It wakes him with a jolt and nearly sends him crashing to the floor. He squints and stares about the room. The clock says 1:23 p.m. With a terrible taste in his mouth, he props his head up and listens, waiting to see if the sound is real or if it had come to him in a dream.

Again the doorbell.

"Argh, what now?" he says, and sorely stands from his chair with a frustrated grunt. He isn't expecting visitors. He rarely receives them, period. People leave him alone, and he them. It's a sound arrangement in his mind.

He clears his throat and leaves the room, suspicious of who may be standing on his stoop. At the door, he stares through the peep hole at two bodies, one male, one female, identities unknown. He sighs and clears the crust from the corners of his eyes before opening the door.

He stares at the smiling faces, not returning the smile. "Can I help you?" he asks.

"Hello, sir," the female says. "We're wondering if you have a few minutes to listen to the words of the Lord today."

The hermit frowns, shrugs his shoulders, and says, "Of course. Is he here now?"

The female smiles and drives her eyes to her feet. "Well, not directly from him, sir, but he gave us all his words. It's our mission in this world to make sure that everyone has heard them, for they are important."

"I see," he says, and eyeballs the male with suspicion. "Important to whom? To him, or to you?"

"Well, to all of us, sir," the male responds. "Aren't you concerned with why you are here on earth?"

The hermit wipes his mouth with the back of his hand. "Not particularly," he says. "It's too small an issue."

Perplexed, the male and female frown and stare at the hermit, mouths agape.

"Well... I mean... I'm sorry," the female's voice trembles. "If I may ask, sir, what do you think happens after you die?"

"I've not the slightest clue," the hermit says. "I imagine it will be the same as before I was born. Timeless. Unconscious. Non-existent."

"But..." the male interjects. "Are you not afraid of going to hell for not leading a righteous life?"

"Not in the least. I'm not afraid of, nor concerned with death or its repercussions. Everything dies. There's no tragedy to it. The tragedy is fearing the inevitable. Whatever happens after death, happens, but I'm here now, alive, living; I think I should treasure that as I see fit, you know. It's one shot, and it's quick."

"Are you an atheist then?"

The hermit shrugs his shoulders and purses his lips.

"I suppose... I mean... I just never think about it. I don't feel the need for spirituality in my life. I'm happy, and if I were to die tonight, I would die satisfied. I'm not sure what else I can tell you. I don't feel the need to add anything to my life."

The female dances awkwardly in place and glances at the male like a wounded animal. The male shakes his head and stares at the ground, trying to work out the words, but coming up with nothing more than, "Well, I'm sorry you feel that way."

"There's nothing to be sorry about," the hermit says. "I don't apologize for who I am; I accept it. It's both liberating and solidifying."

The two bodies nod and stand with defeated postures. "But I wish you good luck on your adventures," the hermit continues. "And I hope you find whatever it is you're looking for. Good day."

Without another word, he shuts the door and finds himself craving another cigarette while watching the jaded visitors waddle down the length of his drive.

"People..." he says. "I'll never understand."

In the office, he lights a cigarette and stares at the photographs of the unknown object as if in a trance. The dot is right in the middle of the constellations Orion, Monoceros, Canis Minor, and Gemini, but he can't find past evidence of the object, and it doesn't have the typical characteristics of an asteroid. Searching online reveals nothing. It seems no one else caught a glimpse of the mystery.

He feels nervous and excited, and his arms and legs are racked with tension. He stares at the screen, his thoughts fractured and chaotic, his mind tired. He yawns and looks at the clock. 1:57 p.m. The sun won't set until about 8:00 p.m. Till then, he decides to try and get a few extra hours of sleep.

It's an arduous ordeal. For three hours he tosses, and turns, and passes in and out of consciousness before finally getting up in a calm but pensive mood. Wanting to clear his mind, he decides to add a few paragraphs to his memoir before the glare of the sun leaves the atmosphere and allows him a direct view of the unknown.

"I live on the outskirts of a town called Rosethorn. It's a small and quiet place, out of the way, and nearly forgotten, which is why I chose it. Not only does it allow me an unobstructed view of the night sky, it also suits my personality quite well. Like the town, I too am a small and quiet person, out of the way, and nearly forgotten; but there's nothing bitter or hostile about it, it's just the way I prefer my life. I don't hate people, I just don't understand them, and it seems to go both ways.

I'm quite like my passions, in fact. During the day, I may as well be hidden behind the glare of an atmosphere; at night, I may as well be one of those distant lights staring back at the earth, watching events unfold, not really understanding the social machinations of the alien world.

People often assume I'm sad because I prefer not to participate in society. Some assume I'm angry, evil, or just plain crazy, but I'm none of the above. To these people, I'm like the night sky. They know I'm there, but they hardly ever lay eyes on me. I'm a distant and mysterious world. People wonder what I'm doing, what I'm thinking, and why I like to be alone, but none of them ever actually ask me. They assume and gossip and accuse, and it's just another aspect of society I do not understand. Surely all the baseless conjectures about other people leaves the conspirators feeling exhausted, fruitless, and frustrated, but I know nothing of it. Boredom seems to be a potent driver of malice, and all I see are people mistaking distraction for happiness, and hostility for passion.

Personally, I prefer stars to people. The universe to the world. The ruthless expanse of space is enough to fizzle out the most hardened human ego and reduce a god to a humble spec of dust. That's what I understand; this immense, symbiotic system we are all a part of. It makes sense to me, but it seems to be a difficult subject to convey to the average citizen. Some say the universe is creepy. The size of it scares them. The reality of our true size is too devastating to think about. There needs to be a reason for it all. None of that makes any sense to me. The universe is a fantastically baffling thing. It's ancient, diverse, and absolutely impossible; yet there it is, and here we are. Despite our penchant for illusions of grandeur, there are certain questions that have no concrete answers; for all we know, we're not even asking the right questions.

It seems to me like there are too many stars and planets out there for any of us to take ourselves seriously. There are too many for us to be alone, or possibly even unique...'

He reviews the paragraphs and sighs, unsure if he'll use them, but it's an issue he'll deal with later on. Outside, dusk is creeping through the sky, and he busies himself with his equipment. When the shades fade dark enough to expose the sparkling lights beyond, he points his telescope with electric excitement to coordinates: RA 06h 45m 23s : DEC 06° 17' 24" and squints his eye into the lens.

Nothing.

There is nothing unusual.

"Ah... Come on," he says, and pulls away shaking his head.

He tries again.

Nothing.

Frustrated, he turns to his desk and double checks the coordinates. They are correct. He stares at the images on the screen. The thing should be there, or at the very least, it should be close. Back at the telescope, he sees Orion, Monoceros, Canis Minor, and Gemini up at the top, but all objects there belong. There isn't a trace of what he'd seen last night.

"How can that be?" he says, and shakes his head. "Where could it have gone?"

He decides to scan the sky blindly, slowly dragging the lens to the right, past Monoceros, and Canis Minor, and then back to the left, past Orion... Nothing.

"Son of a bitch!" he snarls, and pulls up last night's images on the screen with a dejected heart. There it is, right in the middle of the same constellations he's looking at, but it's no longer visible. What could it have been? What could move that quickly?

He scans aimlessly in the same general area, looking for dots that don't belong. According to the differing coordinates of his photographs, he calculates the thing should be moving through space at about eighteen thousand kilometers per hour, placing it somewhere near Monoceros, but it isn't there.

"Damn it!" he says. "My one chance at discovering something and I lose it! Just great!"

Frustrated, irritated, he decides to point the glass farther past Monoceros, toward Hydra, but before he can get a decent view, a violent explosion blows out the windows of his office and hurls him brutally against the back wall.

Darkness.

Chapter 3

Reality returns to him like a thickening fog, and muffled groans follow twitching limbs as consciousness coalesces. It feels like his head's been split open with an axe, and a bolt of panic rips through him when he feels the back of his skull and sees blood on his hand. Dizzy and disoriented, he shakes his head and tries to make sense of the situation. The room is destroyed. The furniture is torn and mangled. The telescope is shattered on the floor.

"What the hell?" he whimpers, and shifts his weight over jagged shards of glass. He can't believe he wasn't ripped apart like everything else, despite the sufficient damage he's suffered. He finds the clock amid the carnage–it reads 11:23 p.m. He figures he's been out about two hours.

He rubs his face with a shaky hand and winces in pain. It feels like it's been shredded, burned, and his body feels sluggish and weak. Outside, he sees yellow and orange flashes of light dancing against the dark sky, and he's suddenly aware that the house is shaking. Vibrating. He hears a steady, thundering roar, but he can't place the sound.

Using his desk for support, he climbs to his feet with ebbing equilibrium and stands staring at a shocking sight. The forest behind the house is ablaze. The flames lick the dark heavens with a ferocious roar, and a convoy of emergency vehicles are parked chaotically in the field where professionals scurry like ants through the strobing madness. An ill feeling creeps through him and his mind reels with questions. What could have caused such a huge explosion? A bomb? An airplane? His limbs tremble, and he's still dizzy, but he's filled with the urge to find out what happened. He charges through the mess and runs toward the carnage. It's a three hundred meter dash through the field to the scene, and the dense hay quickly tire his legs, but he tears toward his destination with an inexplicable, irrational compulsion. Out of breath, his eyes fill with tears, and he fights with himself to make it just a little–

He faceplants the ground and hot pain spreads through his face. Writhing, he fights to catch a breath and continue on with his mission. In little time, he's back to his feet and looking at what he'd tripped on. At first he thinks it's nothing more than an unruly mound of earth, but a moment later, he swears he can see appendages. He squints his eyes and leans forward, too timid to approach the thing just yet. He thinks it's just a mound, but then changes his mind again; it's definitely something with limbs. Cautiously, he scans his surroundings before kneeling beside it, astonished. Gasping in disbelief, his heart begins pounding heavily. He doesn't know what to think, or do. He looks to the fire, then back to the shadow on the ground, and suffers a mess of emotions ranging from elation to fear. He glances at the fire once more and watches panicked people rushing in aimless directions to contain the disaster.

No one knows, he thinks.

No one knows.

Chapter 4

Staring in the mirror, he drags a gentle finger over the flesh and winces whenever he catches the invisible tips of hay slivers. The flying glass from the explosion cut him deeply in some places, especially under his lip, and on his forehead, but the hay is what hurts most. It has scraped areas left untouched by the glass and left him looking like a giant scab with blinking eyes and stern lips. He leans in closer to the mirror and cocks his head to accentuate the light. His eyes look tired, and dreary, and his forehead is still seeping blood. No matter, at least the pain is gone from his head. It's only surface pain now.

He brushes his teeth with great care, gargles mouthwash, and dances in pain when a drop of the alcoholic antiseptic breaches his lips and runs down his chin. He spits out the concoction and stares into the mirror again. He still can't make much sense of what happened last night, but it no longer matters. His damaged house, his equipment, and his face are minimized in his mind–he has something incredible in his possession.

From the bathroom, he walks to the kitchen and pours himself a cup of coffee, and then heads to the office. A disaster. There is shattered glass, melted plastic, and splintered wood everywhere. He stares at the devastated telescope on the floor and sighs. He barely got two days out of the thing. Through the unobstructed frames in the wall, he sees a charred and decimated forest. The flames moved to the east over night and the convoy of emergency personnel ran off after it. Thin, light columns of smoke still rise from the charred remains, but the flames are extinguished. He sighs, has a drink of coffee, and drags his eyes across the disaster of his workspace. He spots his pack of cigarettes hiding under a pile of papers, and decides to light one.

"What the hell," he says. "I should have died. Look at this place. A cigarette isn't unreasonable, is it?"

He takes in the first drag with his eyes closed, savoring the filthy delicacy, and on the exhale he feels a slight tingle spread through his arms–the drug. Expelling another cloud, he rifles through his desk drawers looking for something specific. In the bottom right drawer he finds a video camera, and smiles. Fumbling with the device, he leaves the office, reaches the stairwell to the basement, and heads down calmly, quietly, turning on the light at the bottom. He crushes the cigarette under his boot and pads across the concrete floor to the cold cellar. Carefully, he turns the knob, listens, pulls on the heavy steel door, enters the small room with numb, trembling limbs, and shuts the door behind him.

He slides the power button on the camcorder and turns the lens on himself.

"Last night, something incredible happened. I was searching the heavens with my telescope for an unidentified object I'd photographed the night before in the Monoceres region. I couldn't find it anywhere, but while I was searching, a sudden, unexpected explosion violently rocked my house and knocked me unconscious for about two hours. When I woke up, the woods behind my house were on fire and an army of emergency personnel were working frantically to extinguish the blaze. Um... Anyway... I'm not exactly sure why, I was pretty disoriented at the time, but like a mindless moth I ran toward the fire with this indescribable urge to reach it. It was so overwhelming and powerful that I don't even remember thinking anything in particular. I just had to get there. On my way, however, I tripped over something that sent me face first to the ground. I thought it was a mound of earth at first, but when I inspected the shadow closer, I found... Well... Just look!"

He turns the camera and captures something unimaginable.

"Look at this!" he exclaims. "How can this be real? How can it possibly be here? It's absolutely mind blowing."

On the wooden bench pushed up against the wall, the camera records the image of a body–the body–upon which he'd tripped.

"Amazing!" he says, and places the camera on a shelf so that both he and the body are framed in the shot. He stands next to it, smiling, and shakes the tension out of his arms.

"Now," he says to the camera. "I will measure the body and record its features." He grabs a measuring tape from a shelf below where the camera sits. "First off, I'm unsure whether this being is still alive or not. I doesn't seem to be breathing, but it may be surviving through some process we are unaware of. At this point, it does not appear to have died, but I have no way of qualifying that." He pulls out the tape and stretches it along the length of the body. "Okay, the body is exactly one point four meters in length. It is... Seventy centimeters in girth around the chest, and... fifty-nine centimeters around the waist. It appears to walk, or to have walked, on two legs." Returning the tape to the shelf, he picks up the camera and brings it over the body.

"As you can see, it has a large, almond shaped head, with

tiny leaf-like ears on either side, not unlike our own, but not quite the same, either. The eyes are rather small, but concentrated, and set in a very similar way to our own. Even unconscious, or dead, it still appears quite intelligent. It has no protruding nose like ours, but it does have two tiny orifices set just below the eyes on either side of the face. The mouth is similar to our own, and it does appear to have carnivorous teeth." He steps back and frames the whole body into the shot once again. "Its skin is warm, and appears scaly, but it feels perfectly smooth and firm to the touch. It's gray-ish in color, but almost luminous, perhaps even translucent for the first few layers of skin, covering deeper scales that seem to act like inner armor. It shines silver down here in the glare of the exposed light bulb. As you can see, it has arms similar to humans, only longer and far inferior in girth. The hands are about the same size as an adult human man, except there are six fingers on each, and each digit is webbed to the next about halfway up, ending at the first of three knuckles. Its legs are..." He returns the camera to the shelf and steps back into the shot with his measuring tape, bending over the thing. "Its legs are sixty-five centimeters in length, skinny, and with forward facing knees like our own, but it has these large, fanned out feet, again with six partially webbed digits. The chest is devoid of features, no nipples or navel, although there is a barely noticeable seam running the vertical length of its torso. And... Wait... Okay, under the arms, just below the armpits, are what look like nipples, three on each side, and set in a triangular pattern. Um... It also appears to have genitals in the same general area as humans; this particular case looks like a vagina, but set sideways, and to be honest, calling it either male or female at this point is an unfounded guess. It could be anything. Also, if I tip it over slightly, on its back, slightly higher than the human version, is what looks like an anus. Ah... I haven't weighed it, but from carrying it in my arms I would guess that it weighs about forty kilograms. It also has a distinct scent, but it's like nothing I've smelled before. It's not foul, nor is it sweet. It reminds me of lemon grass, maybe, with a touch of nutmeg? I don't know, I can't be sure."

He leans over the torso and takes in a whiff of air. No, he can't place the smell, but it seems oddly familiar despite being completely alien. He leans in closer to the head once more and stares intently at the perplexing black eyes, when he's startled to the ground in sheer terror.

Doorbell.

"Son of a bitch!" he hisses, but doesn't move immediately. "Scared the shit out of me."

He stares at the body from the floor with his back flattened against the wall. It doesn't stir. It doesn't look like its breathing, but it still doesn't look dead in any way. As alien as it is, it's still alive.

The doorbell rings again and his whole body cringes. "Damn it!" he snaps. "Who the hell is this now, someone who wants to talk to me about the good word of the tooth fairy?"

He doesn't want to leave, and just as he decides to ignore the visitor, the bell tolls once more. Shaking his head, he sighs, stares at the body, and licks his lips in indecision. It would only take two minutes, but they would be–

Again with the doorbell.

"What the fuck?" he snarls, and angrily stomps out of the room. He shuts the door and makes sure it's securely latched before sprinting up the stairs, ready to exact verbal repercussions on the uninvited, unwelcome, unexpected goddamn idiot who decided to–

It's a cop. His chest suddenly feels heavy, and he dances in place with his eye buried in the peep hole. The officer rings the bell again, and then checks his flanks and stares expectantly at the door. Reluctantly, the hermit turns the locks and opens the door.

"Yes, officer?" he says.

The cop frowns and cocks his head to the side like a confused puppy. "Sir, can I ask what happened to your face?"

His face. He'd forgotten about it. It looks like he's taken a buck shot blast and survived. He stares at the uniform before him, his mind completely blank.

"Sir? Are you all right? Were you home last night?"

"Yes," the hermit suddenly snaps to attention. "Yes, I'm fine, thank you. I was home last night, yes. The ah... the explosion blew out my windows in the office and cut me up."

"Can you tell me what you saw, sir? We're collecting statements from around town so we can piece together what happened."

"Was it an asteroid?"

"I'm sorry, I'm not at liberty to comment at this time, sir, but your statement will be useful in our investigation."

The hermit tongues his teeth and stares at the officer. "Yeah, all right. I was home taking photographs of stars when my windows blew in and knocked me unconscious. When I woke up the whole forest was on fire, and my head felt like an axe had gone through it. That's about it; just been taking care of these cuts since."

"So you didn't see anything fall from the sky? Anything strange going on in space?"

The hermit frowns.

"No. I didn't see anything. It totally got me by surprise; and everything in space is strange."

The constable nods and scribbles a few lines in his report. The hermit stands uneasily, nervous.

"Do you have insurance on your home, sir?"

"Of course."

"Have you called them yet?"

"Not just yet, no. I'm getting my papers in order."

"All right, well, I recommend you call them as soon as possible. Is there anything else you would like to add to your statement? Your insurance company will be asking for this report."

The hermit purses his lips and stares at the ground.

"Nope," he says. "That's about it. That's all I know."

"Fair enough, could you print and sign your name at the bottom here please?" the officer says and hands the pad over. After the signature, the constable rips a carbon copy from his book and hands it to the hermit. "Here's your copy, sir. I thank you very much for your help, and have a good day."

"No problem," the hermit says and nods before shutting the door and watching the cop get into his car and drive away.

He sighs and mechanically brings his hand up to rub his face, and then curses viciously as if a thousand electric needles in his skin had been turned on. He shakes his head and forgets about it, his mind once again consumed with what's hidden in the basement.

The being down there could mean things he's never imagined before. Even if it is dead, the evidence is clear. It's magnificent proof of the extended complexity, grace, and variation to be found in the universe. It's proof that mankind isn't as important as people like to think; it isn't unique or special in any way, in fact. That being meant truth. It meant knowledge, and understanding, and enlightenment. Millions of questions run through his mind. What if it's still alive? How would it react if it woke up? Would it be peaceful, hostile, or just plain scared? Wouldn't anyone else be terrified? He frowns when he realizes he's still standing in the foyer and staring at the floor.

His mind races incoherently, and he decides that another cigarette is in good order. The last twelve hours of his life have been testing, frightening, and quite baffling. He doesn't know what he'll do with the body downstairs, but he feels like he should be cautious. Some people would probably want to keep it hidden. Others would want to destroy it. And yet others would want to cage it and charge people to see it. Others would certainly want to worship it. Study it. Torture it. Treat it like a sub-animal despite the very likely possibility that it's far more advanced than all of the primitive apes on earth poking and prodding it with their primitive technology. Yes, he will have to take care with his decisions, and be meticulous in recording all of the information he can gather about it. Most importantly, though, he will have to keep it secret for as long as possible; he will need to protect it.

Leaving the foyer, he returns to the office, places the police report on the desk and trades it for the pack of cigarettes. Inside, he counts only five tobacco sticks and feels a sudden panic. He's been doing well at quitting the nasty habit, but what's happened to him is unprecedented–he will need more.

He lights a cigarette and stares at the mess of the room, the broken glass, the shattered equipment, but none of it feels pressing, or even discouraging. Downstairs, he has everything he needs. Wonder, amazement, power. Of all the people on earth, he feels the luckiest to have ever lived. After spending long years staring at the distant heavens, longing for a single discovery he can call his own, the damn thing falls right into his backyard. He chuckles. As chaotic as it all seems, how can anyone deny that statistics have a venerable sense of humor?

Inhaling his last drag, he crushes the butt in the ashtray and begins feeling antsy. He should check on the mystery in the basement and find out as much about it as he can before... Before what? Before something happens. Before it wakes up, or before he's found out. It's his discovery, and he will be taking credit for it, regardless of what happens. Walking through the suspended cloud of smoke, he leaves the office and walks back to the cellar door.

He listens, pulls on the door, listens once more, and then turns on the light. Inside, the thing doesn't stir. The room is quiet. The camera is still recording.

He pokes his head into the lens' frame and smiles. "Well, I guess I'll have to edit this video. Two visitors in two days, my life truly is being thrown into a whirlwind of madness." He clears his throat and swallows a slab of anxiety over his adam's apple. He still can't believe what he's looking at. "Ah... So I don't remember where we were before the interruption, but I'm just looking at this thing now, and it seems to be changing shades. It's getting slightly darker. I don't know if that's a good thing or not. I suppose only time will tell. The smell hasn't changed. Also, I notice that the body is completely devoid of hair, and... Yes, unbelievably, it is still warm, which makes me think that it is still alive and may even wake up eventually. Again, I'm not sure if that's a good thing, or what I should do if it does, but I suppose only–"

Doorbell.

The hermit stares at the ceiling, completely dumbfounded. Never in his life had three people shown up unannounced, but now that he has a secret to keep, to protect, a goddamn parade of prying strangers are making the rounds. It's ridiculous, and plainly–

The bell.

"Come on, goddamn it!" he snaps, and his face flushes. Out of the room again, he locks the door, trots across the concrete floor, sprints up the stairs, and enters the foyer with balled fists. His mind races with thoughts laced with rage, worry, paranoia. He peeks through the peep hole and sees a man staring dumbly around himself, waiting for someone to answer his call.

"Who the hell is this now?" he hisses, and opens the door.

"Hello, sir. How are you today?" the man says.

"I'm fine, thank you," the hermit replies curtly. "Is there something you need?"

The man smiles widely, fakely, further irritating the hermit.

"Actually," the man says. "I'm just going around the neighborhood informing people of their options for the repair of the damages sustained by last night's explosion. Has your home been damaged at all, sir?"

"What?" the hermit says, and frowns gravely. "What is it you want from me, exactly?"

The man chuckles and seems uncomfortable, but he doesn't lose his composure.

"I sell windows," he says. "The company I work for also takes care of the installation and maintenance if that's what you need. We are fully certified to accept insurance work, and–"

"No," the hermit interrupts him. "I'm not interested." The man's request is so far removed from his state of mind that it fills him with an overwhelming passion for unwarranted rage.

"But, sir, windows are very expensive if paying out of pocket. And if you so choose to–"

"Get off of my property," the hermit snaps. "I didn't ask

to see you."

"Hey, man, I'm just doing my job," the man says in defense. "I didn't mean to bother you in any way."

With that, the hermit slams the door in the man's face. Enraged, he heads back to the office and lights another cigarette. He can't believe it. In the basement is the greatest discovery ever made, and it seems to be attracting every fool out of the woodwork. He paces through the mess of the office and runs a hand through his hair. His face hurts; the cuts are warm and itchy. He wants to return downstairs and document the discovery, but his emotions are standing in the way of doing it calmly and meticulously. He sighs and looks at his computer. Amazingly, the machine has survived the disaster. He sits down and types out his thoughts in an effort to soothe his mind.

'The thing is, if this thing does wake up, I'll be facing a tremendous amount of challenges. There are so many things to consider. Communication, for one. Intelligence, for another. There isn't really much hope for communication, I think, because the considerations go beyond linguistics. On earth, language is a surmountable barrier, and communication is always possible regardless of the spoken words because our concepts are all the same. If you're at home and someone knocks at the door, whether you speak French, English, German, Spanish, Russian, etc..., is inconsequential. In all of those languages, you can communicate to someone else, "Hey, come to the door, we have a visitor." But what if there is no concept of a door, or a home, or a friend? How is communication possible then?

And what about its intelligence level? It looks so smart, to the point of creeping me out. It's small, compact even, but it seems so powerful and dominating. It might learn our languages with ease, but what does that mean for us? We are intelligent, but nowhere nearly as intelligent as we like to think. We are primitive compared to this thing, insects with greater egos than brains. What if it has no ego and it's all brains? Did it come here on purpose? From where?

And even beyond all of that, it's small in stature, but just from feeling it's body, I get the impression that it has far more strength than a human is endowed with. In fact, judging from the strange biology, I wouldn't be surprised to find that this being is some sort of warrior. The scales under its skin look like armor. It's eyes look determined, and ruthless. I don't know... I don't know anything right now, I'm just guessing, but I can't get it out of my head. I can't decide what to do. Everything I know is useless to me at the moment. I am both excited and terrified. Perhaps I'm taking on something that is far more powerful than I realize. Maybe I'm making a mistake. Everything is a maybe...'

He's forgotten his cigarette in the ashtray and he groans miserably when he notices. The compulsion to pollute himself is unsatisfied. He grabs the pack and stares at the cigarettes, biting his bottom lip in indecision. He lights another one and swivels his chair to stare at the destroyed forest. He wonders if they found the remnants of a ship. A fully intact one? How far away is the impact site? From his vantage point, he can't see anything but jagged timbers and charred destruction. There is no mound, no crater, no evidence of a crash. If that's the case, then what caused the explosion, and where did the body lying in the cellar come from?

He puffs on his cigarette and stares absently at the remains of the forest, pondering on what the body in his basement means not only to himself, but to the world. It is the paramount of all discoveries, one so unbelievable that even with hard proof, many will never believe it. They will cry hoax, call him a hack, and possibly even the devil. But those people don't matter. The scientific community is the only one he cares about. Will they take him seriously? If they don't, then the body is insignificant; but if they do, what will their reaction be? Will the scientists of the world be in favor of sharing the information with the public, or will secret government officials seize and destroy the thing before anyone can know of it and cast him out as a crackpot? Every possibility is filled with infinite variables.

He takes another drag and exhales the smoke slowly. "What do I do now?" he says.

Chapter 5

He shifts the transmission into park and frowns at the building. Joe's is the name of the only convenience store in Rosethorn. Aside from it, there is one restaurant in a perpetual cycle of bankruptcy and re-opening, one small bank, and a single grocery/hardware/supply store. Haircuts are performed in people's homes. Shopping is done on the internet. The old church is the main point of convergence for the town's folks. A place to gather, pray, and then stand outside in the parking lot and gossip about other residents. He normally tries to avoid all of these, but a gnawing compulsion has coerced him out of his house and into the lot of Joe's convenience store.

Stepping out of the car, he glances around quickly and hurries his steps. He wants to buy cigarettes and then make a straight line home. There are two other cars in the lot aside from his own, and it brings him silent relief. With his head down in an attempt to hide his damaged face, he walks through the door and avoids the proprietor's casual glance. Standing in front of the counter, a tall, thick wall of potato chips behind him, he avoids eye contact and asks for four packs of cigarettes. The proprietor knows who he is, and he knows the hermit prefers silence over conversation, so he obliges politely as a matter of principle. Everyone is allowed the choice of their choices.

The proprietor reaches his hand into the bulkhead above the counter and fetches the hermit his order, but before the transaction can be completed, the hermit hears a coarse voice belch out from behind him.

"Well, Jesus Christ. How're you doing there, good fellow?"

He knows who it is; it's his nearest neighbor. He's a tall, fat, greasy, smelly man with degenerated black teeth and gums that produce a noxious gas potent enough to be used in warfare. Despite this, seemingly ignorant of it, he curses along fantastically with an infallible, incurable case of verbal diarrhea. The hermit sighs and feels his shoulders drop lower. Surely he could have come into contact with a better mutant.

Dejected, he turns around and feigns a smile. The neighbor is a man of good intentions, after all; he doesn't mean to be repulsive.

When the hermit speaks, his voices cracks, and he suddenly feels nervous.

"Hey, how are you?"

"I'm good," the neighbor boasts. "Where the hell have you been, anyway? Seems I haven't talked to you in years. Christ, did the explosion do that to your face?"

The hermit clenches his jaw in annoyance, determined to cut the conversation short.

"Yes," he says. "Not sure what happened. Windows blew in, did this to my face."

"Well, goddamn, what a show, huh?" the neighbor says. "There were flames well over a hundred feet high; half the forest burned down. Some people say they saw something fall out of the sky, some meteor, or maybe even a UFO. Anyhow, who knows? The word is they haven't found a goddamn thing out there. Have you heard anything?"

The neighbor stares expectantly, smiling obnoxiously, burning layers away from the sensitive membranes of the hermit's nasal cavity.

"I haven't heard anything," the hermit says, and leaves it at that, turning to pay the proprietor and leave with his cigarettes. His mind is suddenly occupied with the neighbor's words. Something had fallen out of the sky. Where in the universe had a being like the one in his basement come from?

"Well, I guess we'll have to wait and see," the neighbor carries on. "Mrs. Wallace says the light in the sky woke her up and she saw a ball of fire crash off in the distance, but who knows? She's a fan of grandpa's medicine, if you know what I mean."

"Right," the hermit replies and clutches his packages of cigarettes in both hands and nods to the owner. "Well, it's been nice talking to you, but I have to get going. Pretty busy with the insurance company. You know how it is. I'll see you later."

"All right," the neighbor says and smiles widely, poisonously. "But don't make it another decade. You're a good man, take care of yourself."

Without another word, the hermit gets to his car and lights a cigarette with a desperate hand. He starts the engine and shakes his head, grinning. For all his faults and blemishes, he still likes the neighbor. The man means well. He's just been corrupted by the small town hive... And severe gingivitis.

In minutes, he parks his car in the garage and notices a new development in the mystery of the explosion. It seems the decimated forest is now being patrolled by the military. Edged up against the tree line, he sees armored vehicles and soldiers standing guard. Helicopters circle in the sky. Temporary barracks are being erected in the field. He lights a second cigarette and stares. There's something in those woods, he thinks. Something important, and maybe even dangerous. The body in his basement came from somewhere, and it got there somehow. They certainly suspect something is wrong, but they don't know about him or his secret, and they will not find out until he's ready to let them. He enters the house and makes a pot of coffee, watches the news, and eats peanut butter toast topped with a layer of honey. Satisfied, he heads down to the cellar, listens intently, opens the door, and steps inside.

He's left the camera running all night, just in case. The body appears much darker now, almost... healthy looking. The scales are no longer visible, and the top layers of skin no longer appear translucent. The chest isn't moving, and it still doesn't appear to be breathing in any common way, but it certainly no longer appears dead.

With a chill racing up his spine, the hermit speaks to the camera.

"Um... I'm quite perplexed to tell you the truth. As you can clearly see, the being has changed colors. In fact, it appears to have almost fully recovered from its injuries. Of course, I don't know that for sure, but from what I know of biological processes here on earth, it appears to be healthy tissue, whatever it is. Ah–I'm feeling kind of nervous now. I'm not sure what I should do. If this thing wakes up–which, man, I just feel like it's about to–how is it going to react? It's in a cellar, on what is almost certainly an alien planet... I guess I'm just sort of freaked out by the likelihood of hostility. I suppose I can't blame it; I'd be terrified in its position."

He turns from the camera and approaches the body with timid steps. He scratches his arm nervously and stands visibly uncomfortable.

"I... I can't tell you why, but I suddenly feel a terrible compulsion to pour water on its skin. I haven't experimented with it at all, I've only observed, but I don't know what to do anymore. I don't know who to call, and to be honest, I kind of don't want to reveal it to anyone. Despite the possible consequences, I want to see what happens. I took care of it this far, I just–I just don't trust it anymore."

Just outside the cellar, the hermit fills a cup of water from the laundry sink and returns inside, shutting the door behind him.

"Well," he says. "Before I do anything else, I just have to do this."

When the water hits the skin, steam erupts chaotically, in spite of the fact that the body emits no high levels of heat. In seconds, the water is absorbed into the skin and the thing starts changing color. The hermit steps back in amazement, suddenly on guard against threats. He watches the skin turn much lighter, and then darken again, and glisten to life.

The hermit is awestruck. Drooling in disbelief. What happened? He can't make sense of it. He reaches out and touches the skin with his hand, where a navel should be but isn't, and he hears a muffled groan and sees the body on the bench twitch grotesquely.

The hermit fills the room with a piercing howl and collapses to the ground in pure terror. His eyes are huge, but he sees nothing. He questions his sanity. Was it real? Did it just twitch? Is it waking up? Shit!

On his hands and knees, he claws blindly for the door handle, desperate to get out of the room, but before he can get a grip on it, he receives a blow to the back that hurls him across the basement with his face plastered against the door. The opposing concrete wall ends his awareness.

The last thing he remembers is the scalding water pouring on him from somewhere.

Chapter 6

Deep breath! Deep breath!

The hermit coughs painfully. His chest burns, and his head feels swollen and raw. Blood is pouring into his eyes, and he rubs them forcefully against the back of his hands and stares about himself. He's in the basement, but it's flooded with water. The hot water tank is ripped out from the corner of the room and the pipe is filling the space like a pool. He can't remember what happened.

He gets to his hands and knees and wades through thirty centimeter deep water to reach the bottom step, but he suddenly doesn't dare ascend. Upstairs, he hears something moving around. He clambers out of the water, away from the sound of pouring water, and listens intently to the mysterious sounds above. Something scrapes across the floor, and the hermit is at attention like a hunting hound. He hears a bang, a chair maybe, and then glass breaking, a groan, a whine, another bang. He holds his breath, excited, terrified, completely baffled as to what to do. He can hear it breathing suddenly, whining. It stomps along the floor, away from him, then toward. Without warning, a roar erupts through the air and the hermit cowers in surprise. His heart skips tempo. It sounds like a bear, but it's nothing of the sort.

Something made of glass is thrown against the wall and shatters on the floor, and a strange pronunciation of some sort of language is spoken. The hermit can't believe it. It is intelligent. It's most surely an apex predator.

He hears another string of indefinable sounds, organized language, and then a piercing shriek. The thing stomps heavily against the floor and approaches the top of the stairs where it could catch sight of the cowering hermit. He sees a shadow shoot past the door at the top and then hears a window smash. The thing is escaping.

The hermit spends an extra moment listening from the stairs, his entire body contracted as if he were having a seizure. Sure that the thing has escaped, he bolts up the stairs and searches quickly around the kitchen. The place is ransacked. To his left, he sees the shattered glass of the window polluting the floor. He's most definitely lost the being to the outside world.

He lunges for the door and slips the locks, but before he can step outside he is grabbed from the back and thrown against the wall. Shaking with panic, his vision blurred, he kicks his feet aimlessly, trying to fend off an alien threat he can't see until it grabs him by the throat and squeezes. Its hands are incredibly hot, and powerful, and they close around his throat until he thinks his eyeballs are going to pop from their sockets. He can't breathe. He's going to die.

He flails his arms and claws at the floor to get free from its grip, but it's too strong. The being brings its face closer to his own and snarls a string of angry phonetics. "Vafurum nomeira zietglisting bart!" But when it receives no answer, it loosens its grip and screams, "Vafurum nomeira zietglisting bart!"

"I don't know!" the hermit cries and gasps for air. "I don't speak your language!"

The being releases his throat and places its hands on the hermit's head. Instantly, it feels like his brain are being mangled. He sees vivid flashes of colorful lights and his eyes cross. His legs twitch uncontrollably and there's an involuntary growl coming from his mouth. He fights against it, but he's no match for the cosmic magic.

Then, as suddenly as it came on, the scrabbled madness stops and the colorful lights disappear. He takes in a desperate breath and looks wide eyed about the room. The being stands to his side, no longer touching him, but staring at him like a opportunistic predator stares at a potential meal. Terrified, shattered, the hermit squirms on the floor and croaks, "Please, just go. I'm sorry. Just go. Don't kill me."

The being leans in and seems to sniff him. The hermit cowers and guards himself against another attack, but before he can protest much further he hears something that stuns him and causes all his fear to vanish.

"Sp... Speak."

The hermit sits up quickly, stupefied.

"Yes!" he cries. "Yes! Speak! You can speak English?" The being shakes its head and stares at the hermit with its black eyes.

"You... Speak... A strange language," it says.
"Wh..." the hermit mumbles, no longer trusting his own sanity. "That's incredible! Incredible! We can communicate?"

"Earth..." the being says.
The hermit nods as excitement overwhelms his other emotions.

"This planet is called earth," he says.
The being nods. "Where?" it says.

"Where?"

"Where?"

"Ah..." the hermit shrugs. "I... I don't know how you measure space. I mean, where are you from?"

The being stares pensively.

"In your words, I am... From the place called... Andromeda."

"The Andromeda galaxy!" the hermit exclaims. "I... I... How can you be speaking to me? How can this be happening?"

"I took it from your mind."

"From my mind?"

"I took everything from your mind."

The hermit wrings his hands, immediately uncomfortable with the idea, and struggles to find the words to continue the astonishing conversation. The only question he can think of is, "Are you here to kill us?"

After a pause, the being says, "No."

The hermit stares at the floor, his mind reeling, his breath quick and shallow. "Please," he says. "You must tell me how you've travelled here from the Andro—" His words are cut short by a sudden, piercing wail cutting through the night air. The being instantly looks up in surprise, in recognition, in relief. It moves away from the hermit and looks through the window at the charred forest. The soldiers patrolling the perimeter are confused and sweeping spotlights in search of the source of the high pitched sound. Helicopters circle above them in wide orbits. The hermit shuffles his weight on the floor, sorely trying to get to his feet. His throat feels crushed. His head is pounding. His body is exhausted. He manages to stand and approach the being, but he keeps his distance and watches the visitor's head bob up and down, forward and backward, seemingly about to leap through the ceiling and be lost forever.

"Wait," the hermit urges. "You must understand how... This is an unprecedented opportunity to... Look, you have to tell me something. Tell me something to help us. Does your race use numbers? Mathematics? Can you see that in my—"

The wail grows to such an intensity that he's forced to block his ears with the palms of his hands. The being grows agitated in response to the sound. It seems desperate and determined. The hermit backs a few steps and keeps a keen eye on it. It dances strangely, moaning, searching, and then says, "Thank you, kind being. All answers are within you." And before the hermit can respond he's knocked back to the floor when the being bursts through the window and heads for the soldiers guarding the forest. Sick with worry, the hermit screams for it to stop, it will be killed and experimented on, but it pays him no mind.

He scrambles to his feet and runs out the door. In the dark, he sees the being racing through the hay field with astonishing speed, but he runs after it nonetheless. The soldiers notice the thing in the field and flash a light on it. Without warning, they open fire, but it hardly stops the being. It increases its speed and crashes straight through the line. Chaos ensues. The helicopters bank sharp turns and concentrate their spotlights into the forest. The wail again grows in power, and even the soldiers can't help but bring their hands to their ears.

The hermit races through the field, desperate to see something, unsure of himself. His legs burn with lactic acid, and his lungs are unable to keep up. He's already cursing the goddamned cigarettes.

Far ahead of him is the tree line which he can't make visual sense of. It's all too hectic and altogether alien. The soldiers point a spotlight on him and order him to stop where he is, but the voice is muffled by the incessant high-pitched drone in the air. Blinded by the light, he knows they're about to open fire on him, but he can't stop, he can't let it go, he has to try and–

A monstrous roar rips through the night and he falls to his knees with his palms pressed against the sides of his head. He tries to shake it off and get his bearings, but before he can get back to his feet, a shaft of blistering white light rips through the darkness and reaches into space. Astonished, the hermit stares with a gaped mouth–and then an explosion erupts from within the wrecked woods and shoots a ball of light from the horizon. The object soars into the sky, blinks its light, tumbles end over end, recovers, and disappears into space with impossible speed.

The night settles into a deafening silence. The hermit, kneeling in the field, stares straight up with welling tears. It's gone. It's over. His chance at making one of the greatest contributions in the history of science has disappeared into the night like an elusive firefly. A moment later he's surrounded by soldiers jabbing guns in his face and screaming at him to lay face down on the ground. The hermit obliges, devastated, beaten. A soldier handcuffs him with unnecessary force and then heaves him up to his feet and stares at him with unblinking eyes.

"What are you doing out here?" the soldier asks. "What did you see?"

The hermit remains quietly defeated. He feels like he's lost an important part of himself. He's lost his dream. He lets the soldiers drag him to one of their vehicles and put him inside.

He stares at the burned woods, sick with emotion, maddened by thoughts. What now? He wonders. What now?

Chapter 7

Exasperated, the hermit shakes his head and slams a fist against the table. The military interrogator stares back at him with a firm mouth, his eyes concentrated, his demeanor stoic. The hermit has explained the circumstances of the situation, but no one believes him.

"An alien? A being from outer space? That's what you're telling me?" the interrogator responds.

"Yes," the hermit exclaims. "Look, like I said, I have proof. I recorded the whole thing with my camera. I had it in the cold cellar for a few days before it woke up; it's all on the camera."

The interrogator shakes his head while the hermit speaks. "We've checked," he says. "There is nothing in your house aside from a tremendous mess and two meters of water in the basement."

He'd forgotten about the water, and at the mention of it, he looks at the ceiling and sighs. It's hopeless, but he doesn't understand why. There had been a major explosion in Rosethorn, yes; the explosion had been caused by an unidentified craft, yes; and the military obviously knew something about it–why else would they have cordoned off the area? He hadn't dreamed the whole thing after all. Had he?

The interrogator leans back in his chair and sighs without breaking eye contact with the hermit. A moment later, he leans back to the table, clicks a ballpoint pen, and begins asking questions.

"Do you take any medications?"

"No."

"Have you ever?" the interrogator presses. "You know, maybe for depression, or pain management? There's no shame in it. Millions of people take them every day."

"I don't take any pills," the hermit says.

"Anger problems?"

He shakes his head.

"I need you to vocalize your answers, please."

"I don't have any anger problems. I'm only frustrated at the moment due to the circumstances."

The interrogator nods without empathy.

"Have you ever experimented with drugs?"

"Yes."

"What kinds?"

"Marijuana. A little bit of cocaine, but mostly psilocybin,

and LSD."

"Do you prefer hallucinogens, then?"

"I suppose."

"And do you still take any of these drugs?"

"I smoke marijuana. I haven't done acid in a long time."

"Uh huh. Did you used to do much?"

"I suppose. It's a good drug."

"And you enjoy that sensation, do you? Losing control."

"I like experiencing things I cannot explain. Acid isn't necessarily about losing control; it's a very personal drug capable of changing a man's perceptions of life forever. I would even call it an intense spiritual experience. At least, it's what people call spiritual."

"Right," the interrogator says. "Are you a spiritual man, then?"

"Not at all."

"What do you believe in?"

"Nothing."

"Nothing at all? No religion or philosophy about the meaning of life?"

"Nothing at all."

"A man of science."

"Yes; but that has nothing to do with my lack of beliefs. Science is also full meaningless questions. Some questions are simply too big to ask, there's nothing wrong with admitting that."

"Uh huh. Would you say you get along easily with others?"

"No."

"You live alone. No friends or family?"

"Yes."

"And you like it that way?"

"Yes."

"Why?"

"People annoy me. It's neither their fault nor mine. It's just the way my brain works. I like being alone. I strive for it."

"Are you depressed?"

"Never."

The interrogator stares intently for a moment.

"Do you ever lose track of time?"

The hermit makes an offended grimace.

"No."

"Do you ever suffer from nightmares? Maybe wake up not quite sure if you're still dreaming?"

"I'm not crazy."

"Do ever see things? Apparitions? Lights? Things you can't explain?"

"Yes. I told you. I saw a light. The explosion was a result of a–"

"Of an alien craft slamming into the ground? A craft flown by a being which you nursed back to health like an injured little puppy?"

"Then why are you guys there? The military had probably never even heard of Rosethorn before the explosion. Why? Why would the government spend money on a trip there?"

"That is a matter of National Security. But what I can tell you is that it does focus on human concerns. These are matters of war, not space. Now why are you lying to me? Why did you try to cross the perimeter? Who do you work for?"

"No one. Goddamn it! I'm telling you the truth!"
The interrogator scoffs with an amused air.

"I don't believe you," he says. "In fact, I think you're bat-shit crazy, and I want to know exactly what you were looking for in a secured area. That's why, on the other side of that glass stands a psychiatrist who is coming in here to talk to you. You have until the end of that conversation to tell the truth. Otherwise, I'll make sure you end up in a sanitarium for the rest of your life."

Enraged, the interrogator stands from his chair and leaves the room. A moment later, a short, balding man with round glasses and pudgy cheeks walks in and sits opposite the hermit.

"Hello," the psychiatrist says.
"Hi."

"How are you feeling?"
The hermit snorts.

"Oh, I'm doing pretty fantastic. Jesus Christ. Look, I'm not crazy. Do you think I'm crazy?"

"I don't know, but I'm not trying to be intrusive. I only want to understand and try to help you. I've listened to your story and there is one part I'm particularly interested in. Do you mind if we talk about it?"

"What is it?"
"You said you spoke to the being."
"Yes."
"How do you think that was possible?"

"It said it took it from my mind. It put its hands on my head and it felt like electricity was being pumped into my brain. I saw bright colors and my body twitched uncontrollably. After it let me go, it gradually gained the ability to speak. I don't know. It was all pretty frantic. I thought I was going to die."

"Did you feel any different after that?"

"I... I don't think so. I mean..."

"Do you feel any different now?"

"I..." The hermit frowns and stares at the table top. "I don't think so."

"Any unusual feelings or thoughts? A loss of interest in things you previously liked? An interest in new things?"

The hermit looks up at the psychiatrist.

"There... There is one thing... I think."

"Please."

"I don't know. I have these... These numbers running through my head. They're... Constant, but I don't know what they mean. I've never been any more than mediocre at math."

"Are these equations?"

"I... I don't know. Maybe. I can't..."

"Here," the psychiatrist says and slides a pen and pad across the table. "Can you write them down?"

The hermit shrugs. "I guess so. I don't..."

He scribbles a string of numbers across the pad, nine distinct lines, and returns it to the psychiatrist. The doctor looks at it with his head cocked to one side. After a moment he returns the pad to the table and stares at the hermit. The hermit shakes his head and lowers his eyes.

"Are you all right?"

"It's just... All of this happened so suddenly. I don't know what to think, or what's going to happen. I'm afraid. And these numbers, I can't make sense of them, and I can't seem to stop them. I can't control it."

"Do you have a headache right now?"

"No. Just the numbers. Do you think the alien gave them to me? Do you think it messed with my head?"

The psychiatrist stares with a tinge of pity.

"I am not doubting your story, but I need to ask you... Are you absolutely certain of your story? I need you to be honest with me, for the sake of your case."

"Yes," the hermit says and nods. "I am absolutely, positively, enthusiastically certain of my story. I am telling you the truth, every word of it."

The psychiatrist nods.

"Well, I'm here to help you, but in order to do that I will need to do a full physical and psychological assessment. Will you participate?"

The hermit purses his lips and squints his eyes. How could all of this have happened, he wonders. No one believes him, not even this doctor, but what other choice does he have?

"Yes," he says. "I will answer your questions and do your tests."

Chapter 8

A sudden pain rips through his bicep and races up his neck. He can't breathe. He's dying. He's dying! Panicked, he tries to scream, but it comes out as an imperceptible moan and he drools all over himself. He tries again and receives the same result. He tries to breathe and calm his thundering heart, but to no avail. He tries to move, to squirm out of his chair, but he can't feel a thing; he hasn't felt a thing in years.

Six years ago, during the psychological assessment with the psychiatrist, things had started out fine. He'd answered the questions with ease, convinced of his sanity, and certain of his story. But as the days went on, strange changes began happening. The numbers would not stop running through his mind, and the madness took on a decisive hold. They became the sole focus of his attention. Doctors spoke, but he didn't understand. They asked for answers, but he could think of no words, only numbers. He spent days and nights awake, babbling numbers, writing them down on anything he could get his hands on. Rendered psychologically unresponsive, it soon became obvious that there was nothing anyone could do for him, and whatever credibility he might have had dissolved in sync with his sanity. The psychiatrist, true to his interest in redeeming the hermit from suspicion, took the scribbled numbers to a mathematician for review. The results were less than enthusiastic. One dreary morning, the psychiatrist entered the hermit's room and found him staring out the window, his lips moving soundlessly, repeating numbers. The doctor said, "I've taken your numbers to a mathematician, just to see if maybe they're some sort of flash of genius on your part."

"Yes," the hermit said, suddenly at attention. "And?" The psychiatrists sighed. "And," he said. "The numbers are complete gibberish."

"What?"
"They are useless. I'm sorry, but they mean nothing. They are random. I was really hoping for a better outcome. I'm sorry things had to end like this."

The hermit said nothing and returned his stare out the window, his lips resuming their silent mumble. The doctor lowered his eyes, sighed, and nodded resolutely. There was nothing anyone could do for him.

Ultimately deemed insane, they wheeled him into this ghastly place, clothed him with a robe, and stuck an IV in his arm.

Since then, he's been sitting around in a wheel chair, completely fried and speaking unintelligibly, drooling and pissing himself. He doodles the numbers everywhere, not sure of what they are, and no longer caring. They are meaningless to him. They are not answers. They are curses, and they have ruined him. He's lost everything. His house. His life. His mind. He's especially lost his mind.

None of that matters much anymore, however, because he's been waiting for this moment for a long time. Squirming in a chair with death baying at the nape of his neck. Terrified and satisfied. The numbers do have an end, after all.

He throws his head back and moans again, weakly flailing his arms. There are no orderlies around, only other patients lost in their own government approved drug induced psychosis. He drags his eyes across them. They drool and moan and stare at phantasms a thousand kilometers away. He's all alone, the way he's always liked it; and like everyone else, regardless of the life they've led, he's alone in death. He regrets nothing, aside from the numbers. He's run through the situation countless times in his head. If only he hadn't chased after the being toward the woods. If only he hadn't approached it at all. What then? In the end, however, it makes no difference, for reality takes no notice of hypothetical pasts.

Another bolt of pain tears through his arm, his neck, his chest. It comes on strong and he growls strangely, his vision grays, and his whole body feels like it's ablaze. In his mind, all he sees are the same old numbers. The meaningless, madness inducing numbers. With a final gasp, he feels a disconnection, rather different than the mundane disassociation of medication. He feels warm, calm, and satisfied. The numbers stop and the world dims like an outgoing kaleidoscope. The energy is restored to the universe.

Chapter 9
Epilogue

Two years later, the hermit is an obscurity in the annals of history. He's neither left a mark nor a stain on the comedy of humanity. At the sanitarium, a young orderly is charged with clearing the stock room of old and useless items. Dutifully, she scours through shelves of file boxes, knick knacks, and miscellaneous artifacts of the insane. Half a day into her toil, she comes across a notebook and quickly checks the contents before shredding it. She smiles when she sees the scribbled pages. They're covered in numbers, equations, she guesses, but she's the first to admit her uselessness in mathematics. Her friend, however, is quickly becoming a world renown mathematician. She decides to keep the book, against regulations, and hands it to her friend two days later.

"What do you think?" she says. "Is it all advanced and stuff?"

The friend stares at the numbers with a furrowed brow. They seem random and not organized in any conventional form.

"I don't know. It looks like garbage to me. Where'd you get this?"

"At the sanitarium," she says, and laughs.

"The sanitarium," he says. "Was the guy a mathematician or something?"

"I don't know. I found it in a box. It's anonymous."

"Huh," the friend says and looks at the page again. He shrugs. "Can I keep it?"

"That's why I gave it to you," she says.

He puts the book in his pocket and forgets about it.

A year later, the orderly is paged to the front desk to meet a visitor. She thinks it's a mistake, no one ever visits her at work; but when she rounds the corner into the long hallway leading to the front, she sees her friend standing there, beaming with a wide smile. Surprised, confused, she says, "Hi. Is everything okay?"

"I need to talk to you," he says quickly, irrationally. "Can we talk somewhere?"

"Sure... Ah, let's go outside."

They sit on a bench and he launches into an excited rant.

"Do you remember that book you gave me, with the numbers in it?"

"Yeah."

"Well, are you sure you don't know who it belongs to?"

"There's no way to tell. Whoever it was is probably dead. Why? What's wrong?"

"Nothing is wrong. Look, they seemed like gibberish at first. Just... Well, craziness, stuff you'd expect from a sanitarium. But for whatever reason I kept looking at them, and just sort of messing around with them on the side, for fun. And then I started seeing patterns, and over time, I've been able to reconstruct them into proper equations, and... And..."

"What is it? You're scaring me."
"And they basically solve physics," he exclaims. "They answer everything we've ever wondered, and more. It gives us things that we will be learning about for the next hundred years. They're... They're brilliant. I mean, I can't, I can't believe you found this in a box. Do you realize what this means?"

"I guess so, I mean..."
"Everything is about to change, and fast. From now on, we will be able to compute faster, travel farther, and conquer nature in every respect. We will have definitive answers on how the universe formed, and maybe even why it did in the first place. It's all in these beautifully elegant and simple sets of equations. We've been fixated on describing the symptoms of these equations for hundreds of years now, instead of simply describing the causes. The rest is all effect. We've been overcomplicating everything for years, and because of your chance decision to keep that notebook, you've set our world ahead by eons. You can quit your job now if you want. Neither one of us will ever be working out of necessity again."

The young orderly isn't quite sure what to say. The day had begun like any other; what did this all really mean? She lowers her eyes to the ground and tries to make sense of what he's telling her.

"My God," he continues, oblivious of her confusion. "Can you believe it? The answers to the universe, sitting in a box in the store room of a sanitarium. The poor person who wrote them down wasn't crazy at all, he or she was just too brilliant for anyone to recognize. It's as mind blowing as the equations themselves."

The End

THE DEVIL'S LAST RITES

Day 1: July 27th, 1847

The first time they tried to kill me was about a week ago. An angry mob dragged me to the gallows, kicked me in the gut, pulled a bag over my head, and placed a noose around my neck. Blind and breathless, I clambered back to my feet in time for the floor to give way beneath me and certify my doom. For reasons I cannot explain, I suppose any type of superstition is possible, the rope snapped before my neck did and I hit the ground with a dramatic thump. I realized I was still alive when spectators began arguing vehemently about what to do next, as if no one was being properly entertained at my hanging. Some proclaimed that they shouldn't have tried to kill me in the first place; others called for a second attempt. On the ground, I reeled from the shock of having survived certain death, and I could easily sense the pungent fear seizing hold of the crowd in response. These were a superstitious folk, after all, and some of them were getting downright hysterical about it. I couldn't see them through the bag, but I could imagine their terrorized stares, their faces gray and drawn. From what I could hear, some were even debating the possibility of my invincibility. I couldn't help it; I burst out laughing, and the sound of my voice may as well have been a bomb. The crowd instantly backed away from me with hurried footsteps through the mud. I won't lie, I loved their fear. I loved the irony of their failure to kill me. I laughed, but I had no illusions about the ordeal. My death was called for in the name of the greater good. God's will, they said, but it's funny how they always seemed to choose his wishes for him. Nevertheless, justice had been demanded and it had failed to be delivered. If necessary to appease the communal ego, it would come at the cost of freedom and innocence. My dilemma was far from over.

After a general outpouring of emotions, they picked

my sore mass from the ground and locked me in a tiny concrete room for four days. Like an animal, I was fed every twelve hours, watered every six, and the rest was all introspective nightmares. I knew they would never release me, and they would never let me live. The time in the box was only to impose the maximum amount of torture and entertainment before their next attempt at my execution.

When they opened the door after what seemed like an eternity, I inhaled a breath of fresh air and smiled. In truth, it smelled like shit and mud, but after days of choking on the foul effluence oozing from my pores, anything different was a welcomed relief.

Thrown face first into the muck, fists and boots unleashed a senseless beating on me before I was dragged away through the mud. I was too weak to resist, and too tired to care. With malicious grimaces, they pulled me through a dense crowd of onlookers who spat and kicked at me as I passed by. Little girls, no more than five or six years old, slapped me in the face; little boys ensured the proper punishment of my testicles. I winced and yelped, but I would not bring about the pinnacle of entertainment they were aiming for. I would not scream, and I would not plead in order to satisfy their sick compulsions before mass began and their humble hats would have to be pulled back on.

Once through the crowd, they threw me against a stone wall, tied my arms, blindfolded my eyes, and then murmured amongst themselves while I stood trembling and weak, not really knowing what was to become of me. It all sounded very exciting. Parents herded their children together and massaged their shoulders in anticipation of the big event about to unfurl. My death.

I heard feet sloshing around me in the mud, and then the hammer of a rifle being pulled back. If they couldn't hang me, by God, they were going to shoot me. I didn't care. Four days in the box had been more than enough time to make peace with myself, turn my regrets into points of pride, and understand that all things died, but only those who didn't comply to vague doctrines died tortuously.

I heard the voice of my executioner, Elvin Kass, the town's elected Sheriff. He was a fat and stupid man who had once shot and killed another over accusations in a card game, but the Lord had since forgiven him, and given him a promotion to head executioner.

"We are here today to witness the public execution of

Aldous Crawler," he said. "Though the Lord decided to spare him from death by hanging, proper justice has not yet been brought down upon his head for his heinous crimes."

"I didn't do anything," I cried.

"Shut up!" Elvin snapped, and kicked me in the gut, knocking the air from my lungs and the turds from my bowels. "As I was saying," he continued. "Justice has not been rendered. Children, rejoice in the love of God, and pray to him each and every day so that he may cleanse the earth of such monsters. Remember this day vividly in your minds and strive to fight against this type of evil in any way you can. We must not allow the devil to take over our lands!"

With that, a cacophony of applause arose and was pro-ceeded by prayers, songs, and a long awaited sense of safety. Yes, safety at all cost. Appease the illusion. Sedate the brutes. Kill all threats, real or perceived.

"Aldous Crawler!" Elvin announced. "For your crimes against humanity, for which you refuse to take responsibility, we as a community, guided by the eternally wise hand of our Lord and Savior, sentence you to suffer in the deepest pits of hell. We will not tolerate evil of your kind! May you serve as an example of what true justice is, and may God have mercy on your soul; other-wise, may you burn in hell for all eternity."

I heard him hold his breath to steady his aim; then he pulled the trigger. The boom was deafening, shocking, and the air suddenly smelled thick of gunpowder. At first, I couldn't tell if I'd been shot. I couldn't feel anything. I couldn't hear anything. But as far as I could tell, I was still breathing.

And then I heard Elvin's voice roar through the shocked silence.

"My Lord in heaven!" he cried, choking on his breath. "Why do you spare this vile, decadent creature of evil in our com-munity? Please, please, do not forsake us. He has been given fair trial, proven guilty, and rightfully sentenced to death!"

When he finished speaking to the sky, an eerie silence hung in the air and all I could hear was Elvin's frustrated breath, as if he expected a direct response to come down from the clouds. Once again, I lost myself in big, roaring chuckles that caused an audible shudder to pass through the crowd. I didn't know how I'd survived two executions, but some force was obviously on my side. Perhaps Elvin's precious lord and savior simply liked me bet-ter? I wasn't sure, but I was awfully happy that none of his divine convictions had any real bearing; otherwise, the crazy bastard might have killed me! Ha! Ha! The fool! If the rope and bullet couldn't kill me, I was sure the laughter was about to. I hoped the onlooking cowards had been thoroughly entertained, because I'd been so entertained, damn it, I was ready to die. They could all kiss my ass.

Elvin's indignant rage tensed the air like an electrical storm. Once more, I heard him load his weapon, curse the very air I breathed, and try to put a bullet into my blindfolded face. This time, he didn't miss his shot, but he didn't hit me either. He pulled the trigger, and in the silent anticipation of the deed being done, I heard a benign click, a failure to ignite any powder whatsoever.

I didn't have supernatural powers, nor did I believe in any sort of superstition–but at that moment, I wondered if I had over-looked something. Perhaps there was a god up there looking down on me, protecting me from the lunatics in the streets.

Immediately after the harmless click of his gun, perhaps more out of humiliation than anything else, he grabbed the barrel with both hands and smashed the stock into the ground 'till it shat-tered into splinters.

Still I laughed. I laughed 'till my blindfold was soaked through with tears and my stomach started to hurt. My cheeks burned. My chest was tight. And once again, I was assaulted by a throng of boots and fists on every part of my body. It was hardly enough to wipe the smile from my face. Screw the bastards. I had a reputation to uphold; I was the goddamned devil.

Back into the concrete room I went, bruised and bleeding, shot at twice, but overall no worse for the wear. Four more days I sat while they busied themselves concocting another diabolical plan to deal with the demon in the concrete cell. Death had to be delivered. It was the only sensible thing to do.

After a week of malnutrition and no sleep, they eventu-ally found a solution to my possible invincibility. If I couldn't be hanged, and I couldn't be shot, perhaps a more romantic, slower mode of execution would do the trick. Plus, it would be more fun for the kids.

They pulled me out of the room for another round of public assault. I felt like my insides were bone dry. I was so thirsty, and hungry, and dizzy. After the communal beating, I was thrown to the feet of Elvin Kass like a mangled dog and received a sharp kick to the ribs. I fell over on my side and gnashed my teeth as the pain engulfed me. Elvin grinned and spat into my face.

"Hello, Devil," he said. "Welcome to the end of your life. You must cease to exist, for you are a plague in this world. You are vile, and infected with evil. You were never meant to live, demon, and it is our duty to send you back to hell."

"Boo!" I said, and laughed, making a mockery of the mockery named Elvin Kass.

He snorted, completely offended, and slapped me across the face. He towered over me with his chest out and his hands raised to the sky. Behind him a dense crowd pushed against each other to catch a glimpse of the immortal devil.

Elvin said, "You, Aldous Crawler, creature of hell; the manner of your death has been put to a community vote... and I am proud to announce that the method of execution has been decided upon. You are hereby sentenced to death by way of scaphism."

Scaphism! I'd read about it before. It was an ancient Persian method of execution, and if it sounded terrible and disgusting in a book, it was nothing compared to the reality of it. The crowd cheered at the declaration and chanted in unison, "Kill the devil. Kill the devil. Kill the devil."

Elvin said, "Do you understand the terms of your punishment, devil?"

I smiled through the cake of blood and mud on my face and said, "There's no use. You've already lost."

"You seem confused, devil," he replied. "It is you who has lost. Back to hell you go. Let's get on with it!"

They picked me out of the mud, bound my arms and legs, threw my tired body onto a wagon, and hustled the horses down to the lake. On the shore, they kicked me from the platform to the ground with a solid thump. All around me, the crowd screamed obscenities and kicked and jabbed and spat at me.

They dragged me closer to the lake, stripped me naked, threw me into a row boat, tied my hands and feet to the edges, and covered every inch of my badly beaten body with honey. My head was then steadied, and a funnel was shoved down my throat, through which equal amounts of milk and honey were forced into my stomach. They poured the concoction 'till I convulsed and puked all over myself. They waited 'till I was done emptying my stomach, then continued guzzling the mess down my throat. Three times I puked, and three times they ensured I was filled back up to the top. Once I was bursting at the seams, they placed a second row boat over top of me, upside down, with my hands and feet protruding from the sides, and tied it down.

I thought, well, at least I won't drown. They'd taken all necessary safety precautions to ensure I'd experience the maximum amount of torture. I felt them drag the boat into the water. Elvin said, "Hear us, Devil! Today you are being sent back to hell where you belong. Do not return here, or you will be met with the same punishment as you are about to suffer. In the name of God, may you plead for mercy, and burn in hell."

"Amen." The crowd said in sync.

They pushed the boat into the water and I floated away from the shore. Immediately, the heat inside my tomb rose and my digestive system panicked. The milk and honey forced adverse effects, and I couldn't do anything but allow a gross exodus from both ends of my body. The stench was ungodly, putrid, and only served to continue my repulsive convulsions. In minutes, I found myself exhausted and soiled with a mess of biological refuse. As such, my crypt floated away from the beach 'till the tether stopped the momentum near the middle of the lake.

So here I am, my third unwilling confrontation with death, and this one far more cruel and disgusting than I ever expected. From the seam in between the two boats, I can see the angry congregation staring at me. They're screaming obscenities and cursing me to eternal damnation. This time, they've had enough practice after all, I believe they got it right. I will not survive this punishment, but I'm not dead yet, and I am not going anywhere 'till I am done dealing with these demented lunatics. They think they're in total control, but they know nothing of what they've done. For now, they ridicule and assault me, but in time they will learn of their mistake. The longer I live, the bigger their failure.

Day 2: July 28th, 1847

Do you know what the worst part of scaphism is? It isn't so much the unbearable stench, the heat, the bugs, the thirst, or the guarantee that cankerous infections will ravage your limbs while you watch that gets to you. That pain is physical, and it can be handled. What truly breaks you is when an entire community of men, women, and children pull you in to shore just before the morning temperatures give way to hellish degrees, remove the boat above you, and fill you to the gills with more milk and honey than you could handle in a month. Once topped up, they pour an extravagant amount of honey over your body, replace the boat above, and send you back out to bake in the middle of the lake. This fulfills three goals for the community. A spiteful satisfaction from your suffering, an infliction of more torture, and a sufficient amount of nutrition to ensure you live long enough to experience it.

And I'm a bad guy.
I've just been released from the first communal feeding since yesterday, but I know there will be more. Once a day, just before the sun hits its zenith, they will pull on the tether of my boat, reel me in, and fill me with more delectable refreshments. A complimentary meal, free of charge. Surely I'm causing someone grief. It's a lot of food to be wasting on a quiet fool. The only thing I do have to look forward to is the increasingly offended contortions their faces will make as, day after day, they open my rancid sarcophagus. This is day one, and I'm already lying in a bed of shit and vomit. If I live for another week, or even just another three days, my god, I will smell fantastic! Wafting from my final tomb will be a miasma foul enough to knock the birds out of the sky. I can't wait! I only hope that by then my own sense of smell will have been completely obliterated, for ignorance truly is bliss. Yes, that's what I see when I stare at the beach. Bliss. Justice. Ignorance. I see the shore over there polluted with hypocrisy, lies, and propaganda. I see brainwashed children guided by brainwashed parents. I see fools of all ages.

But listen, this isn't about them, it's about me. They can take my life away, but they sure as hell can't take me away from me.

At the moment, and forevermore, I'm not alone inside my tomb. In fact, I'm the minority. Already, the space is filled with mating insects of every species, shape, size, and color. I am a prospering nest of maggots, beetles, worms, parasites, and a host of other things I have never before seen the likes of. I suppose the upside is I'll learn a few things concerning the life cycle of various bugs before I go. It will serve no other purpose aside from the pleasure of learning something new one last time. It's the only true way of escaping reality. Focus the mind on attaining knowledge, no matter how obtuse the subject may seem. There is something to be learned from everything, good and bad.

Outside, the sun beams with abnormal intensity. Inside, I'm suffering one hundred percent humidity and the digestive equivalent of swallowing needles and washing them down with a gallon of boiling horse piss; not to mention the millions of bugs starting to grow prone to biting and boring into my skin. It's starting already. I am decaying and watching it happen.

This is what happens when one dimensional solutions are applied to three dimensional problems. These people fear me like I'm some sort of preternatural beast escaped from the clutches of hell, but I am no such thing. I'm an educated man, and I have a deep appreciation for the great arts of the world. I keep to myself, read books on every subject of interest, and generally behave the way it comes naturally to me. No one seems to like that, however. Not anywhere. But this isn't to take credibility away from my tormentors, for they are also well read. The problem is the book never changes. It's insanity in a loop, over and over again, ad infinitum. It can't possibly be good for your brain, and it's certainly not a pragmatic way of gaining knowledge about yourself or the world around you. There's so much out there, too much out there. But they don't seem to care. They say I am a beast, a gargoyle, a monstrosity, but not a single one knows the truth about me.

You see, all I ever wanted to do as a young man was write books. I wanted to write pages of substantial ideas to mull over. I wanted to offer differing points of view and alternative observations of the world. I aspired to write about life like the greats; like Dante, whose own masterpiece is helping me tremendously at the moment. To me, the point of the divine comedy is that one must pass all the way through hell in order to get out of it. It's an elegant concept that can be applied to any and all tribulations. Unfortunately, I lack a monumental amount of that brand of intuitive knowledge and talent. I've tried a few times, but I've never published any of it. I do it to settle the fragmented thoughts dancing inside my head. I used to dream about publishing my work in an effort to get other people to question their own thoughts and beliefs, to help people find or understand themselves in a clearer way, but

I've learned a long time ago that no one has the freedom of thought when their opinions differ radically from the general mass illusions. In that case, you're having "dangerous thoughts." Dangerous thoughts; what does that even mean? Dangerous to whom, the status quo? Who decides?

Zang! Here we are again with the vomit and the diarrhea. My surroundings are so foul, so unbelievably offensive, it's hard to stop myself from spewing uncontrollably from both ends. The bugs, on the other hand, seem absolutely delighted with the denouement. Fresh food. A paradise of decomposing rot.

I can barely move my hips. Every minute, I'm further mummified inside a hardening crust of my own insides. The honey on my skin is so thick, and so dry, I feel like I can't sweat the heat out of my blood. My head feels like it's swelling, but the pinnacle of my pain is found in my guts. The milk sloshing inside of me is turning sour, chunky, corrosive.

This is some people's idea of justice.
Justice is just another word for gross vengeance.

With the sun peaking in intensity, and after only twenty four hours in my floating tomb, I won't deny that I am suffering. My mood surely isn't as light as it was, but I'm still refusing to give those bastards the satisfaction of my pain. It's my pain, and they can't have it! Every time they pull me in to shore, I will smile. Every time they frantically cover their mouths after removing the boat above me, I will laugh maniacally. And every time they curse me back to hell, I will say that I forgive them, if only to throw their own insanity back into their faces.

If for nothing else, I'm proudest of the fact that I got these self-righteous automatons to use their imagination for once. Sure, it's coming at the cost of my life... maybe... but at least they had to dig deep into those stunted minds to think outside the box and come up with an original punishment for a man of my distinction. I'm the goddamn devil! I deserve a proper doom!

Ha. Ha. What can I say? I've been the devil round these parts for some time.

As a child, I was raised in a poor family. My father was a drinking man; my mother was a punching bag. I grew up in chaos, but I didn't let it stand in my way. I buried my face in books day after day, and ignored the madness, the rage, the violence. I used to crawl into bed, close my eyes, and wish that I could do something to stop my father from hurting us, from hurting my mother like she was a piece of trash, but I was afraid of standing up to his wrath.

And then one night, he killed her. He pressed a boot firmly against her chest and shot her in the face.

I was only a boy then, about fifteen, but to this day I can feel the astute shock that tore through me at the sound of that shot. A scar tissue memory. I leaped from my bed and climbed out the window in the grip of an oppressive panic. From the stable, I stole my father's unsaddled horse, along with a musket, and raced into the darkness with heavy tears streaming from my eyes. He was outside screaming at me as I blew past the house, but I refused to stop. I ran the horse hard and fast until her breath could no longer sustain our escape and my heart could beat at a reasonable pace. That night I tried sleeping under the stars next to a small fire, but I was irrationally paranoid of hearing my father's angry voice creep up behind me. It never came; nor did sleep. I sat in the darkness stoking the fire with a stick, losing myself in devastated fits of tears. I imagined the fear my mother must have felt, the total domination, the ultimate, unwilling submission. I regretted leaving her; I felt I should have stayed and shot my father in retaliation. I should have avenged my mother's death. I should have done something, anything, but it was too late. I was never going back.

I watched the sun crown the distant mountains and color the clouds pink before mounting my father's mare and riding her toward unknown destinations. For a week I explored the towering mountains, the wild plains, the dense, uninhabited wilderness, and hunted hare or fowl when the pangs of hunger took hold of me. I spent nights camped on the edge of rivers, or lakes, and spoke to the horse in an effort to stow my loneliness. I told her every flavor of terrible things I wished I would have done to my father, and what I would do if I ever saw him again. I felt betrayed, and emotionally maimed. Something in me had died along with my mother, and although I wasn't able to pinpoint exactly what it was, the general sense of hatred it left me with grew more powerful over the years. In many ways, that void became me.

Eventually, growing tired of my aimless travels, I came upon a cotton farm advertising labor for hire. The job provided room and board as well as a small income. After meeting the owner and answering a few questions, I was hired, assigned a room, and the very next day I began working. There was a sense of pride that came with being responsible for myself. I enjoyed working hard and easily got along with other workers. The experience forced me to grow up quickly, but it wasn't much of a hassle. My friendship with fellow workers was enough to cull my sharp sense of loneliness in little time. Suddenly, I was a man, depending on myself for survival. I spent three years in toil, saving up, and hardening my independence. The last thing I wanted was to end up like my father. I never did find out what happened to him for murdering my mother, but if he was publicly impaled, then he got what he deserved. He was an evil, spiteful, and harmful man that didn't deserve a woman as precious as my mother, nor a son to stick around after she was gone. He deserved no family, no friends, and no forgiveness.

When I turned eighteen, I found myself with a pocket full of money and a consuming urge to move on with my life and settle some roots somewhere. My employer was sad to see a good worker go, but happy for a young friend getting on with his life. He sold me a beautiful white mare with a long mane. I named her Hera, after the goddess, and hit the road in search of new adventures. Once again, I was a citizen of the wilderness. I reveled in the freedom of the open ground, the cool wind racing across my face, the blazing sun, the smell of trees, the captivating vistas, the distant sounds of the calm nights. The experience made me realize what was beautiful about being human; there was a fundamental part in all of us, an impenetrable grit made up of convictions that could not be reached by anyone lest we allowed them. No matter the force, the idea, the torture, that part remained intact 'till we allowed it to break. Otherwise, we were all untouchable.

After traveling four days, I came flying into a small town in the middle of the night, suffering mean pangs of hunger. Naturally, everything was closed. The streets were little more than mud ruts lined with carriages of every shape and color, and nothing about the place impressed anything of meaning on me upon first inspection; but as I've learned over the years, meaningful things are often discovered at the most unexpected and inopportune times.

There was an inn edged on the main street, at which I stopped, despite the fact that there were no lights inside. I gently rapped on the door and listened for signs of acknowledgement. When none came I decided to return to my horse and brave the hunger 'till morning, but before I could remount my mare, I heard a woman's voice calling after me. I turned and stared up at a young girl leaning out of a second story window, saying, "Sir? Have you just come into town?"

I said I had. I was hungry, too, but I would settle for just a room 'till breakfast was served, if it was at all feasible.

"No problem at all," she said and smiled warmly. "One

moment, I will be right down."

Shrugging my shoulders, I smiled and looked forward to resting my bones in a comfortable bed. When she crept open the door, I knew I was in love. Working on the farm, young girls were a sparse sight. I had never known the love of a woman, and the sensational euphoria of holding such a soft and delicate creature in my arms at night was nothing more than wishful imaginations I'd entertained in the depths of loneliness. I won't kid you, I had thought about it. Good Lord, for years I'd longed for nothing else. And after working hard, fending for myself, and discovering what I was made of, I felt ready for love. I felt comfortable with who I was, and willing to share it, and assimilate it into something new. Unfortunately, she brought out such a shy aspect of my personality that I felt as tough my limbs were made of wax and I'd forgotten how to speak.

"Welcome to Mason Manor," she said. "Where have you come from?"

"I've been traveling," I replied, "On my horse..." and found that I couldn't speak any other words. I stood there and stared dumbly, feeling my cheeks flush with hot blood. She smiled and stared at the floor. Her fiery red hair and green eyes were incredibly intoxicating, and when she smiled, the dimples in her cheeks made her look kind hearted, patient, and full of love. It turned me into a bumbling fool, unable to take part in even the simplest of conversations. Not knowing what else to do to break the awkward tension between us, I paid her for a room, to which she escorted me, and bid me good night.

"I'm terribly sorry for having awoken you," I finally managed to say before she left. She bit her bottom lip and stared at me with wide eyes. God, my heart melted.

She said, "It's no problem at all, Mr..."
"Aldous," I said. "Aldous Crawler. Aldous is fine, if that's what you'd like to call me. Or... I mean... Yes. I'm sorry, your name is?"

"I'm Anne," she smiled, and blushed in response to my stupid mumbling. "I will let you get some rest... Aldous," I still remember her eyes when she spoke my name. I knew I was in love, and I hoped that what I saw in her eyes wasn't merely a figment of my imagination.

"Thank you," I said, and with a shy nod, she left and closed the door behind her.

I didn't sleep a second. I lied on the bed with a candle burning on the table and stared at the ceiling, dreamily repeating her name.

"Anne. Oh, Anne. I think we should get married, Anne." I waited impatiently for the sun to rise and breakfast to be served so that I could see Anne once more. In my mind, I imagined that she hadn't slept either, that her mind had been preoccupied with passionate thoughts of the strapping young lad freshly come to town. Oh, how I wished for it.

When the time came, I dressed, washed my face, and headed downstairs with the hunger of a wolf. Not even on the last step, she noticed me from across the room and made her way to greet me with that beautiful smile of hers.

"Good morning... Aldous," she said. "Good morning, Anne," I said, and I could tell by the sparkle in her eyes that she had indeed thought about me all night. I was ecstatic, and suddenly, my entire mission in life seemed to change. Where was I going, after all? What was I looking for? Was it Anne? Was she the answer to the void I felt inside, the loneliness, the missing piece of my puzzle? I was convinced that she was, and just like that I felt like I'd grown two inches taller, the room seemed brighter, the air fresher, the people friendlier. I sat at a table and ordered ham and eggs. Anne served me personally, and then sat and talked about the weather and answered my questions about the town.

Six month later, we married. It was the happiest day of our young lives, and the first time I felt like I'd found crucial answers to the gnawing questions lingering in the depths of my soul. I had found myself. We had found each other. We were hopelessly in love, but we soon found out that despite having formed a powerful bond and filled our heads with a future full of love and happiness, the reality proved a little more difficult to bring to fruition. For one thing, Anne's father, Mr. Wilson, hated my guts. The main reason was because I'd never bothered to ask for his daughter's hand prior to our marriage. To be fair, I had a very good reason–I didn't care. Whether he approved or not made no difference to me, and I couldn't see why it mattered. I loved his daughter with a deep, fundamental passion. In addition, I had only ever depended on myself, on my own terms. I believed in hard work, in being kind to others, and in helping those in need in any way I could, but I'd always done so purely out of nature. It was innate, intuitive, and as such I felt no need or desire to subscribe to any type of tradition, culture, religion, or philosophy. I was who I was because of who I was. No more, no less. But that kind of attitude didn't resonate well with others, and especially not with an elder hardcore traditionalist. If you had asked Mr. Wilson what I'd done to incur such a dramatic insult on his person, he'd have told you I sodomized his wife while eating a live puppy.

Compounding the problem, he wasn't happy with the fact that I was bedding his daughter in his own house, which was the Mason Manor. Perhaps he was only jealous I wasn't bedding him, but no one aside from myself would have dared to speak of such things. The bottom line was that his disapproval hurt Anne, his only daughter, and I thought that a far greater offense than anything I had or hadn't done. I wondered what kind of selfish, inconsiderate, self-important bastard would do such a terrible thing to his own flesh and blood, but I soon discovered the answer. Ancient traditions and blind complacency made people like Mr. Wilson vindictive, shallow, and irrationally hostile to any contrarian. It made no difference that I loved and took care of my wife or that I served her as equally as she served me; I'd offended him by not taking part in his imaginary play. How could I care? In the face of vindication, the only defense was an opposite stance, or a complete lack of acknowledgement. Anne and I were a team, a partnership, and it was no one else's business. We were happy, in love, and ready to forge a strong future together; no grumpy old man was going to stand in our way in order to satisfy his own ends.

Thus, every morning I rose, made love to my wife, and then headed downstairs for breakfast with a smile on my face. I never noticed the old man's indignant eyes nor his wife's blushing stare when I came down the stairs. I didn't care, and I wasn't below suggesting that perhaps a good fucking would do them both some good.

Thankfully, perhaps for all of us, our arrangement at the Mason Manor didn't last long. I took employment as a lumberjack, and in no time at all we purchased a cozy little house on the edge of town. The old man no longer had to put up with our boisterous lovemaking, and I no longer had to brave his beady eyed little scowls of hatred–but if I thought we were going to live happily ever after, I was gravely mistaken.

In this small, secluded town, I was an outsider, a stranger, an untrustable threat. I was to be treated with suspicious glares wherever I went, and spoken to with an air of distant caution, as if my very breath threatened to fill the air with disease. As was common, it was a place where everyone not only knew each other well, most were related in one way or another, even some husbands and wives. They stocked the local population with incestuous children, who in turn grew up to continue the pattern, furthering the degeneracy. An idiot child from a cousin or sister was a common occurrence. No one batted an eye at that sort of thing; but filling someone's daughter with fresh seed from an unrelated bloodline was absolutely unacceptable. Naturally, rumors arose, fantasies brewed, and the next thing I knew I was being treated badly by citizens for reasons neither stated nor defined. I was bad, and should be treated as such. Dark forces began conspiring against me, for they were unfamiliar with my brand of ardor. I was young, in love, and a little bit eccentric. Worst of all, I was confident without beliefs, a thing so far beyond their scope of understanding it became proof of my being in cahoots with the Antichrist, imbued with powers, and filled with evil ambitions.

As a result of our differing opinions, the town's folks and I locked into a long term relationship about as healthy as mine and Mr. Wilson's. Defiantly, I walked the streets and smiled at the pouting lips, tipped my hat at the scowling faces, and replied with a flattered "Thank you" to all vilified insults hurled my way. Before long, I couldn't go out for a loaf of bread or a pint of beer without getting into some sort of verbal confrontation. Everywhere I went I heard snickering voices; there's the louse, the knave, the beast, the devil.

The Devil! Labelled as such by people who claimed to pray semi-professionally for love, and I was barely twenty years old. I had never bestowed ill will or action on any of them, but reality was disregarded in favor of rumors, gossip, and petty imaginations. Not subscribing to the politics or religion of the place was considered a grave offense, a downright hostile threat, and one they seemed determined to oust me for. They vied to grind me down, pound me into dust, and manipulate me into either converting to their ways or running out of town. It wasn't going to go well, for I would always chose spite over submission. It was in my soul.

The solution seemed simple to me at the time. I kept my head down, minded my business, and ignored the relentless compulsion of others to meddle in my affairs. It worked for a time, and I was happy with my life. I worked hard during the day, relaxed with my wife in the evenings, and repeated the process day after day. A year and a half after our nuptials, Anne announced that she was pregnant, and nine months later she gave birth to a beautiful little girl we named Angela. My life changed. I was a father, a thing I couldn't have conceived of only two years before. I was suddenly impervious to the universal hate my presence aroused around town. The citizens became less than petty, they were harm-less, and they could all go to hell. The birth of my daughter solidi-fied my convictions and rendered me invincible in the face of the hostilities forced against me. Anne and Angela became my life, my very reason for living. Angela brought such joy to Anne and I that we needed nothing else. We were a family, closely knit, passion-ately in love, and completely enraptured with our life together.

Of course, such a wonderful, beautiful happiness wouldn't be tolerated by the town's folks. Our precarious relationship was bound to escalate to a disastrous climax; and it did, beginning when Angela was a little over a year old. On a regular evening like any other, I was in the general store for milk and flour, when a man I had never met before simply couldn't let it go.

"You're that demon fellow, aren't you?" he said, leaning closer to my ear from behind. "What are you here for, demon? Do you not have babies to eat somewhere else?"

I forced my lips into a smile and did my best to ignore the fool.

"Hey, I'm talking to you, you dirty asshole. I want to know what right you think you have to walk these streets. You weren't born here, so why are you here?"

I replied more out of amusement than malice, but the action proved to be a decisive blow in a long and drawn out battle of wills. I said, "I'm here to sleep with your mother and your wife. Sometimes at the same time."

His eyes blazed with fury as he took the hat from his head, leaned in toward me, and snarled, "You disgusting, disre-spectful, animal! How dare you insult my family's blood?"

"I apologize," I said. "I didn't mean to take the job away from you, but your mother doesn't seem to mind replacing you with me."

The words had scarcely left my lips before his fist slammed into my face. I stammered backward, dizzy with surprise, shaking with rage. I connected a solid punch with his chin and sent him crashing into a stack of potatoes crates behind him, but he was hardly keen on accepting defeat. He jumped to his feet and tackled me to the floor. The game was up. We struggled to near exhaustion, snarling at each other like rabid dogs, but neither would give up. In a moment of confusion, I cocked my head back and smashed it into his face. He went limp and stared straight up with silly eyes, but by the time I got back to my feet he was lucid again, enraged, insane. He lunged for me with homicide in his eyes. I dodged his attack, and he tripped on a bushel of beans and crashed headlong through a window. He lied unconscious and bloody on the floor.

With shock and terror, onlookers backed out of the store and left me panting and slightly regretting my actions. I just wanted to get home. I bolted from the store but came face to face with the Sheriff at the time, who wasted no time in locking me behind bars for the night, calling me drunk. I was no such thing, but I was worried. My wife and child were waiting for me, and I wouldn't be home for a while. I felt terrible; however, the fight had been a necessary climax to the unnecessary harassment that had gone on for far too long. I spent the night tossing and turning on my cot, replaying the fight in my head. I didn't know it at the time, but I had just forged a demented relationship with a man who would spite me for many years to come. Elvin Kass would never forgive me for standing up for myself and making a fool of him in a store full of his friends.

Things changed drastically after that. Wherever I went, people reacted with fear, agitation, and violence. They threw bottles and garbage at me from blind corners. Men, women, and children spat on me in the streets. I was even fired from my job with unreasonable passion on behalf of my employer, and if I thought I was going to find other sources of income, I was dreaming. As far as the citizens were concerned, I was about to be taught a lesson–and indeed I was.

I took up quail hunting after my loss of employment in order to supplement our lack of funds. I would hunt until I had either shot enough birds or the light of day failed, and I would then return home slowly through town, purposefully smiling at every fool who stared at me with disdain. I was doing just that one warm summer evening, trudging through the streets and stirring the blood of the psychologically invalid citizens by showing them that they would never wipe the smile from my face, when I was suddenly aware of a drastic change in their demeanor. I couldn't quite define what it was, but the bad energy in the air felt oppressive. I was used to braving scowling stares wherever I went, but on that evening, something ominous and powerful seemed to emanate from every pair of eyes I caught. They were full of hatred, but it wasn't the superficial type I was used to; this was deeper, and far more meaningful, somehow. As always, I kept my head up and my shoulders back and I ignored the callous bastards. As I approached my house, however, I noticed the pungent smell of smoke in the air, and then I saw the glow contrasting the darkening sky. An oppressive sense of worry came over me, though I still didn't quite know why. With a lump in my throat, I walked farther and noticed with a shock that it was my house in flames. Panicked, I dropped my birds and ran, slipped, tripped, and clawed my way through the mud, desperate to catch sight of my family huddled outside in fear, but still alive. I couldn't see them. I couldn't see anyone, in fact, and I remember thinking it was the oddest thing. No curious souls stood in the street to watch the tragedy unfold. No one prayed to the good Lord for the safety of everyone involved. No one cared.

The roof glowed red, timbers exploded, flames licked at the black night air, and I was sick with a desperation so intense I couldn't even begin to describe it. I crashed through the door and hit the floor in the middle of the inferno. I couldn't see anyone. I couldn't hear them.

"Anne!" I screamed at the top of my lungs, but the sound of my voice was inaudible over the roar of the fire. The place billowed with thick smoke that was highlighted with thrashing flames behind it, under it, over it, around it.

"Anne! Angela!"
Nothing. I looked around and tried to find a way up the stairs, but my eyes were burning badly and my lungs couldn't handle the acrid smoke.

It was hopeless. It was done.
I fell to the floor and cried. I smashed my fists against the floor, desperate to wake from the terrible nightmare, but it was no more a dream than the hateful town's folks were. The heat bubbled my skin, seared my throat, and forced me to curl into a fetal position and await certain death.

I wanted to die. If I couldn't have my family with me in this confused and convoluted thing we called life, then what was the point? They were my life. They were my everything, my very breath. If they were forced to die in such a horrific way, then I felt I had a responsibility to join them. Choking on the smoke, I couldn't stop my grief stricken imagination from reeling. Involuntarily, I imagined my daughter's little face contorted with the pain of flames licking at her tiny body. I imagined my wife frantically trying to get to the baby and being overcome with smoke and fire. I saw destruction, annihilation, death. They were dead.

They were dead.
Goddamn it.

Fortunately, or unfortunately, depending on your perception, I lost consciousness, fully prepared to die. But then I opened my eyes again and found myself lying outside in the mud. To my right, a young boy was running away from me. That's all I remember about that point in time. That child, running away from me. Since then, I've attributed my survival to that boy with both appreciation and chagrin, though I still have no idea who he was, or why he saved me. It doesn't matter much anymore, I suppose.

After the fire, the investigator of the blaze told me he couldn't find evidence of foul play, but I could tell he was lying. It was arson. Standing in the middle of the charred half timbers, I could smell the gunpowder. An explosion had gone off. Someone had intentionally set my house ablaze. Someone was responsible for the death of my family. Someone... Maybe everyone.

In my tomb now, with the worst of the heat over and the evening gaining over the land, I'm staring back at the shore, thinking of my long lost family. It was such a long time ago, and yet, I can still remember their faces with such clarity that I hardly ever welcome the memories.

In the line of respectable citizens braving the heat of the sun for a chance to watch me die, I know that one of them is responsible for that fire. I've always suspected Elvin Kass, my executioner, but I've never been able to prove it. I see him there, staring at me from a distance, impatiently waiting for the righteous moment when they pull me in and find that my heart has ceased beating, and all I can feel inside is a deep, burning regret that I didn't kill the son of a bitch the first time I met him. Instead of causing him to crash through a window, I should have snapped his neck.

Too late. The sun is now only a faint glow on the horizon and I can't see the shore anymore. There won't be a moon out tonight. It will be me and my mind trying to contend with the creeping cold of night. Luckily, I have good memories, and they usually do bring me good dreams. I feel no pain, no torture. I am tired now.

Day 3: July 29th, 1847

Two of them puke violently; the rest gag, and choke, and fill me with malicious pride. The smile on my face is in stark contrast to the unhealthy stew of filth I've been soaking in for the last two days. I laugh and laugh and hurl insults at them 'till they shove the funnel down my throat and fill me with more dairy. It feels like my insides are soggy, mushy, and almost immediately, my bowels react and explode all over the place.

I see the septic liquid splatter and I smile around the funnel jabbed into my mouth. You've got some on your cheek there, good sir. Some in your hair, ma'am. Some has fouled your shirt there, cocksucker. I hope it's full of disease. I hope it seeps inside them and eats their souls. I hope it makes them suffer terrible deaths. Who better than I to wish for such a thing? I am the devil, the Antichrist, the object of their worst nightmares. They fear me, and they should. They're killing me, but I am hardly done dealing with them. Even stuck inside my tomb, losing strength by the minute, I am winning. I still have the upper hand. I still have their fear.

When they pull the funnel from my mouth I puke all over myself, and my tormentors retreat instantly as if I'd burst into flames. I feel shooting pains in my crotch. I wonder if it's bugs boring into my testicles? Are they in my brain yet? In my stomach and intestines? Certainly, it's only a matter of time before that sort of thing comes about.

I hear them chanting a prayer and I suddenly burst out laughing at how ridiculous it all is. What are they praying for? Peace? Love? Understanding? I can't tell, but the one thing they aren't asking the Lord for is forgiveness for their actions. A few of them say they're justified; therefore, they are. They hold their children up on their shoulders to watch and learn; this is how you treat people who scare you. It's your right, your duty, to punish them in the name of your beliefs.

Learn, children. There is no greater danger in the world than abstract beliefs contradicting your abstract beliefs. That's abstract madness, and something physical must be done to fight against those abstract threats. Otherwise, there's no telling what kind of abstract harm it may bring.

Learn, children, so you can teach your own children not to stand for intimidation. Teach them that those who are smarter than you, those who question what they are told, and those who think they know better than the Lord will be segregated, labelled, belittled, harmed, and destroyed. It's God's will, found right here in these various sentence fragments taken out of context.

They replace the boat above me and praise the Lord. They mock my suffering and my degradation. They wish me death and damnation. Through the seam, I stare at the children watching their parents. They laugh and cheer and sing and clap, but they don't understand why, and they never will. They will never question the validity of their parents' actions. They won't ever regret or even remember it. They are doomed to continue the lunacy, to mold their own children in the same vein, and to punish anyone who makes them uncomfortable.

There is a little girl hanging on to the leg of the man tying the boat closest to my head. She stares at me through the seam with bright almond shaped eyes. She burns with curiosity and inquisitiveness... Her enemies. She sucks on her thumb and stares, occasionally looking up to her father, who reassures her, "It's okay, honey. The devil can't hurt you any more. Can you say bye bye to the devil? Bye, Devil. All the way to hell!" And she waves and smiles and shrugs her shoulders. I feel bad for her. Her life is ruined. Predestined and meaningless. I wish I could reason with someone, even a child, but there is no one. No one. These kids are brainwashed adults in six year old bodies. I feel like I should do something to help them along.

I whisper, "Hey, little girl." She catches my voice and leans in closer like a cat who's just spied a mouse behind a door. "Can you hear me?" I ask.

She nods that she can.

"Good," I say. "I'm the devil, and I'm going to kill you in your sleep."

A shrill scream pierces the air and the girl runs away crying for her mother. Everyone stares, unanimously terrified. I see a new pair of eyes lean in to the seam. They are angry and tinged with genuine terror.

"What did you say to my daughter, you foul beast?" the father screams.

I laugh, then choke, then puke, but the spite keeps riding high.

I say, "You can't kill the devil." I say, "I will be back to plunge your children into the darkness of sin." I say, "You've already lost, you just don't know it yet." I say, "When I'm God, everyone dies!"

"Burn in hell!" The eyes recede and the heel of a boot thumps harmlessly against the side of the boat.

I laugh and stare at the children.

"Enough of this!" Elvin Kass says. "Get him out there!"

A group of boys sword fight with sticks, taking turns to deliver a valiant death to the devil. Victorious conquests against evil! I wonder how long this sort of convoluted psychosis has gone on for? How long has it been passed down through generations? These parents' parents? Grandparents? Hundreds of years? Thousands? How long will it continue? How many more people will be subjected to this type of treatment for reasons outside of their control? Even one is too many.

I feel the boat get hung up on the shore, and the men hiss curses under their breaths.

Elvin screams, "What's the problem?"

The men bark orders at each other and I then feel the mass move once more. I become buoyant in the water.

A voice says, "Suffer well, demon. You've earned it."

I can't speak anymore. My outbursts took what little energy I had. Floating away, I stare through the seam and see women cuddling with their children, waving at my barge, assembling for prayer.

Down on your knees. Hands together. Eyes closed. Open your hearts to God's love. Open your hearts to his love. Love his love. Love his wrath. Love his murder.

From the middle of the lake, they're nothing but distant figures. Geared automata. They can have their false happiness. They think they've won, but they know nothing of what the devil– I–am capable of. I am not finished with them.

For now, however, I'm tired, and weak, and decomposed. The heat is stifling and the bugs are hard at work gnawing, burrowing, and reproducing. So be it. My mind keeps involuntarily escaping into sordid hallucinations anyway. I wake without sleeping. I sleep without waking. I dream of my family; gone so long, yet still so close. I cry. I wonder who my child would be today. Would she be a strong, independent free-thinker? A beautiful, intelligent woman filled with the courage to guide her life as she saw fit?

I suppose that's the magic. She is whoever I want her to be, whenever I want her to be. Because the truth is, due to the hands of the people on the beach, she is no one. She is gone. She is dead.

Everything costs something, and my payment is due. I am the devil, the dark prince, the evil one, and my beating heart is the greatest weapon I have. I have a vested interest in living just a little while longer.

Day 4: July 30th, 1847

Early morning, I'm so cold. The repulsive stew I fester in by day hardens with the cool of night. There's a certain calm that comes with that, but it's a peace found in madness. When the sun sets, I definitely start to lose my grip. All night I see things, say things, and feel things, but I am barely ever conscious of my physical torture.

I can't seem to shiver... Or breathe. I don't feel like I'm here. I'm watching, but it doesn't feel like it's happening to me. I wonder how much longer I have? Is this the edge of a slow death? Is this what it feels like? Dissociative? That seems cruel in light of the intense vividness of life.

The sun is crowning the horizon and beginning to light the day. I can only stare at the bleary darkness through the seam of my crypt. A thick fog blankets the lake, and I can hear the occasional bird or bat cut through the chilled air in search of breakfast. Inside my hardened cocoon, I still feel the occasional bite or burrow, but there's no pain. I am being eaten alive. I am first hand witness to the separation of the mind from the body. I'm here, and yet I am not. A paradox, like the rest of life.

I'm growing tired of thinking, but I can't seem to help it. It's all I have left. With the sun clearing the horizon and burning away the fog, I can vaguely see the beach. I see the congregation assembling there for yet another day of watching me die. I see Elvin Kass speaking to the crowd and pointing his hands up to the sky, justifying their actions through the force of an ill-conceived communal responsibility. He looks like a broken marionette, twisting and writhing about, mindless like he's always been. When he's done stomping about, the bodies link together and proclaim the glory of God to the cloudless sky. The sight makes me chuckle. I just don't understand. How is anyone suppose to reason with that brand of insanity?

The temperature is rising quickly, and I'm starting to feel my cocoon soften and reveal the true scope of damage I've suffered.

Last night, the darkness awoke a vast array of nocturnal creatures, all very hungry and very attracted to my biological musk. Swarms of bugs I couldn't see crawled into the casket while I spent the opaque night drifting in and out of consciousness. Terrible dreams, worse reality. I'd come out of soul-crushing nightmares and into moments of lucid reality where spider-like legs shuffled over my face, prickly wings tickled the insides of my ears, and furry things bore into my nostrils. I'd scream at the top of my lungs, and then be overtaken once more by ghoulish hallucinations and doom-riddled emotions.

I can see my skin is covered with sores, burrows, nests, and eggs. General necrosis. It hurts to breathe this morning too. Maybe I have bugs in my lungs. My decomposing stomach. My shredded intestines.

I suddenly feel a tug on my boat. Time for breakfast. On the way, I smile and choke and puke a little bit of greenish liquid from my nose. I can't wait for them to smell me. Through the seam, I watch the trees and boulders that frame the distant shore pass by. There's no wind and the humidity just hovers in the air, stagnant and all encompassing. I hear water splashing against the boat, and the cries of birds circling above. For a moment, I can't tell if I've fallen asleep or not. Am I moving? Am I here? Am I alive?

"Are you ready for breakfast, Devil?" I hear them taunt and curse me, and then I feel the thump of the boat as it meets the sand. Snickering bodies circle my tomb, grunting as they push and pull my sarcophagus up the slope. I see hands fumbling about at the restraints and in no time at all the boat above me first shifts, then lifts away. Instantly, the crowd jumps back with repulsed cries, and I hear some of them gag and puke. I laugh. The arrogance of these people. The hypocrisy.

"I can't believe he's still alive." I hear one of them say. I cough and it causes sharp pains to flash through me, but I manage a breath anyway.

"The... The..." I mumble, not even sure if anyone can hear me 'till Elvin says, "Hang on, hang on... I think the devil is trying to say something. Are you trying to repent for your sins, Devil?"

"The..." I struggle again, and despite the horrid stench, a few heads hover above me to listen.

"Well... Say it, Demon!" "The... Devil is hungry," I gasp, and laugh, and startled bugs escape from my mouth and ears. Instantly, hurried hands form the sign of the cross and the crowd backs farther away.

"That's it!" Elvin says. "Give me the funnel!" This time it feels like he's pouring fire down my throat. It won't go down. It just keeps bubbling and splashing everywhere. Elvin forces the funnel deeper, ripping open my throat, and pours more milk into me. I think I'm going to explode. He pulls the thing from my mouth and covers me with honey. A mass uprising of insects form a cloud around his head, and then attack the golden liquid.

I stare at the blue sky, not even sure if any of it is real anymore. I hear voices but I'm not making much sense of what they're saying. Birds cross my view. Insects. Death. And then I'm aware of eyes staring at me, standing next to Elvin, covering his nose with a rag. It's Father Robin, the town priest slash emperor.

"If you're still alive by this time tomorrow," he says. "We are burning the boat. May God condemn you to hell, fiendish beast."

In that case, I will live one more day purely out of spite. I will force them to kill me by their own hands. The cowards.

I hear the boat being dragged through the sand, the water splashing, the voices receding. Back I go. I watch the trees on the opposite shore. The perched birds. The glistening water. The heat is unbearable. The bugs are unbearable. But my spite is now so intense I'm proud of it. My spite is the only reason I'm still alive. They took everything from me, multiple times, and then they ask me what my problem is? I am the devil for a reason, and I am armed with a power so subtle it's the stuff of genius. I am the devil, enjoying my hot putrid bath, waiting.

I reach the end of the tether and the boat pulls gently to one side and spins. I watch, incapable of doing anything else. I catch sight of the congregation again. I see them linked together, praying, chanting, celebrating. Elvin is again hurling his hands in the air, proclaiming more nonsense. Father Robin is talking to the children, probably promising them a place in heaven for their positive contributions to the community.

After my family died, Father Robin approached me and asked if I would allow him to perform a public cleansing of my soul in order to purify myself and show folks that I was willing to repent. He said it might be beneficial for me in light of my tragic situation; which, of course, he was so terribly sorry to hear about.

He shoveled bullshit down my throat, and there was something odd about the way he stared at me. He claimed to be a man of God, but his eyes betrayed him. He was shallow, crooked, and controlling.

I've always believed it unwise to accept the advice of a man who has never seriously contemplated suicide. He hasn't lived, nor questioned enough things to have anything reasonable or responsible to say. That man is a fool, with nothing but foolish ideas running through his mind like shiny diamonds made of polished shit.

I declined, but he persisted and tried to dominate me with his eyes.

"Are you sure, Aldous? It would be better for you, for the community, and our country as a whole, if you would just accept the love of God into your heart. Open yourself to him and he will help you through this terrible time. We will help you. You must be cleansed."

I was rabid.

"Listen, Priest," I snapped. "You god-fearing lunatics killed my family! And for what?"

"What are you saying?"

"Shut up! I'm going to find who did this, Priest, and when I do, I will do unholy things in retaliation. You scared little wimps think I'm evil now, you just wait 'till I get my hands on the stupid bastard who thought it'd be a good idea to do something so terrible not only out of complete ignorance, but of arrogance. Now get away from me. I hope you had nothing to do with this, Priest, because I'll gut you like a pig."

I was furious, and devastated.

I was so devastated.

The priest protested and urged me to denounce the devil and surrender myself to the love of God.

I laughed.

"You want me to surrender?"

"To the Lord, my son."

"I don't surrender, Priest. Not ever. Plus, I don't trust you. You're an evil man underneath your big divine costume. Witches, were-wolves, demons, and God all make for excellent vehicles to advance political agendas. Vague, perceived, unrealistic threats; those are your favorite tools, and I want nothing to do with them. Leave me to myself, Priest. Nothing will stop me from avenging the memory of my family."

After that, there was a drastic change. When I went into town for water or groceries I was no longer faced with snarling simpletons hurling insults my way, throwing things at me, and trip-ping me in the mud. No. Now, people hushed their conversations, stared at me with suspicious eyes, and hurriedly stepped out of my way, desperate to not touch me in any way. God only knows what Elvin and that foolish priest had told them about me.

At first I rather enjoyed this new development. Get out of my way! Don't touch me! Don't talk to me! Don't even think about me! It was a beautiful reality. I hated each and every one of those deluded and delusional lunatics, and I was proud of walking into silent streets and parting fools on either side of me like I was some sort of monarch. I was the devil. The ultimate source of their fears. The children stared at me as though I had enormous horns mounted on my forehead, but none of that bothered me; what did, what caused a seething hate to bubble inside of me, was their eyes. They stared at me with eyes that were filled with guilt, as if every one of them had had a hand in setting fire to my family. The bastards. I hated them so much. So goddamned much.

I spent the first week without my family outside of town. I mounted my horse and rode the wind like I had when I was eighteen. I only wanted to think. I slept under the moon, and hunted for food. I rode aimlessly, taking in the scenery, trying to deal with the terrible emotions washing through me. I missed them so much. My little girl. My wife. Our life together. It was unbearable.

I thought about moving away–just pointing my horse in one direction and riding it out for a week 'till I arrived somewhere new and anonymous–but I couldn't do it. I didn't want to leave my family's memory. As painful and punishing as it was, it was mine. They were mine, and for me to jump ship felt like an insult to my wife, to my child. No, I could not do it, and I certainly wasn't keen on letting the town have that glory. I decided to stay and rub it in their faces. I would make my presence known. I would hold those responsible to terrible punishments. Nothing as drastic as scaphism, but something far more sensational.

Two weeks after the fire, I paid a visit to Mr. Mayer, the town bank manager, to inquire on the possibility of using my savings to acquire a new property. I didn't know exactly what I was looking for; I only knew that I wanted a place on the fringe of town. I'd had my fill of morons for five lifetimes. To my surprise and amusement, not only did Mr. Mayer happily agree to help me, he came to reveal his own personal feelings about the town and it's influx of stupidity. He explained that he was a lot more like me than I realized, and how he acted in public was merely a front to ensure his monopoly on the money game in town.

Naturally, I suspected a trap. But upon further conversation he clarified his true feelings concerning Elvin Kass, and Father Robin, and the rest of the flock following them like dumb birds, and subsequently earned my tentative trust. Only time would prove his sincerity. We shook hands and stared sternly into each other's eyes as if solidifying our subtle friendship, and our search for a property began. I wanted somewhere tucked away, somewhere I could think, and mourn, and come to grips with my broken heart.

Two days later I rode with Mr. Mayer to lake Saint Claire, about ten miles from town, where he showed me a small log cabin fronting the water. The place was swallowed by dense bush. Distant. Forgotten. Alone.

The cabin was large and open on the inside. A decent wood stove stood in the corner, the chimney seemed in order, and the windows and roof showed no drastic evidence of water damage. I could work on it and make it my own. I made a fair deal with Mr. Mayer and moved in immediately. I could keep the existing furniture, whatever there was. An old sleeping bag on an old bed. Two and half wooden chairs. A dust pitted mirror.

It was perfect.

For months, I toiled at grooming the landscape and repairing the shack. I worked hard at making it my home, and it felt good to be working toward something meaningful. It felt like I was carving a new path and forging ahead with a purpose, no matter how feeble. It helped to distract me during the day; however, once the sun set and the moon rose, I missed my family with rabid emotional psychosis. I suffered bouts of helpless rage, agonizing loneliness, and atrophied optimism. I no longer had a decent reason to live. I only had my shack and my marred thoughts to carry me through the darkness that had crept into my life. Everything was so dark.

I asked Mr. Mayer if there was a possibility that he could get me some books, seeing as I had also lost those precious things in the fire. He smiled and said it was no trouble at all, and added that in the meantime he would be glad to lend me whatever books he had in his private collection, the one for the real side of his personality.

I was ecstatic. I wanted to–no–I needed to focus my mind. I needed to learn something, to teach myself something, and to keep focussed on positive things for the future. In Mr. Mayer's collection, I found two books on chemistry, and one on mathematics. These I snatched up immediately. Mr. Mayer, recognizing the importance we both placed on scientific knowledge, offered me ink, dip pens, and papers in order to study. I thanked him, and truly appreciated the gesture. He helped me more than I had expected him to, and I was forever in his debt.

Finally, I was home. My cabin faced east and blessed me with beautiful sunrises every day. With Mr. Mayer's help, Jack was his first name, I was able to get my hands on a variety of seeds and plant myself a garden. I toiled the earth at the side of the cabin and filled it with a vast assortment of vegetables. For meat, I hunted hare and fowl; and once a month, to the beautiful chagrin of everyone in town, I jumped on my horse and rode to the market for anything else I needed.

Jack helped me further by providing me with income in exchange for firewood. It wasn't much, but it was enough for a man like me. Coupled with what I still had as savings, I could afford to live alone, hunt wildlife, grow vegetables, and delve my mind in the study of science and mathematics. That was all I wanted, and it was all I had.

I loved it, and for two years, the arrangement was without a hitch. No one bothered me; I bothered no one. I studied, and practiced, and in time, once again with Jack's help, I was able to locate more advanced books on the subjects.

But two years of peace couldn't possibly last without problems. I was a hermit hiding in the bush, keeping to myself; people didn't like that. Two years before, they hated my guts, wished me ill, and demanded I leave them alone; two years later, they wanted nothing more than to know what I was doing. Suspicions became rumors, and rumors became truths. Bored psychological grudges bubbled through the populace, and each day gained toward an ultimate, untimely climax. I may have left town, but I was still an evil force, a wizard, an occultist. No one knew exactly what I was doing out there in the bush. It was ripe with possibilities. Some said I performed ritualistic dances in the dead of night to conjure up demons and curse the town. Others claimed to have witnessed me flying through the sky, showering them with diabolical laughter. And still others decided I was the dark Lord himself, preparing to unleash a terrible evil on the community. Most said something should be done about that; the others were told.

They feared me because they didn't understand me, and instead of dispelling their concerns with just a tinge of empathy, or even a basic conversation, they regressed further into ignorance and colored me evil. Did they really think that if I'd been privy to those types of powers I would have stayed holed up in my cabin? Damn it. If I ever had access to supernatural forces I would have flattened the place a week after moving into it. Goddamned lunatics. Nevertheless, imaginations once again conspired against me without any proof of malevolence or malice on my part, 'till something unexpected happened and seemed to give credence to their raw emotions.

Someone found a dog lying in the street with its eyes ruptured and chunks of fur missing from its coat. A potent, caustic stench emanated from the carcass and forced onlookers to examine the beast from a distance. In little time, a crowd converged around the scene and began conspiring. There were no obvious signs of foul play, no bullet or stab wound, and despite its final, agonized posture, some claimed to have seen it trotting around town only a day before, healthy and friendly. What could have done such a thing? Naturally, they cried devil.

Yes, it was my fault. I prowled the streets at night stalking dogs. I stepped in people's flower beds and pissed on their tomatoes. I scratched at their windows in the dead of night and cast spells on their children.

But then it happened again; this time they found four dogs and two cats. Suddenly, when I went to the market, people avoided me like a leper. Their righteous little eyes were filled with a burning desire to attack, if not for the monstrous fear gripping at their insides.

I smiled and threw my shoulders back. I would be lying if I said I didn't enjoy their fear. I loved it. It gave me power. If I'd been a crooked man I could have picked up anything I wanted, declared that it was mine, and no one would've dared to say anything to the contrary. But I wasn't crooked, I paid for the things I took; 'till people began refusing to sell me things. They didn't want me sniffing around their booths and contaminating their products. They didn't want my money. They didn't want anything to do with me. They prayed for the good Lord to strike me dead and clear the air of my stench.

After that, I insisted on going to the market once a week, purely out of spite, but it was difficult to get my hands on anything useful. After a few visits, I stopped going and disappeared.

The years went on, and with them, the problem escalated. After the cats and dogs, someone found a horse, then a sheep, and then, nearly ten years after vanishing from their view, a farmer awoke one morning to find his entire stock of cattle dead. The carcasses looked like the other animals they'd found. Sick, savaged, cursed. I suddenly found myself in grave trouble.

Who else could possibly be responsible for such a thing? Elvin Kass and his troop of funny little soldiers came knocking on my door, screaming for me to face the consequences of what I had done. I went with them, but not without chanting ominous gibberish on the way. I wasn't saying anything real, but believe me, I was getting my effort's worth. I sang, and they cowered like frightened bugs, afraid to make eye contact with me.

Boo.

They propped me up before the Sheriff's office where dense walls of angry protesters closed in on me. I was pummeled with garbage and saliva, and cursed to enough corners of hell to guarantee me employment as a guide when I got there. I smiled. They had wonderful imaginations, and charismatic personalities, and beautiful screaming voices. I thought they were going shoot me dead. I know Elvin wanted to put a bullet in my skull; but, in good standing with the code of "justice" they ascribed to, they first had to prove my intentional malevolence. There was nothing to prove. Things died, sometimes in strange ways; I even went as far as offering up the suggestion that perhaps the Lord was simply angry with them for the way in which they blew his ideas out of proportion, context, and logic–but no one seemed to agree.

I escaped punishment and returned to my cabin a free man, but it hardly came without a cost. I must admit I grew paranoid and tired of the nonsense, but I felt helpless against it. I expected people to come and burn my place to the ground in the middle of the night, or shoot me dead in the street on a whim; luckily, it never happened. I was left alone, and it's a good thing I enjoyed it, because the choice had long ago been taken away from me. The only person who would occasionally speak to me was Jack. I say occasionally, because I understood as well as he did that our camaraderie was strictly forbidden in the eyes of the majority. It would ruin everything he'd ever worked for, and I was hardly keen on destroying such a thing. He was a hard working, dedicated, and honest man; the last thing I wanted was to give him super powers too.

But he did visit, and when he did we'd spend hours talking about life, chemistry, mathematics, and beyond. I asked him once how he managed to do so well amongst the town's folks since he was so different on the inside from what he portrayed. He replied, "We're all actors to some degree, Aldous, I just happened to figure out the mechanics of this place early on and how I could use them to my advantage. I'm not a bad man, you know, but I do owe my success in this world to my self-awareness. Dealing with these people, a man has no choice but to pretend unless he wants to be... Well... I don't have to tell you. The people in this town are bigots who use their beliefs to justify their bigotry. As you know, bigotry is narrow-minded psychology; a man comes into a place like this talking about God, and government, and justice–all is well, and he is accepted. That's your problem here, Aldous. You refuse to pretend that you are anything but yourself, and people don't like that much. In any case, it's something I must admit I truly envy about you. I may look successful, but I don't actually have the courage to be anything but a coward. You're a fighter, and as such, you stand like a fathomless threat that won't back down, 'till death do you part. You are who you are, and not only proud of it, but uncompromising. It's a breath of fresh air for a man like me to meet a man like you, and I apologize on behalf of my town for what has happened to you."

"Ha!" I said, and leaned back into my chair. "Thank you, good sir. I appreciate your friendship more than you know. You are my only friend, and for that I am grateful."

We shook hands and had a drink, and that was the last time I ever saw Jack Mayer. On his way home that night, he was spotted leaving my property, and ultimately declared a servant of the devil. A dark accomplice. A social cannibal.

It ruined him. He lost his business, his home, his every-thing, and it was all because of our friendship. In response, Jack Mayer hung himself from the rafters of his home. The lunacy of it all was impalpable, yet there it was; imagination solidifying into reality.

I heard of his death indirectly, and on a day already filled with extraordinary circumstances. Almost a week after our final conversation, I went to the market filled to the gills with smug ar-rogance, lusting for a confrontation. It had become sport by then, after all, but when I arrived I found myself lumbering about in confusion. No one stepped back when I approached anymore, and no angry eyes followed my trajectory through the crowd. I didn't exist. I was a ghost. A forgotten threat. A bored story. Surprised, I tested their devotion. I leaned over booths and rubbed up against people. I picked up and examined their fruits and vegetables. I pissed in the middle of the street. No one cared. They simply car-ried on as if I existed in an alternate dimension. I stumbled through the mud with my head held high, determined to keep my resolve, but I was feeling a sharp sense of rejection in response to their indifference. I seethed with pangs of resentment. They couldn't get to me. No matter what. They could never get to me.

They were getting to me.

An unreasonable rage flared through me and my mind reeled with tragic thoughts. They wouldn't give me their fear. They wouldn't let me get to them. What had happened? How could they ever think of being safe from me, the devil?

I trudged down the street, pissed off and wanting to go home, when I overheard a group of pecking puppets talking about Jack's death. I stopped in my tracks and fixed my evil eyes on them. A three-chinned blob of lard under the guise of self-appointed divinity was telling the others how Jack had been found dangling from the end of a rope; a note that read "The cost of truth is too high"; a fireplace filled with the flaky ashes of consumed books, one could only guess at what kinds of subjects they'd contained; you never truly knew your neighbors, after all; the devil had tainted his soul; he possibly may have even been a secret homosexual; who knows what he was doing in the bush with the evil being; how horrible of him to be human–what was he thinking; the money had corrupted him; God hated his guts, and rightly so.

Flabbergasted, I shook my head and frowned. Jack Mayer was dead? Jack Mayer had killed himself? Because of me? Because of them? Because of himself? How could it have happened? Could I have done something to help him? Anything? I could have avoided him. Yes, there was no doubt about it. Without my friendship, Jack Mayer would still be alive; with my friendship, Jack Mayer was dead. I felt the brunt of responsibility weigh heavily on my shoulders, knowing it wasn't so, yet unable to take it in any other way. Such a sharp, maniacal anger came over me that I had to fight with myself not to bludgeon the mob of righteous blubber 'till they became one with the mud.

I went home dominated by an ugly fury and kicked, and punched, and hurled anything I could reach. "Those bastards!" I screamed. "Those arrogant, pretentious apes! And they call me evil! They call ME evil! How deluded can people be?" I swung an axe through my table, fell off balance, and landed on top of the splintered heap out of breath and out of patience. The town had taken everything from me. Everything! And at the end of it all, I'd let them get to me! How had that happened? Mine was an unshakable spite, a dedicated malice fortified by the actions of mindless fools. There's was an ignorant evil, far worse than anything intentional, and it had taken my self-respect, my family, my friends, and ultimately, my will to continue. News of Jack's suicide pummeled me with sadness. How could I not hate them? They had done their utmost to push me over the edge, to destroy and mock who I was. I was a sub-creature, a dispensable brute by duty, by unanimously ratified principles, by the loving violence of the Lord. What did they expect would happen? That I would turn? That I would repent what they thought I should and forgive their actions as good intentions? What was the final climax? When did someone take a final stand in their own defense? They had wanted a devil for so long, why shouldn't they get one? They had asked for it repeatedly, compulsively. I owed them nothing if not retaliation.

When I stood from the rubble of my table I sighed and ran my trembling hands through my hair. I felt foolish for letting them get to me. I felt guilty about Jack. I felt a solid resolve to never let myself be compromised again. Never again. I would never give up on myself, and they would never succeed in pushing me the way an innocent banker had gone. They would have to kill me themselves.

For months, no one saw my face. I vanished from their lives, though I'm sure a vast spectrum of rumors were abound. I kept to myself and studied furiously. I lived my own life, with my own thoughts, and my own convictions. Back in town, however, animals continued to turn up dead under unexplainable circumstances. The occurrences were sporadic, and seemingly devoid of pattern, and all the praying in the world wasn't incurring the slightest sign of divine intervention. It was the devil's work. The evil in the woods. The silhouette under waxing moons.

I never showed my face.

Then, quite suddenly on a calm July morning, one hundred and twenty six people died, and all hell broke loose. My cabin was set on fire and I was thrown in the mud by a mob of jabbing gun barrels. Elvin Kass stomped his boot in between my shoulder blades and screamed, "This time you die, Devil!"

Day 5: July 31st, 1847

I'm laughing so hard that blood is gushing from my nose. The sun's been up for a while now, and since the first rays lit the sky I've been keeping myself busy by screaming fantastically hilarious things, hoping the calm air above the water is carrying my voice to the beach.

"Elvin!" I scream. "The Devil has come for you, Elvin. You and your disciples have lost! You have lost and I have won! I am inside you, Elvin. I am inside all of you, rotting your souls and your stupid little brains. You're all coming to hell with me! Ha! Ha! Ha!"

The screaming isn't doing me any favors. I am on the edge of death, finished, but I had a rough night, and the fact that I've lived through two of their execution attempts and braved the third like a champion is the ultimate spiteful triumph, and the funniest goddamn thing I've ever heard of in my life.

In last night's stifling darkness, I was tortured so badly by my own mind I didn't even notice the onslaught of bugs. I was hurled into madness of the kind I've never experienced. I had vivid dreams of being with my wife and daughter, and I hugged them, and kissed them, and cried with joy, but they kept bursting into flames and turning to ashes in my hands. Then things chased and slashed at me from the shadows. I saw fantastic flashes of twirling lights, as though I was imploding. I couldn't tell what was fact or madness; either way was equally punishing.

Right now, I'm up to my neck in shit in every possible sense of the expression. I can see my fastened wrists from the corners of my eyes. Variously sized and colored larvae are crawling out from under my skin. My arms are black, and atrophied, and dry. I desperately need water. The pain that flashed through my head a few days ago hasn't gone away, it's just forced a disconnection between my senses and reality. Everything is a dream. Everything is funny. I'm still alive! Ha! Ha! And those bastards on the beach are doomed!

Staring through the seam, I'm mad with satisfaction at what I see. I will not be receiving another feeding today, and they will not be burning my boat, either. I know this, because I am what they say I am, and even in death I will get what I deserve. Across the expanse of glittering water, I watch the congregation. They are still praying, but on this day their penitent words of praise are motivated by fear.

Yesterday, when the sun set, no one went home. They stayed on the beach and braved the cold, lied in the sand, and never lit a lantern. They stayed there, because they're sick, and they can no longer move. Hence my joy. This morning, I'm watching tiny bodies heave violently and squirm in the sand like the bugs in my skin, convinced that they've made a grave mistake and the Lord is now punishing them for it. They are turning on each other, blaming each other for things said and done. But it is not the Lord who punishes them, it is I, their devil, who is claiming the vengeance I am due.

Just before their first attempt at executing me, I told them I was going to take them with me. I was the devil, and they could never get rid of me. I made them shit their goddamned Sunday pants. And now look, over there on the beach, they're all coming to hell with me. In fact, by the looks of it, some have already beaten me there. I've been telling them for days that I've been winning, but these people lack a tremendous amount of faith in reality. Their greatest downfall has always been their idea of me, the thing they thought I was. That's power to me. It's opportunity. Many of those who judged me were only children the last time I'd seen them, and the fear was especially pronounced in their eyes when they stared at me. To them, I was nothing but legend. A dark wizard holed up in the bush, screaming spells, and molesting animals as a matter of principle. An apex predator. I felt the power it gave me, and it felt good.

See, after they arrested me, they burned my house down, again, and circled me like snarling dogs. Bound and gagged, they threw me onto a wagon and paraded me to the Sheriff's office.

Elvin got in my face. His breath smelled like he'd been swilling ten day old horse piss. He grinned and punched me in the face to the surprised delight of the crowd. They applauded his brave courage, and he bowed gracefully, thanking the Lord in the sky. They then kicked and stomped me into the mud and accused me of having cursed them with some sort of devil plague. One hundred and twenty six people had died in one day; someone was responsible for it. They demanded that I heal the ones I'd sickened and resurrect those I'd killed. I pissed myself laughing trenched half a foot in the mud. I had no hope.

"Will you repent your curse, Devil?" Elvin screamed. I wasn't doing a goddamned thing, so they snuggled a noose around my neck and tried to hang me. Two weeks later, proof of my evil is apparent. They have pushed me for far too long, and for no valid reasons. I've always been a stranger to these people. Not one of them has ever taken the time to have a decent conversation with me. Not one of them knows who I am, or what I like, or what I care about in life; which, ironically, isn't all that different from their own desires. But not one of them ever cared beyond blindly believing what they were told about a quiet man hiding in the bush.

Well, good. Through the seam, I see women caressing tiny bodies in agony. I see lumbering sloths puking violently. I see Elvin on his hands and knees, cursing me from the edge of the beach. Thick clouds are beginning to obscure the sun and everything looks ominous. I taunt Elvin again, pushing the limits of my strength.

"You've lost, Elvin. How does it feel? How does it feel to be beaten by the devil?"

I watch and smile. I love their suffering and their pain. I love it more than they've loved mine.

If any of them would have taken the time to have a chat, have a drink, and discuss the trivialities of life like adults, they would have known that for many years I've been studying all kinds of fascinating subjects; most notably, chemistry. I've developed a deep, fundamental love of it. The fact that some things can be turned into other things simply by processing them in a certain way evokes passion in me like nothing else. It's magical. It's logical. And it's the solution to my burning compulsion for revenge against the residents of this disturbed little town.

I spent years studying and distilling chemicals. After Jack's demise, I was able to order books and equipment from the post office in a neighboring town. I was also able to befriend a botanist who had access to nearly any plant I required for experiments.

In time, my experiments and knowledge grew in complexity. True to my nature, I pushed myself harder and harder to create complex concoctions, useful potions, and deadly poisons.

Of course, as any scientific man will tell you, proper experiments need subjects; so what if some dog, or cat, or cow dies? Things die. They were right, however; I did kill them. But that was only practice aimed at perfecting my craft. I wanted something special, something new, something previously unheard of; and after five years of arduous, meticulous work, I achieved my goal. In the end, I came up with two very distinct, yet equally potent poisons derived from the same fungus. With their intricacies perfected, I'd reached the pinnacle of my efforts. I had mastered my craft and found a way to avenge the unwarranted qualms of my past. There was only one thing left to do before I died, and I knew my death would be a swift one. At least, I thought so at the time.

In the silence of night, I mounted my mare and trampled to town. In minutes I stood at my destination, trembling anxiously, drunk with self-righteousness. In front of me, the top of two wells starkly contrasted the inky night. Every resident in town drank from these. Triumphantly, I poured a vial into each well. The first potion, named Anne's Wrath, caused an instant death when administered, and one hundred and twenty six people died on the same day. The second potion, however, named Angela's Last Laugh, brought about a slow and tortuous death that took days, exactly like the ones I see happening on the beach at this very moment.

Ha! Ha! They have no idea what happened. All this time they thought they were winning a war against Satan, and now they believe they're being punished by God himself!

"Ha! Ha! Ha! Do you feel the evil coursing through your veins, Elvin? That's my evil! That's my pain! I'm watching you die first, Elvin! I'm watching you all die!"

I see him throw a fist in the air. He tries to scream but a mess of bloody vomit is all that comes out. He collapses face first on the edge of water, his limbs limp and useless. Behind him, a heap of bodies are huddled together, some trying to comfort the already dead. Father Robin lays sprawled before them, his face in the sand, and a murder of crows are already pecking at his head.

I have won, and the proof is in rigor on the beach, losing animation by the minute. I make no apologies for my actions. I am detestably inhuman, I am aware of that, but I wasn't born as such. I'm evil by experience, by design, and by popular demand. All I see over there is victory. I see the end result of decades worth of clashing tensions. I see the smiles of my mother, my wife, my little girl, my friend... and... I see... I see... a boy coming to the beach from the woods. Like an apparition, he bounds from the trees and lands in the sand with great theatrics. He wields a branch like a sword and fights an invisible enemy amongst the corpses, seemingly unaffected by the carnage around him. He dashes forward and slices the branch through the air, then falls back in defense, recovers, kicks, and delivers a coup de grace on the priest left overs baking in the sand. He raises his hands in the air and waves to his imaginary audience as if he were Jerónimo Sànchez de Carranza thanking his spellbound fans. He takes a bow and it suddenly hits me like a kick to the face; I know this boy. I've seen him before.

The night my family died, lying in the mud in the heat of the fire, I saw this very child running away from me in the darkness. But that was twenty years ago. It was... It was so long ago.

The boy faces the water and bows, and then stops abruptly as if startled by the sight of my barge. He stares at it, at me, and I'm suddenly full of odd emotions and racing thoughts. The boy approaches the water and stands next to Elvin's corpse, unbothered by its presence. He stares as if to make sense of something paranormal, and then runs out on top of the water. Astonished, I watch him sprint across the glistening body with complete disregard for the laws of physics. When he reaches my tomb, he kneels on the water and stares through the seam with inquisitive eyes.

"Does it hurt?" he asks.

I smile and close my eyes.

"Not at all," I say. "Not at all."

The End

Other Titles by Andy Malice

A Rhapsody Interlude:

Jessica Sanders is hunting a killer who has put her exceptional detective skills to shame. He has left an ugly trail of carnage across her city, and has, consequently, placed her at the forefront of the biggest ongoing homicide case in the nation. He has to be stopped, and fast–but when her first break in the case forces her to engage in a twisted mind game with the killer, she soon finds herself pushed to the limit in a desperate race to stop the haunting psychopath known as, The Fleshcrafter.

ISBN:978-0-9879371-4-8
(Also available as an e-book)

Crypto Fools:

Have you ever felt the rush of jumping from an airplane? How about the exhilaration of back-packing an unknown land? What is the wildest thing you have ever done? Regardless of the answer, Mickey Tyler wants to know–Have you ever been kidnapped? Are you interested?

He's been asking this question to people in an attempt to end his long standing existence as a late twenty something nobody slumming through life with no direction. He wants to leave his mark on the world. He wants to make something of himself and achieve every one of his wildest dreams. He wants it all, until he gets it.

ISBN:978-0987937131
(Also available as an e-book)